VAL McDERMID

The Last Temptation

HarperCollins*Publishers*

HarperCollins*Publishers*
77–85 Fulham Palace Road, London W6 8JB

The HarperCollins website address is:
www.harpercollins.co.uk

This paperback reissue edition published 2006

1

First published in Great Britain by
HarperCollins*Publishers* in 2002

Copyright © Val McDermid 2002

Val McDermid asserts the moral right to
be identified as the author of this work

ISBN-13 978 0 00 786994 7

Typeset in Meridien by Palimpsest Book Production Limited,
Polmont, Stirlingshire

Printed and bound in Great Britain
by Clays Ltd, St Ives plc

For Cameron Joseph McDermid Baillie:
not much of a gift by comparison,
but the best I can do.

Acknowledgements

Moving off one's home turf carries with it many risks. Those who assisted in minimizing those risks include: Pieke Bierman and Tom Wortche, who found the Irish pub in Berlin and provided many other important and invaluable research sources besides; Jeanet van Wezel, who showed me Leiden; Jurgen and Marita Alberts, who introduced me to Bremen; Ron Mackay, who smuggled me in where I shouldn't have been; Hartmut Geisser, who took me on the Spree and shared a lifetime's experience of the world of commercial *schippermen*; Captain Kirk Schoorman and Nils Clausen for their insights into life on the water; Adrian Muller for assistance with the Dutch police organization; and Dr Sue Black for her help with pathological detail. Thanks too to the British Council, who first took me to Köln and Berlin, and to LitFest Köln, who allowed me to renew my acquaintance with their city.

I would also like to thank Gill Lockwood and the staff of the ACU at Leeds General Infirmary, the CDU and SM4 at St Mary's Hospital, Manchester, without whose efforts this book would have been much easier to write . . . And all of those who gave support of various kinds at crucial stages in the writing – Lisanne, Julia, Jane, Diana, Kate, Leslie and, more than anyone, Brigid.

I have taken some diabolical liberties with the geography of various European cities and the organization of assorted law enforcement agencies. But this is a work of fiction, which means the reader must forgive my playing fast and loose with reality. At least I got the rivers right.

The last temptation is the greatest treason:
To do the right deed for the wrong reason.

Murder in the Cathedral
T. S. Eliot

Only when it is responsible for providing psychological diagnoses for state purposes does psychology really become important.

Max Simoneit, scientific director of
Wehrmacht Psychology, 1938

NORTH SEA

HOLLAND

AMSTERDAM

Leiden

DEN HAAG

Utrecht

Osnabruck

Mittelland

ROTTERDAM

Nieuwe
Maas

Wharves

R. Lek

R. Waal

Neder Rijn

Arnhem

Münster

Dortmund Ems Kanal

R. Maas

R. Rhine

Wesel

Duisburg

Düsseldorf

KÔLN

R. Maas

R. Rhine

Bonn

Koblenz

R. Maas

Mainz

Bingen

0	10	20	40	60	80	100 km

0	10	20	30	40	50	60 miles

Case Notes

Name: Walter Neumann

Session Number: 1

Comments: The patient has clearly been troubled for some time with an overweening sense of his own infallibility. He presents with a disturbing level of overconfidence in his own abilities. He has a grandiose self-image and is reluctant to concede the possibility that he might be subject to valid criticism.

When challenged, he appears offended and clearly has difficulty masking his indignation. He sees no need to defend himself, regarding it as self-evident that he is right, in spite of all evidence to the contrary. His capacity for self-analysis is clearly limited. A typical response to a question is to deflect it with a question of his own. He shows a marked reluctance to examine his own behaviour or the consequences of his actions.

He lacks insight and the concept of a wider responsibility. He has mastered the appearance of affect, but it is unlikely that this is more than a convenient mask.

Therapeutic Action: Altered state therapy initiated.

1

Blue is one colour the Danube never manages. Slate grey, muddy brown, dirty rust, sweat-stained khaki; all of these and most of the intermediate shades sabotage the dreams of any romantic who stands on her banks. Occasionally, where boats gather, she achieves a kind of oily radiance as the sun shimmers on a skin of spilled fuel, turning the river the iridescent hues of a pigeon's throat. On a dark night when clouds obscure the stars, she's as black as the Styx. But there, in central Europe at the turning of the new millennium, it cost rather more than a penny to pay the ferryman.

From both land and water, the place looked like a deserted, rundown boat repair yard. The rotting ribs of a couple of barges and corroded components from old machinery, their former functions a mystery, were all that could be glimpsed through the gaps in the planks of the tall gates. Anyone curious enough to have stopped their car on the quiet back road and peered into the yard would have been satisfied that they were looking at yet another graveyard for a dead communist enterprise.

But there was no apparent reason for anybody to harbour idle curiosity about this particular backwater. The only mystery was why, even in those illogical totalitarian days, it had ever been thought there was any point in opening a business there. There was no significant population centre for a dozen miles in any direction. The few farms that occupied the hinterland had always required more work to make them profitable than their occupants could provide; no spare hands there. When this boatyard was in operation, the workers had been bussed fifteen miles to get to work. Its only advantage was its position on the river, sheltered from the main flow by a long sandbar covered in scrubby bushes and a few straggling trees leaning in the direction of the prevailing wind.

That remained its signal selling point to those who covertly used this evidently decaying example of industrial architecture from the bad old days. For this place was not what it seemed. Far from being a ruin, it was a vital staging post on a journey. If anyone had taken the trouble to give the place a closer look, they would have started to notice incongruities. The perimeter fence, for example, made of sheets of prefabricated reinforced concrete. It was in surprisingly good repair. The razor wire that ran along the top looked far more recent than the fall of communism. Not much to go on, in truth, but clues that were there to be read by those who are fluent in the language of deviousness.

If such a person had mounted surveillance on the apparently deserted boatyard that night, they would have been rewarded. But when the sleek black Mercedes purred along the back road, there were no curious eyes to see. The car halted short of the gates and the driver climbed out, shivering momentarily as cold damp air replaced the climate-controlled environment. He fumbled in the pockets of his leather jacket, coming out with a bunch of keys. It took him a couple of minutes to work his way through the four unfamiliar padlocks, then the gates swung silently open under his touch. He pushed them all the way back, then hurried back to the car and drove inside.

As the driver closed the gates behind the Mercedes, two men emerged from the back of the saloon. Tadeusz Radecki stretched his long legs, shaking the creases out of his Armani suit and reaching back into the car for his long sable coat. He'd felt the cold as never before lately, and it was a raw night, his breath emerging from his nostrils in filmy plumes. He pulled the fur close around him and surveyed the scene. He'd lost weight recently, and in the pale gloom cast by the car's headlamps the strong bones of his face were a reminder of the skull beneath the skin, his darting hazel eyes the only sign of the vitality within.

Darko Krasic strolled round to stand beside him, angling his wrist up so he could see the dial of his chunky gold watch. 'Half past eleven. The truck should be here any minute now.'

Tadeusz inclined his head slightly. 'I think we'll take the package ourselves.'

Krasic frowned. 'Tadzio, that's not a good idea. Everything's set up. There's no need for you to get so close to the merchandise.'

'You think not?' Tadeusz's tone was deceptively negligent. Krasic knew better than to argue. The way his boss had been acting lately, not even his closest

5

associates were prepared to risk the flare of his anger by crossing him.

Krasic held his hands up in a placatory gesture. 'Whatever,' he said.

Tadeusz stepped away from the car and began to prowl the boatyard, his eyes adjusting to the gloom. Krasic was right in one sense. There was no need for him to involve himself directly in any aspect of his business. But nothing was to be taken for granted just now. His mindset had been shaped by his grandmother, who, in spite of the noble blood she insisted flowed in her veins, had been as superstitious as any of the peasants she'd so despised. But she'd dressed up her irrational convictions in the fancy clothes of literary allusion. So, rather than teach the boy that troubles come in threes, she'd enlisted Shakespeare's adage that 'When sorrows come, they come not single spies, but in battalions'.

Katerina's death should have been sorrow enough. Tadeusz prided himself on never allowing his face to give him away, either in business or in personal relationships. But that news had transformed his face into a howling mask of grief, tears flooding his eyes as a silent scream tore through him. He'd always known he'd loved her; he just hadn't grasped how much.

What made it worse was that it had been so ridiculous. So very Katerina. She'd been driving her Mercedes SLK with the top down. She'd just left the Berlin ring road at the Ku'damm exit, so she'd probably still been going too fast when a motorbike shot out from a side street in front of her. Desperate to avoid hitting the careless rider, she'd swerved towards the pavement, lost control of the powerful roadster and careered into a newspaper kiosk. She'd died in the arms of a paramedic, her head injuries too appalling to comprehend.

The biker was long gone, unaware of the carnage he'd left in his wake. And mechanical examination had discovered a fault in the circuit that controlled the anti-lock braking in the Merc. That, at any rate, was the official version.

But once his initial grief had receded to the point where he could function again, Tadeusz had begun to wonder. Krasic, ever the loyal lieutenant, had reported that in Tadeusz's temporary absence there had been a couple of more or less subtle attempts to move in on his business. Krasic, who had stoically refused to be distracted by his boss's bereavement, had dealt ruthlessly with the threats, but as soon as Tadeusz showed signs of life again, he had laid out the full story before him.

Now, the word was out. Tadeusz wanted the biker. The police officers on his payroll had been little help; information from witnesses was scant. It had all happened so fast. It had just started to rain, so passing pedestrians had their heads down against the weather. There were no surveillance cameras in the immediate area.

The private investigator Tadeusz had hired to re-interview the witnesses had come up with a little more. One teenage boy had been enough of a wannabe rider himself to have noticed that the machine was a BMW. Now, Tadeusz was waiting impatiently for his police contacts to provide a list of possible candidates. One way or another, whether her death had been an accident or a more cruel design, someone was going to pay for it.

While he waited, Tadeusz knew he had to keep himself occupied. Usually, he left the planning on the ground to Krasic and the competent cadre of organizers they'd built around them over the years. He dealt in the big picture and the details were not his concern. But he was edgy. There were threats out there in the shadows, and it was time to make sure that all the links in the chain were still as sound as they had been when the systems were set up.

And it did no harm now and again to remind the peons who was in charge.

He walked over to the water's edge, gazing down the river. He could just make out the leading lights of a huge Rhineship, the grumble of its engine drifting across the water. As he watched, the barge angled into the narrow, deep channel that would bring it alongside the boatyard wharf. Behind him, Tadeusz heard the gates opening again.

He turned to see a battered van drive in. The van cut away to one side, over by the Mercedes. Moments later, he heard the electronic beep of a reversing warning. A large container lorry backed into the boatyard. Three men jumped out of the van. Two made their way towards the wharf, while the third, dressed in the uniform of a Romanian customs officer, headed for the back of the truck, where he was joined by the truck driver. Between them, they removed the customs seal from the container, unfastened the locks and let the doors swing open.

Inside the container were stacked cases of canned cherries. Tadeusz curled his lip at the sight. Who in their right mind would contemplate eating Romanian canned cherries, never mind importing them by the truckload? As he looked on, the customs man and the driver started to unload the boxes. Meanwhile, behind him, the barge glided up to the wharf, where the two men expertly helped it moor.

Swiftly, a narrow passage between the cardboard boxes appeared. There was a moment's pause then, suddenly, bodies surged through the gap and leapt to the ground. Bewildered Chinese faces gleamed sweating in the dim lights that glowed from vehicles and the barge. The stream of humanity slowed, then stopped. Around forty Chinese men huddled tight together, bundles and backpacks clutched to their chests, their frightened eyes flickering to and fro across the alien boatyard like horses who smell the taint of blood. They were shivering in the sudden cold, their thin clothes no protection against the chill of the river air. Their uneasy silence was more unsettling than any amount of chatter could have been.

A whisper of a breeze gusted a waft of stale air from the back of the lorry towards Tadeusz. His nose wrinkled in distaste at the mingled smells of sweat, urine, and shit, all overlaid with a faint chemical tang. *You'd have to be desperate to choose this way to travel.* It was a desperation that had made a significant contribution to his personal wealth, and he had a certain grudging respect for those with courage enough to take the path to freedom he offered.

Swiftly, the truck driver, the two men from the van and the barge crew organized their cargo. A couple of the Chinese spoke enough German to act as interpreters and the illegals were readily pressed into service. First they emptied the truck of its cherries and chemical toilets, then hosed down the interior.

Once it was clean, they formed a human chain and transferred boxes of canned fruit from a container on the barge to the lorry. Finally, the Chinese climbed aboard the barge and, without any apparent reluctance, made their way into the now empty container. Tadeusz's crew built a single layer of boxes between the illegals and the container doors, then the customs official affixed seals identical to the ones he'd removed earlier.

It was a smooth operation, Tadeusz noted with a certain amount of pride. The Chinese had come into Budapest on tourist visas. They'd been met by one of Krasic's men and taken to a warehouse where they'd been moved into the container lorry. A couple of days before, the barge had been loaded under the eyes of customs officials near Bucharest with an entirely legal cargo. Here, in the middle of nowhere, they'd rendezvoused and been swapped. The barge would take far longer than the lorry to reach Rotterdam, but it was much less likely to be searched, given its documentation and customs seals. Any nosy official with serious doubts could be referred to the local customs who had supervised the loading. And the lorry, which was far more likely to be stopped and searched, would continue to its destination with an unimpeachable cargo. If anyone had seen anything suspicious enough at the airport or the warehouse to alert the authorities, all they would find would be a truckload of canned cherries. If officials noted the Hungarian customs seals had been interfered with, the driver could easily shrug it off as vandalism or an attempt at theft.

As the customs official crossed back to the truck,

Tadeusz intercepted him. 'A moment, please. Where is the parcel for Berlin?'

Krasic frowned. He'd almost begun to think that his boss had had sensible second thoughts about the Chinese heroin the illegals had brought with them to pay part of their passage. There was no reason for Tadzio to change the systems that Krasic had so punctiliously set up. No reason other than the foolish superstitions he'd been prey to since Katerina's death.

The customs man shrugged. 'Better ask the driver,' he said with a nervous grin. He'd never seen the big boss before, and it was a privilege he could well have done without. Krasic's ruthlessness in Tadeusz's name was a legend among the corrupt of Central Europe.

Tadeusz cocked an eyebrow at the driver.

'I keep it in the casing of my CB radio,' the driver said. He led Tadeusz round to the lorry cab and pulled the radio free of its housing. It left a gap large enough to hold four sealed cakes of compressed brown powder.

'Thank you,' Tadeusz said. 'There's no need for you to be troubled with that on this trip.' He reached inside and extracted the packages. 'You'll still get your money, of course.'

Krasic watched, feeling the hair on the back of his neck stand up. He couldn't remember the last time he'd crossed a frontier with so much as a joint of cannabis. Driving across Europe with four kilos of heroin seemed like insanity. His boss might be suffering from a death wish, but Krasic didn't want to join the party. Muttering a prayer to the Virgin, he followed Tadeusz back to the limo.

11

2

Carol Jordan grinned into the mirror in the women's toilet and punched the air in a silent cheer. She couldn't have had a better interview if she'd scripted it herself. She'd known her stuff, and she'd been asked the kind of questions that let her show it. The panel – two men and a woman – had nodded and smiled approval more often than she could have hoped for in her wildest dreams.

She'd worked for this afternoon for two years. She'd moved from her job running the CID in the Seaford division of East Yorkshire Police back to the Met so she'd be best placed to step sideways into the elite corps of the National Criminal Intelligence Service, NCIS. She'd taken every available course on criminal intelligence analysis, sacrificing most of her off-duty time to background reading and research. She'd even used a week of her annual leave working as an intern with a private software company in Canada that specialized in crime linkage computer programs. Carol didn't mind that her social life was minimal; she loved what she was doing and she'd disciplined herself not to want more. She reckoned there couldn't be a detective chief inspector anywhere in the country who had a better grasp of the subject. And now she was ready for the move.

Her references, she knew, would have been impeccable. Her former chief constable, John Brandon, had been urging her for a long time to move away from the sharp end of policing into the strategic area of intelligence and analysis. Initially, she had resisted, because although her early forays into the area had given her a significantly enhanced professional reputation, they'd left her emotions in confusion, her self-esteem at an all-time low. Just thinking about it now wiped the grin from her face. She gazed into her serious blue eyes and wondered how long it would be before she could think about Tony Hill without the accompanying feeling of emptiness in her stomach.

She'd been instrumental in bringing two serial killers to justice. But the unique alliance she'd formed with Tony, a psychological profiler with more than enough twists in his own psyche to confound the most devious of minds, had breached all the personal defences she'd constructed over a dozen years as a police officer. She'd made the cardinal error of letting herself love someone who couldn't let himself love her.

His decision to quit the front line of profiling and retreat to academic life had felt like a liberation for Carol. At last she was free to follow her talent and her desire and focus on the kind of work she was best suited to without the distraction of Tony's presence.

Except that he was always present, his voice in her head, his way of looking at the world shaping her thoughts.

Carol ran a frustrated hand through her shaggy blonde hair. 'Fuck it,' she said out loud. 'This is my world now, Tony.'

She raked around in her bag and found her lipstick. She did a quick repair job then smiled at her reflection again, this time with more than a hint of defiance. The interview panel had asked her to return in an hour for their verdict. She decided to head down to the first-floor canteen and have the lunch she'd been too nervous to manage earlier.

She walked out of the toilet with a bounce in her stride. Ahead of her, further down the corridor, the lift pinged. The doors slid open and a tall man in dress uniform stepped out and turned to his right without looking in her direction. Carol slowed down, recognizing Commander Paul Bishop. She wondered what he was doing here at NCIS. The last she'd heard, he'd been seconded to a Home Office policy unit. After the dramatic, anarchic and embarrassing debut of the National Offender Profiling Task Force that he'd headed up, no one in authority wanted Bishop in a post anywhere near the public eye. To her astonishment, Bishop walked straight into the interview room she'd left ten minutes before.

What the hell was going on? Why were they talking to Bishop about her? He had never been her commanding officer. She'd resisted a transfer to the nascent profiling task force, principally because it was Tony's personal fiefdom and she had wanted to avoid working closely with him for a second time. But in spite of her best intentions, she'd been sucked into an investigation that should never have needed to happen, and in the process had broken rules and crossed boundaries that she didn't want to think too closely about. She certainly didn't want the interviewers who were considering her for a senior analyst's post to be confronted by Paul Bishop's dissection of her past conduct. He'd never liked her, and as Carol had been the most senior officer involved in the capture of Britain's highest profile serial killer, he'd reserved most of his anger about the maverick operation for her.

She supposed she'd have done the same in his shoes. But that didn't make her feel any happier with the notion that Paul Bishop had just walked into the room where her future was being decided. All of a sudden, Carol had lost her appetite.

'We were right. She's perfect,' Morgan said, tapping his pencil end to end on his pad, a measured gesture that emphasized the status he believed he held among his fellow officers.

Thorson frowned. She was all too aware of how many things could go wrong when unfathomable emotions were dragged into play in an operation. 'What makes you think she's got what it takes?'

Morgan shrugged. 'We won't know for sure till we see her in action. But I'm telling you, we couldn't have found a better match if we'd gone looking.' He pushed his shirtsleeves up over his muscular forearms in a businesslike way.

There was a knock at the door. Surtees got up and opened it to admit Commander Paul Bishop. His colleagues didn't even glance up from their intense discussion.

'Just as well. We'd have looked bloody stupid if

we'd come this far and then had to admit we didn't have a credible operative. But it's still very dangerous,' Thorson said.

Surtees gestured to Bishop that he should take the chair Carol had recently vacated. He sat, pinching the creases in his trousers between finger and thumb to free them from his knees.

'She's been in dangerous places before. Let's not forget the Jacko Vance business,' Morgan reminded Thorson, his jaw jutting stubbornly.

'Colleagues, Commander Bishop is here,' Surtees said forcibly.

Paul Bishop cleared his throat. 'Since you've brought it up . . . If I could just say something about the Vance operation?'

Morgan nodded. 'Sorry, Commander, I didn't mean to be so rude. Tell us what you remember. That's why we asked you to come along.'

Bishop inclined his handsome head gracefully. 'When an operation is perceived as having reached a successful conclusion, it's easy to sweep under the carpet all the things that went wrong. But by any objective analysis, the pursuit and ultimate capture of Jacko Vance was a policing nightmare. I would have to characterize it as a renegade action. Frankly, it made the Dirty Dozen look like a well-disciplined fighting unit. It was unauthorized, it ran roughshod over police hierarchies, it crossed force boundaries with cavalier lack of respect, and it's nothing short of a miracle that we managed to salvage such a favourable outcome. If Carol Jordan had been one of my officers, she would have faced an internal inquiry and I have no doubt that she would have been demoted.

I've never understood why John Brandon failed to discipline her.' He leaned back in his chair, his heart warmed by the soft glow of righteous revenge. Jordan and her bunch of vigilantes had cost him dear, and this was the first real chance he'd had for payback. It was a pleasure.

But to his surprise, the interview panel seemed singularly unimpressed. Morgan was actually smiling. 'You're saying that, when she's in a tight corner, Jordan cuts through the crap and does her own thing? That she doesn't have a problem showing initiative and dealing with the unexpected?'

Bishop frowned slightly. 'That's not quite how I would have put it. More that she seems to think the rules don't necessarily apply to her.'

'Did her actions endanger either herself or her fellow officers?' Thorson asked.

Bishop shrugged elegantly. 'It's hard to say. To be honest, the officers involved were less than candid about some aspects of their investigation.'

Surtees, the third member of the panel, looked up, his pale face almost luminous in the fading afternoon light. 'If I may summarize? Just to check we're on the right track here? Vance hid behind the facade of his public celebrity as a television personality to murder at least eight teenage girls. His activities went entirely unsuspected by the authorities until a classroom exercise by the National Offender Profiling Task Force threw up a puzzling cluster of possibly connected cases. And still no one outside the group took the case seriously, even after one of their number was savagely killed. I'm right in saying that DCI Jordan had no involvement in the case until after

17

Vance killed outside his target group? Until it was clear that unless some action was taken to stop him, he would almost certainly kill again?'

Bishop looked slightly uncomfortable. 'That's one way of putting it. But by the time she came on board, West Yorkshire were already investigating that case. They were taking appropriate measures and conducting a proper inquiry. If Jordan had wanted to make a contribution, that would have been the correct channel to go through.'

Morgan smiled again. 'But it was Jordan and her motley crew that got the result,' he said mildly. 'Do you think Jordan displayed strength of character in the way she acted in the Jacko Vance investigation?'

Bishop raised his eyebrows. 'There's no doubt that she was stubborn.'

'Tenacious,' Morgan said.

'I suppose.'

'And courageous?' Thorson interjected.

'I'm not sure whether I'd characterize it as courage or bloodymindedness,' Bishop said. 'Look, why exactly have you asked me here? This isn't normal procedure for appointing an NCIS officer, even at senior rank.'

Morgan said nothing. He studied his pencil on its rotating journey. Bishop hadn't asked why he was here when he thought there was an opportunity for putting the shaft in on Jordan. It was only when he realized that he was talking to people who didn't share his managerial view that he'd pushed for an answer. In Morgan's book, that meant he didn't deserve one.

Surtees bridged the gap. 'We're considering DCI Jordan for a very demanding role in a key operation.

18

It's highly confidential, so you'll understand why we're not able to provide you with details. But what you have told us has been very helpful.'

It was a dismissal. He couldn't believe he'd been dragged across London for this. Bishop got to his feet. 'If that's all . . . ?'

'Do her junior officers like her?' Thorson caught him on the back foot.

'*Like* her?' Bishop seemed genuinely puzzled.

'Would you say she has charm? Charisma?' she persisted.

'I couldn't say from personal experience. But she certainly had my officers on the profiling task force eating out of her hand. They followed where she led them.' Now the edge of bitterness was impossible to disguise. 'Whatever feminine wiles she used, it was enough to get them to forget their training, forget their loyalties and chase off all over the country at her bidding.'

'Thank you, Commander. You've been very helpful,' Surtees said. The panel sat in silence while Bishop left the room.

Morgan shook his head, grinning. 'She really got under his skin, didn't she?'

'But we learned what we needed to know. She's got guts, she shows initiative and she can charm the birds off the trees.' Surtees was scribbling notes on his pad. 'And she's not afraid to confront danger head-on.'

'But nothing like this. We'd have to cover her back in ways we've never considered before. For example, she couldn't be wired. We couldn't risk that. So any product is going to be compromised for lack of corroboration,' Thorson objected.

Surtees shrugged. 'She has an eidetic memory for aural stimulus. It's in the notes. She's been independently tested. Anything she's heard, she can recall verbatim. Her reports are probably going to be even more accurate than the muffled crap we get from half the surveillances we mount.'

Morgan smiled triumphantly. 'Like I said, she's perfect. The target won't be able to resist.'

Thorson pursed her lips. 'For all our sakes, I hope not. But before we make a final decision, I want to see her in action. Agreed?'

The two men looked at each other. Morgan nodded. 'Agreed. Let's see how she performs under pressure.'

3

The sun was slanting at an awkward angle as Tony Hill drove up the long hill out of St Andrews. He pulled the sun visor down and glanced in the rear-view mirror. Behind him, the green of the Tentsmuir Forest contrasted with the blue sparkle of the Firth of Tay and the North Sea beyond it. He glimpsed the jagged grey skyline of the town, ruins cheek by jowl with imposing nineteenth-century architecture, each indistinguishable from the other at this distance. It had become a familiar sight over the past eighteen months since he'd taken up his post as Reader in Behavioural Psychology at the university, but he still enjoyed the tranquillity of the view. Distance lent enchantment, turning the skeletons of St Regulus Tower and the cathedral into gothic Disney fantasies. Best of all, from a distance he didn't have to deal with colleagues or students.

Although his professor had acted as if acquiring someone with his reputation had been a major enhancement of their departmental prospectus, Tony wasn't sure he'd lived up to expectations. He'd always known he wasn't really suited to the academic life.

He was bad at politics, and lecturing still left him sweaty-palmed and panicky. But at the time he'd been offered the job, it had seemed a better option than continuing with work he no longer felt fit for. He'd started out as a clinical psychologist, working at the sharp end in a secure mental hospital, dealing with serial offenders. When the Home Office had started taking an interest in the effectiveness of offender profiling in police investigations, he'd been one of the obvious candidates to run the feasibility study.

It had helped his reputation almost as much as it had damaged his psyche that in the course of the study, he'd been directly caught up in the capture of a psychopathic killer who had been targeting young men. In the process, his own vulnerabilities had come close to destroying him. The degree of his involvement still gave him screaming nightmares from which he woke drenched in sweat, his body racked with echoes of past pain.

When the profiling task force was set up according to the recommendations he'd made, he'd been the inevitable choice to take charge of training a hand-picked team of young police officers in psychological profiling techniques. It should have been a straight-forward assignment, but it had turned into an excursion into hell for Tony and his charges. For a second time, he had been forced to confound the rules that said his should be an arm's-length role. For a second time, he had ended up with blood on his hands. And the absolute certainty that he didn't want to have to do any of it ever again.

His participation in the shadow world of offender profiling had cost him more than he cared to tot up.

Two years later, and he was still never free of the past. Every day, when he went through the motions of a professional life he didn't really believe in, he couldn't help thinking of what he had walked away from. He'd been good at it, he knew. But in the end, that hadn't been enough.

Impatient with himself, he ejected the Philip Glass cassette. Music gave him too much space for idle speculation. Words, that's what he needed to divert him from his pointless introversion. He listened to the tail end of a discussion about the emergence of new viruses in sub-Saharan Africa, his eyes on the road that wound through the picturesque scenery of the East Neuk. As he turned off towards the fishing village of Cellardyke, the familiar pips announced the four o'clock news.

The comforting voice of the newsreader began the bulletin. 'The convicted serial killer and former TV chat show host Jacko Vance has begun his appeal against conviction. Vance, who once held the British record for the javelin, was given a life sentence at his trial eighteen months ago for the murder of a police officer. The appeal is expected to last for two days.

'Police appealed for calm in Northern Ireland tonight . . .' The words continued, but Tony wasn't listening any longer. One last hurdle and then it would finally be over. One more anxiety would, he hoped fervently, be laid to rest. Intellectually, he knew there was no chance of Vance's appeal succeeding. But while it was pending, there would always be that niggle of uncertainty. He'd helped put Vance away, but the arrogant killer had always maintained he would find a loophole that would set him free. Tony hoped the road to freedom was only a figment of Vance's imagination.

As the car wound down the hill towards the seafront cottage Tony had bought a year ago, he wondered if Carol knew about the appeal. He'd e-mail her tonight to make sure. Thank God for electronic communication. It avoided so many of the occasions for awkwardness that seemed to occur when they were face to face, or even talking on the phone. He was conscious of having failed Carol, and, in the process, himself. She was never far from his thoughts, but to tell her that would have been a kind of betrayal he couldn't bring himself to perform.

Tony pulled up in the narrow street outside his cottage, parking the car half on the kerb. There was a light on in the living room. Once, such a sight would have set the cold hand of fear clutching his heart. But his world had changed in more ways than he could ever have dreamed of. Now, he wanted everything to stay the same; clear, manageable, boxed off.

It wasn't perfect, not by a long way. But it was better than bearable. And for Tony, better than bearable was as good as it had ever been.

The throb of the engines soothed him, as it always had. Bad things had never happened to him on the water. For as long as he could remember, boats had protected him. There were rules of life on board, rules that had always been clear and simple, rules that existed for good and logical reasons. But even when he'd been too young to understand, when he'd inadvertently done things he shouldn't have, the punishment had never descended on him until they went ashore. He'd known it was coming, but he had always managed to hold the fear at bay while the engines rumbled and the mingled smells of men's unwashed bodies, stale cooking fat and diesel fumes filled his nostrils.

The pain had only ever been visited on him when they left their life on the water behind and returned to the stinking apartment by the fish docks in Hamburg where his grandfather demonstrated the power he held over the young boy in his care. While he was still staggering to recover his land legs, the punishments would begin.

Even now when he thought about it, the air in his lungs seemed to condense. His skin felt as if it were writhing over his flesh. For years, he'd tried not to think about it because it made him feel so fractured, so fragile. But slowly he had come to understand that this was no escape. It was merely a postponement. So now he made himself remember, almost treasuring the terrible physical sensations because they proved he was strong enough to defeat his past.

Small transgressions had meant he would be forced to crouch in a corner of the kitchen while his grandfather fried up a hash of sausage, onions and potatoes on the stove. It smelled better than anything the cook on the barge ever served up on the boat. He never knew if it tasted better, because when the time came to eat, he would have to wait in his corner and watch while his grandfather tucked into a steaming plate of fried food. Drenched in the appetizing aroma, his stomach would clench with hunger, his mouth become a reservoir of eager saliva.

The old man would gorge his meal like a hunting

dog home in his kennel, his eyes sliding over to the boy in the corner with a contemptuous glare. When he finished, he would wipe his plate clean with a hunk of rye bread. Then he'd take out his bargee's clasp knife and cut more bread into chunks. He'd take a can of dog food from the cupboard and tip it into a bowl, mixing the bread into the meat. Then he'd put the bowl in front of the boy. 'You're the son of a bitch. This is what you deserve until you start to learn how to behave like a man. I've had dogs that learned faster than you. I am your master, and you live your life as I tell you.'

Shaking with anxiety, the boy would have to get down on all fours and eat the food without touching it with his hands. He'd learned that the hard way too. Every time his hands came off the floor and moved towards dish or food, his grandfather would plant a steel-capped boot in his ribs. That was one lesson he'd taken to heart very quickly.

If his misdemeanours had been minor, he might be allowed to sleep on the camp bed in the hall between his grand-father's bedroom and the squalid cold-water bathroom. But if he'd been judged unworthy of such luxury, he'd have to sleep on the kitchen floor on a filthy blanket that still smelled of the last dog his grandfather had owned, a bull terrier who'd suffered from incontinence for the last few days of its life. Cowering in a ball, he'd often been too scared to sleep, the demons of bewilderment keeping him edgy and uneasy.

If his unintentional sins had been on a more serious scale still, he would be made to spend the night standing in a corner of his grandfather's bedroom, with the glare of a 150-watt bulb directed into his face in a narrow beam. The light that leaked into the room didn't seem to bother his grandfather, who snored like a pig through the night. But if the boy sank exhausted to his knees or slumped in standing sleep against the wall, some sixth sense always woke the old man. After that had happened a couple of times, the boy had learned to force himself to stay awake. Anything to avoid a repetition of that excruciating pain in his groin.

If he had been judged as wantonly wicked, some childish game a contravention of protocol that he should have instinctively understood, then he'd face an even worse punishment. He would be sent to stand in the toilet bowl. Naked and shivering, he'd struggle to find a position that didn't send shooting cramps up his legs. His grandfather would walk into the bathroom as if the boy were invisible, unbutton his trousers and empty his bladder in a stinking hot stream over his legs. He'd shake himself, then turn and walk out, never flushing after himself. The boy would have to balance himself, one foot in the bottom of the pan, soaking in the mixture of water and urine, the other bracing on the sloping side of the porcelain.

The first time it had happened, he had wanted to vomit. He didn't think it could get any worse than this. But it did, of course. The next time his grandfather had come in, he'd dropped his trousers and sat down to empty his bowels. The boy was trapped, the edge of the seat cutting into the soft swell of his calves, his back pressed against the chill wall of the bathroom, his grandfather's warm buttocks alien against his shins. The thin, acrid smell rose from the gaps between their flesh, making him gag. But still his grandfather behaved as if he were nothing more substantial than a phantom. He finished, wiped himself and walked out, leaving the boy to wallow in his sewage. The message was loud and clear. He was worthless.

In the morning, his grandfather would walk into the bathroom, run a tub of cold water, and, still ignoring the boy, he'd finally flush the toilet. Then, as if seeing his grandson for the first time, he would order him to clean his filthy flesh, picking him up bodily and throwing him into the bath.

It was no wonder that as soon as he'd been able to count, he'd measured off the hours until they returned to the barge. They were never ashore for more than three days, but when his grandfather was displeased with him, it could feel like three separate lifetimes of humiliation, discomfort and misery. Yet he never complained to any of the crewmen. He never realized there was anything to complain about. Isolated from other lives, he had no option but to believe that this was how everyone lived.

The understanding that his was not the only truth had come slowly. But when it came, it arrived with the force of a tidal wave, leaving him with a formless craving that hungered for satisfaction.

Only on the water did he ever feel calm. Here, he was in command, both of himself and the world around him. But it wasn't enough. He knew there was more, and he wanted more. Before he could take his place in the world, he knew he had to escape the pall that his past threw over every single day. Other people seemed to manage happiness without trying.

For most of his life, all he had known was the tight clamp of fear shutting out any other possibilities. Even when there was nothing concrete to cause trepidation, the faint flutter of anxiety was never far away.

Slowly, he was learning how to change that. He had a mission now. He didn't know how long it would take him to complete. He wasn't even sure how he would know he had completed it, except that he would probably be able to think about his childhood without shuddering like an overstrained engine block. But what he was doing was necessary, and it was possible. He had taken the first step on the journey. And already he felt better for it.

Now, as the boat ploughed up the Rhine towards the Dutch border, it was time to firm up the plans for the second stage. Alone in the cockpit, he reached for his cellphone and dialled a number in Leiden.

4

Carol looked at the three interviewers in blank incomprehension. 'You want me to do a role-play for you?' she said, trying not to sound as incredulous as she felt.

Morgan tugged the lobe of his ear. 'I know it seems a little . . . unusual.'

Carol couldn't stop her eyebrows rising. 'I was under the impression that I was being interviewed for the job I applied for. Europol Liaison Officer with NCIS. Now, I'm not sure *what's* going on.'

Thorson nodded understandingly. 'I appreciate your confusion, Carol. But we need to evaluate your undercover capabilities.'

Morgan interrupted her. 'We have an ongoing intelligence-gathering operation that crosses European frontiers. We believe you have a unique contribution to make to that operation. But we need to be sure that you have what it takes to carry it through. That you can walk in someone else's shoes without tripping yourself up.'

Carol frowned. 'I'm sorry, sir, but that doesn't sound much like an ELO's job to me. I thought my role would be essentially analytical, not operational.'

Morgan glanced at Surtees, who nodded and picked up the conversational baton. 'Carol, there is no doubt in this room that you will make a terrific ELO. But in the process of dealing with your application, it's become clear to all of us that there is something very specific that you and you alone can provide in the context of this single, complex operation. For that reason, we would like you to consider undertaking a day-long undercover role-play so we can observe your reactions under pressure. Whatever the outcome of that, I can promise that it will not adversely affect our decision about your fitness to join NCIS as an ELO.'

Carol swiftly processed what Surtees had said. It sounded to her as if they were saying the job was hers regardless. They were telling her she had nothing to lose by playing along with their eccentric suggestion. 'What exactly are you asking me to do?' she said, her face guarded, her voice neutral.

Thorson took the lead. 'Tomorrow, you will receive a full brief on the role you are to assume. On the appointed day, you will go where you've been told and do your best to achieve the goals set out in your brief. You must remain in character from the moment you leave home until one of us tells you the role-play is over. Is that clear?'

'Will I have to deal with members of the public, or will it just be other officers?' Carol asked.

Morgan's ruddy face broke into a grin. 'I'm sorry, we can't tell you any more right now. You'll get your brief in the morning. And as of now, you're on leave. We've cleared that with your management team. You'll need that time to do some research and prepare yourself for your role. Any more questions?'

Carol fixed him with the cool grey stare that had worked so often in police interview rooms. 'Did I get the job?'

Morgan smiled. 'You got *a* job, DCI Jordan. It may not be the one you expected, but I think it's fair to say you're not going to be a Met officer for very much longer.'

Driving back to her Barbican flat, Carol was barely conscious of the traffic that flowed around her. Although she liked to think that, professionally, she always expected the unexpected, the course of the afternoon's proceedings had caught her completely unawares. First, the appearance out of the blue of Paul Bishop. Then the bizarre turn the interview had taken.

Somewhere around the elevated section of the Westway, Carol's bewilderment started to develop an edge of irritation. Something stank. An ELO's job wasn't operational. It was analytical. It wasn't a field job; she'd be flying a desk, sifting and sorting intelligence from a wide variety of sources across the European Union. Organized crime, drugs, the smuggling of illegal immigrants, that's what she'd be focusing on. An ELO was the person with the computer skills and the investigative nous to make connections, to filter out the background noise and come up with the clearest possible map of criminal activity that could have an impact on the UK. The nearest an ELO should ever come to primary sources was to cultivate officers from other countries, to build the kind of contacts that ensured the information that made it through to her was both accurate and comprehensive.

So why did they want her to do something she'd never done before? They must have known from her file that she'd never worked undercover, not even when she was a junior detective. There was nothing in her background to indicate she'd have any aptitude for taking on someone else's life.

In the stop-start traffic of the Marylebone Road, it dawned on her that this was what troubled her most. She didn't know whether she could do this. And if there was one thing Carol hated even more than being blindsided, it was the thought of failure.

If she was going to beat this challenge, she was going to have to do some serious research. And she was going to have to do it fast.

Frances was chopping vegetables when Tony walked in, Radio 4 voices laying down their authoritative counterpoint to the sound of the knife on the wooden board. He paused on the threshold to appreciate something so ordinary, so comfortable, so relatively unfamiliar in his life as a woman preparing dinner in his kitchen. Frances Mackay, thirty-seven, a teacher of French and Spanish at the high school in St Andrews. The blue-black hair, sapphire blue eyes and pale skin of a particular Hebridean genetic strain, the trim figure of a golfer, the sharp, sly humour of a cynic. They'd met when he'd joined the local bridge club. Tony hadn't played since he'd been an undergraduate, but it was something he knew he could pick up again, an accessible part of his past that would allow him to build another course of brickwork in his perpetual facade; what, in his own mind, he called passing for human.

Her playing partner had moved to a new job in Aberdeen and, like him, she needed someone regular with whom she could construct a bidding understanding. Right from the start, they'd been in tune across the green baize. Bridge parties had followed, away from the club, then an invitation to dinner to plan some refinements to their system before a tournament. Within weeks, they'd visited the Byre Theatre, eaten pub lunches all along the East Neuk, walked the West Sands under the whip of a northeast wind. He was fond, but not in love, and that was what had made the next step possible.

The physiological cure for the impotence that had plagued most of his adult life had been at hand for some time. Tony had resisted the pull of Viagra, reluctant to use a pharmacological remedy for a psychological problem. But if he was serious about making a new life, then there was no logical reason to hang on to the shibboleths of the old. So he'd taken the tablets.

The very fact of being able to get into bed with a woman and not have the dismal spectre of failure climb in alongside was novel. Freed from the worst of his anxiety, he'd escaped the tentative awkwardness he'd always experienced during foreplay, already dreading the fiasco to come. He'd felt self-assured, able to ask what she needed and confident that he could provide. She certainly seemed to have enjoyed it, enough to demand more. And he'd understood for the first time the macho pride of the strutting male who has satisfied his woman.

And yet, and yet. In spite of the physical delight, he couldn't shake off the knowledge that his solution was cosmetic rather than remedial. He hadn't even treated the symptoms; he'd simply disguised them. All he'd done was find a new and better mask to cover his human inadequacy.

It might have been different if sex with Frances had been charged with an emotional resonance. But love was for other people. Love was for people who had something to offer in return, something more than damage and need. He'd schooled himself not to consider love an option. No point in yearning for the impossible. The grammar of love was a language beyond him, and no amount of pining would ever change that. So he buried his angst along with his functional impotence and found a kind of peace with Frances.

He'd even learned to take it for granted. Moments like this, where he stood back and analysed the situation, had become increasingly rare in the circumspect life they had built together. He was, he thought, like a toddler taking his first clumsy steps. Initially, it required enormous concentration and carried its own burden of bruises and unexpected knocks. But gradually the body forgets that each time it steps forward successfully it is an aborted tumble. It becomes possible to walk without considering it a small miracle.

So it was in his relationship with Frances. She had kept her own modern semi-detached house on the outskirts of St Andrews. Most weeks, they would spend a couple of nights at her place, a couple of nights at his and the remainder apart. It was a rhythm that suited them both in a life with remarkably little friction. When he thought about it, he considered that calm was probably a direct result of the absence of the sort of passion that burns as consuming as it does fierce.

Now, she looked up from the peppers her small hands were neatly dicing. 'Had a good day?' she asked.

He shrugged, moving across the room and giving her a friendly hug. 'Not bad. You?'

She pulled a face. 'It's always horrible at this time of year. Spring sets their teenage hormones raging and the prospect of exams fills the air with the smell of neurosis. It's like trying to teach a barrel of broody monkeys. I made the mistake of setting my Higher Spanish class an essay on "My Perfect Sunday". Half the girls turned in the sort of soppy romantic fiction that makes Barbara Cartland sound hard-boiled. And the lads all wrote about football.'

Tony laughed. 'It's a miracle the species ever manages to reproduce, given how little teenagers have in common with the opposite sex.'

'I don't know who was more intent on counting the minutes till the bell at the end of the last period, them or me. I sometimes think this is no way for an intelligent adult to earn a living. You knock your pan in trying to open up the wonders of a foreign language to them, then someone translates *coup de grâce* as a lawnmower.'

'You're making that up,' he said, picking up half a mushroom and chewing it.

'I wish I was. By the way, the phone rang just as I came in, but I had a couple of bags of shopping so I let the machine pick it up.'

'I'll see who it is. What's for dinner?' he added, as he walked towards his office, a tiny room at the front of the cottage.

'*Maiale con latte* with roast vegetables,' Frances called after him. 'That's pork cooked in milk to you.'

'Sounds interesting,' he shouted back, pressing the play button on the answering machine. There was a long bleep. Then he heard her voice.

'Hi, Tony.' A long moment of uncertainty. Two years of literal silence, their only communication irregular flurries of e-mail. But three short syllables were all it took to penetrate the shell that he'd grown round his emotions.

'It's Carol.' Three more syllables, these ones entirely unnecessary. He'd know her voice through a sea of static. She must have heard the news about Vance.

'I need to talk to you,' she continued, sounding more confident. Professional, then, not personal after all. 'I've got an assignment that I really need your help with.' His stomach felt leaden. Why was she doing this to him? She knew the reasons he'd drawn a line under profiling. She of all people should grant him more grace than this.

'It's nothing to do with profiling,' she added, the words falling over each other in her haste to correct the false assumption she'd feared, the one he'd so readily made.

'It's for me. It's something I've got to do and I don't know how to do it. And I thought you would be able to help me. I'd have e-mailed, but it just seemed easier to talk. Can you call me, please? Thanks.'

Tony stood motionless, staring out of the window at the blank faces of the houses that opened straight on to the pavement on the other side of the street. He'd never really believed Carol was consigned to his past.

'Do you want a glass of wine?' Frances's voice from the kitchen cut across his reverie.

He walked back into the kitchen. 'I'll get them,' he said, squeezing past her to get to the fridge.

'Who was it?' Frances asked casually, more polite than curious.

'Someone I used to work with.' Tony hid his face in the process of pulling the cork and pouring wine into a couple of glasses. He cleared his throat. 'Carol Jordan. A cop.'

Frances frowned in concern. 'Isn't she the one . . . ?'

'She's the one I worked with on the two serial killer cases, yes.' His tone told Frances it wasn't a subject for discussion. She knew the bare bones of his history, had always sensed there was something unspoken between him and his former colleague. Now at last this might be the chance to turn over the stone and see what crept out.

'You were really close, weren't you?' she probed.

'Working on cases like that always brings colleagues close together for the duration. You've got a common purpose. Then afterwards you can't bear their company because it reminds you of things you want to wipe off the face of your memory.' It was an answer that gave nothing away.

'Was she calling about that bastard Vance?' Frances asked, conscious that she'd been headed off at the pass.

Tony placed her glass by the side of the chopping board. 'You heard about that?'

'It was on the news.'

'You didn't mention it.'

Frances took a sip of the cool, crisp wine. 'It's your business, Tony. I thought you'd get round to it in your own good time if you wanted to talk about it. If you didn't, you wouldn't.'

His smile was wry. 'I think you're the only woman I've ever known who didn't have the nosy gene.'

'Oh, I can be as nosy as the next person. But I've learned the hard way that poking my nose in where it's not wanted is a great recipe for screwing up a relationship.' The allusion to her failed marriage was as oblique as Tony's occasional reference to his profiling experiences, but he picked it up loud and clear.

'I'll give her a quick ring back while you're finishing off in here,' he said.

Frances stopped what she was doing and watched him walk away. She had a feeling tonight would be one of those nights when she was wakened in the chill hours before dawn by Tony shouting in his sleep and thrashing around beneath the bedclothes. She'd never complained to him; she'd read enough about serial killers to have an idea what terrors were lodged in his consciousness. She enjoyed what they shared, but that didn't mean she wanted to partake of his demons.

She couldn't have known how very different that made her from Carol Jordan.

5

Carol leaned back on the sofa, one hand clutching the phone, the other kneading the fur of her black cat, Nelson. 'You're sure you don't mind?' she asked, knowing it was a formality. Tony never offered anything he didn't mean.

'If you want my help, I'll need to see whatever brief they give you. It makes much more sense for you to bring it with you so we can go through it together,' Tony said, sounding matter of fact.

'I really appreciate this.'

'It's not a problem. Compared to what we've worked through in the past, it'll be a pleasure.'

Carol shuddered. Someone walking across her grave. 'You heard about Vance's appeal?'

'It was on the radio news,' he said.

'He's not going to succeed, you know,' she said, more confidently than she felt. 'He's just another guest of Her Majesty, thanks to us. He tried every trick in the book and a few others besides at the trial, and we still managed to convince a jury that was predisposed to love him. He's not going to get past three law lords.' Nelson protested as her fingers dug too deeply into his flesh.

'I'd like to think so. But I've always had a bad feeling about Vance.'

'Enough of that. I'll head straight out to the airport tomorrow as soon as the brief arrives and get a flight to Edinburgh. I can pick up a hire car there. I'll call you when I have a better idea of my ETA.'

'OK. You're . . . you're welcome to stay at my place,' he said. Over the phone, it was hard to sift diffidence from reluctance.

Much as she wanted to see where two years apart would have brought them, Carol knew it made sense to leave herself a back door. 'Thanks, but I'm putting you to enough trouble. Book me in at a local hotel, or a bed and breakfast place. Whatever's most convenient.'

There was a short pause. Then he said, 'I've heard good reports of a couple of places. I'll sort it out in the morning. But if you change your mind . . .'

'I'll let you know.' It was an empty promise; the impetus would have to come from him.

'I'm really looking forward to seeing you, Carol.'

'Me too. It's been too long.'

She heard a soft chuckle. 'Probably not. It's probably been just about right. Till tomorrow, then.'

'Good night, Tony. And thanks.'

'Least I can do. Bye, Carol.'

She heard the click of the line going dead and cut off her own handset, letting it fall to the rug. Scooping Nelson up in her arms, she walked across to the wall of windows that looked out across the old stone church, incongruously preserved in the heart of the modern concrete complex that had become home. Only this morning, she'd looked across the piazza with a sense of elegiac farewell, imagining herself packing up and moving to Den Haag to take up her post as a brand-new ELO. It had all seemed very clear, a visualization that held the power to bring itself into being. Now, it was hard to picture what her future would hold beyond sleep and breakfast.

The *Wilhelmina Rosen* had passed Arnhem and moored for the night. The wharf he always used when they tied up on the Nederrijn was popular with the two crewmen he employed; there was a village with an excellent bar and restaurant less than five minutes' walk away. They'd done their chores in record time and left him alone on the big barge within half an hour of tying up. They hadn't bothered asking if he wanted to accompany them; in all the years they'd been working together, he'd only once joined them on a night's drinking, when Manfred's wife had given birth. The engineer had insisted that their captain should wet the baby's head with him and Gunther. He remembered it with loathing. They'd been down near Regensburg, drinking in a series of bars that were familiar with the needs of boatmen. Too much beer, too much schnapps, too much noise, too many sluts taunting him with their bodies.

Much better to stay on board, where he could savour his secrets without fear of interruption. Besides, there was always work to be done, maintaining the old Rhineship in peak condition. He had to keep the brasswork gleaming, the paint smart and unblistered. The old mahogany of the wheelhouse and his cabin shone with the lustre of years of polishing, his hands following a tradition passed down the generations. He'd inherited the boat from his grandfather, the one good thing the bastard had done for him.

He'd never forget the liberation of the old man's accident. None of them had even known about it till morning. His grandfather had gone ashore to spend the evening in a bar, as he did from time to time. He never drank with the crew, always preferring to take himself off to a quiet corner in some bier keller far away from the other bargees. He acted as if he was too good for the rest of them, though his grandson thought it was probably more likely that he'd pissed off every other skipper on the river with his bloody-minded self-righteousness.

In the morning, there had been no sign of the old man on board. That in itself was remarkable, for his regularity of habit was unshakeable. No illness had ever been permitted to fell him, no self-indulgence to keep him in his berth a minute after six. Winter and summer, the old man was washed, shaved and dressed by six twenty, the cover of the engines open as he inspected them suspiciously to make sure nothing evil had befallen them in the night. But that morning, silence hung ominous over the barge.

He'd kept his head down, busying himself in the bilges, stripping down a pump. It occupied his hands, avoiding any possibility of showing nervousness that might be remarked on later if anyone had become suspicious. But all the while, he'd been lit up by the inner glow that came from having taken his future into his own hands. At last, he was going to be the master of his own destiny. Millions of people wanted to liberate themselves as he had done, but only a handful ever had the courage to do anything about it. He was, he realized with a rare burst of pride, more special than anyone had ever given him credit for, especially the old man.

Gunther, busy cooking breakfast in the galley, had noticed nothing amiss. His routine was, perforce, as regular as his skipper's. It had been Manfred, the engineer, who had raised the alarm. Concerned at the old man's silence, he'd dared to crack open the door to his cabin. The bed was empty, the covers so tightly tucked in that a five-mark piece would have trampolined to the ceiling off them. Anxiously, he'd made his way out on deck and begun to search. The hold was empty, awaiting that morning's load of roadstone. Manfred rolled back a corner of the tarpaulin and climbed down the ladder to check it from stem to stern, worried that the old man might have decided to make one of his periodic late-night tours of the barge and either fallen or been taken ill. But the hold was empty.

Manfred had started to have a very bad feeling. Back up on deck, he edged his way round the perimeter, staring down into the water. Up near the bows, he saw what he was afraid of. Jammed between the hull and the pilings of the wharf, the old man floated face down.

The inference was obvious. The old man had had too much to drink and tripped over one of the hawsers that held the barge fast against the wharf. According to the postmortem, he'd banged his head on the way down, probably knocking himself unconscious in the process. Even if he'd only been stunned, the combination of alcohol and concussion had combined to make drowning a foregone conclusion. The official finding had been accidental death. Nobody doubted it for a minute.

Just as he'd planned it. He'd sweated it till the verdict was in, but it had all turned out the way he'd dreamed it. He'd been bewildered to discover what joy felt like.

It was his first taste of power, and it felt as luxurious as silk against his skin, as warming as brandy in the throat. He'd finally found a tiny flicker of strength that his grandfather's constant and brutal humiliations had failed to extinguish, and he'd fed it the kindling of fantasy, then more of the hot-burning fuel of hatred and self-loathing until it flared bright enough to fire him into action. He'd finally shown the sadistic old bastard who the real man was.

He'd felt no remorse, neither in the immediate aftermath nor later, when attention had turned away from his grandfather's death to the latest gossip of the rivermen. Thinking about what he'd done filled him with a lightness he'd never known before. The craving for more of it burned fierce inside him, but he had no idea how to satisfy it.

Improbably, the answer had come at the funeral, a gratifyingly small gathering. The old man had been a bargee all his adult life, but he had never had any talent for friendship. Nobody cared enough to give up a cargo to pay their last respects at the crematorium service. The new master of the *Wilhelmina Rosen* recognized most of the mourners as retired deckhands and skippers who had nothing better to do with their days.

But as they filed out at the end of the impersonal service, an elderly man he'd never seen before

45

plucked at his sleeve. 'I knew your grandfather,' he said. 'I'd like to buy you a drink.'

He didn't know what people said to get out of social obligations they didn't want. He'd so seldom been invited anywhere, he'd never had to learn. 'All right,' he'd said, and followed the man from the austere funeral suite.

'Do you have a car?' the elderly man said. 'I came in a taxi.'

He nodded, and led the way to his grandfather's old Ford. That was something he planned to change, just as soon as the lawyers gave him the go-ahead to start spending the old man's money. In the car, his passenger directed him away from the city and out into the countryside. They ended up at an inn that sat at a crossroads. The elderly man bought a couple of beers and pointed him to the beer garden.

They'd sat down in a sheltered corner, the watery spring sunshine barely warm enough for outside drinking. 'I'm Heinrich Holtz.' The introduction came with a quizzical look. 'Did he ever mention me? Heini?'

He shook his head. 'No, never.'

Holtz exhaled slowly. 'I can't say I'm surprised. What we shared, it wasn't something any of us like to talk about.' He sipped his beer with the fastidiousness of the occasional drinker.

Whoever Holtz was, he clearly wasn't from the world of commercial barge traffic. He was a small, shrivelled man, his narrow shoulders hunched in on themselves as if he found himself perpetually in a cold wind. His watery grey eyes peered out from nests of wrinkles, his look sidelong rather than direct.

'How did you know my grandfather?' he asked.

The answer, and the story that came with it, changed his life. Finally, he understood why his childhood had been made hell. But it was rage that welled up inside him, not forgiveness. At last, he could see where the light was. At last, he had a mission that would shatter the glacial grip of fear that had paralysed him for so long and stripped him of everything that other people took for granted.

That night in Heidelberg had simply been the next stage in that project. He'd planned scrupulously, and since he was still at liberty, he'd clearly made no mistakes that mattered. But he'd learned a lot from that first execution, and there were a couple of things he'd do differently in future.

He was planning a long future.

He powered up the small crane that lifted his shiny Volkswagen Golf from the rear deck of the *Wilhelmina Rosen* on to the dock. Then he checked that everything was in his bag as it should be: notepad, pen, scalpel, spare blades, adhesive tape, thin cord and a funnel. The small jar containing formalin, tightly screwed shut. All present and correct. He checked his watch. Plenty of time to get to Leiden for his appointment. He tucked his cellphone into his jacket pocket and began to attach the car to the crane.

6

The applause broke in waves over Daniel Barenboim's head as he turned back to the orchestra, gesturing to them to rise. *Nothing quite like Mozart to provoke good-will to all men,* Tadeusz mused, clapping soundlessly in his lonely box. Katerina had loved opera, almost as much as she loved dressing up for a night out in their box at the Staatsoper. Who cared where the money came from? It was how you spent it that counted. And Katerina had understood about spending with style, spending in ways that made life feel special for everyone around her. The prime seats at the opera had been her idea, though it had seemed entirely fitting to him. Coming tonight had felt like a rite of passage, but he hadn't wanted to share his space, least of all with any of the several preening women who had made a point of offering their condolences in the foyer ahead of the performance.

He waited till most of the audience had filed out, gazing unseeing at the fire curtain that shut off the stage. Then he stood up, shaking the creases out of his conservatively tailored dinner jacket. He slipped into his sable coat, reaching inside a pocket to turn his phone back on. Finally, he walked out of the opera house into the starry spring night. He brushed past the chattering groups and turned on to Unter den Linden, walking towards the spotlit spectacle of the Brandenburg Gate, the new Reichstag gleaming over to the right. It was a couple of miles to his apartment in Charlottenburg, but tonight he preferred to be out on the Berlin streets rather than sealed off inside his car. Like a vampire, he needed a transfusion of life. He couldn't stand to play the social game yet, but there was an energy abroad in the city at night that fed him.

He had just passed the Soviet War Memorial at the start of the Tiergarten when his phone vibrated against his hip. Impatiently, he pulled it out. 'Hello?'

'Boss?'

He recognized Krasic's deep bass. 'Yes?' he replied. No names on a cellphone; there were too many nerds out there with nothing better to do than scan the airwaves for stray conversations. Not to mention the various agencies of the state, constantly monitoring their citizens as assiduously as they ever had when the Red Menace still surrounded them.

'We have a problem,' Krasic said. 'We need to talk. Where will I find you?'

'I'm walking home. I'll be at Siegessäule in about five minutes.'

'I'll pick you up there.' Krasic ended the call abruptly.

Tadeusz groaned. He stopped for a moment, staring up at the sky through the budding branches of the trees. 'Katerina,' he said softly, as if addressing a present lover. At moments like this, he wondered if the bleak emptiness that was her legacy would ever dissipate. Right now, it seemed to grow worse with every passing day.

He squared his shoulders and strode out for the towering monument to Prussia's military successes that Hitler had moved from its original site to form a traffic island, emphasizing its domineering height. The gilded winged victory that crowned the Siegessäule gleamed like a beacon in the city lights, facing France in defiant denial of the past century's defeats. Tadeusz paused at the corner. There was no sign of Krasic yet, and he didn't want to loiter there looking obvious. Caution was, in his experience, its own reward. He crossed the road to the monument itself and strolled around the base, pretending to study the elaborate mosaics showing the reunification of the German people. *My grandmother's Polish heart would shrivel in her breast if she could see me here,* he thought. *I can hear her now. 'I didn't raise you to become the Prince of Charlottenburg,' she'd be screaming at me.* At the thought, his lips curled in a sardonic smile.

A dark Mercedes pulled up at the kerb and discreetly flashed its lights. Tadeusz crossed the round-about and climbed in the open door. 'Sorry to spoil your evening, Tadzio,' Krasic said. 'But, like I told you, we've got a problem.'

'It's OK,' Tadeusz said, leaning back against the seat and unbuttoning his coat as the car moved off down Bismarckstrasse. 'My evening was spoiled by a bastard on a BMW, not by you. So, what's this problem?'

'Normally, I wouldn't bother about something like this, but . . . That package of brown we brought up from the Chinese? You remember?'

'I'm not likely to forget. I haven't had my hands on the product for so long, it's not as if I could confuse it. What about it?'

'It looks like there's some sort of crap in it. There's four junkies dead in S036, and according to what I hear, there's another seven in hospital in intensive care.'

Tadeusz raised his eyebrows. East Kreuzberg, known locally by its old GDR postal code, was the heart of the city's youth culture. Bars, clubs, live-music joints kept the area round Oranienstrasse buzzing towards dawn every night. It was also home to many of the city's Turks, but there were probably more vendors of street drugs than of kebabs in the scruffy, edgy suburb. 'Since when have you given a shit about dead junkies, Darko?' he asked.

Krasic shifted his shoulders impatiently. 'I don't give a shit about them. There'll be four more tomorrow queuing up to take their place. Thing is, Tadzio, nobody pays any attention to one dead junkie. But even the cops have to sit up a bit when there are four bodies on the slab and it looks like there are more to come.'

'How can you be sure it's our junk that's killing them? We're not the only firm on the streets.'

'I made some inquiries. All of the dead ones used dealers who get their supplies from our chain. There's going to be heat on this.'

'We've had heat before,' Tadeusz said mildly. 'What makes this so special?'

Krasic made an impatient noise. 'Because it didn't come in the usual way. Remember? You handed it over to Kamal yourself.'

Tadeusz frowned. The hollow feeling in his stomach had returned. He recalled the bad feeling he'd had about this deal, the unease that had stolen up on him in the Danube boatyard. He'd tried to avoid the fates by changing the routine, but it seemed that the measures he'd taken to sidestep trouble had simply brought it to his door by a more direct route. 'Kamal's a long way from the street dealers,' he pointed out.

'Maybe not far enough,' Krasic growled. 'There have always been cut-outs between you and Kamal before. He's never been able to say, "Tadeusz Radecki personally supplied me with this heroin," before. We don't know how much the cops know. They might be just a step or two away from him. And if he's looking at a deal that will save him too much hard time, he might just think about giving you up.'

Now Tadeusz was really paying attention, his languid disinterest a distant memory. 'I thought Kamal was solid.'

'Nobody's solid if the price is right.'

Tadeusz turned in his seat and fixed Krasic with his sharp blue eyes. 'Not even you, Darko?'

'Tadzio, I'm solid because nobody can afford my price,' Krasic said, clamping a beefy hand on his boss's knee.

'So, what are you saying?' Tadeusz moved his leg away from Krasic, unconsciously making physical the distance he knew existed between them.

Krasic shifted in his seat, turning to stare out of the window past Tadeusz. 'We could afford to lose Kamal.'

Two months ago, Tadeusz would simply have nodded and said something like, 'Do whatever it takes.' But two months ago Katerina had still been alive. He hadn't yet had to revise his understanding of loss. It wasn't that he harboured some sentimental notion that Kamal could be to someone what Katerina had been to him; he knew Kamal, knew his venality, his power games, his pathetic strutting attempts at being someone worth reckoning with. But his experience of the wrench of sudden death had opened up a channel for empathy in quite unexpected directions. The idea of having Kamal killed on the off-chance that it might be for his personal benefit sat uncomfortably with Tadeusz now. Side by side with this was the consciousness that he could not afford to reveal what Krasic would surely see as a weakness. One would be very foolish indeed to show too much of the soft underbelly to a man like Krasic, however loyal he had always been. All this flashed through Tadeusz's head in an instant. 'Let's wait and see,' he said. 'Getting rid of Kamal right away would only draw the cops' attention in that direction. But if there's any sign that they're moving towards him . . . you know what to do, Darko.'

Krasic nodded, satisfied. 'Leave it with me. I'll make some calls.'

The car swept past Schloss Charlottenburg and turned into the quiet side street where Tadeusz lived. 'Talk to me in the morning,' he said, opening the door and closing it behind him with quiet finality. He walked into the apartment building without a backward glance.

Even though the sky outside was grey and overcast, Carol's eyes still took a few moments to adjust to the gloomy interior of the little quayside pub where Tony had suggested they meet. She blinked rapidly as she registered the quiet country music playing in the background. The barman looked up from his paper and gave her a quick smile. She glanced around, taking in the fishing nets draped from the ceiling, their brightly coloured floats dulled by years of cigarette smoke. Watercolours of East Neuk fishing harbours dotted the wood panelling of the walls. The only other customers appeared to be a couple of elderly men, their attention firmly on their game of dominoes. There was no sign of Tony.

'What can I get you?' the barman asked as she approached.

'Do you do coffee?'

'Aye.' He turned away and switched on a kettle that perched incongruously among the bottles of liqueurs and aperitifs below the gantry of spirits.

Behind her, the door opened. Carol turned her head and felt a tightening in her chest. 'Hi,' she said.

Tony crossed the few yards to the bar, a slow smile spreading. He looked as out of place in the bar as he always had everywhere outside his own rooms. 'Sorry I'm late. The phone just wouldn't stop ringing.' There was a moment's hesitation, then Carol turned to face him and they hugged, her fingers remembering the familiar feel of his well-worn tweed jacket. The couple of inches he had on her made him a good fit for her five feet and six inches. 'It's good to see you,' he said softly, his breath whispering against her ear.

They parted and sized each other up. His hair had started to thread with silver round the temples, she noted. The wrinkles round his dark blue eyes had deepened, but the ghosts that had always flickered in his gaze seemed to be finally at rest. He looked healthier than she'd ever seen him. He remained slim and wiry, but he felt firmer in the hug, as if his compact frame had built a subtle layer of muscle. 'You look well,' she said.

'It's all this fresh sea air,' he said. 'But you – you look terrific. You've changed your hair? It's different somehow.'

She shrugged. 'New hairdresser. That's all. He styles it a bit more sharply, I think.' *I can't believe I'm talking about hairdressing,* she thought incredulously. *Two years since we've seen each other, and we're talking as if there had never been more between us than casual acquaintance.*

'Whatever, it looks great.'

'What can I get you?' the barman interrupted, placing a single cup with an individual coffee filter in front of Carol. 'Milk and sugar in the basket at the end of the bar,' he added.

'A pint of eighty shilling,' Tony said, reaching for his wallet. 'I'll get these.'

Carol picked up her coffee and looked around. 'Anywhere in particular?' she asked.

'That table in the far corner, over by the window,' he said, paying for the drinks and following her to a spot where a high-backed settle cut them off from the rest of the room.

Carol took her time stirring her coffee, knowing he would recognize the displacement activity with his usual cool detachment, but unable to stop herself. When she looked up, she was surprised to see he was staring just as intently at his beer. Some time in the past two years he had absorbed something new into his behaviour; he'd learned to give people a break from his analytical eye. 'I appreciate you taking the time for this,' she said.

He looked up and smiled. 'Carol, if this is what it takes to get you to come and visit, all I can say is it's a small price to pay. E-mail's all very well, but it's also a good way to hide.'

'For both of us.'

'I wouldn't deny it. But time passes.'

She returned his smile. 'So, do you want to hear my Mission Impossible?'

'Straight to the point, as always. Listen, what I thought, if it's OK with you, is that we could get you settled in at your hotel then go back to my place to discuss what they've got lined up for you. It's more private than a pub. I only suggested meeting here because it's easier to find than my cottage.'

There was something more that he wasn't saying. She could still read him, she was relieved to find. 'Fine by me. I'd like to see where you're living. I've never been here before – it's amazingly picturesque.'

'Oh, it's picturesque, all right. Almost too picturesque. It's very easy to forget that passions run as high in picture postcard fishing villages as they do on the mean streets.'

Carol sipped her coffee. It was surprisingly good. 'An ideal place to recuperate, then?'

'In more ways than one.' He looked away for a moment, then turned back to face her, his mouth a straight line of resolve. She had a shrewd idea what was coming and steeled herself to show nothing but happiness. 'I'm . . . I've been seeing someone,' he said.

Carol was aware of every muscle it took to smile. 'I'm pleased for you,' she said, willing the stone in her stomach to dissolve.

Tony's eyebrows quirked in a question. 'Thank you,' he said.

'No, I mean it. I'm glad.' Her eyes dropped to the gloomy brown of her coffee. 'You deserve it.' She looked up, forcing a brightness into her tone. 'So, what's she like?'

'Her name's Frances. She's a teacher. She's very calm, very smart. Very kind. I met her at the bridge club in St Andrews. I meant to tell you. But I didn't want to say anything until I was sure something was going to come of it. And then . . . well, like I said, e-mail is a good place to hide.' He spread his hands in apology.

'It's OK. You don't owe me anything.' Their eyes locked. They both knew it was a lie. She wanted to ask if he loved this Frances, but didn't want to hear the wrong answer. 'So, do I get to meet her?'

'I told her we'd be working this evening, so she's not coming over. But I could call her, ask if she'd like to join us for dinner if you'd like?' He looked dubious.

'I don't think so. I really do need to pick your brains, and I have to go back tomorrow.' Carol drained her coffee. Picking up her cue, Tony finished his drink and stood up.

'It's really good to see you, you know,' he said, his voice softer than before. 'I missed you, Carol.'

Not enough, she thought. 'I missed you too,' was what she said. 'Come on, we've got work to do.'

7

All violent death is shocking. But somehow murder in a beautiful nineteenth-century house overlooking a tranquil canal, a medieval seat of learning and an impressive church spire provoked a deeper sense of outrage in Hoofdinspecteur Kees Maartens than the same event in a Rotterdam back street ever had. He'd come up the ranks in the North Sea port before finally managing a transfer back to Regio Hollands Midden, and so far his return to his childhood stamping grounds had lived up to his dreams of a quieter life. Not that there was no crime in this part of Holland; far from it. But there was less violence in the university town of Leiden, that was for sure.

Or so he'd thought until today. He was no stranger to the abuse that one human – or several combining in the same blind fury – could inflict on another. Dockside brawls, pub fights where insults real and imaginary had provoked clashes out of all proportion, assaults and even murders that turned sex workers into victims were all part of a day's work on the Rotterdam serious crimes beat, and Maartens reckoned he had grown a second skin over years of exposure to the ravages of rage. He'd decided he was impervious to horror. But he'd been wrong about that too.

Nothing in his twenty-three years at the sharp end had prepared him for anything like this. It was indecent, rendered all the more so by the incongruity of the setting. Maartens stood on the threshold of a room that looked as if it had been fundamentally unchanged since the house had been built. The walls were covered from floor to ceiling with mahogany shelving, its ornate beading warm with the muted gleam of generations of polishing. Books and box files filled every shelf, though he couldn't see much detail from here. The floor was burnished parquet, with a couple of rugs that looked worn and dull to Maartens. *Not something I would have chosen in so dark a room*, he thought, conscious that he was avoiding the central focus of the room with all his mental energy. Two tall windows looked out across the Maresingel to the historic town centre beyond. The sky was a washed-out blue, thin strips of cloud apparently hanging motionless, as if time had stopped.

It had certainly stopped for the man who occupied the hub of this scholar's study. There was no question that he was dead. He lay on his back on the wide mahogany desk that stood in the middle of the floor. Each wrist and ankle was tied to one of the desk's bulbous feet with thin cord, spread-eagling the dead man across its surface. It looked as if his killer had tied him down fully dressed, then cut his clothes away from his body, exposing the lightly tanned skin with its paler ghost of swimming trunks.

That would have been bad enough, a profanation

Maartens hoped his middle-aged body would be spared. But what turned indignity into obscenity was the clotted red mess below the belly, an ugly wound from which rivulets of dried blood meandered across the white flesh and dripped on to the desk. Maartens closed his eyes momentarily, trying not to think about it.

He heard footsteps on the stairs behind him. A tall woman in a tailored navy suit, honey blonde hair pulled back in a ponytail, appeared on the landing. Her round face was serious in repose, her blue eyes shadowed beneath straight dark brows. She was pretty in an unremarkable way, her understated make-up deliberately making her appear even more bland and unthreatening. Maartens turned to face Brigadier Marijke van Hasselt, one of his two team co-ordinators. 'What's the story, Marijke?' he asked.

She produced a notebook from the pocket of her jacket. 'The owner of the house is Dr Pieter de Groot. He's attached to the university. Lectures in experimental psychology. Divorced three years ago, lives alone. His teenage kids come to visit every other weekend. They live just outside Den Haag with the ex-wife. The body was discovered this morning by his cleaner. She let herself in as usual, saw nothing out of the ordinary, did the ground floor then came on up here. She glanced in the study door and saw that –' Marijke gestured with her thumb at the doorway. 'She says she took a couple of steps inside the room, then ran downstairs and called us.'

'That's the woman who was waiting on the doorstep with the uniformed officer when we got here?'

'That's right. She wouldn't stay in the house. Can't say I blame her. I had to talk to her in the car. Tom's rounded up some of our team and set them on door-to-door inquiries.'

Maartens nodded approval of her fellow co-ordinator's action. 'Later, you can go over to the university, see what they can tell you about Dr de Groot. Is the scene-of-crime team here yet?'

Marijke nodded. 'Outside with the pathologist. They're waiting for the word from you.'

Maartens turned away. 'Better let them in. There's bugger all else we can do here till they've done their stuff.'

Marijke looked past him as he moved towards the staircase. 'Any idea on the cause of death?' she asked.

'There's only one wound that I can see.'

'I know. But it just seems . . .' Marijke paused.

Maartens nodded. 'Not enough blood. He must have been castrated around the time of death. We'll see what the pathologist has to say. But for now, we're definitely looking at a suspicious death.'

Marijke checked her boss's dour face to see if he was being ironic. But she could see no trace of levity. In two years of working with Maartens, she seldom had. Other cops protected themselves with black humour, an instinct that sat comfortably with her. But comfort was the one thing that Maartens seemed inclined to prevent his team ever experiencing. Something told her they were going to need more than Maartens's austerity to get them through a murder as horrible as this. She watched him descend, her heart as heavy as his tread.

Marijke crossed the threshold of the crime scene.

The *recherche bijstandsteam* had a fixed system, even though murders didn't happen often enough on their patch to be routine occurrences. Her role while Maartens briefed the forensic team and the pathologist was to make certain the crime scene remained secure. She took latex gloves and plastic shoe covers out of the leather satchel she always carried with her and put them on. Then she walked in a straight line from the door to the desk, which brought her level with the dead man's head. This study of the dead was her job, the one Maartens always avoided. She was never sure if he was squeamish or simply aware that he was better occupied elsewhere. He was good at putting people to tasks that suited them, and she had never flinched at the sight of the dead. She suspected it was something to do with being a farm girl. She'd been accustomed to dead livestock since early childhood. Marijke really didn't care how much noise the lambs made.

What she cared about was what this body could teach her about victim and killer. She had ambition; she didn't intend to end her career as a brigadier in Hollands Midden. Every case was a potential stepping stone to one of the elite units in Amsterdam or Den Haag, and Marijke was determined to shine whenever she got the chance.

She stared down at the corpse of Pieter de Groot with a clinical eye, one fingertip straying to touch the distended abdomen. Cool. He'd been dead for a while, then. She frowned as she looked down. There was a circular stain on the polished surface of the desk, forming a nimbus round the head as if something had been spilled there. Marijke made a mental note to point it out to the scene-of-crime team. Anything out of the ordinary had to be checked out.

In spite of her intention to scan methodically every inch of the body and its surroundings, her eyes were irresistibly drawn to the crusted blood surrounding the raw wound. The exposed flesh looked like meat left unwrapped overnight on a kitchen counter. As she realized what she was seeing, Marijke's stomach gave an unexpected lurch. From a distance, she'd made the same assumption as Maartens. But de Groot hadn't been castrated. His genitals were still attached to his body, albeit smeared grotesquely with blood. She sucked in a mouthful of air.

Whoever had killed the psychologist hadn't removed his sexual organs. His murderer had scalped his pubic hair.

Carol leaned on the window sill, the steam from her coffee making a misty patch on the glass. The weather had closed in overnight, and the Firth of Forth was a rumpled sheet of grey silk with slubs of white where the occasional wave broke far from shore. She longed for her familiar London skyline.

It had been a mistake to come here. Whatever she'd gained professionally from the trip was more than cancelled out by the rawness of the emotion that Tony's presence had stirred up in her. Bitterly, she acknowledged to herself that she had still been clinging to a sliver of hope that their relationship might finally catch fire after an appropriate gap of time and space. The hope had crumbled like a sand-castle in the sun with his revelation that he had moved forward, just as she had always hoped he would.

Except that she wasn't the companion he had chosen to share the journey with.

She hoped she hadn't let the depth of her disappointment show as they'd left the pub, forcing her face to smile the congratulation of a friend. Then she'd turned away, letting the sharp north-easterly wind give her an excuse for smarting eyes. She'd followed his car up the hill away from the picture-postcard harbour to the small hotel where he'd arranged a room for her. She'd taken a defiant ten minutes to repair her make-up and arrange her hair to its best advantage. And to change out of her jeans into a tight skirt that revealed more than anyone in the Met had ever seen. She might have lost the battle, but that didn't mean she had to beat a bedraggled retreat. *Let him see what he's missing*, she thought, throwing down a gauntlet to herself as much as to him.

Driving back to his cottage, they'd said little of consequence, making small talk about life in a small town. The cottage itself was much as Carol had expected. Whatever this woman meant to Tony, she hadn't stamped her identity over his space. She recognized most of the furniture, the pictures on the wall, the books lined up on shelves along the study wall. *Even the answering machine,* she thought with a faint shudder, ambushed by memory.

'Looks like you've settled in,' was all she said.

He shrugged. 'I'm not much of a homemaker. I went through it with a bucket of white paint then moved all the old stuff in. Luckily most of it fitted.'

Once they were settled in the study with mugs of coffee, present constraints somehow slipped away and the old ease that had existed between them reasserted itself. So while Tony read the brief that Morgan had couriered to Carol that morning, she curled up in a battered armchair and browsed an eclectic pile of magazines ranging from *New Scientist* to *Marie Claire*. He'd always read a strange assortment of publications, she remembered fondly. She'd never been stuck for something to read in his house.

As he read, Tony made occasional notes on a pad propped on the arm of his chair. His eyebrows furrowed from time to time, and occasionally his mouth quirked in a question that he never enunciated. It wasn't a long brief, but he read it slowly and meticulously, flipping back to the beginning and skimming it again after he'd first reached the end. Finally, he looked up. 'I must admit, I'm puzzled,' he said.

'By what, in particular?'

'By the fact that they're asking you to do something like this. It's so far outside your field of experience.'

'That's what I thought. I have to assume there's some aspect of my experience or my skills that overrides my lack of direct undercover work.'

Tony pushed his hair back from his forehead in a familiar gesture. 'That would be my guess. The brief itself is more or less straightforward. Pick up the drugs from your source, exchange the parcel of drugs for cash and return it to your first contact. Of course, I'm assuming they'll throw spanners in the works along the way. There wouldn't be any point in it otherwise.'

'It's supposed to be a test of my abilities, so I think it's fair to expect the unexpected.' Carol dropped the magazine she was reading and tucked her legs underneath her. 'So how do I do it?'

Tony glanced at his notes. 'There's two aspects to this – the practical and the psychological. What are your thoughts?'

'The practical side's easy. I've got four days to go at this. I know the address for the cash pick-up and I know the general area where I'm going to be doing the handover. So I'm going to check out the house where I've got to go for the money. Then I'm going to get to know the various routes from A to B like the back of my hand. I need to be able to adjust to any contingencies that crop up, and that means knowing the terrain well enough to change my plans without having to think twice. I need to think about what I'm going to wear and how easily I can adapt my appearance to confuse anyone who's watching me.'

He nodded, agreeing. 'But of course, some of the practicalities are conditional on the psychological aspects.'

'And that's the bit I don't have a handle on. Which is why I'm here. Consulting the oracle.' Carol gave a mock salute.

His smile was self-mocking. 'I wish my students had the same respect for my abilities.'

'They've not seen you in action. They'd change their tune then.'

His mouth narrowed in a grim line and she saw a shadow in his eyes that had been missing before. 'Yeah, right,' he said after a short pause. 'Sign up with me and see circles of hell that Dante could never have imagined.'

'It goes with the territory,' Carol said.

'Which is why I don't live there any more.' He

looked away, his eyes focused on the street beyond the window. He took a deep breath. 'So. You need to know how to walk in someone else's shoes, right?' He turned back to face her, a forced expression of geniality on his face.

'And under their skin.'

'OK. Here's where we start from. We measure people by how they look, what they do and what they say. All our assessments are based on those things. Body language, clothes, actions and reactions. Speech and silence. When we encounter someone, our brain enters into a negotiation between what it's registering and what it has stored in its memory banks. Mostly, we only use what we've got locked up there as a control to judge new encounters. But we can also use it as a sampler on which to base new ways of acting.'

'You're saying I already know what I need to know?' Carol looked dubious.

'If you don't, even someone as smart as you isn't going to learn it between now and next week. The first thing I want you to do is to think about someone you've encountered who would be relatively comfortable in this scenario.' He tapped the papers with his pen. 'Not over-confident, just reasonably at home with it.'

Carol frowned as she flicked back through her memories of criminals she'd gone head to head with over the years. She'd never worked with the Drugs Squad, but she'd encountered both dealers and mules more often than she could count when she'd been running the CID in the North Sea port of Seaford. None of them seemed to fit. The dealers were too cocky or too fucked up by their own product, the mules too lacking in initiative. Then she remembered Janine. 'I think I've got someone,' she said. 'Janine Jerrold.'

'Tell me about her.'

'She started out as one of the hookers down at the docks. She was unusual, because she never had a pimp. She worked for herself, out of an upstairs room in a pub run by her aunt. By the time I came across her, she'd moved on to something a bit more lucrative and less physically dangerous. She ran a team of organized shoplifters. Occasionally, we'd lift one of the girls, but we never got our hands on Janine. Everybody knew she was behind it. But none of her girls would grass her up, because she always looked after them. She'd turn up to court to pay their fines, cash on the nail. And if they got sent down, she made sure their kids were looked after. She was smart, and she had so much bottle.'

Tony smiled. 'OK, now we've got Janine in our sights. That's the easy bit. What you have to do now is construct Janine for yourself. You need to mull over everything you've seen her do and say, and work out what ingredients went into the mix to make her the woman she is now.'

'In four days?'

'Obviously, it's going to be a rough draft, but you can work something up in that time. Then comes the really hard bit. You've got to shed Carol Jordan and assume Janine Jerrold.'

Carol looked worried. 'You think I'm up to it?'

He cocked his head on one side, considering. 'Oh, I think so, Carol. I think you're up to just about anything you set your mind to.'

There was a moment of silence, electric and pregnant. Then Tony jumped to his feet and said, 'More coffee. I need more coffee. And then we need to plan what we're going to do next.'

'Next?' Carol said, following him into the hall.

'Yes. We haven't got much time. We need to start role-playing right away.'

Before Carol could answer, there was the unmistakable sound of a key turning in the lock. They both swivelled round to face the front door, their faces rigid with surprise. The door swung open to reveal a trim woman in her late thirties. She pulled her key out of the lock, giving them both a smile whose warmth evaded her eyes. 'Hi, you must be Carol,' Frances said, pushing the door to behind her, stuffing her keys into her pocket and holding out her hand. Her eyes were scanning Carol from head to toe, taking in the short skirt with a slight raise of the eyebrows.

Carol shook it automatically.

'Carol, this is Frances,' Tony gabbled.

'Why on earth are you hanging around in the hall?' Frances asked.

'We were going to make more coffee,' Tony said, backing into the kitchen doorway.

'I'm sorry to butt in,' Frances said, steering Carol into the living room. 'I feel so stupid about this. But I left a pile of fourth-year jotters that I was marking last night. I was in such a rush, I clean forgot them this morning. And I need to give them their essays back tomorrow.'

Yeah, right, thought Carol, watching with a cynical eye as Frances picked up a pile of school notebooks tucked away round the far side of the sofa.

'I was just going to sneak in and fetch them. But if you were breaking for a cup of coffee, I might as well join you.' Frances turned and fixed Carol with a sharp stare. 'Unless I'm interrupting something?'

'We'd just reached a natural break,' Carol said stiffly. She knew she should say something along the lines of how pleased she was to meet Frances, but while she might have what it took to go undercover, she still didn't feel comfortable lying in a social situation.

'Tony?' Frances called. 'I'll stop for a quick coffee, if that's OK.'

'Fine,' came the reply from the kitchen. Carol was reassured to hear he sounded as enthusiastic as she felt.

'You're not at all how I'd imagined you,' Frances said, chilly dismissal in her voice.

Carol felt fourteen again, snagged on the jagged edge of her maths teacher's sarcasm. 'Most people don't have much idea about what cops are really like. I mean, we've all been to school, we know what to expect from teachers. But people tend to rely on TV for their images of police officers.'

'I don't watch much TV myself,' Frances said. 'But from the little that Tony has said about you, I was expecting someone more . . . mature, I suppose is the word. But look at you. You look more like one of my sixth-year students than a senior police officer.'

Carol was spared from further sparring by Tony's return. They sat around for twenty minutes making small talk, then Frances gathered up her marking and left them to it. After he saw her out, Tony came back into the room shaking his head ruefully. 'Sorry about that,' he said.

'You can't blame her,' Carol said. 'Probably just as well you weren't showing me the view from the upstairs rooms, though.'

It should have been a cue for laughter. Instead, Tony looked at the carpet and stuffed his hands in the pockets of his jeans. 'Shall we get on?' he said.

They'd worked on various role-plays for the rest of the evening, not even stopping over dinner. It was demanding work, taking all Carol's concentration. By the time the taxi came to take her back to her hotel, she was worn out from the combination of exercising her imagination and exorcizing her emotions. They said their farewells on the doorstep, stepping into an awkward hug, his lips brushing the soft skin under her ear. She'd wanted to burst into tears, but had held herself tightly in check. By the time she'd returned to the hotel, she felt only a hollowness in her stomach.

Now, as she stared out across the sea, Carol allowed herself to acknowledge her anger. It wasn't directed at Tony; she acknowledged he had never held out an unfulfilled promise to her. Her fury was all turned against herself. She had no one else to blame for the emotional heartburn that plagued her.

She knew she had two choices. She could let this rage fester inside her like a wound that could poison her whole system. Or she could finally draw a line under the past and use that energy to drive her forward into the future. She knew what she wanted to do. The only question was whether she could manage it.

Case Notes

Name: Pieter de Groot

Session Number: 1

Comments: The patient's lack of affect is notable. He is unwilling to engage and shows a disturbing level of passivity. Nevertheless, he has a high opinion of his own capabilities. The only subject on which he seems willing to discourse is his own intellectual superiority. His self-image is grandiose in the extreme.

His demeanour is not justified by his achievement, which seems best described as mediocre. However, his view of his capacities has been bolstered by a nexus of colleagues who, for unspecified reasons, have demonstrated a lack of willingness to question his own valuation of himself. He cites their failure in this respect as a demonstration of support for his own estimation of his standing in the community.

The patient lacks insight into his own condition.

Therapeutic Action: Altered state therapy initiated.

8

The laden Rhineship ploughed on towards Rotterdam, its glassy bow wave barely altering as the brown river widened, the Nederrijn imperceptibly becoming the Lek, then taking in the broad flow of the Nieuwe Maas. For most of the morning, he'd been blind to the passing scenery. They'd drifted through small, prosperous towns, with their mixture of tall town-houses and squat industrial buildings, church spires stabbing the flat grey skies, but he couldn't have described a single one of them, save from memory of previous trips. He'd registered neither the grassy dykes that obscured the lengthy stretches of flat country-side nor the graceful sweeps of road and rail bridges that broke up the long reaches of river.

The pictures he kept seeing were very different. The way Pieter de Groot had crumpled to the floor when he'd hit him on the back of his head with the sap he'd made himself, sewing the soft chamois leather with tight stitches then stuffing it with bird-shot. He couldn't imagine himself ever doing what de Groot had done, trusting a stranger enough to turn his back on him within five minutes of meeting.

Anyone that careless of his safety deserved what was coming to him.

More thrilling pictures. The panic in the heartless bastard's eyes when he'd come round to find himself bound naked to the top of his own desk. Curiously, his terror had subsided when the bargee had spoken. 'You're going to die here,' he'd said. 'You deserve it. You've played at being God. Well, now I'm going to teach you what happens when somebody plays God with you. You've fucked up people's heads for too long, and now it's your turn to get fucked up. I can make it fast because, believe me, you don't want it to be slow. But if you scream when I take the gag out of your mouth, I'm going to hurt you so much you'll be begging to die.' He'd been surprised by the reaction. His first victim had struggled, refusing to accept it was pointless. That, it seemed to him, was a natural response. It had irritated him, because it had made his work more difficult. But he'd respected it. It was how a man should behave.

The professor in Leiden, though. He'd been different. It was as if he instantly recognized that the person staring down at him was beyond the reach of any argument he could raise against his fate. He'd given up the ghost there and then, his eyes dull with defeat.

Cautiously, he'd taken the gag from the man's mouth. The psychologist hadn't even tried to plead. In that moment, he'd felt a terrible kinship with his victim. He didn't know what had happened in the man's life to give him this capacity for resignation, but he identfied an echo of his own learned behaviour and hated de Groot all the more for it. 'Very

76

fucking sensible decision,' he'd said gruffly, turning away to hide his unease.

He didn't want to think about that moment.

More beautiful pictures. The heaving chest, the convulsive jerking and twitching of a body fighting to stay on the right side of eternity. It made him feel better to replay his newly minted memories like this. He couldn't remember anything else that had ever made him feel so light-hearted.

And afterwards, the other pleasure he'd discovered, an unforeseen. Now at last he was able to show those whores who was boss. After he'd killed the professor in Heidelberg, he'd been astonished to find, driving back to the boat, that he wanted a woman. He was mistrustful of the urge that had so humiliated him in the past, but he told himself that he was a different man now, he could do what the hell he wanted.

So he'd made a detour to the back streets near the harbour and picked up a whore. She'd had a place to take him to, and he'd paid extra for the privilege of tying her up, spread-eagling her over the stained bed as he'd spread-eagled his victim over his desk. And this time, there had been no mortification. He'd been hard as a rock, he'd fucked her with brutal speed, he'd made her groan and beg for more, but it hadn't been her he'd seen, it had been the mutilated body he'd left behind. He felt like a god. When he'd finished, he'd untied her and forced her on to her stomach so he could celebrate his new potency by sodomizing her too. Then he'd left, throwing her a handful of coins to demonstrate his contempt.

He'd driven back to the boat on a high such as he'd never known, not even after he'd killed the old man.

It wasn't what he'd learned from Heinrich Holtz after the funeral that had lifted the curtain of darkness inside him or helped him to forgive his grandfather. Sometimes he wondered if he possessed the ability to forgive; so many responses that other people took for granted had been squeezed out of him. If they'd ever been there in the first place.

But what he had understood was who he could use to make a new library of memories that would bring him joy and light. For a long time, he had brooded, wondering how he could make his torturers pay. What had finally illuminated the road to his release was the terrible humiliation he'd suffered at the hands of that bitch of a Hungarian whore. It wasn't the first time he'd been taunted, but it was the first time someone had sounded just like his grandfather. A dizzying blackness had engulfed him, blocking out everything except an insatiable rage. In an instant, he'd had his hands round her throat, so tight her face had turned purple, her tongue poking out like a gargoyle. But in that moment when he had literally held her life in his hands, he'd suddenly realized it wasn't her he wanted to kill.

He'd fallen away from her, gasping and sweating, but simultaneously clear-headed, his feet set on a new path. He'd staggered into the night, an altered man. Now, he had a mission.

His pleasure in the remembrance of things past was broken by the arrival of Manfred with a steaming mug of coffee. He didn't begrudge the interruption, however. It was time something brought him back to earth. He'd been steering all morning on automatic pilot, which wasn't good enough for the stretch of river that lay ahead. The congested waters of Rotterdam were a deathtrap for the inattentive skipper. As the Nieuwe Maas swept through its wide bends towards the various side channels leading to wharves and moorings, tugs and barges and launches were constantly on the move. They could shoot out insouciantly from blind corners at outrageous speed. Avoiding collisions required all his attention to the radar screen as well as to the waters around him. Up in the bows, Gunther scanned the waterway, a second pair of eyes for what lay ahead, where the skipper's view was often obscured.

For now, he had to concentrate on getting them to safe harbour. The boat was all that mattered, for without the boat he was nothing; his mission would be scuppered. Besides, he was proud of his skills as a Rhine skipper. He had no intention of becoming the butt of dockside laughter.

Later, there would be plenty of time to indulge himself, to let the darkness fold back and bask in the light. While they were unloading, he could return to his memories. And perhaps plan how he would add to his store.

Brigadier Marijke van Hasselt wrinkled her nose. Not minding the dead was one thing; enduring the assorted stenches and sights of a postmortem was something that required rather more fortitude. The early stages had been fine. Nothing bothered her about the weighing and measuring, the freeing of head and hands from their plastic coverings, the scraping from under each individual fingernail, all meticulously recorded on audio and video tape by

Wim de Vries, the pathologist. But she knew what lay ahead, and it wasn't a prospect for the delicate of stomach.

At least de Vries wasn't one of those who relished the humiliation of the police officers who had to attend postmortems. He never brandished organs like a gleeful offal butcher. Rather, he was calm and efficient, as respectful of the dead as the disassembling of their physical secrets allowed him to be. And he spoke plainly when he found something the attending officer needed to know. All of which was a relief to Marijke.

Delicately, he continued his external examination. 'Some traces of froth in the nostrils,' he said. 'Consistent with drowning. But none in the mouth, which surprises me,' he added as he shone a light into de Groot's mouth. 'Wait, though . . .' He peered more closely, reaching for a magnifying glass. 'There's some bruising at the back of the throat here, and contusions on the insides of the lips and cheeks.'

'What does that mean?' Marijke asked.

'It's too early to be precise, but it looks as if something was forced into his mouth. We'll know more later.' Efficiently, he took a series of swabs from the body's several orifices then began to pay attention to the external injuries.

'The excision of the pubic hair is quite neat,' he said. 'Only a few signs of tentative cuts on the navel here.' He pointed with a latex-covered fingertip. 'You see? I've never seen this before. Pubic scalping, I suppose you'd have to call it. Your perpetrator has been careful not to damage the genitals themselves.'

'Was he still alive when it happened?'

De Vries shrugged. 'The scalping was done very close to death itself. He was either just dead or dying when it happened.' He continued to examine the body, pausing at the left side of the head. 'Nasty bump here.' His fingers probed the lump. 'Slight abrasion of the skin. Blunt force trauma. He took a blow to the head some time before he died.' He nodded to the technician. 'Let's roll him.'

Marijke stared down at the pattern of lividity on de Groot's back. The hollow of his neck, the small of his back, the thighs above the crook of his knees were stained purple as a bruise with the blood that had drained there, drawn downwards by the inexorable force of gravity. Where he had been pressed against the surface of the desk, the flesh remained a ghastly white; the shoulders, the buttocks, the calves. It reminded Marijke of a strange abstract painting. De Vries pressed a thumb against the shoulder of the corpse. When he withdrew it, there was no change. 'So,' he said, 'hypostasis is in the second stage. He has been lying dead in this position for at least ten to twelve hours. And he hasn't been moved after death.'

Now came the part Marijke hated. The body was replaced on its back and the dissection began. She slid her eyes sideways. To the casual observer, it would look as if she was paying close attention to what de Vries was doing, but in reality, she was staring at the tray of instruments as if her life depended on committing them to memory in some perverse version of Kim's Game. The dissecting knife, for incisions and removal of organs, with its metal two-piece handle and four-inch disposable blades.

The brain knife with its fine twelve-inch blade for making thin sections of the delicate tissue. The scissors and scalpels and forceps for things she didn't want to think about. The oscillating-bladed Stryker saw for cutting bone without destroying the surrounding tissues. The T-shaped chisel called the skull key, for extra leverage when prying apart the bones of the cranium.

So it was she missed the moment when de Vries cracked open the chest and the pale distended lungs ballooned out of the cavity. 'I thought so,' he said, satisfaction creeping through his professional demeanour and demanding her attention like a leg-winding cat.

'What's that?' She dragged her reluctant eyes from the surgical tools.

'Look at the state of the lungs.' He poked a finger into the grey tissue that bulged through the space between the ribs. It left a clear indentation. 'He's been drowned.'

'Drowned?'

De Vries nodded. 'No doubt about it.'

'But you said he died in the position where he was found.'

'That's right.'

Marijke frowned. 'But there was no water there. He was tied to his office desk. It's not like it was a bathroom or a kitchen. How could he be drowned?'

'Very unpleasantly,' de Vries said, his tone neutral, his eyes fixed on the work of his hands. 'Judging by the state of the mouth and the windpipe, I think some sort of funnel or tube was forced into his airway and water was poured down it. You said he was tied down, and I can see the marks of the ligatures for myself. He couldn't have put up much of a struggle.'

Marijke shuddered. 'Jesus. That's cold.'

De Vries shrugged. 'That's your province, not mine. I just read what the body has to say. Thankfully, I don't have to deal with the mind behind it.'

But I do, the detective thought. *And this is a very nasty one.* 'So the cause of death would be drowning?' she asked.

'You know I can't say that for sure at this stage. But it certainly looks that way.' De Vries turned back to the cadaver, slipping his hands into the abdominal cavity and lifting out the mass of the internal organs.

Drowning, she thought. *Not something you'd come up with in the heat of the moment. Whoever did this, he planned it very carefully. He came equipped for what he had to do.* If this was a crime of passion, it was a very strange passion indeed.

Carol closed the heavy door of her flat and leaned against it, kicking off her shoes. She crossed one leg over the other and bent to massage the liberated toes. She'd spent the whole day tramping around the back streets of Stoke Newington, Dalston and Hackney, looking at the world around her with the eyes of a criminal. It wasn't so different from the cop's take on the world. They were both looking for possible escape routes, possible targets of crime, possible gaps in security. But before, she'd been the hunter. Now she had to calculate what the quarry might need.

She'd memorized back alleys, vacant lots, hiding places. She'd checked out pubs with rear exits, kebab shops whose back door might be accessible to someone with quick enough wits and sharp enough elbows, gypsy cab firms whose drivers parked round the corner from the main drag, ready for a swift getaway. She'd learned which houses offered easy access to back gardens that could double as escape routes. She'd spent three days among the traffic fumes, stale cooking smells and cheap perfume of the streets, dressing to blend with the heterogeneous mixture of those hoping they were upwardly mobile and those living with the knowledge they were going nowhere but down. She'd eavesdropped on accents from five continents, checked out who attracted attention as they passed by, who was ignored.

It wasn't anywhere near enough, but it would have to do. Tomorrow she would spend polishing her performance, then it would be time for the real thing.

9

It was like picking a scab. The agony was exquisite, but the activity was irresistible. Tadeusz sat at the polished slab of burl oak that served as the desk in his home office, sorting through his photographs of Katerina. There were the public shots; the pair of them arriving at a film premiere, her radiant looks causing the snappers to take her for some minor starlet; a charity dinner, Katerina feeding him a piece of lobster with her fingers; Katerina at the formal opening of the day-care centre she'd helped raise funds for. There was a series of studio portraits that he'd persuaded her was the only birthday present he wanted from her. That the camera had loved her was clear from their sensuous quality.

Then there were the dozens of snaps he'd taken of her, some casual, others painstakingly set up. Katerina in Paris, posed with her head at an angle so the Eiffel Tower was reflected in her mirrored shades; Katerina in Prague, Wenceslas Square the dramatic backdrop; Katerina in the market place in Florence, rubbing the gleaming bronze nose of the wild boar statue for luck; and Katerina in a bikini sprawled on a sun lounger, one leg cocked at the knee, reading a trashy airport novel. He couldn't even remember if that last one had been taken on Capri or Grand Cayman. For some reason, it had ended up out of sequence among the Prague photographs. So much for every picture telling a story.

He'd always meant to put the photographs into albums, but there had never been time while she'd still been alive, while he'd been adding to the archive constantly. Now, he had all the time in the world to arrange the images of Katerina in whatever sequence he desired. Tadeusz sighed and reached for one of the leather-bound albums he'd chosen himself earlier that week from a photographic supplies wholesaler. He flipped open another wallet of snapshots and began to trawl through, discarding the images of landscapes and interesting architectural details, winnowing out the best shots of Katerina and arranging the first three on the page. Painstakingly, he mounted them, then wrote next to them in his neat hand, 'Katerina, Amsterdam. Our first weekend together.' He'd have to check the exact date in his diary, a realization that angered him. It seemed wrong that every detail wasn't carved in memory, a small token of disrespect that Katerina didn't deserve.

The buzz of the video entryphone interrupted him and he closed the album, getting to his feet and crossing the hall to the small screen sunk discreetly into the wall by the apartment door. Darko Krasic stood outside, half-turned towards the avenue, his eyes shifting back and forth in a constant surveillance. Even here in the respectable streets of Charlottenburg, his lieutenant didn't take his safety for granted.

Krasic always quoted his father, a fisherman. 'One hand for the boat, one hand for yourself.' Tadeusz didn't mind what some might have seen as paranoia; as far as he was concerned, it was directed towards keeping him safe as much as Krasic, and therefore a bonus rather than a cause for concern.

He buzzed Krasic in at the ground floor, putting the apartment door on the latch and heading through to the kitchen to make a pot of coffee. He'd barely taken the beans from the freezer when Krasic strode in, head down and shoulders wide, a man looking for somewhere to put his belligerence. He knew better than to direct it at his boss, however. 'We've got trouble,' he said in a surprisingly calm voice.

Tadeusz nodded. 'I heard the radio news earlier. Another two dead junkies in some shitty nightclub in Oranienstrasse.'

'That makes seven, counting the one who died in intensive care.' Krasic unbuttoned his overcoat and took a cigar case from his inside pocket.

'I know.' He dumped the beans in the grinder and killed all prospect of conversation for a few seconds. 'I can count, Darko.'

'So can the media. They're kicking up a real stink, Tadzio. This isn't going to go away. The cops are under a lot of pressure.'

'That's what we're paying them for, isn't it? To take the pressure and leave our people alone?' He tipped the ground coffee into a cafetiere and poured the hot water over it.

'Some things they can't ignore. Seven dead, for example.'

Tadeusz frowned. 'What are you saying, Darko?'

'It's gone past the point where our normal protection can take care of things. They're going to arrest Kamal tonight. We've had our card marked, that's as far as our man can stick his neck out right now.' He lit his cigar and puffed luxuriously.

'Fuck. Can we control what happens?'

Krasic shrugged. 'It depends. If he's looking at seven murder charges, Kamal might think it's worth taking the risk of giving me up. Or even you. If they offer him immunity, he might decide his best chance is to take us off the streets. Give himself a breathing space and trust to the witness protection programme.'

Tadeusz pressed the plunger down slowly, his mind flipping through the options. 'We're not going to let it go that far,' he said. 'Time for the pawn sacrifice, Darko.'

Darko allowed himself a thin smile. Tadzio hadn't lost it. 'You want me to make sure he never gets as far as the police station?'

'I want you to do whatever it takes. But make it look good, Darko. Give the press something to take their minds off all those dead wasters.' He poured two cups of coffee, pushing one towards the Serb.

'I've already got one or two ideas on that score.' He raised his cup in a toast. 'Leave it with me. You won't be disappointed.'

'No,' Tadeusz said firmly. 'I won't be. Now, losing Kamal leaves us with a gap. Who's going to fill it, Darko? Who's got what it takes to walk in a dead man's shoes?'

It had been a long day, but Brigadier Marijke van Hasselt was too wired for sleep. She'd delivered the results of the postmortem – death by drowning, as de Vries had tentatively predicted early on in the autopsy – at a briefing with her boss, Maartens, and her opposite number, Tom Brucke. Though none of them had said it in so many words, they really didn't have a single lead.

They'd masked the insecurity this inevitably produced with the familiar police routines that they all knew in their bones. Briskly, Maartens had outlined the ground rules for the investigation, assigning tasks to one team or the other, acting as if this was a directed inquiry that already had its terms of reference clearly mapped out. But they all knew they were groping in the dark for Pieter de Groot's killer.

Most murders were easy. They fell into one of three broad categories: domestic disputes jacked up one step too far; drunken brawls that escalated beyond the initial intent; or the incidentals of other criminal activity, usually connected to drugs or violent robbery. The Leiden killing didn't fit any of these categories. Nobody in the victim's immediate circle had an obvious motive, nor was this the kind of murder that arose from the engorged or embittered passions of domestic relationships. Besides, the ex-wife and the current girlfriend both had alibis, the one at home with her children, the other visiting her sister in Maastricht.

Maartens had remarked that they needed to take a look at his professional life. He couldn't imagine that anyone at the university would have turned to murder to solve some scholastic dispute, but with so few threads to grasp, they had to be sure they weren't missing the obvious. He'd heard that passions could run high in the rarefied atmosphere of academic research, and there were some very strange people around in higher education, especially in areas like psychology.

Marijke had said nothing, unwilling to provoke further her boss's prejudice against university graduates like herself. Although Maartens was every bit as clued in about modern policing as any of his colleagues, he still clung to some of the old-school attitudes of his youth, and she didn't want what was an already complicated investigation made any more awkward. She'd acknowledged his assignment of the university connection to her team with a quick nod. It would almost certainly be a complete waste of time, and it would have to wait until after the weekend, but she'd make sure the job was done thoroughly.

Tom Brucke's team had begun their canvass of the neighbourhood, but so far they'd drawn a blank. Nobody had seen or heard anything that had any apparent relevance to the murder. It wasn't the sort of area where a strange car would immediately be noticed by the neighbours, and few people paid attention to individual pedestrians on a street where there was regular foot traffic. Whoever had killed Pieter de Groot, he hadn't drawn attention to himself.

Marijke had spent the rest of the day supervising a search of de Groot's home, to see if there was anything that might be construed as a clue to the bizarre scenario that had been played out in the upstairs room. But there was nothing. She wondered about what was missing, however. There was no sign of a diary, desk calendar or personal organizer in the office. She couldn't believe a man like de Groot wouldn't have some sort of *aide memoire* for his appointments in his home office. She'd even had one of the technicians check over his computer to see if he kept an electronic diary, but that had drawn a blank too.

But sometimes absences held their own clues. To Marijke, this lack said that whoever had killed Pieter de Groot was no casual caller. He'd been expected, and he'd taken care to remove all trace of that appointment. If she was right, there was a chance that there might be a duplicate note of the arrangement in de Groot's diary at the university. She made a note to herself to make sure she was there when they entered his office, and set one of her officers the task of getting them admission first thing in the morning.

Eventually, she grudgingly accepted there was nothing more for her to do. Her team was busy with the tedious routine of sifting material and information that would probably prove useless. They didn't need her. The best way she could serve the inquiry now was to go home and let her mind turn over what little they knew. Sleep, she always found, was the best possible state in which to uncover new angles of approach.

But sleep wasn't going to come any time soon, Marijke knew. She poured herself a glass of wine and settled herself down in front of her computer. Some months previously, she'd become a subscriber to an on-line newsgroup for gay police officers. Not that there was any problem with being a lesbian and a Dutch police officer, nor did she have a ghetto mentality. But sometimes it was helpful to have what she thought of as a room of one's own and, via the newsgroup, she'd developed close friendships with a handful of other officers whose take on the world chimed comfortingly with her own. More than that, she'd formed a bond of particular intimacy with a German colleague. Petra Becker was a criminal intelligence officer in Berlin and, like Marijke, senior enough not to be entirely comfortable with close confiding relationships with her colleagues. Like Marijke, Petra was also single, another damaged survivor of the attrition of their career on relationships. They'd been cautious with each other at first, escaping from the newsgroup into private live chat rooms where they could write more openly about thoughts and feelings. They were both aware that each had found some special connection to the other, but they were equally reluctant to push for a face-to-face encounter in case it shattered what they valued.

And so they had developed the habit of spending an hour or so in each other's virtual company several nights a week. Tonight there was no prior arrangement in place, but Marijke knew that if Petra was at home and awake, she'd be in one of the public chat rooms on the gay police site, and that she'd be able to tempt her away from the crowd into private discussion.

She connected to the website and clicked on the <chat> icon. There was a list of public discussion areas, and she went straight to the Debating Forum, a room where people tended to talk about policy and its impact on their work. Half a dozen people were engaged in a heated argument about undercover operations, opinions flying as fast as fingers could type, but Petra wasn't one of them. Marijke exited and entered the Lesbian Issues area. This time, she was lucky. Petra was one of three women rehashing a recent Danish case of alleged lesbian rape, but as soon as she saw Marijke's name on her screen, she escaped and took her into a private area where they could exchange on-screen messages without anyone eavesdropping.

Petra: hello, love. how are you tonight?

Marijke: I just got in. We caught a murder today.

P: that's never fun.

M: No. And this was a really nasty one.

P: domestic? street?

M: Neither. The worst kind. Ritualistic, organized, no obvious suspects. Clearly personal, but in an impersonal sort of way, if you see what I mean.

P: who's the victim?

M: A professor at the university in Leiden. Pieter de Groot. His cleaner found the body. He was in his study at home, staked out naked on his desk. He'd been drowned by having a funnel or a pipe shoved down his throat, then water poured through it.

P: very nasty. was he one of those scientists who do animal experiments?

M: He was an experimental psychologist. I don't know much detail about what he did. But I don't think this is about animal rights. I think this was a one-on-one. There's more, you see. Whoever did this, they didn't stop at killing. There's mutilation as well.

P: genital?

M: Yes and no. The killer left his prick and balls intact, but scalped his pubic hair. I've never seen anything like it. It was almost worse than if he'd been castrated. That would have made more sense, more typical of what the sexually motivated killer would do.

P: you know, this is ringing bells with me. some bulletin i glanced at. not one of ours, a cry for help from another force.

M: You mean there's been a case like this in Germany?

P: can't say for certain. but something's niggling at the back of my mind. i'll do a computer trawl in the office.

M: I don't deserve you, do I?

P: no, you deserve much better. so, now we got the shop talk out of the way, you want to get personal?

Marijke smiled. Already, Petra had reminded her that there was more to life than murder. At last, she could see a route that might take her to sleep.

10

The *Wilhelmina Rosen* sat unusually high in the water. She'd discharged her cargo that morning, but someone at the shipping agency had screwed up, and the load that should have been stowed that afternoon had been delayed till the following day. He wasn't unduly anxious. He could probably make up the day once they were under way, even if it meant bending the rules about how long their watches should be. And the crew were happy enough. They weren't going to complain about a night ashore in Rotterdam, since it wasn't a delay that would put a dent in their pay.

Alone in his cabin, he unlocked a small brass-bound chest that had belonged to his grandfather and contemplated its contents. The two jars had originally contained pickled gherkins, but what floated inside now was infinitely more grisly. Preserved in formalin he'd stolen from a funeral parlour, the skin had lost its flesh tints and assumed the colour of tinned tuna. Fragments of the small muscles were darker, standing out against the skin like a cross-section of tuna steak grilled rare. The hair remained curled, though now it had the harsh dullness of a bad wig. Still, there could be no doubting what he was looking at.

When he had first fantasized about this, he'd known he would need some souvenir to remind himself how well he'd done. He had read books about murderers who had excised breasts, removed genitalia, stripped the skin from their victims to clothe themselves. None of this seemed right. They were weirdos and perverts, whereas he was driven by a motive far more pure. But he wanted something, and he needed it to hold meaning for him alone.

He ranged over the indignities he'd been forced to suffer at the hands of the old man. There was no blurring at the edges of his memory. Even commonly repeated tortures failed to merge into one big picture. Every detail of every mortification was pinprick sharp. What could he take that would keep his purpose fresh, clear and meaningful?

Then he'd remembered the shaving. It had happened soon after his twelfth birthday, a day unmarked by gifts or cards. The only reason he knew it was his birthday was that he'd caught a glimpse of his birth certificate a few months before when the old man had been sorting through some papers. Until then, he'd had no date to call his own. He'd never had so much as a birthday card, never mind presents, cakes and parties. But who could have been invited to any party of his? He had no friends, he had no wider family. As far as he was aware, the only people who even knew his name were the crew of the *Wilhelmina Rosen*.

He'd known he was born some time in the autumn, because around the turning of the leaves, the litany of rage that poured into his ears would alter. Instead of, 'You're eight years old, but you still act like a baby,' the old man would snarl, 'You're nine now, time you learned what it is to take some responsibility.'

Around the time he turned twelve, he'd noticed the changes. He'd grown taller, his shoulders straining the seams of his flannel work shirts. His voice had become unreliable, shifting registers as if he were possessed by a demon. And around his cock, dark wiry hairs had started to sprout. He'd imagined this would happen eventually. He'd spent too long living in close confinement with three adult males not to have grasped that at some point his body was going to duplicate theirs. But the reality was simply another source of anxiety. He was leaving childhood behind, without any clear idea of how he could ever become a man.

His grandfather had noticed the changes too. It was hard to imagine how he could be more brutal, yet he seemed to regard it as a challenge to find fresh sources of humiliation. Things had reached a new level of horror when a hawser snapped one morning as they were docking in Hamburg. It had been one of those things that was nobody's fault, but the old man had decided that someone had to pay the price.

When they'd got back to the apartment, he had ordered the boy to strip. He'd stood shivering in the kitchen, wondering which of the familiar agonies awaited him, while his grandfather had raged through to the bathroom, swearing and insulting him. When the old man had returned, he was carrying his cut-throat razor, the blade open and gleaming like silver in the dimness of the afternoon light. Terror had risen like bile in his throat. Convinced he was going to be castrated at the very least, he'd sprung at the old man, fists flying, desperate to escape whatever lay ahead.

He hadn't even seen the punch that hit the side of his head like a mallet. All he knew was a moment of crushing pain, then oblivion. When he'd opened his eyes, it was dark. There was a dribble of dried vomit running from his cheek to the floor and a burning pain in his groin that was sufficiently frightening to render insignificant the dull throb in his head. He lay for long minutes, curled on the cold linoleum, afraid to allow his hands to explore for fear of what they might find.

Eventually, he dared. His fingers crept down his stomach, tentative and slow. At first, he encountered only the cold, smooth flesh of his stomach. Then, just above the pubic bone, there was a sudden change in texture and a jagged stab of pain that made him suck his breath in sharply. He clenched his jaw and pushed himself up on one elbow. It was too dark to see anything, but he decided he'd risk turning on a light. It might bring even more wrath down on his head, but he couldn't bear not knowing what had happened to him.

Almost crying with the several pains that movement brought, he managed to get to his knees, where he paused to let a nauseating dizziness pass. Using the table as a prop, he dragged himself to his feet and tottered the few steps to the kitchen light switch. He leaned against the wall and flicked the switch with trembling fingers. Dim yellow light filled the dingy room, and he steeled himself for a glance.

The skin around his genitals was red raw. Every

trace of pubic hair had been erased, along with the top layer of skin. There were pinprick scabs of blood where the razor had gone deeper still, but the cruel scraping of the tender skin was the source of the burning pain that coursed through his groin. He'd been more than shaved, he'd been skinned. He'd been reminded forcibly that he wasn't fit to think of himself as a man. He hated himself then, contempt swallowing him like a black tide.

Looking back now, he realized his panicky rebellion had been a turning point. From then on, his grandfather had been less ready to inflict his tortures. The old man began to keep his distance, relying on the verbal flaying that could still reduce the teenage boy to quivering incompetence. He thought about running away, but where would he run to? The *Wilhelmina Rosen* was his only world and he doubted his ability to survive in any other. Gradually, as he had emerged into his twenties, he comprehended that there might be another way to gain freedom. It had been a painfully slow process, and in the end, he had won.

But that victory still hadn't been enough. He'd known that before Heinrich Holtz had told his story in the beer garden. What Holtz had given him was a glimpse of how he could finally get his own back. He'd given him a way to be a man.

He picked up one of the jars and swirled it round, watching the contents move in a slow *danse macabre*. He smiled as he unzipped his jeans.

Tadeusz Radecki was far too smart to be nothing more than a gangster. He'd built a legitimate business empire of video-rental stores that provided him not only with a justifiable income to keep the tax authorities happy, but also allowed enough leeway in its accounting procedures to permit a serious amount of money laundering. If his business rivals had ever seen his company's books, they'd have wondered how he could achieve such high rental levels per video and probably fired their own marketing teams out of pique. But that wasn't going to happen. Tadeusz made sure his public business was above reproach. Not for him the shady back-street video stores with their under-the-counter hardcore, or the wraps of drugs that changed hands in the video boxes. It might be his wares they were peddling, but there was no way he wanted any official connection to them.

That afternoon, he'd been visiting his flagship store at the top of the Ku'damm, where they did as much business selling videos as they did renting them out. He'd gone to check out the revamp that the most stylish shopfitters in the city had been carrying out, and he'd been impressed with the result. Clean lines, moody lighting and a coffee bar in the middle of the shop floor came together to produce the perfect ambience for browsing and spending.

After the tour of the shop, the manager had taken him up to his office for a celebratory glass of wine. As they'd entered, the TV screen had been showing a news channel. A reporter stood in a street Tadeusz recognized immediately as Friesenstrasse in Kreuzberg. Behind him was the unmistakable four-storey building that housed the GeSa, the detention centre where all newly arrested criminals were brought. It wasn't somewhere Tadeusz was personally familiar with; he knew the street principally because he always bought his reading material at the Hammett crime bookshop there.

The reporter's mouth was opening and closing soundlessly, his frowning face indicating the seriousness of what he was revealing to the waiting world. Then the picture changed to amateur video footage of a man being hustled out of a car towards the heavy grey door of the GeSa, a uniformed officer on either side of him. Suddenly, a woman ducked under the barrier that prevented cars from driving straight into the yard from the street. The officers on duty in the guard post were caught unawares, only emerging from their booth as the woman ran up behind the prisoner and his escort, waving something in front of her. She stopped a couple of yards away from them, directly behind the prisoner. In an instant, his head blossomed scarlet, like a blob of spaghetti sauce splattered on a kitchen surface. The police officers peeled away from him as he crumpled. They hit the deck with their pale faces turning towards the woman. Even at that range, it was possible to see their eyes stretching wide in panic.

Tadeusz stared at the screen, appalled. He'd only seen the sniper's victim for a few seconds, and then only in three-quarter profile. But he knew who the dead man was. He was aware of the shop manager saying something and he turned away from the screen. 'Sorry?' he said.

'I said, it's funny how real-life shootings never look half as dramatic as the ones we sell.' He reached for the open bottle of red wine on his desk and poured two glasses.

'I don't think I've ever seen a real-life shooting before,' Tadeusz lied. 'I'm quite shocked they're showing it in all its glory on the early evening news.'

The manager laughed as he handed a glass to his boss. 'I'm sure the moral guardians of the nation's youth will be clogging the TV station switchboard with complaints as we speak. Cheers, Tadeusz. Good decision to choose those guys. They've made a great job of the shop floor.'

Tadeusz raised his glass mechanically, reaching for his mobile with his other hand. 'Yes. Now I need to find a way to justify the expense of doing up the rest of the chain. Excuse me.' He touched a couple of keys to speed-dial Krasic. 'It's me,' he said. 'We need a meeting. I'll see you at my place in half an hour.' He ended the call without waiting for Krasic's response, then sipped his wine. 'Lovely stuff, Jurgen, but I'm afraid I've got to run. Empires to build, new worlds to conquer – you know how it is.'

Twenty minutes later, he was pacing the floor in front of his TV screen, flipping channels to see if he could find a local news station that was running the footage of Kamal's assassination. Finally, he caught the tail end of the video and immediately raised the volume. The studio anchorman took up the story. 'The dead man, whose name has not yet been released, had been arrested in connection with the seven heroin deaths in the city in the past week. Sources close to the investigation say that the woman who fired the fatal shot was the girlfriend of one of the addicts who died after shooting up with contaminated drugs. Already, there are calls for an inquiry into how the woman found out about the arrest before the prisoner had even been taken into formal custody.' He glanced down at his papers. 'And now over to our correspondent at the Reichstag, where representatives have been debating new measures to combat the spread of BSE . . .'

Tadeusz hit the mute button. He'd heard all he needed to know. When Krasic finally arrived five minutes late, complaining about the traffic, he launched straight in. 'What the hell are you playing at?'

'What do you mean, Tadzio?' Krasic stalled. It was clear from the troubled look in his eyes that he knew exactly what his boss meant.

'Fuck it, Darko, don't play stupid games with me. What possessed you? Having Kamal taken out on the steps of the fucking police station? I thought we were trying to take the limelight off this investigation, not turn it into the lead story across the country? Jesus, you couldn't have gone for a more public display.'

'What else was I supposed to do? There wasn't enough time to stage a convenient road accident . . .' His voice tailed off as he realized what he'd said.

The colour drained from Tadeusz's face. He looked terrifying in the shadows cast by the subtle lighting of the room. 'You insensitive bastard,' he snarled. 'Don't think you can divert me away from this fiasco by reminding me of Katerina.'

Krasic turned away and scowled. 'That's not what I meant. I just meant that I didn't have enough time to set something up that would look accidental. So I reckoned if it was going to end up looking like murder, it needed to look like a domestic, not something to do with the business. So I got Marlene to do the dirty.

103

She's been working for us, shifting product in Mitte for the past couple of years. She's not a user herself. And she's smart enough to play the distraught girlfriend, deranged with grief. She'll get away with next to nothing when it comes to court. And she won't grass us up. She's got a six-year-old girl I've promised we'll take care of. She knows me well enough to understand what that means. One word out of place and the kid gets taken care of, though not in the way she wants. Boss, it was the only way. It had to be done, and it had to be done like this.' There was no plea in Krasic's voice, just a convinced finality.

Tadeusz glared at him. 'It's all going to shit,' he complained. 'This was supposed to go away. Instead, Kamal's whole life is going to come under the microscope.'

'No, boss, you're wrong. It's Marlene they're going to be looking at. Before we're done, we'll have turned her into the heroine who rid the city of some vile drug-dealing scum. Like I told you, she's not a user. Her life looks clean. And we can put up plenty of people who'll make her sound like Mother fucking Teresa. Photographs of the six-year-old looking lost. Stuff about how she was trying to get her boyfriend off the junk. Besides, now they've seen how we dealt with Kamal, nobody else is going to say a thing to the cops. Trust me, Tadzio, it's for the best.'

'It had better be, Darko. Because if it all goes to shit, I know exactly who to blame.'

11

Tony glanced at the clock as he left the seminar room. Five past eleven. Carol would almost certainly have embarked on her quest by now. He wondered where she was, how she was doing, what she was feeling. Her visit had unsettled him more than he cared to admit. It wasn't just that she had disturbed him on a personal level; he'd been expecting that and had done what he could to armour himself against the turbulent currents he knew would be swirling beneath the surface of any encounter between the pair of them.

What he hadn't anticipated was how she would stir him up on a professional level. The pleasure he'd taken in the preparation they'd done had been the mental equivalent of a cold shower. It had snapped his synapses to attention in a way that no interaction with undergraduates had ever done. It had reminded him that he was operating at about half his capacity here at the university, and while that might have been sensible as a kind of convalescence from the harrowing he'd undergone at the hands of Jacko Vance, it was no way to spend the rest of his life. If he'd needed further reinforcement, it had just fallen into his lap.

He'd always feared this moment. Deep down, he'd known the siren call of what he did best might rise again to waken him from the slumberous existence he'd chosen. And he'd done everything in his power to guard against that moment. But the combination of the news of Jacko Vance's appeal and the return of Carol Jordan had been too strong for his fortifications.

Things had changed since he'd last been in the front line, he knew that. Quietly, privately, the Home Office had taken a sideways step from using professional psychologists as consultants on complex serial murder investigations. The publicity that had been generated by their earlier policy had given them too many sweaty-palmed moments for them to be willing to continue it indefinitely. Not everyone was as talented as Tony; and few were as close-mouthed. Although there were still a handful of experts who were called in on an ad hoc basis, the police had been busy behind the scenes building their own skills base at the National Crime Faculty at Bramshill. Now there was a new breed of criminal analyst, officers trained in an impressive mixture of psychological skills and computer navigation. Like the FBI and the Canadian RCMP, the Home Office had decided that it was better to rely on police officers trained in specialist areas than to call on the sometimes questionable skills of clinicians and academics who, after all, had no direct experience of what it took to catch a criminal. So, in one sense, there was no longer a place for Tony doing what he believed he had a unique talent for. And after the last debacle there was no way any politician would agree to give him any training or developmental role.

But perhaps there was something else he could offer. Perhaps he could find a niche that would allow him occasionally to flex his analytical muscles in pursuit of the profoundly disturbed minds who committed the most unreadable of crimes.

And perhaps this time, with Carol almost certainly moving to some new role in Europol, he could escape the turmoil that had accompanied his last two excursions into the minds of serial killers. It was certainly worth thinking about.

The only question now was who he could reach out to in a tentative approach. The Vance appeal would have reminded people of his existence. Maybe this was the perfect time to jog their memories a little more, to persuade them that he alone had something to throw into the ring that nobody else had. Not only did he understand how the mind of the serial offender worked; he was one of the few people on the planet who had actually been responsible for putting some of them where they could do no more harm.

It wouldn't hurt to try.

That Monday morning in Berlin, Petra Becker was also thinking about serial offenders. It would be a terrific boost to her career if she managed to be the person who made the links that demonstrated there was a serial killer working across European borders.

But first she had to find the case she'd been reminded of. Petra sat and frowned at her computer, the severity of her expression a sharp contrast to the spiky exuberance of her short dark hair. Parallel lines furrowed her broad forehead and her eyebrows shadowed her blue eyes, turning them navy. She knew she'd read about it relatively recently, but she'd dismissed it as being of no interest. Petra worked in intelligence. Her team were responsible for gathering information on organized crime, building a basic case, then passing it on to the appropriate law enforcement bodies. With European borders allowing free passage to the criminal as well as the law-abiding following the Schengen Agreement, that frequently meant colleagues in other countries, often using Europol as a conduit. In the past three years, Petra had investigated areas as diverse as product tampering, drug running, credit-card fraud and human trafficking. Murder wasn't normally on her beat, except when the investigating officers thought there might be a connection to organized crime. It was, she thought cynically, a way of handing off any difficult case that looked remotely like a scum-on-scum killing, the sort of scuzzy case that most police forces didn't lose any sleep over if they couldn't nail a culprit.

So the case she was looking for would have come in as a possible gangland killing. But if it had been tossed aside because it didn't fit any of their parameters, it wouldn't be in any of the holding files on the computer. It might even have been deleted from the main system, on the basis that it was just clutter.

Petra, however, was too anally retentive to dump case information without a trace. You never knew when something written off by everyone else might just feed into a subsequent investigation. So she'd developed the habit of taking brief notes even on the apparently irrelevant. That way, she could always go back to the original investigating officers and pull the details again.

She called up the folder that contained her notes and checked the recent files. There were four murder cases from the past seven weeks. She dismissed a drive-by shooting in a small town between Dresden and the Polish border and the murder of a Turk in Stuttgart. He'd bled to death following the amputation by machete of both hands. Petra had thought it was probably more to do with some domestic settling of scores than any organized criminal activity, since the local cops hadn't come up with a single thing to connect the dead man to anything more illegal than an expired visa.

That left two cases. A very strange murder in Heidelberg and the crucifixion of a known drug dealer in Hamburg. Her notes said nothing about pubic scalping, but she seemed to recall it had featured in one or other of those cases. She checked the reference numbers and sent e-mails to both police divisions involved. With luck, she'd have an answer by the end of the day.

Petra headed for the coffee machine, feeling very pleased with herself. She was emptying a sachet of sugar into her cup when her boss, Hanna Plesch, joined her. 'You're looking cheerful,' she said.

'And you're going to put a stop to that, right?' She cocked an eyebrow at her.

'That shooting over at the GeSa on Friesenstrasse – I want you to do a bit of digging, see what you can come up with.' Plesch leaned past her and pressed the button for a black coffee.

Petra stirred her coffee thoughtfully. 'It's hardly our

area, is it? I heard it was being written up as a personal thing. The shooter was the girlfriend of one of the doctored heroin victims, wasn't she?'

Plesch gave a sardonic smile. 'That's the official line. Me, I think it stinks. She's on our files, you know, the woman who did the shooting. Marlene Krebs. We had intelligence that she was dealing in Mitte. Small fry, so we left her alone. But we heard she's tied in to Darko Krasic.'

'Which means she might be a way through to Radecki,' Petra continued. 'So you want me to talk to her?'

Plesch nodded. 'It could be worth our while. She probably thinks she's looking at a light sentence if she plays the sympathy card – woman insane with grief takes revenge on the evil drug pusher who destroyed her lover. If we can persuade her that's not going to happen . . .'

'She might just give us something we can use to build a case against Krasic and Radecki.' Petra sipped her coffee, wincing at the heat.

'Exactly.'

'Leave it with me,' she said. 'I reckon as soon as she finds out who I am and what I know about her, she'll realize she hasn't got a cat in hell's chance of making the deranged lover defence work. Can you let me have whatever we've got on her?'

'It's already on your desk.' Plesch began to move away.

'Oh, and Hanna . . . ?'

She paused and glanced over her shoulder. 'You want something else.' It was a statement, not a question.

'Some*one* else. I need someone out on the street in Mitte. We need to establish that the dead guy really wasn't Marlene's man.'

'Hard to prove a negative.'

'Maybe so. But if we can nail down who Marlene has been shagging, it might rule out a connection to the dead guy. Likewise, if we can establish whether he was involved with anyone on a long-term basis . . .'

Plesch shrugged. 'Probably worth a try. The Shark's got nothing pressing on his plate. Send him out for some red meat.'

Petra's heart sank as she walked back to her desk. The Shark was an ironic nickname for the most junior member of the squad. He'd earned it because he had no taste for blood and was incapable of moving backwards to reassess new data in the light of experience. Nobody thought he would last long on the squad. He wasn't the person she would have chosen to trawl the bars and cafés of Mitte, probing their sources to find out what was to be learned about Marlene Krebs. It showed what a waste of time Plesch thought that was. Still, it was better than nothing. And she could always head out there herself that evening if she'd not managed to pry something useful out of Krebs in exchange for a deal on her sentence.

It wasn't as if she had anything better to do.

Even though it was a raw, damp day, Carol was sweating. She'd carried out the first part of her assignment without a hitch, but she knew she was a long way off being home and dry. The detailed brief had arrived by courier just after seven. She'd ripped open the thin envelope, almost tearing the contents in her haste. There was a single sheet of paper inside. It informed her that she should be at the address she had previously been given by ten a.m. There, she would be provided with the rest of her instructions.

Her first instinct was to arrive right on time at the rendezvous, an anonymous terraced house in Stoke Newington. But that might be the first test in itself. Perhaps she was supposed not to do what was expected of her. Hurriedly, she showered and dressed in the clothes she'd decided Janine Jerrold would have worn for such an assignment. A short black lycra skirt, a white T-shirt with long sleeves and a scoop neck under a fitted fake leather jacket. In her shoulder bag she carried everything she needed to change her look. A baseball cap, aviator frames with clear glass lenses, a pair of denim leggings and a lightweight waterproof kagoule in a nasty shade of pale blue. Also in the shoulder bag was an illegal CS gas spray and a metal comb with a sharpened tail. They were both relics of her days in CID in the port of Seaford, items she'd confiscated and never got round to handing in. She wasn't quite sure how her watchers would react if she had to resort to them, but she was supposed to be showing initiative and acting like a real drugs courier. She could always argue the point afterwards.

Having decided to arrive early, Carol set out from her flat just after eight. She took a circuitous route to her destination. There would, she was sure, be followers, but she had no intention of making it easy for them. Taking advantage of the rush-hour commuters would be one way of improving her edge. Even so, she still jumped off the tube at the last possible moment, doubling back three stops before emerging at street level and catching a bus.

When she turned into the quiet side street, there was no one on her heels. But that didn't mean there weren't keen eyes on her. She climbed the three steps to the front door she'd been directed to. The paintwork was filthy with London grime, but it looked in reasonably good condition. She pressed the doorbell and waited. Long seconds passed, then the door opened a couple of inches. A pale face smudged with stubble and topped with a spiky crest of black hair peered at her. 'I'm looking for Gary,' she said, as instructed.

'Who are you?'

'Jason's friend.' Again, following her orders.

The door swung open, the man taking care to stay out of sight of the street as he let her in. 'I'm Gary,' he said, leading the way into the front room. He was barefoot, wearing faded 501s and a surprisingly clean white T-shirt. Dingy net curtains hung at the window, obscuring the street. The carpet was an indeterminate shade between brown and grey, worn almost to the backing in front of a sagging sofa that faced a wide-screen NICAM TV complete with DVD player. 'Take a seat,' Gary said, waving a hand at the sofa. It wasn't an appetizing prospect. 'I'll be right back.'

He left her alone with the home entertainment centre. There was a stack of DVDs by the player, but that was the only personal touch in the room, which otherwise was about as welcoming as a police interview room. Judging by the titles, Gary was a fan of violent action movies. There wasn't a single movie Carol would have paid money to see, and several she'd have parted with hard cash to avoid.

Gary was gone less than a minute. He returned with a plastic-wrapped package of white powder in one hand and a roll-up trailing a streamer of unmistakable dope smoke in the other. 'This is the merchandise,' he said, tossing the package towards her. Carol grabbed it without thinking, then realized this meant her fingerprints were now all over it. She made a mental note to wipe the surface as soon as she got the chance. She had no idea whether she'd be carrying the real thing, although she doubted it. But the last thing she needed was to get a tug from some eager copper who wasn't part of the operation and be nailed with a half-kilo of cocaine with her prints all over it.

'So where am I supposed to deliver it?'

Gary perched on the arm of the sofa and took a deep drag from the skinny joint. Carol studied his narrow face, itemizing the features as she habitually did. Just in case. Thin, long nose; hollow cheeks. Deep-set brown eyes. A plain silver ring through the left eyebrow. A jutting jaw with a definite overbite. 'There's a café-bar in Dean Street,' he said. 'Damocles, it's called. The guy you're meeting will be at the corner table at the back by the toilets. You hand over the package and he'll give you a wad. You bring the cash back here to me. That clear?'

'How will I know it's the right guy? I mean, what if he can't get that table.'

Gary rolled his eyes. 'He'll be reading *Q* magazine. And he smokes Gitanes. That enough? Or do you want his inside leg measurement?'

'A description would help.'

'Dream on.'

'Or a name?'

114

Gary's grin was crooked, revealing even teeth stained ivory. 'Yeah, right, that'll happen. Look, just do it, huh? I'll be expecting you back here by two.'

Carol tucked the drugs away in her shoulder bag, placing the package between the folds of the denim leggings then rubbing the surface clean through the cloth. She didn't care if Gary saw her. It wouldn't hurt to have a witness to her prudence if he was, as she suspected, one of Morgan's watchers. 'See you later, then,' she said, trying not to show the antagonism she felt. After all, there was no point. He was almost certainly someone like her, a cop thrust into an alien role for some purpose neither of them was allowed to know.

She returned to the street and shivered as a chill gust of wind cut through her thin clothes. The quickest way to Soho would mean turning left and heading back to the main road where she could pick up a bus. Which would be what they were expecting her to do. So she turned right and walked briskly towards the end of the street. From her earlier reconnaissance, Carol knew she could cut through the warren of back streets to a short alley between some shops that would bring her out on the other side of Stoke Newington, from where she could catch a train. They wouldn't be expecting that, she reckoned.

At the corner, she quickened her pace to a trot, hoping to make the next corner before whoever was on her tail could catch up with her. She crossed into the next street, pulling the kagoule out of her bag as she went. Her next turning was almost upon her, and she swung quickly into a gateway, pulling the kagoule over her head and jamming the baseball cap over her blonde hair. Then she walked back into the street, this time adopting a slow, swaggering walk, as if she had all the time in the world.

When she reached the junction, she glanced over her shoulder. Nobody in sight apart from an elderly man clutching a supermarket carrier bag and shuffling down the opposite side of the street. Which meant nothing, she knew. She couldn't allow herself to act as if she'd shaken off her pursuit.

Now the entrance to the alley was in sight. It was a narrow passage between high brick walls, easy to miss if you didn't know it was there. With the adrenaline surge of relief, Carol turned into its gloomy mouth.

She was about a third of the way down when she realized she'd made a bad mistake. Heading towards her were two young men. There wasn't quite enough room for them to walk side by side, but they were so close together she couldn't possibly pass them. They looked like thugs; but these days, most men in their late teens and early twenties did. Carol found herself wondering, idiotically, when exactly it had become fashionable for respectable lads to look like potential muggers. This pair fit the identikit mould perfectly. Heads shaved to stubble, waterproof Nike jackets over football shirts, chinos and Doc Martens. There was nothing to distinguish them from thousands of others. *Maybe that's the point,* she thought as they approached inexorably.

She desperately wanted to look behind her, to check her avenue of escape, but knew that would instantly be seen as a sign of weakness. The gap between her and the two men closed by the second and she could see their gait change almost imperceptibly. Now they were moving more cautiously on the balls of their feet, a pair of predators sizing up the prey. She had to assume they were part of the game. Which meant they'd stop short of doing her serious damage. To think otherwise was too disturbing. Carol was far too accustomed to being a woman in control of her environment to contemplate how easily she'd turned herself into a potential victim.

Suddenly they were upon her, jostling her from either side, backing her into the wall. 'What have we got here, then?' the taller of the two said, his voice a guttural North London taunt.

'Yeah, what's your name, darlin'?' the other leered.

Carol chanced a look at the far end of the alley. It was clear. There were only the two of them.

Her moment's inattention had given them their chance. The taller one grabbed at her bag. 'Give it up,' he demanded. 'Save yourself a beating.'

Carol clung on grimly, leaning against the wall and adjusting her weight. Her left leg shot out in a savage kick, catching him on the inside of the kneecap. He howled in pain and rage, stumbling back and away from her, releasing the bag strap to grab his knee as he crumpled to the ground.

'Fucking cunt,' the other one said in a low voice that was far more frightening than a shout. He sprang towards her, right arm pulling back for a punch. Carol saw it all with slow-motion clarity. As he brought his fist towards her, she let herself drop and his momentum carried him forward into the wall.

It gave her a couple of precious seconds to grab the gas canister from her bag. As her first assailant scrambled to his feet, she let him have the CS gas straight in the face. Now he was really howling, screaming like an animal in a trap.

His mate swung round, ready for a second attack. When he saw her grinning like a madwoman, the spray can at arm's length, pointing straight at him, he raised both hands, palms facing her, in the universal gesture of surrender. 'Fucking take it easy, bitch,' he shouted.

'Get out of my fucking way,' Carol snarled.

Obediently, he flattened himself against the wall. She edged past him, careful to keep the spray pointing at him all the time. His friend was still yelling, his eyes streaming and his mouth contorted in pain. Carol walked backwards in the direction of the street, never taking her eyes off them. The one who had punched the wall had his arm round the other now, and they were staggering towards the far end of the alley, all the bravado knocked out of them like the air from a punctured balloon. She allowed herself a small, private smile. If that was the best Morgan could throw at her, she was going to come out of this with flying colours.

She turned her back on her assailants and walked out into the busy street. It was hard to believe that only a matter of yards from this mid-morning bustle of shoppers and strollers she'd stared physical danger in the face. As the adrenaline surge receded, she became aware of the state she was in. Her upper body was drenched, the double skin of the vinyl jacket and the kagoule acting like a sweatbox on her skin. Her hair under the baseball cap felt plastered to her head. And she was starving. If she was going to complete this mission, she'd be crazy to ignore her body's messages.

Up ahead, she saw the golden arches of a McDonald's. She could get something to eat then use the toilet to clean herself up and switch from the skirt into her denim leggings. With luck it would have a functioning hot-air hand drier. She could maybe even alter her hairstyle, thanks to the sweat of panic.

Twenty minutes later, Carol was back on the street. Her hair was off her face, slicked back with a smear of hair wax. The aviator frames subtly altered the shape of her face. The jacket was zipped up, hiding the T-shirt underneath. She looked different enough from the woman who had rung Gary's doorbell to confuse most casual observers. She knew it wasn't enough to fool the sort of scrutiny she expected to be under, but it might be sufficient to buy her a few extra seconds when it counted.

She took her time getting to the station, browsing shop windows as if she was just another idle shopper wondering what to buy for dinner. But once there, she trotted up the steps to the platform just in time to catch the train. Good thing I checked out the timetable, she congratulated herself as she slumped into a corner seat in a carriage that smelled of dust. It was a breathing space. Time to figure out what came next.

12

Petra walked into the squad room of the GeSa. It was as depressing as every other one she'd been in. The net curtains that blurred the bars over the three windows were the dirty yellow of second-hand nicotine, the walls and floor the same graded shades of grey that characterized the rest of the GeSa. *That fascinating gamut from dove to anthracite,* Petra thought wryly. The Wachpolizisten stationed at the GeSa had tried to brighten up the room with the usual kitsch array of postcards, cartoons and photographs of their pets. A couple of tired plants struggled to cope with the absence of any direct sunlight. It only served to make the place even more depressing.

The room was empty except for a solitary female WaPo who was putting a plastic box full of a prisoner's personal effects on one of the shelves. She turned as Petra leaned on the counter and cleared her throat. 'I'm Petra Becker from Criminal Intelligence. I'm here to see Marlene Krebs,' Petra said. 'You've still got her, right?'

The WaPo nodded. 'She's due to see the judge in a couple of hours, then she'll be transferred, I guess. Don't you want to wait till then?'

'I need to talk to her now. I can use the lawyer's room, yeah?'

The WaPo looked uncertain. 'You better talk to the boss. He's in the report room.'

'That's down at the end of the cell block, right?'

'Behind the fingerprint room, yes. You'll need to leave your gun here.'

Petra took her pistol from its holster in the small of her back and locked it into one of the lockers for visiting officers. Then she headed out of the squad room towards the cell corridor. She glanced up at the electronic alert system the cops sarcastically called the room-service board. None of the alarm lamps was lit; for once the prisoners were being well-behaved, not driving the GeSa team crazy with constant summonses.

The cell block itself was surprisingly sterile and modern. The usual linoleum gave way to red brick tiles on floor and walls. Most of the doors were closed, indicating that they were occupied. A couple were open, revealing a small vestibule, beyond which wall-to-wall bars enclosed four square metres of cell equipped with a bed and a rectangular hole in the floor covered with a chrome grid in case the inmates decided not to ring for a toilet visit and just fouled the cell. It was a mistake most of them made only once; the cost of cleaning the cell after such acts of defiance was billed directly to the prisoners.

Petra wondered which door concealed Marlene Krebs, and how she was coping. Badly, she hoped. It would make her job that much easier.

She found the shift commander in the Schreibzimmer, frowning at one of the Berliner

Modell computers. She explained her mission, and he asked her to wait while he organized an interview. 'We shouldn't really have her here,' he grumbled. 'She should have gone straight to KriPo, but since it happened on our doorstep, they told us to hang on to her.'

'It is only for twenty-four hours max,' Petra pointed out.

'That's about twenty-three too many for me. She's been bleating since she arrived. She wants a lawyer, she wants to use the toilet, she wants a drink. She seems to think this is a hotel, not a detention centre. She acts like we should be treating her like a hero instead of a criminal.' He pushed himself to his feet and made for the door. 'I'll send someone for you in a few minutes. You can take a look at the paperwork – it's in the tray over there.' He gestured with his thumb to a pile of files stacked high above the edges of a filing tray.

He was as good as his word. Within ten minutes, she was sitting in the Anwaltsraum, facing Marlene Krebs across a table bolted to the floor. Krebs could have been any age between thirty and forty, though Petra knew from the report she'd read that the woman was only twenty-eight. Her hair was dyed a harsh black, tousled from a night in the cells. Her make-up was smudged, presumably from the same cause. Krebs had the puffy face and hands of a drinker, and the whites of her pale green eyes were tinged with yellow. However, she also possessed the sleepy sensuality of a woman who is attractive to men and who knows it.

'Marlene, I'm Petra Becker from Criminal Intelligence.' Petra sat back and let the words sink in.

Krebs' face revealed nothing. 'Have you got any cigarettes?' she asked.

Petra took a half-empty pack from her pocket and pushed it towards Krebs. She snatched at it and thrust a cigarette between full lips. 'What about a light, then?' she demanded.

'The cigarette was free. The light will cost you.'

Krebs scowled. 'Bitch,' she said.

Petra shook her head. 'Not a good start.'

'What's this about, anyway? What have I got to do with Criminal Intelligence?'

'It's a bit late to be asking that, Marlene. That really should have been your first question.'

Krebs took the cigarette from her mouth and flicked the tip as if there was ash to be deposited. 'Look, I admit I shot that dope-dealing bastard Kamal.'

'It's not like there's much room for doubt.'

'But I had good reason. He sold my Danni the junk that killed him. What can I say? I was crazy with grief.'

Petra slowly shook her head. 'You're never going to cut it as an actress, Marlene. That routine needs a lot of work before you go in front of a judge. Look, we both know your story is bullshit. Why don't we cut the crap and see what I can do for you?'

'I don't know what you're talking about. I told you. Kamal killed Danni. I loved Danni. Something in me snapped when I heard Kamal had been arrested and I wanted to take revenge for what he had taken from me.'

Petra smiled. It was the lizard smile of a predator who smells the first hint of blood. 'See, Marlene, there's the first problem. The guys who brought Kamal in, they didn't hang around. They went straight to his restaurant, they pulled him out of the front door and into their car. Then they drove here. I've seen the logs. There was barely enough time for you to hear about the arrest, never mind get hold of a gun and get to Friesenstrasse in time to put a bullet in his head.' Petra let Marlene think about that. 'Unless of course someone tipped you the wink that the arrest was about to go down. Why would anyone do that, unless they wanted Kamal dead? So, how did you hear about Kamal's arrest?'

'I don't have to answer you.'

'No, you don't. But you do need to listen to me, because everything I'm saying to you is a stick of dynamite blowing a hole in your mitigation. Marlene, this isn't going to play the way whoever set you up for it said it would. Your story is going to fall to bits as soon as the KriPo start poking around. Now, I know you think they're not going to bother too much with this because it's saved them the hassle of a difficult prosecution with Kamal, not to mention one less scuzzy middle-ranking dealer on the streets. But me, you see, I'm bothered. Because I'm interested in the people above Kamal.'

'You're not making any sense,' Krebs said obstinately. 'Are you going to light this fucking cigarette or what?'

'I told you. Not for free. Come on, Marlene. Face it, you're going away for a very long time. This wasn't a crime of passion, it was an assassination. And we're going to prove it. You're going to be a grandmother before you see freedom again.'

For the first time, there was a flicker of something

behind Krebs' cold eyes. 'You can't prove what isn't true.'

Petra laughed out loud. 'Oh, please, Marlene. I thought your sort believed that's what us cops do all the time? OK, proving what isn't true can sometimes be . . . demanding. But compared to that, proving what we *know* to be true is a piece of piss. I know you were put up to this. And I know the people who did that gambled on us not caring too much about who took Kamal down or why. But they weren't gambling with their own stake. They were using you for chips. So, we already have a hole in your story about time. I think the next hole will be where you got the gun from.'

'It was Danni's gun,' she said quickly. 'He left it in my apartment.'

'Which is about ten minutes drive from Kamal's restaurant and a good twenty-minute drive from here. But the cops only took thirteen minutes to get here from Kamal's. You couldn't possibly have made it here in time, even if someone had called you the minute the cops took Kamal into custody. So calling it Danni's gun makes a second hole in your story.' Petra picked up the cigarette packet and put it back in her pocket.

'Right now,' she continued, 'I've got a team out in Mitte talking to everybody who knows you and who knew Danni. I'd put money on us not finding a single person who can put you and him together. Well, maybe we'll get one or two. But I'd put money on the fact that they'll be tied in as closely to Darko Krasic as you are.'

At the sound of Krasic's name, Krebs reacted. Her thumb flicked the end of the cigarette so hard she broke the filter tip clean off. For one brief moment, something sparked in her eyes. Inside, Petra rejoiced. The first crack had appeared. Now for the crowbar.

'Give him up, Marlene. He's thrown you to the wolves. You talk to me, you can save yourself. You can watch your kid grow up.'

Something shifted behind Krebs' gaze and Petra realized she'd lost her. The mention of her daughter, that's what had done it. *Of course*, she thought. *Krasic has the kid under wraps. That's his insurance policy.* Before she could break Krebs, they'd have to find the daughter. Still, it was worth one last throw of the dice. 'You'll be going in front of the judge soon,' she said. 'You'll be remanded in custody. No matter how smart-mouthed your lawyer is, no matter how many times he plays the card that you're no risk to the public, they're not going to bail you. Because I'm going to tell the prosecutor we've got you on our books as someone with links to organized crime. You're going into the general prison population. Do you have any idea how easy it will be for me to make it look like you're co-operating with us? And do you have any idea how little time it will take Darko Krasic to make sure you never talk to anyone else again? I mean, think about it, Marlene. How long did it take him to set up Kamal?' Petra got to her feet. 'Think about it.' She crossed to the door and knocked to indicate that the meeting was over.

As the WaPo outside opened up, Petra looked back over her shoulder. Marlene Krebs was leaning forward, her loose hair shrouding her face. 'I'll be calling on you, Marlene.'

Krebs looked up. Hate blared across the room at Petra. 'Fuck you,' she said.

I'll take that as a yes, Petra thought triumphantly as she walked back to the Wachte for her gun. She had finally lit a low flame under Darko Krasic that might eventually cook Tadeusz Radecki.

Carol had always enjoyed the ambience of Soho. She'd seen it shift from the seediness of the porn industry's hub to the stylish, gay-orientated café society it had become in the 1990s, but there had never been a time when she hadn't found it fascinating. Chinatown rubbed shoulders with theatreland, leather men shared the pavements with shifty-eyed prostitute's punters, media gurus battled wannabe gangstas for taxis. Although she'd never policed its narrow, traffic-choked streets, she'd spent a lot of time there, much of it in a drinking club on Beak Street where one of her oldest friends, now a literary journalist, was a founding member.

Today, everything was different. She was looking at the world through a different lens. From the perspective of a drugs courier, nothing was quite the same. Every face on the street was a potential cause for concern. Every dodgy doorway could pose some unnamed threat. To walk down Old Compton Street was to tiptoe into the danger zone, antennae bristling and every sense quivering with alertness. She wondered how criminals coped with these levels of adrenaline. Just one morning and she was jittery at some deep level, her stomach clenched and her skin clammy. Simply trying to keep her pace down to a stroll took every ounce of effort she had to give.

She turned into Dean Street, her eyes scanning the pavements and the roadway, constantly checking to see if anyone was taking an interest in her. Something tricky was bound to be lying in wait for her, and she wanted a sense of what that might be.

Carol spotted Damocles up ahead of her on the opposite side of the street. It looked like a typical Soho café-bar, all designer chairs and marble tables, exotic flower arrangements visible through the smoked-glass window. She kept on walking till she reached the next corner, then circled the block so that she came back down Dean Street in the opposite direction.

She was almost level with them when she saw them. She'd never worked Drugs, but she was familiar with the plain clothes cars they used. This one looked like a bog-standard Ford Mondeo, but what gave it away were the twin tail pipes of the exhaust. This had a lot more under the bonnet than the standard engine. The stubby radio aerial sticking out of the rear window was confirmation enough if she'd needed it. The driver sat behind the wheel, ostensibly reading the paper, a baseball cap pulled down to shield the top half of his face.

Where there was one, there would be more. Now she had a better idea of what she was looking for, Carol carried on ambling down the street. There was another car she was fairly sure was Drugs Squad, again with the driver in place behind his newspaper. Directly opposite Damocles, two men were making a very thorough job of cleaning the window of a newsagent's. A third man was bending over a bike, pumping up the rear tyre very slowly, checking the pressure with his fingers every few seconds.

Two car loads, she thought. That meant six or eight officers. She'd clocked five, which meant there were probably another three she hadn't spotted. If she was their target, the chances were that the others were already inside the café. Fine. So be it.

Time for a little improvisation.

What Carol hadn't registered was the battered white van parked behind the Mondeo. Inside, it was fitted out with state-of-the-art surveillance kit. Morgan, Thorson and Surtees perched on swivel chairs, headsets clamped to their ears. 'That's her, isn't it?' Thorson said. 'She's changed the way she looks, but it's her.'

'You can always tell by the walk,' Surtees said, reaching across her to snag a Thermos he'd had filled with café latte from his favourite Old Compton Street bar. 'The one thing it's almost impossible to disguise.'

Morgan stared intently into one of the video monitors. 'She's carrying on to the corner. That's two passes. She'll go in next time.'

'She handled those two thugs well,' Surtees said, pouring out his coffee and pointedly not offering any to his colleagues. Morgan, he knew, would have his inevitable bottle of San Pellegrino stashed somewhere. Thorson he'd never liked enough to want to share anything with.

Thorson glared at him as the rich aroma of the coffee hit. She never seemed to manage to be as prepared for things as that anally retentive bastard Surtees. He always made her feel inadequate. She suspected that Morgan knew that, and that it was one of the reasons he kept them working together. He always liked to keep people on their toes. It meant he got results, but she couldn't help feeling that it was sometimes at the expense of the nervous systems of his team members. She craned her neck to look at the monitor over Morgan's shoulder. 'All units in place, target entering,' she heard through the crackle in her headset. 'On my word, not before.'

Carol had come back into sight, this time moving with a determined stride towards the heavy glass and chrome doors of Damocles. Morgan clicked the mouse linked to the video display and the picture changed to the inside of the café. Another click and the screen split into two images. One showed the whole of the interior, the other focused on the man sitting reading and smoking at a table in the rear. They watched as Carol walked in and made straight for the bar. She chose a stool towards the back of the room, a little distance from the man she'd been told was her contact. But she made no attempt to catch his attention. She said something to the barista, who supplied her with a mineral water.

'A pity we couldn't get audio in place,' Surtees said.

'There's far too much background noise,' Thorson said. 'We tried a mike under the table, but the marble blocked out anything worth hearing.'

Carol reached into her bag and pulled out a packet of cigarettes. She took one out and put it between her lips.

'I didn't think she smoked,' Thorson said.

'She doesn't.' Morgan frowned at the screen. 'What is she up to?'

Carol made a show of searching in her bag and pulling a face in disgust. She looked around her and her eyes lit on the man at the corner table. She hitched herself off the stool, leaving her bag on the bar, and walked across to him. Now her body was between the man and the camera and they couldn't see what was happening. She bent down, then eventually stood up, the lit cigarette between her fingers. 'A long time to light a fag,' Morgan said, suspicion in his voice. 'She's not following the script.'

'Good for her,' Thorson said softly as Carol returned to her bar stool. She sipped her drink and toyed with the cigarette, stubbing it out before it had burned halfway down. Then she was on her feet in a blur of movement, grabbing her bag and heading for the toilets. As she opened the door, her contact jumped to his feet, leaving his magazine, and followed her.

'Oh shit,' Morgan said. 'Is there an exit out there?'

Surtees shrugged. 'I've no idea. It was Mary who checked the place out.'

Thorson coloured. 'There's a fire exit. It's alarmed . . .'

As she spoke, the peal of a security siren screamed. At the same moment, all hell broke loose in their ears.

Carol ran down the narrow service alley between the tall buildings. She didn't have to look over her shoulder to check her contact was behind her; she could hear his heavy footfalls closing on her with every step. They emerged on a narrow side street, the pavements busy with people returning to their offices after lunch. Carol slowed to a brisk walk, her contact falling into step beside her. 'Fucking hell,' he said. 'You trying to kill me?'

'I spotted a geezer from the Drugs Squad sitting outside the café in a car,' she said, still firmly in character. 'Him and his storm troopers turned over a mate of mine's place a couple of months back. They didn't get anything then, and I'm fucked if I was going to let them get anything now.' A nearby police siren swirled through the air. 'We've got to get off the street.'

'My motor's over in Greek Street,' he said.

'They might have clocked that an' all,' Carol said impatiently. She jinked across the road between the traffic-jammed cars, heading for a dingy corner pub. She pushed open the doors. It was still busy from the lunchtime crowd and she squirmed her way to the rear of the room, checking he was still with her. They squeezed into the angle between the bar and the back wall. Carol's hand was in her bag. 'Have you got the money?'

His hand was inside his jacket pocket. He came out with an envelope folded to the size of a twenty-pound note, thick as a London A-Z. Their hands were low, his body blocking them from any curious eyes. Carol passed him the drugs and took the money. 'Nice doing business,' she said wryly, then pushed past him. She looked around for the ladies' toilet, made her way through the throng and dived into a cubicle. She sat on the toilet, head in her hands, shaking. What the hell sort of assignment did they have lined up for her if this was their idea of an exercise?

Gradually, she got her breathing and her heart rate under control. She stood up and wondered if there was any point in trying to change her look again. She pulled off the leggings and replaced them with the skirt, then jammed the baseball cap down over her hair. She might as well give it a try. Now all she had to do was get back to Stoke Newington in one piece. That shouldn't be beyond her, she thought grimly.

Out on the street, there was no sign of pursuit. She made her way by a circuitous route to the Tottenham Court Road underground station and tried not to think about what could still go wrong. At least now she didn't have any drugs on her. Money was always explicable. The only dodgy thing in her possession was the CS gas canister. When nobody was looking, she pushed it into the gap between the seat and the bulkhead of the tube. Not the most responsible thing she'd ever done, but she wasn't thinking like Carol Jordan any longer. She was thinking like Janine Jerrold, one hundred per cent.

Three-quarters of an hour later, she turned back into the street where the day's mission had begun. There was no sign of anything out of place. It was funny how, in just a few hours, normal could seem so rife with potential threat. But at least now the end was in sight. She took a deep breath and marched up to the front door.

It wasn't Gary who answered the door this time. The man on the doorstep had the bulky upper torso of a weightlifter. His reddish hair was cropped close to his head and the glare from his prominent pale blue eyes was unnerving. 'Yeah? What do you want?' he asked belligerently.

'I'm looking for Gary,' she said. Her nerves were buzzing again. He didn't look like a cop, but what if this was another trap?

He pursed his lips then shouted over his shoulder. 'Gary, you expecting some bird?'

A muffled, 'Yeah, let her in,' came from the room she'd been in earlier.

The weightlifter stepped back, opening the door wide. There was nothing in the hall to make her uneasy, so Carol stifled her doubts and walked in. He stepped neatly behind her and slammed the door shut.

It was obviously a signal. Three men stepped out from the doorways leading off the hall. 'Police, stay where you are,' the one who had opened the door shouted.

'What the fuck?' she managed to get out before they were on her. Hands seized her and half-pushed, half-dragged her into the living room. One of them made a grab for her bag. She clung on grimly, trying for the appearance of indignant innocence. 'Get your hands off me,' she shouted.

They pushed her on to the sofa. 'What's your name?' the weightlifter demanded.

'Karen Barstow,' she said, using the cover name she'd been given in the brief.

'Right then, Karen. What's your business with Gary?'

She tried for bewildered. 'Look, what is this? How do I know you're the Old Bill?'

He pulled a wallet out of the pocket of his jogging trousers and flashed a warrant card at her too fast for her to take in a name. But it was the real thing, she knew that. 'Satisfied?'

She nodded. 'I still don't get it. What's going on? Why are you picking on me?'

'Don't play the innocent. We know you're one of Gary's mules. You've been carrying drugs for him. We know the score.'

'That's bullshit. I just came round to give him his winnings. I don't know nothing about no drugs,' she said defiantly. She thrust her bag at him, relieved she'd ditched the CS gas. 'Look. Go on. There's fuck all in there.'

He took the bag and unceremoniously dumped the contents on the floor. He went straight for the envelope and ripped it open. He riffled the bundle of notes with his thumb. 'There must be a couple of grand here,' he said.

'I don't know. I didn't look. You won't find my prints on a single one of them notes. All I know is that my mate Linda asked me to drop off Gary's winnings.'

'It must have been a helluva bet,' one of the other officers said, leaning indolently against the wall.

'I don't know anything about that. You gotta believe me, I don't know what you're talking about. I don't even do drugs, never mind dealing them.'

'Who said anything about dealing?' the weightlifter asked, shoving the money back into the envelope.

'Dealing, running, whatever. I don't have nothing to do with that. I swear on my mother's grave. All I was doing was bringing Gary his winnings.' She was confident now. They had nothing on her. Nobody had seen her hand over the drugs to her contact, she was clear on that.

'Gary says he sent you off with a parcel of drugs this morning,' the weightlifter said.

'I don't know why he'd say that, because it's not true.' She was almost sure what he was saying was a bluff. All she had to do was stick to her story. Let them come to her with anything concrete.

135

'You went out with the drugs and you were due to come back with the money. And here you are with an envelope full of readies.'

She shrugged. 'I told you, it's his winnings from the horses. I don't care what lies Gary's told you, that's the truth and you can't prove any different.'

'Let's see about that, shall we? A little trip down to the station, get a female officer to give you the full body search and see if you're as keen on your bullshit then.'

Carol almost smiled. At least she was on firmer ground here. She knew her rights. 'I'm not going nowhere with you pigs unless you arrest me. And if you arrest me, I'm saying bugger all until I get to see my lawyer.'

The weightlifter glanced around at his colleagues. That was all she needed to see. They didn't have anything on her. They had been lying about what Gary had said, because if he really had thrown her to the wolves, it would be enough to arrest her on suspicion. She got to her feet. 'So, what's it to be? Are you going to arrest me, or am I going to walk out that door? With Gary's money, by the way, because you've got no right to that.' She crouched down and started scooping her possessions back into her bag.

Before anyone could respond, the door opened and Morgan stepped into the room. 'Thank you, gentlemen,' he said. 'I appreciate your help. But I'll take it from here.'

The weightlifter looked as if he wanted to protest, but one of his colleagues put a restraining hand on his arm. The four who had confronted Carol filed out of the door. On his way out, the one who had been lounging against the wall turned back. 'For the record, sir, we're not best pleased with the way this has gone.'

'Noted,' Morgan said curtly. He winked at Carol and held a finger to his lips till they heard the front door close behind them. Then he smiled. 'You have really pissed off the Drugs Squad,' he said.

'I have?'

'That was a real deal that went down out there,' he said, crossing to the sofa and sitting down. 'The Drugs Squad's intention was to pick up the bloke you sold the drugs to. You were supposed to have a fairly hairy time but be given the opportunity to escape. Unfortunately, you didn't play it the way we were all expecting you to. And chummy walked away with a parcel of drugs that was supposed to be back in our hands by bedtime.'

Carol swallowed hard. This was exactly the kind of fuck-up she'd wanted to avoid. 'I'm sorry, sir.'

Morgan shrugged. 'Don't be. Somebody should have had the wit to cover the emergency exit. You, on the other hand, exhibited initiative under pressure. You acted in character throughout. You dealt with those two bruisers from the NCIS football hooligan squad with intelligence and style, you did everything you could to cover your tracks and change your appearance, and you outsmarted the opposition right along the line. We couldn't have asked for a better display of your talents, DCI Jordan.'

Carol stood up a little straighter. 'Thank you, sir. So, do I get the job?'

A shadow crossed Morgan's normally open features. 'Oh yes, you get the job.' He reached into the inside pocket of his jacket and fished out a card. 'My office, tomorrow morning. We'll give you the full brief then. Right now, I'd suggest you go home and make whatever arrangements are necessary to cover your absence. You'll be going away for a while. And you won't be able to go home again until the job's done.'

Carol frowned. 'I'm not going to Europol?'

'Not just yet.' He leaned forward, his elbows on his knees. 'Carol, you get this assignment right, and you can more or less write your own ticket.'

She noted the use of her first name. In her experience, senior officers outside your own team only ever got that informal when the shit was heading for the fan and they hoped you'd be the one standing between it and them. 'And if I get it wrong?'

Morgan shook his head. 'Don't even think about it.'

13

There was never any shortage of work for idle hands on board the *Wilhelmina Rosen*. The old man had set the standard, and he was determined not to fall below it. The crew clearly thought he was obsessive, but he didn't care. What was the point in having one of the most beautiful Rhineships on the water if you didn't maintain it to the highest standard? You might as well be piloting one of the modern steel boxes that had as much personality as a cornflake packet.

Tonight, his task was to restore the brasswork on the bridge to its gleaming patina. He'd been understandably preoccupied with his personal plans, but that morning he'd noticed that it had begun to grow dull. So he'd decided to spend the evening with a bundle of rags and a tin of brass polish, determined to nip his slipshod ways in the bud before they became a new habit.

Inevitably, his mind slipped sideways from the repetitive task to the closer concerns of his heart. Tomorrow, they would be heading back down the Rhine, towards the place where all this had begun. Schloss Hochenstein, standing high on a bluff upriver from Bingen, its gothic windows glaring down on the turbulent waters of the Rhine gorge, its grey stone as forbidding as a thundercloud, the legacy of some almost-forgotten medieval robber baron. For years, the *Wilhelmina Rosen* had motored up and down this stretch of river, his grandfather at the helm never betraying by so much as a sideways glance that the schloss meant anything to him.

Perhaps if it had been situated in a less demanding stretch of water his studied avoidance of so prominent a landmark would have taken on its own significance. In the Rhine gorge, however, skippers had to concentrate every ounce of their attention on the water. It had always been a severe test of the skills of boatmen, with its sharp twists, its rock-studded banks, its unexpected eddies and whirlpools and the very speed of its flow. These days, it was easier because deep channels had been dug and dredged to control the capricious movement of the water. But it still remained a stretch of water where a tourist making a single trip would have stronger memories of the surrounding scenery than a Rhineship skipper who had made the transit a hundred times. And so he had never noticed his grandfather's stubborn refusal to let his eyes range over the prospect of Schloss Hochenstein.

Now he knew the reason for that evasion, he had developed a deep and abiding fascination with the castle. He'd even driven up there one night when they'd been moored a few miles upriver. He'd been too late to buy a ticket and take the tour, but he'd stood outside the ornately carved lintel of the main gateway his grandfather had entered sixty years before. How could anyone look at that grim facade and not sense the horrors those high narrow windows had witnessed? He imagined the stones held captive the screams and cries of hundreds of children. The very walls were a repository of pain and fear. Just looking at it made him sweat, the memories of his own agonies rising sharp and harsh as the day they were inflicted. The schloss should have been razed to the ground, not turned into a tourist attraction. He wondered if any of the guides on the pleasure boats that plied the gorge ever mentioned the recent history that had stained Schloss Hochenstein so indelibly. Somehow, he doubted it. Nobody wanted to be reminded of that part of the past. They wanted to pretend it had never happened. And that was why nobody had ever had to pay for it. Well, he was making the bastards pay now, that was for sure.

He rubbed away at the brass, his mind replaying the conversation he'd had in the beer garden with Heinrich Holtz. Well, not so much a conversation as a monologue. 'We were the ones they called lucky,' he'd said, his rheumy eyes flickering constantly from side to side, never settling on one thing for long. 'We survived.'

'Survived what?' the younger man asked.

Holtz continued as if he hadn't heard the question. 'Everybody knows about the concentration camps. They all talk about the horrors inflicted on the Jews, the gypsies, the queers. But there were other victims. The forgotten ones. Me and your granddad, we were two of the forgotten ones. That's because where we ended up was called a hospital, not a camp.

'Did you know that German psychiatric hospitals

held three hundred thousand patients in 1939, but only forty thousand were still alive in 1946? The rest died at the hands of the psychiatrists and the psychologists. And that's not counting all the children and babies who were slaughtered in the name of racial purity. There was even one so-called hospital where they celebrated the cremation of the ten thousandth mental patient in a special ceremony. Doctors, nurses, attendants, the administrative staff, they all joined in. They all got a free bottle of beer to toast the occasion.

'But you didn't have to be mad to end up in their clutches. If you were deaf or blind, retarded or disabled, you had to be got rid of for the sake of the master race. A stammer or a harelip was enough to see you sent off.' He paused and sipped cautiously at his beer, his shoulders hunching closer than seemed possible.

'Me and your granddad, we weren't mentally or physically handicapped. We weren't mad. We were just badly behaved lads. Anti-social, they called us. I was always up to mischief. I'd never do what my mother told me. My dad was dead, and she wasn't much good at keeping me in order. So I was running wild. Stealing, throwing stones, making fun of the soldiers goose-stepping through the town.' He shook his head. 'I was only eight years old. I didn't know any better.

'Anyway, one morning a doctor arrived at the house with a couple of men in white coats and SS boots. I fought like a tiger, but they just beat the living shit out of me and threw me into the back of what had been an ambulance. Now, it was more like a

142

police van. They chained me to the wall and we set off. By the end of the day, there were a dozen of us in there, scared out of our wits, sitting in our own piss and shit. Your granddad was one of them. We were sitting next to each other, and that was the beginning of our friendship. I reckon that's how we survived. We managed to keep some sort of human contact alive between us, in spite of everything that happened.' Holtz finally met the barge skipper's eyes. 'That's the hardest thing. Remembering you're human.'

'Where did they take you?' the skipper inquired. He knew it was probably the least important thing he could ask, but he sensed already that Holtz's story would be far from pretty. Anything that would derail or even delay it seemed like a good idea.

'Schloss Hochenstein. I'll never forget my first sight of it. You only had to look at it to feel the fear rising up and choking you. A great big castle, like something out of a horror film. Inside, it was always dark, always cold. Stone floors, tiny high windows and walls that seemed to sweat damp. You'd lie shivering in your bed at night, wondering if you'd still be alive in the morning. You never cried, though. If you made a fuss, you got injections. And if you got injections, you died. It was like living in a nightmare you can't wake up from.

'The government had requisitioned the schloss and turned it into what they called the Institute of Developmental Psychology. You see, they didn't just want to kill all us kids who didn't fit the mould. They wanted to use us, alive and dead. The dead had their brains pickled and dissected. The living had their brains fucked with too, only we got to live with the consequences.' Holtz reached into the inside pocket of his overcoat and took out a packet of slim dark cigars. He shook one out of the packet and offered it to the younger man, who declined with a shake of the head and a wave of the hand. Holtz unwrapped it and took his time lighting it.

'You know how scientists do their experiments with rats and monkeys? Well, in Schloss Hochenstein they used us kids.' Holtz fiddled with his cigar, using it as a prop rather than smoking it.

'The smart kids, like me and your granddad, we learned quickly. So we survived. But it was a living hell. How do you think the Nazi interrogators learned their skills? They practised on us. We would be deprived of sleep for weeks at a time, till we were hallucinating and so disorientated we could no longer speak our own names. We were given electric shocks to the genitals to see how long we could keep a secret. The girls were raped before and after puberty to explore the emotional effects. Sometimes the boys were forced to take part in the rapes, so their reactions could be observed. They forced rubber tubes down our throats then poured water straight into our lungs. Your grandfather and I, we survived that. God knows how. For days, I couldn't eat a thing, my gullet felt like one long bruise. But there were a lot who didn't make it. They drowned.

'They used to stage exhibitions. They'd bring in doctors from other hospitals, SS officers, local officials. They'd pick some poor fucking imbecile, some kid with Down's syndrome, or a spastic. The doctors would parade them in front of the audience, talking about how they must be exterminated for the benefit of the people. We were seen as a drain on the resources of the state. They'd say things like, "A dozen soldiers can be trained for what it costs to keep one of these vegetables in an institution for a month."

'And there was no escape. I remember one lad, Ernst, who was brought in with us. His only sin was that his father had been condemned as an enemy of the state for being lazy. Ernst thought he could outsmart them. He tried to win their trust by working as hard as he could. He was always sweeping the floors, cleaning the toilets, making himself useful. One day, he managed to get out of the main building into the courtyard and he made a run for it.' Holtz shuddered at the memory.

'They caught him, of course. We were in the dining hall, eating the slops they served us for dinner, when they dragged him in by the hair. Then they stripped him naked. Four nurses held him down on a table while two of the doctors beat the soles of his feet with canes, counting out loud all the time. Ernst was screaming like a scalded baby. They kept beating him till his feet were lumps of raw meat, the flesh hanging off the bones and the blood dripping off the table on to the floor. Eventually, he passed out. And the institute director was standing there with a clipboard, noting how many strokes of the canes and how long it had taken to get to that point. Then he turned to us and said, as calmly as if he was announcing what was for dessert, that we should all remember what would happen to any part of our bodies that didn't behave as it should.' Holtz passed a hand over his face, wiping a thin sheen of sweat from his forehead.

'Do you know, that sadistic bastard remained a member of the German Society of Psychiatrists till he died in 1974? Nobody wants to admit what was done to us.

'The guilt's too much, you see. It was hard enough for Germany to accept what we did to the Jews. But what was done to us was worse. Because our good German parents let it happen. They let the state take us away, mostly without any protest. They just accepted what they were told, that we needed to be disposed of for the greater good. And afterwards, nobody wanted to hear our voices.

'To tell you the truth, I've made myself forget a lot of what happened back there. That's how I've coped. The scars are still there though, deep down.'

There was a long silence. Finally, the young skipper drained his beer and said, 'Why are you telling me this?'

'Because I know your granddad didn't. We used to meet up for a drink now and then, and he admitted that he'd never told you. I thought he was wrong. I think you deserved to know what made him the man he was.' Holtz reached out with his bony fingers and covered the other man's hand with his. 'I don't know for sure, but I expect it was not easy being brought up by him. But you have to know that, if he was harsh to you, he did it for your own protection. He didn't want to risk you turning into the kind of boy he was, with all the consequences that could bring with it.

'Men like me and your granddad, we might know with our heads that the Nazis aren't coming back, that nobody is going to do to our children and grandchildren what was done to us. But deep down, we're still terrified that there are bastards out there who would do the same thing to the people we love. Those doctors, they didn't come out of nowhere. The monsters weren't just there for one generation. They never paid the price for what they did, you know. They carried on, respected and well rewarded, climbing to the top of their so-called profession, using what they'd learned to train the ones who came after them. There are still monsters out there, only they're better hidden now. Or they're somewhere else. So, you should know that whatever he did to you that might have seemed cruel or heartless, it was done with the best of motives. He was trying to save you.'

He had pulled his hand back then. He couldn't bear the dry papery feel of old skin against his own. His head hurt, a dull ache starting at the base of his skull and spreading outwards like steel fingers squeezing his brain. He felt the familiar blackness rising inside him, swallowing all his pleasure in saying a last farewell to his grandfather. He didn't know how to deal with what he'd just been told, and physical contact with this ruined old man wasn't helping. 'I have to go,' he said. 'My crew. They're waiting.'

Holtz stared down at the table. 'I understand,' he said.

On the drive back to town, they sat in silence, each staring out at the road ahead. When they reached the outskirts, Holtz said, 'You can let me out here. I can catch a bus. I don't want to put you out.' He reached into his pocket and took out a slip of paper. 'I wrote down my address and phone number. If you want to talk some more about this, call me.'

Holtz got out in the gathering gloom of the afternoon and walked off without a backward glance. They both knew they'd never meet again.

He rubbed his temples, trying to replace his bleak thoughts with the joy he'd felt when he'd pushed the old man into the water. But it wasn't working. He put the old Ford in gear and headed back to the docks. He'd always known there must be a reason for what had happened to him. The brutality, the segregation from other kids, the refusal to let him have anything more than a basic education because cleverness got you into trouble; that all had to have come from somewhere. But whatever he had imagined, it hadn't been this. Now at last, he had someone to blame.

Tony pulled up in the drive of Frances's semi-detached house. Everything about it was squared off and neat. Built before developers started putting flourishes on their executive homes, it was entirely plain in its appearance and, unlike several of her neighbours, Frances had steadfastly avoided anything that would break up the straight lines of doors and windows, gable end and garden. No fake Georgian bottle-glass window panes for her, no elaborate front door with panels and mouldings. No island beds or wishing wells in the garden, just neat rectangular borders with roses pruned to within a bud of their lives. At first, Tony had liked the orderliness of it all, a contrast to the blurred edges and confusion of his own life.

But now he acknowledged that there were good reasons why he had chosen an old cottage without a single wall that was plumb, and a patch of garden filled with rambling geraniums and overgrown hebes.

As he had come to know Frances better, he had been reminded that those who impose such regimented order on their surroundings are also inclined to hedge in their internal lives with restrictions and barriers for fear their unruly souls might burst forth and create an unmanageable chaos.

There were times when he longed for chaos.

This evening they were due to play bridge with some acquaintances over in Cupar. Frances, he knew, would have dinner cooking, ready to serve within minutes of his arrival so that they would be sure of getting to Cupar in good time. He wanted to speak to Carol, to find out how her undercover day had gone, but he knew that there would be no chance later. He'd tried to call her before he left the office, but she hadn't been home. Maybe in the ten minutes it had taken him to drive across St Andrews she'd have returned.

He keyed her number into his mobile and waited. Three rings and he was connected to her machine. 'Hi, Carol, it's Tony. I was wondering how . . .'

'Tony? I just walked through the door. Hang on.'

He heard the electronic beep of the machine being turned off. Then her voice again. 'How lovely of you to call.'

'Put it down to professional curiosity. I was interested to hear how it had gone.'

'I was going to e-mail you later, but this is better still.'

Even several hundred miles away, he could hear the elation in her voice. 'You sound like you're on a real high. How was it?'

Her low chuckle was infectious. He could feel the

smile spreading across his face. 'I suppose that depends on your point of view.'

'Start with your point of view.'

'Brilliant. There were a couple of moments where I was absolutely bricking it, but I never felt as if it was slipping out of my control. All the work we did together made me feel confident I could handle whatever they threw at me, and I did.'

'I'm glad,' he said. 'So, who didn't think it was brilliant?'

'Oh God,' she groaned. 'I am numero uno on the Drugs Squad shit list tonight.'

'Why? What happened?'

Laughter bubbled up in Carol's voice as she outlined the fiasco to Tony. 'I know I should be mortified, but I'm too busy being pleased with myself.'

'I can't believe they had so little confidence in you,' Tony said. 'They should have realized you're smart enough to spot a surveillance. You've set up enough of them over the years. From there, it's not a big step to working out that you'd come up with some way to evade the take-down. So, what else did they throw at you?' He settled back in the driving seat and let Carol take him through the day. When she finally ran out of steam, he said, 'Hey, you should be proud of yourself. One day on the streets and already you've stopped thinking like the hunter and begun to think like the prey. I'm impressed.'

'I couldn't have done it without you.'

He smiled. 'You've no idea how much of a kick I got from feeling I was back in the game again, however peripherally. My life is so predictable these days, it was great fun to sit down and work with you again. In fact, it was even better than before, because there were no lives at stake this time.'

'Maybe you should think about getting back into harness,' Carol said.

Tony sighed. 'There's no place for people like me in today's offender-profiling strategy.'

'It wouldn't have to be front line. You could train. Think about it, Tony. If the Home Office don't want to take a chance, maybe you should think about Europe. All those intelligence officers in Europol need to learn how to profile crimes and criminals, so they can determine what's connected. There must be a place for someone with your talents,' Carol said insistently.

'Yeah, well, we'll see. So, did they tell you whether you've got the job?'

'They did. And I have. But I still don't know what it is. They're going to brief me tomorrow. Here's the best bit: if I perform well, I get to write my own ticket. The world's going to be my oyster.'

Tony couldn't help the prickle of misgiving raising the hairs on the back of his neck. For them to have made Carol a promise of that magnitude, the assignment that lay ahead of her was bound to be fraught with risk. It had to be the kind of enterprise that would provoke an instinctive refusal. With this much sugar coating, the pill would of necessity be an extremely bitter one. 'That's great,' he said. His eye caught the digital clock on the dashboard. He was cutting it tight if he was going to have time to eat before they had to leave for Cupar.

'Listen, Carol, I've got to go now. But I want you to promise me that you'll call as soon as you know what they want from you. I'm not saying this because I have any doubts about your ability. It's just . . . it sounds like you're going to need all the help you can get, and they're probably going to put you in a position where help won't be easy to come by. I want you to know that I'm here for you. Whatever you need from me, you've got it.'

There was a moment's silence, then she said, 'You've no idea how much that means to me. Thank you. I'll be in touch.'

'Take care.'

'And you. Thanks for calling.'

He ended the call, shoved his phone back in his pocket, and got out of the car. When he walked in, he could smell the fragrant aroma of a rich tomato and meat sauce. As he passed the open door of the darkened living room, he heard Frances speak. 'I'm in here,' she said.

Tony followed the sound of her voice into the living room. He couldn't see much detail, but he could make out Frances's shape silhouetted against the window. 'I heard your car and I couldn't work out why you hadn't come in,' she said. 'So I came to have a look, make sure everything was all right.'

'The phone rang just as I pulled up.' *Some lies are a necessary veneer*, he thought sadly.

'You were ages,' Frances said.

He couldn't see her face, but there was something in her voice that twisted inside him. 'Sorry about that. I hope dinner isn't spoilt.'

'I think my cooking's a wee bit more robust than that.' Frances turned so her back was to the street. Now her face was even more obscured. 'Was it Carol?'

152

'What makes you think that?' As soon as the words were out, he realized how much of a revelation they were. In part, it was a professional response. Answer a question with a question, don't let the subject take control of the interview. But it was also the instinctive response of someone who has something to conceal. The innocent man would have said, 'Yes, it was Carol, she's very excited because she's got the job she was after.' However, where Carol Jordan was concerned, Tony could never be an innocent man.

'She's the only person you wouldn't want to talk to with me listening in the background.'

Tony flushed. 'What's that supposed to mean?'

'It means you've got something to hide where Carol Jordan is concerned.'

'You're wrong. She was talking to me about a confidential police assignment, that's the only reason I took the call in the car.'

Frances snorted. 'Do you think my head buttons up the back? You took the call in the car because you knew I'd spot the obvious.'

Tony took a couple of steps towards her. 'I haven't a clue what you're talking about, Frances.'

'Don't play games with me. You're in love with her. Christ, I only had to be in your company for five minutes to work that one out.'

'No,' he said. 'You're wrong.'

'I'm right. And I've got far too much self-respect to put up with having my nose rubbed in it.'

'Look, Carol is a former colleague, a friend. How can you be jealous of someone I've never even slept with?'

'Well, more fool you. You should have tried the

little blue pills a bit sooner, shouldn't you? Because she's obviously gagging for it.'

Her words hit like a slap to the cheek. 'Leave Carol out of this. Whatever you've got into your head, it's between you and me.'

'That's the trouble, Tony. It's not between you and me. It's always been between you and Carol, only you never let me see that before. You kept it hidden away, pretending you wanted to be with me when the truth is she's the one you want.'

'You're so wrong, Frances. There's no future for me and Carol. All there is between us is a very difficult past. I'm with you because I want to be.'

Suddenly Frances picked up a small crystal vase from the window sill and hurled it at him. 'You lying bastard,' she shouted as he dodged to one side. It crashed into the wall with an incongruous tinkle of smashed glass. 'I'm not a masochist, Tony,' she panted, anger stealing her breath. 'Life is too damn short to fritter away my emotions on a man who's desperate for somebody else. So get the hell out.'

There was nothing he could think of to say. It surprised him how little he cared that it was clearly over. He turned and headed for the door.

'Leave your keys on the hall table on the way out,' Frances shouted at his retreating back.

Tony carried on walking. To his surprise, the prevailing emotion he felt was relief. Relief and a sudden surge of hope. He hadn't felt this optimistic in years.

14

Sometimes, Petra wished Marijke van Hasselt didn't live so far away. Tonight, it would have been good to settle down with a bottle of wine and discuss the day's events with someone who didn't have anything at stake but who understood the intricacies of police work. At least tonight Marijke was on-line too, she saw with a lightening of her spirits. They moved into a private chat room and Petra went straight to the question that interested her most. Anything to take her mind off the dead ends of the Kamal/Marlene inquiry.

P: so, how's the murder going?

M: A lot of work and not much progress. I spent today at the university interviewing his colleagues and students, but we didn't get a single lead worth pursuing.

P: what, you finally found a victim everybody loves?

M: Plenty of people didn't like de Groot, but nobody with anything that looks remotely like a motive. You don't kill somebody just because he failed your thesis or blocked your promotion.

P: god, you dutch are so civilized . . .

M: What's even more annoying is that we didn't find an appointments diary. Apparently he had one of those Palm Pilots that he always carried. But no sign of it.

P: the killer probably took it with him to cover his tracks.

M: So, did you manage to track down what it was that jogged your memory when I told you about de Groot?

P: i've narrowed it down to a couple of possibilities, but i haven't heard back from either of them. you know what these provincials are like, no sense of urgency.

M: FWIW, there's nothing in our records anywhere in Holland that corresponds to the de Groot murder.

P: so, you're running round in the dark? nothing from forensics?

M: Not so far. It's all been very frustrating, going through the motions without any sense of what we should be looking for.

P: there's nothing harder to work than this kind of killing.

M: I know. Take my mind off it. Tell me about your day.

P: frustrating. i'm trying to prove a negative – a woman who claims she was the lover of a man who is now dead, but i don't think they even knew each other. i think there's a chance we could use this as a lever to lift the lid on a major figure in organized crime. this guy has always kept his hands clean, kept his distance from the sharp end. we've never laid a finger on him, and i want to be the one who nails him. the only trouble is, she's got a kid, and i suspect that our man has spirited her away some-where to use as a pressure point over her. so i need to find the kid as well.

M: Any joy?

P: not so far. if she doesn't turn up in school tomorrow, i'm going to tell plesch we should put out a national appeal for her as missing. act like she might be the victim of a paedo. it'll drive the mother nuts and it'll make whoever is taking care of her very, very nervous.

M: As long as you don't make them so nervous they do something stupid.

P: i don't think these guys would use anyone who'd panic for something this sensitive. if anything happens to the kid, they've lost their pressure point on the mother. more than that, they're going to turn her into a vengeful fury who will be out to get their blood.

M: But how safe will the mother be if you get your hands on the kid?

P: her life won't be worth a pocketful of euros. which means, as soon as we get the kid, we take the mother out of the general prison population and put her somewhere very, very safe.

M: Sounds like you're pushing really hard on this one.

P: i want to get this guy so bad i can taste it. but the other thing is that i heard a rumour there's some kind of major operation being planned against him that would take the ball out of our court. so i feel like time isn't on my side.

M: Be careful. It's hard to do your best work when you're looking over your shoulder. That's when we make mistakes, no?

P: i know. part of me realizes it doesn't matter who gets him, as long as we take him down. but i'm greedy.

M: As if I didn't know that.

P: so, you want to satisfy my greed?

M: I thought you'd never ask . . .

Petra smiled. Sometimes, distance really didn't matter so much after all.

Morgan's office was exactly what Carol would have conjured up if she'd been asked to imagine it. It was a large cubicle partitioned off from an open plan office space. The frosted glass panels that were supposed to provide an illusion of privacy had been turned into memo boards. Maps, photographs and sheets of paper with single words or phrases written in sprawling capitals in thick magic marker were sellotaped to the glass, completely obscuring its inhabitant and his activities from anyone outside the room.

The filing cabinets and cupboards that lined the walls were piled high with files and reference books. The computer on the desk was an island of straight lines marooned in a zigzag sea of paper. It all looked chaotic, but Carol suspected that Morgan would be able to lay his hands on any single document in a matter of moments. There was nothing personal in the room; no photographs of family or of Morgan shaking hands with the powerful or famous. The only thing that marked the space out as his was the jacket hanging on a peg on the back of the door. Not on a hanger, just dangling limp from the hook.

He'd met her at the lift, hustled her through the outer office so fast she'd had the chance for nothing more than the most superficial impression of an array of mostly empty desks. The occupants of the remainder barely raised their heads as they passed, then returned indifferent to their monitors or their phone calls. He'd thrown open his office door and stood back, saying, 'Give me five minutes. There's something I've got to sort out. Tea or coffee?'

She'd been sitting in the visitor's chair for fifteen minutes when Morgan pushed the door open with his hip, a mug in each hand. 'There you go,' he said, putting one down on the pile of papers nearest Carol. 'Sorry I kept you.'

He moved round behind his desk, pushing the chair sideways so the computer didn't obscure her view of him. His cramped office only served to emphasize how big he was. He topped six feet easily, and he had the breadth to go with it. But even though he was in his mid-forties, he hadn't lost definition. She could see the swell of his shoulder muscles under his shirt, and there was no depressing splay of material and straining buttons across his stomach. He had a square, blunt face with eyes set wide enough apart to give him a

159

look of guilelessness that Carol knew was entirely misleading. Now, he was smiling at her, the skin round his eyes crinkling into deep lines. 'Cracking job yesterday,' he said. 'The Drugs Squad were spitting feathers, of course, but it's their own fault it all went down the Swanee. I had their guv'nor on to me last night, giving me earache, but like I said to him, it doesn't do to underestimate the opposition, especially when the opposition's got one of my team playing for them.'

'You don't mind that there's a bag of coke out on the streets that shouldn't be there?' Carol asked, partly because she didn't want to appear complacent, but mostly because she wanted to remind Morgan that she was still a copper.

'Sometimes you have to accept a bit of collateral damage. I'm looking at a much bigger picture.' Morgan picked up his coffee and took a sip. He flashed a quick glance of assessment at her over the rim, then relented. 'Besides, they picked the bugger up last night. They knew he wouldn't have had time to shift the gear, so they kicked his door in about half an hour after I sent them packing. Caught him in the middle of stepping on it so he could shop it out for twice the price. So your conscience can rest easy, DCI Jordan.' He gave her a knowing grin. 'Nice to see that going undercover hasn't blunted your copper's instincts.'

Carol said nothing. She reached for her mug and took a tentative taste. It was almost as good as she would have made herself, which made it about three hundred per cent better than anything she'd ever tasted in a police establishment. Her respect for Morgan rose even higher.

He leaned across the desk and pulled a folder out from under a pile of scribbled notes. He flicked it open, checking the contents, then slid it over to Carol. 'Go on,' he said as she stared at the blank cover. 'Take a look.'

Carol flipped the file open. She found herself staring down at a 10x8 black-and-white photograph of a remarkably handsome man. It wasn't a posed studio-shot, but had the graininess of something snatched while its subject wasn't looking. He was in three-quarters profile, looking off at something to the right of the photographer, a slight frown provoking a line between his eyebrows. His glossy dark collar-length hair was swept back from a high forehead, falling over delicate ears in a slight wave. The eyes were deep-set above wide Slavic cheekbones. His nose had the curve of a hawk's bill, and his full lips were slightly parted, giving a faint glimpse of white teeth. He looked as sharp and polished as a diamond.

'Tadeusz Radecki. Tadzio to his friends,' Morgan said. 'He's genetically Polish, though he was born in Paris and educated in England and Germany. Currently lives in a palatial apartment in Berlin. His grandmother was some sort of countess. Plenty of blue blood, but his old man had a gambling habit and there wasn't much dosh left by the time Tadeusz finished with university. So he decided to become an entrepreneur. On paper, he owns a very successful chain of video-rental outlets in Germany. He moved in big time after the wall came down and cashed in on all those Ossies who'd been starved of Hollywood culture.'

Carol waited. She knew there was more, much

more. But she'd never seen the point in asking questions simply for the satisfaction of hearing her own voice. Morgan leaned back in his chair, locking his hands behind his head. 'Of course, that's not the whole story. Our man Tadzio realized early on that there was more money to be made on the wrong side of the law than on the right side. Through his family contacts, he started doing a bit of gunrunning for the warlords in the former Yugoslavia after that all fell to bits. He had the contacts in the old Soviet Union to supply the material, and he set himself up as a middle man. Clean hands again. It worked out very nicely for him. He made a packet and he also acquired his right-hand man, a lethal little Serb called Darko Krasic.

'With the profits from the gunrunning, Tadzio and Darko invested in some serious protection and started shifting large amounts of drugs. They always took care to stay far enough away from the street-level stuff to keep their hands out of the muck while making sure their noses stayed right in the trough. In the last few years, they've taken the lion's share of the hard drugs market in central Germany, as well as financing some major international deals, including shipping heroin into the UK. They've stayed on top mostly because Darko has a reputation for being a totally ruthless bastard. You double-cross him, you die. And not in a nice way.'

Morgan sat up straight again and indicated to Carol she should move forward in the file. The next photograph showed a railway marshalling yard. The doors of a freight container stood open, revealing half a dozen bodies sprawled in a heap. 'Remember that?' he asked.

Carol nodded. 'Eight Iraqi Kurds found dead in a container at Felixstowe. Last summer, was it?'

'That's right. There had been a hold-up loading the ferry on the other side of the Channel, and the poor sods had basically fried alive as their air supply gave out. They were the victims of Tadeusz Radecki's latest business venture. It's questionable what adds more to the total of human misery, his drug running or his people smuggling. But we're not interested in how many addicts he's created for our German colleagues to deal with; what matters to us is putting a stop to his involvement in bringing illegals into this country in numbers we can only guess at.'

Carol started to turn to the next picture in the file. 'Hang on,' Morgan said. It wasn't a tone to argue with. She dropped her hand. 'He's a big player, then?' she asked.

'One of the biggest. He had the capital to get in on the ground floor. And he already had the infrastructure set up. If you're bribing bureaucrats to move your drugs around with impunity, it doesn't take a lot more to get them to turn a blind eye to truckloads of human flotsam. He's bringing them in from China, from the Middle East, from the Balkans, from Afghanistan. As long as they've got the cash or the drugs to pay their way, he'll take them where they want to go. And where most of them want to go is here.'

'What happens to them when they get here? Does he link in to some organized network? Or are they just dumped and left to get on with it?'

Morgan smiled. 'Good question. We think it depends on how much money they can come up with.

163

For a price, they get papers and some even get a job. But if they don't have enough money to pay for that, they get dumped somewhere that's already over-loaded with asylum seekers and they just join the rest of the crowd.'

'I suppose it would be naive to ask why the German police haven't arrested Radecki?'

'The usual reason. Lack of evidence. Like I said, he keeps his distance. There are firewalls between him and the business at street level. And the video shops make a great money laundry for a sizeable chunk of the proceeds. So he's got an apparently legitimate source for living very high on the hog. The German organized crime squad have been trying to get a line on Krasic and Radecki for a long time, but they've never been able to make anything stick. There's prob-ably only a handful of people who could actually tie Radecki to any of this, and they're too scared to talk. Take a look at the next shot.'

Carol turned over to the next picture. It showed the corpse of a man lying on a short flight of stone steps. Most of his head was missing. It wasn't a pretty sight.

'That was one of the people the Germans thought might be able to put Radecki in the frame. They arrested him two days ago on the grounds that he was the supplier of a dodgy batch of smack that killed off half a dozen addicts. He got a bullet through the brain right on the steps of the police station. That's how fearless these guys are.'

Carol felt the strange mixture of apprehension and excitement that always came with the prospect of the chase. She had no idea what Morgan had in store for her, but whatever it was, it was clearly going to take her into the big time. 'So where do I come in?'

Morgan suddenly found the contents of his cup deeply interesting. 'Radecki had a lover. Katerina Basler. They'd been together four years. If he had a chink in his armour, it was Katerina.' He met Carol's eyes. 'By all accounts, he was besotted with her.'

'Was?'

'Katerina died two months ago in a car crash. Radecki was devastated. Still is, we hear. After she died, he went to pieces. Shut himself away in his fancy apartment, let Krasic deal with the day-to-day running of the operation. But now he's back. And that's where you come in. Take a look at the next photograph.'

Carol obediently turned the page. The skin on her arms turned to gooseflesh as she stared down at her mirror image. The woman in the photograph had long hair, but, that apart, on first impressions she could have been looking at her twin. Coming face to face with her doppelgänger in a police file was one of the most unsettling things that had ever happened to her. Her hands felt clammy and she realized she was holding her breath. Discreetly she exhaled, as if the release of spent air might blow the illusion away. 'Jesus,' she said, her tone a protest against this apparent violation of her uniqueness.

'It's uncanny, isn't it?'

Carol studied the picture more intently. Now, she could see differences. Katerina's eyes were a couple of shades darker. Their mouths were distinct in shape. Her chin was stronger than Katerina's. Side by side, you could have told them apart without any difficulty.

Yet that first impression of identity lingered on for Carol. 'It's weird to think there's someone else out there with the same face. What a bizarre coincidence.'

'They do sometimes happen,' Morgan said. 'You can imagine how gobsmacked I was when I saw your face looking up at me from an application form. That's when we had the idea for this operation.'

Carol shook her head in wonder. 'She could be my sister.'

Morgan's smile reminded Carol of a lion's yawn. 'Let's hope Tadzio thinks so.'

15

The *Wilhelmina Rosen* was under way, carving a passage through the murky waters. It was a stretch without locks or complex navigation, so Gunther was at the helm, leaving him free to settle down in the cabin with a stack of paperwork. Bills of lading, receipts for fuel, payroll accounts all sat waiting for his attention. But his mind kept slipping away from the task.

Heinrich Holtz's story had opened up so many questions. His fellow crewmen might think him simple and straightforward, but there had always been much more going on behind his eyes than he'd revealed. He'd always had to live in his head, starved as he had been of the company of his contemporaries. The only thing that had kept the inner darkness at bay had been reading, though his grandfather had tried to deny him even that. As a teenager, he'd become adept at smuggling books on board, battered paperbacks bought from charity shops and market stalls. He'd read late at night in the privacy of his tiny berth in the bows, devouring violent adventure novels, biographies and true crime, dropping them overboard once he'd finished with them, lest the old man catch him in something that would at the very least be scorned as a waste of time. It had taught him to look beyond the surface to what lay beneath.

So the revelation of the secret of Schloss Hochenstein was the key that had unlocked the closed mansion of his past. He still had to wander down the corridors and explore the rooms before he could have any understanding of what really lay within. Some of those rooms remained obstinately dark, with no possibility of illumination. His grandmother, for example. She had been dead before he was born. He had no idea if she had borne the brunt of his grandfather's sadism or if her love had been enough to calm his rage while she lived. There was no way of telling.

He knew almost nothing of his mother. His grandfather had only ever referred to her as a whore, or a bitch who had fouled her own doorstep. There wasn't even a photograph of her among the old man's personal effects. He might have passed her a hundred times on the street and he would never have known. He liked to think that the electric current of his hatred would alert him to the bitch's presence, but he knew that was wishful thinking.

From his birth certificate, he had gleaned a few facts. She was called Inge. She had been nineteen at the time of his birth, her occupation listed as a secretary. Where his father's name should have been, there was a blank. Either she hadn't known who he was, or she had had her own reasons for keeping silent. Perhaps he was a married man. Perhaps he was a callow fool she didn't want to be tied to for the rest of her life. Perhaps she was trying to protect him from the wrath of her own father. All these options were equally possible, given that he knew nothing of the kind of person she had been, or whether she had been as brutally oppressed by the old man as he had. It didn't stop him despising her for leaving him to face the fate she had escaped.

After the old man's funeral, he had asked the crew what they knew of his mother. They'd never have dared open their mouths while the old man was alive, but with him safely despatched, Gunther had told what little he knew.

Inge had been brought up very strictly. Her mother had kept her close, forcing her into the mould of proper German womanhood. But when she had died, Inge had seized her chance. Whenever the old man came home, she was demure as ever, putting his meals on the table, making sure the apartment was clean and neat, dressing modestly and speaking only when she was spoken to. While the *Wilhelmina Rosen* was out of port, however, it was a different story.

Gunther had heard from other boatmen that Inge was regularly seen in the dockside bars, drinking with sailors until the early hours. Naturally, there were boyfriends, enough to earn her the reputation of a good-time girl, if not quite a slut.

She must have known she was dancing with the devil, he thought. Watermen have a strong sense of community and a confined world; word of her indiscretions was bound to make its way back to her father's ears. But before that could happen, she'd fallen pregnant. What surprised him, now he came to think about it, was that she hadn't got rid of him. It wasn't that hard to come by an abortion in Hamburg in the mid-1970s. She must have wanted to keep him very badly if she was prepared to withstand the wrath of her father.

According to Gunther, she managed to hide the pregnancy for the first five or six months, swaddled in baggy sweaters. When her father had found out, he had been enraged almost beyond speech. Life on board had been hell for a few weeks, the old man in the foulest of tempers and the crew unable to do right for doing wrong. He could imagine only too well what it must have been like, and felt grateful to have missed it.

There followed an ominous silence for a couple of months. Then one morning, after a three-day lie-over in Hamburg, the old man had arrived at the quayside in a laden car. The crew had watched open-mouthed as he had calmly unloaded a crib with two full sets of bedding, several carrier bags of baby clothes and a box containing bottles, formula and sterilizing tablets. Finally, the old man had wheeled a pram up the gang-plank. It contained a baby.

No one had the nerve to ask the old man what had become of Inge, and they'd sailed before rumours could reach them. But when they'd next hit their home port, Gunther had made a beeline for the bars to garner what gossip he could. As he'd suspected, the old man had come home to find Inge ensconced with the baby. He'd thrown her bodily out of the apartment, tossing her clothes down the stairs after her. He'd changed the locks and set about bringing up baby himself.

Inge, it was reported, had left town. One of her ex-boyfriends worked on a cruise ship and he'd found her a job on board, waitressing. When the ship came back to Hamburg, Inge was gone. She'd handed in her notice in Bergen and walked off into the Norwegian night without a forwarding address. That was the last anyone in Hamburg had heard of her, as far as he could tell.

He wondered what had become of her, but in a remote, unemotional way. Even as a child, he had never entertained fantasies of rescue. It had never occurred to him to dream that his mother would sweep on board, wrapped in mink and dripping with diamonds, to take him away from his personal hell and envelop him in the lap of luxury.

These days, when he thought of her, he imagined she had probably ended up selling herself in one way or another, either formally as a prostitute or informally as the wife of someone she could see as a protector. It was, he thought, a damn sight more than she deserved.

But Heinrich Holtz's story had made him realize there was no point in blaming his mother or his grandfather. Might as well blame the bullet or the gun for killing. The finger that had pulled the trigger on his own particular fate hadn't been the old man. It had been the psychologists who thought that people were a legitimate resource for their experiments.

Everybody acted as if all that had ended with the Nazi era. He knew better. He'd done his research. He'd learned from his experience at the hands of his grandfather that there was no point in rushing to vengeance. It was necessary to know the enemy, to study their strengths as well as their weaknesses. After the funeral, he'd made it his business to read everything he could find about the theory and practice of psychology. At first, it had been like reading a foreign language. He'd had to read and reread till the words blurred and his head ached, but he'd struggled on. Now, he could use their own weapons against them. Now, he knew their truths almost as well as he knew his own. He could wrap up his ideas in their secret jargon. Which of them would have believed that a mere boatman could infiltrate their world?

He knew they were still using people as their guinea pigs. They were still fucking with the heads of their victims, still hiding behind the guise of professional scientific curiosity to wreak damage. Even when they were supposed to be helping, they just made things worse. While they were still out there, his would not be a unique fate. Other poor sods would be as crippled as he had been. His task was clear. He had to send out a message that could not be ignored.

There was no point in making an example of one or two. He had to cut a swathe through their ranks. He'd chosen his victims meticulously, plodding through reams of published papers in the journals of experimental psychology. He was only interested in those who might be regarded as the legitimate professional descendants of his persecutors – the Germans, of course, and their treacherous collaborators, the French, the Belgians, the Austrians and the Dutch. He'd ignored anyone who experimented on animals, looking instead for those evil bastards who not only used humans as the stepping stones for their own advancement, but who boasted of it in print. It was sickening, the way they detailed how they manipulated their subjects, twisting their minds and their behaviour. He'd been surprised that there weren't more of them, but he supposed that not all of them were stupid enough to expose their own cruelties. It took a while, but finally he had a list of twenty names. He'd chosen to start with the ones who were based nearest the waterways, but if the need arose he could travel further afield later in his campaign.

Now, he had to be very, very careful. He had to plan every move with the precision of a military operation. And, so far, it had paid off handsomely.

He looked out of the porthole at the brown water surging past. Bremen would be next. The jar was ready and waiting.

Petra Becker was as cross as a cat whose mouse has been taken from it by a squeamish human. She'd had another frustrating day trying to prove a negative. They'd tracked down the man that Marlene Krebs was sleeping with, but he'd given them nothing useful. Marlene was a free agent, he'd shrugged. Yes, he'd heard she'd been seeing Danni, but he didn't care so long as she practised safe sex, which she always did with him. You didn't want to take chances with junkies, he'd added self-righteously.

Danni's girlfriend had denied any knowledge of his supposed affair with Marlene, but they hadn't lived together and she couldn't say for sure where he'd been on the nights he hadn't been with her.

Between them, Petra and the Shark had found three people who claimed to have known about the affair. The KriPo detectives were satisfied with that, but Petra wasn't. One of the three had convictions for minor dealing, another worked in one of Radecki's video stores. And the third owed so much to the local loan sharks that he'd have admitted to sleeping with the Chancellor if the price had been right. She didn't believe any of them. But that was a long way from being able to disprove the story that Marlene still stuck so doggedly to.

She'd come back to the office determined to get the next phase of her strategy off the ground. None of her usual sources had been able to give her any leads on Marlene's daughter's whereabouts. All she'd been able to establish was that Tanja had been picked up from school on the day of the shooting in a big black Mercedes. Nobody had noticed who was driving the car, or anything useful like the number plate. She could be anywhere by now. Given Radecki's network, she might not even be in Germany.

But they had to try. So she'd marched into Hanna Plesch's office and laid out her idea. Plesch had heard her out, frowning. Then she'd shaken her auburn head. 'It's too risky,' she said.

'It's the only way. If we run it big as a missing child, we're bound to get a response. Wherever she's being held, someone must have seen her. Or, at the very least, noticed something a bit suspicious. We need to find the girl so we can make it safe for Marlene to tell us what she knows.'

'And what if they decide to cut their losses and kill the kid? What do we say to the media then? Do you really think Krebs will give you the time of day if she thinks you're the one who got her daughter killed?' Plesch stared her down. She was clearly as determined as Petra was.

'We don't have any other choice,' Petra said obstinately.

'Petra, we're getting nowhere with this. We might have to accept it's another dead end. We'll keep working the case, but I won't put a child's life at risk.'

'The child's already at risk.'

'Krebs knows that. And she knows what she has to do to keep her child alive. You're not going to change that. Petra, you might have to let this one go. There'll be other chances.'

Petra glared at her boss. 'Not from what I hear.'

'Meaning?'

'The word is that there's going to be a big operation mounted against Radecki. And it's not going to be ours. Boss, I've worked my arse off for years trying to build a case against that bastard, and if this is going to be our last chance to put him away, I don't want to leave any stone unturned.'

Plesch looked away. 'This job is not personal, Petra. You don't have some sort of divine right to be the one who finally cracks Radecki's organization. It doesn't matter who closes him down, as long as somebody does.'

'You're confirming there is something going down? Something that takes it away from us?' Now her blood was up and she didn't care that she was overstepping the mark. Her eyes were narrowed and there were patches of colour on her cheeks and neck.

'Don't push me,' Plesch said, getting to her feet. 'Just go out there and do your job. We need to talk about this some more, but not now. Listen to me, Petra. We've worked together long enough for you to understand that there are times when you have to trust me. This is not a good time for you to rock the boat. Don't go down the high-risk road. It's not necessary and it's not desirable.' She forced a smile. 'That's an order, by the way. You don't expose the child.'

Petra had walked out fuming, her hands clenched into fists at her side. Only later, when her initial anger had subsided, had she analysed what Plesch had said to her. She had verified, albeit indirectly, that something major was going to change in the Radecki investigation. But she seemed to be suggesting that there would be a role for Petra if she kept her nose clean. It was a long way from a promise, but it made her feel slightly less raw about Plesch's dismissal of her plan.

She slouched in her chair and logged on to her internal e-mail. She wasn't expecting anything interesting, but it was better than staring at the wall. She scanned the short list of new mail. The only thing that piqued her attention was a reply to her request for information from the police in Heidelberg. Given the way things had been panning out for her over the past couple of days, she refused to allow herself to feel eager, but she opened the e-mail anyway. Her eyes flicked down the screen, taking in the key details: *Walter Neumann, 47. Lecturer in psychology at the Ruperto Carola University of Heidelberg.*

Petra felt a blip on her mental radar. Another academic, another psychologist. This was promising. She scrolled on down. Three weeks previously, he'd been found by a student in his apartment near the Altstadt campus. His computer had been smashed to the floor and he'd been spread-eagled on his back across his desk. The details were identical to the information Marijke had given her about de Groot's murder in Leiden, right down to the cause of death – drowning – and the cutting away of the pubic hair and the skin attaching it to the body.

'Bingo,' she said softly. OK, the rules said it took three to make a series when it came to murder, but two killings with such an off-the-wall MO couldn't be coincidence. What puzzled her was why this had ever crossed the desk of the organized crime unit. She carried on reading, and found the tenuous explanation at the very end of the document.

Initial investigations have produced no personal motive for this murder. However, according to our intelligence, Neumann was involved in the drugs scene. He had allegedly been a long-time user of cannabis and amphetamines, and the narcotics squad responsible for dealing with the university had heard rumours that Neumann dealt drugs to his students. Although we have no firm evidence of his involvement in drug dealing, it seems possible that so bizarre a murder may have come about as a result of his involvement with the organized crime that exists in the drug culture. In short, that this may be an execution designed to send a message we cannot read to others who might be tempted to transgress the unwritten codes of such people.

'Pompous bullshit,' Petra muttered as she read the final paragraph. 'Translation: we can't make head nor tail of this, so let's offload it to someone else.' Nevertheless, she was for once glad of the buck-passing of her colleagues in the provinces. Without

177

their laziness and incompetence, she'd never have been able to make the connection between this murder and Marijke's case in Leiden.

The question was, what should she do now? There was no effective operational co-operation between the police forces of separate countries in the European Union. Interpol had no role to play here. Europol was for intelligence-sharing and the development of policing strategies, not cross-border operations. If she made this official, it would get bogged down in bureaucratic red tape and departmental politics.

But if she and Marijke worked the two cases together, sharing information and pooling leads . . . Since the Radecki investigation looked set to be snatched from under her, she needed to find another path to glory. This might just be it.

Petra hit the reply button. *Please send full pathology and forensic reports re Walter Neumann. We would prefer hard copies if possible. This matter is both urgent and highly confidential.*

She sent the message then sat back in her chair, a small smile of satisfaction on her face. If Plesch was right and there was a place for her in whatever was planned against Radecki, all well and good. But if she was only humouring her, this would be her insurance policy.

16

Three days really wasn't enough. Carol stared into her wardrobe, frowning. Some of her clothes would work, but most of them wouldn't. Morgan had given her a budget for new outfits that had made her eyebrows climb, but shopping to spend it was going to take her the best part of the day. Then she'd have to pack for her new identity, making sure she didn't include anything that would give a hint of her reality.

Her brother Michael had already agreed to take care of Nelson; he planned to drive down that evening from his home in Bradfield and take the cat back to the stylish loft apartment they'd once shared there. At least Michael hadn't asked awkward questions, like why he was being asked to cat-sit indefinitely while his sister went off to some unspecified destination; as soon as she'd said she couldn't explain for operational reasons, he'd dropped the subject.

The one thing she wished was that she'd had the chance to confide in Tony. She knew his insights would be helpful, and, more than that, his support would give her confidence. But an assignment this sensitive wasn't something she could trust either to the phone lines or to electronic communication. She had called him after her briefing session with Morgan, and had hated having to hold out on him. She'd made it clear that her reluctance was based purely on her misgivings about the security of their means of communication and, like Michael, he hadn't pressed her.

Carol flicked through the hangers, selecting possible garments and throwing them on the bed behind her. She was grateful that she would have to abandon most of what she had chosen to reflect her own personality. The thought that Carol Jordan might have much in common with this new creation, Caroline Jackson, even on the most superficial level, was not something she felt comfortable with. It bothered her slightly that the names were so similar, even though Morgan had explained the operational reasons for it. 'We like to keep the first name as close to your own as possible, so you don't get those horrible moments where someone says your name and you don't connect at all. And we've found it helps if the initials are the same too. Those who know about these things say it makes it all psychologically easier and less likely that you'll trip yourself up.'

Carol reached the end of the possible choices from her wardrobe and closed the double doors. She walked around her bedroom, stroking the familiar objects on her dressing table and bookshelves as if the action of her fingers would imprint them on her memory, accessible whenever she needed to touch base with who she really was. She paused in front of three photograph frames that faced her bed. Michael, his arm around the woman he'd been living with for the past two years, his expression open and delighted. Her parents at their silver wedding party, her mother's head on her father's shoulder, a look of indulgent affection on her face; her father, looking directly into the camera, his familiar quirky smile lifting the corners of his eyes. And finally, a snatched snapshot of her with Tony and John Brandon, her former boss, taken at the police party that had celebrated the resolution of the first case they'd worked together. They all had the slightly bleary look of people who were heading towards drunk but hadn't quite got there yet.

Her reverie was interrupted by the rude blurt of the entryphone buzzer. Carol frowned. She wasn't expecting anyone. She walked through to the living room and grabbed the handset. 'Hello?' she said.

Through the crackle of static she heard a tinny voice say, 'Carol? It's me. Tony.' She held the phone away from her ear, staring at it as if it were an unfamiliar artefact. Her free hand automatically moved to the door release button while she tried to get her head round what she'd just heard. Like a sleepwalker, she replaced the handset and crossed to open her front door. Outside the excellent soundproofing of her flat, she could hear the whine of the lift machinery.

The lift door slid open and she tensed herself for the familiar jolt that came with the sight of him. The harsh lighting bleached his skin tones to wood ash, turning him monochrome. Then Tony stepped forward and recovered his humanity. His hair had been cut since she'd seen him last, she noted as he walked towards her, looking unusually pleased with himself. 'I hope this isn't a bad time,' he said.

Carol stepped back and waved him in. 'What are

you doing here?' she said, unable to suppress the laugh bubbling under her voice.

Tony walked in, touching her gently on the elbow and leaning forward to give her a chaste kiss on the cheek. 'Forgive me if I seem presumptuous, but you sounded on the phone like a woman who could use a little moral support. And from what I know of you, I didn't imagine you would be opening yourself up enough to be getting it anywhere else.' He spread his hands out in a gesture of munificence. 'So, here I am.'

'But . . . shouldn't you be at work? How did you get here? When did you get here?'

Before he could answer, Nelson appeared, alerted by a familiar voice. The cat wound himself round Tony's legs, sinuously shedding black hairs all over his blue jeans. Tony immediately dropped into a crouch to scratch the cat between the ears. 'Hello, Nelson. You're looking handsome as ever.' Nelson purred, narrowing his eyes and watching Carol as if to say he could teach her a thing or two. Tony looked up. 'I flew down on the shuttle from Edinburgh this morning. I don't have any teaching commitments today, so I thought I'd take a chance on catching you at home.'

'An expensive chance,' Carol said. 'You could just have phoned, made sure I'd be home.'

Tony stood up. 'Sometimes I get fed up with being prosaic.'

Before she could stop herself, Carol said, 'And what does Frances think about that?' As soon as her words landed, they altered the landscape of his face. It was as if a physical shutter had closed down behind his eyes.

'What I do is no longer any concern of Frances,' he said. His tone of voice deflected discussion as effectively as armour plating.

Carol couldn't help a squirm of delight in her stomach. It couldn't be coincidence that Frances had been consigned to history so soon after her visit. Which meant . . . all sorts of things she couldn't begin to permit herself to consider. It should be enough that he was here now, with her; his choice, not her request. 'Come and sit down,' she said. 'Coffee, yes?'

'Oh, please. They can map the human genome, but they still can't make a decent cup of coffee on a plane.'

'Make yourself at home,' Carol said, gesturing towards the twin sofas that sat at right angles, making the most of her view. 'I won't be a minute.' She headed for the kitchen.

Rather than settling down, Tony roamed the room. Much of the contents were familiar, but some were new. There were a couple of large Jack Vettriano prints from his film noir series in heavy distressed gilt frames that would have been totally out of place in the cottage where Carol had been living previously but which looked strong and moody on these high white walls. The CD collection had expanded to include a tranche of contemporary guitar bands whose names he recognized but whose music was completely alien to him. He'd never seen the brightly coloured gabbeh that dominated the centre of the room either.

But there was nothing that didn't chime with his understanding of Carol. She was still the person he knew. He stood at the window and gazed down at the old church, incongruous among the modernity of its surroundings. He wasn't sure he'd done the right thing, coming here like this. Sometimes, however, risks had to be taken. Otherwise, how would he know he was alive?

Carol's voice cut through his introspection. 'Coffee,' she said, placing a cafetiere and two mugs on the low glass table.

He turned to face her and smiled. 'Thanks.' He took off his jacket, revealing a black V-necked sweater in fine wool; a more fashionable look than he used to go for, Carol noted. They settled down with their drinks, each on a separate sofa, but close enough at the angle between them to have touched if they'd felt able to. 'So,' he said. 'Do you want to talk about it?'

Carol tucked her feet under her and cradled her mug in both hands. 'I'm dying to talk about it. They're sending me in deep. Total immersion undercover.'

'This is Europol?' he asked.

'Not exactly. It's a UK operation. To tell you the truth, the lines are a bit blurred. I'm not sure where Special Branch ends and Customs and Excise begins on this one. And I wouldn't be surprised if the intelligence services have got a finger in the pie too.' She gave a wry little smile. 'All I know for sure is that my own chain of command goes through Superintendent Morgan, who is attached to NCIS. And that's all I'm supposed to need to know.'

Tony was experienced enough as an interviewer of serial offenders not to let his unease show. But already he didn't like the sound of this. In his limited experience of British policing, grey areas always heralded deniability. If the time came when someone had to be shot down in flames, the only person visible in the sights would be Carol. That she wasn't admitting this even to herself was worrying. 'What's the assignment?'

Carol relayed everything Morgan had told her about Tadeusz Radecki. 'Morgan said that when he saw my Europol application, he couldn't believe his eyes,' she continued. 'Katerina was dead, but here was her double, applying to work at the sharp end of intelligence. And so he came up with the idea of mounting an operation using me as the bait to sucker Radecki in.'

'You're going undercover to try to seduce Radecki?' Tony felt the ground shift under his feet. He'd thought the honey trap had died with the Cold War.

'No, no, it's much more subtle than that. It's a sting. According to Morgan, Radecki used to have a sweet little deal going with a gangster in Essex, Colin Osborne. Osborne would funnel Radecki's illegal immigrants in via a couple of clothing sweatshops he ran in the East End. Every few months he'd tip off a contact in Immigration and get them hustled away to detention centres. Then he'd replace them with the next shipment from Radecki. He managed to keep his own nose clean, because the sweatshops were always set up using false names and credit references.'

'Neat,' Tony said.

'Very. Anyway, Osborne got himself killed in a gangland shooting about six weeks ago. And everybody's still squabbling over who gets which piece of turf from his nasty little empire. Meanwhile, nobody is providing a convenient refuge for Radecki's illegals.'

'And that's where you come in?'

'That's exactly where I come in.' She grinned. 'I turn up in Berlin with a proposition for Radecki. I'm Caroline Jackson.' She gestured with her thumb towards the small office that opened off the living room. 'I've got a file half an inch thick with Caroline's back story. Where she went to school, when she lost her virginity, when her parents died and how, where she's lived over the years, how she's made a living. Now, she's a wealthy businesswoman with some very dodgy contacts.'

Tony raised an admonishing finger. 'Not "she", Carol. It has to be "I" from now on.'

Carol pursed her lips in rueful acknowledgement. 'I own the lease on a former US airbase in East Anglia. I have a factory producing hand-made wooden toys on the site, as well as the former barracks. I also have a source of forged Italian passports. I knew Colin Osborne and knew he was getting workers from Radecki. And now Colin's dead, I'm here to take up the slack. I need workers and I can offer them an even better deal than Colin. They work for me for free for a year and they get legal EU papers. And Radecki gets a market for his illegals.'

Tony nodded. 'I can see how that would appeal to him. So why do they need the added incentive of someone who looks like his dead girlfriend?'

'Well, Morgan said it wasn't the first time they'd thought of putting someone in to pull the scam I'm going to be doing. But there were some reservations because the chances were they'd only be able to get evidence on the final stage of the racket. So, although they would probably net Radecki, they might not be able to roll up his networks behind him. Then I came

186

along. The general idea is that he'll open up further and faster to me than he would to someone else. Assuming I can gain his confidence, I should be able to find out exactly how his operations work. If I play my cards right, we could close down his drug smuggling, his gunrunning and his people trafficking. And that would be a result worth having.'

Her eagerness worried Tony. He knew that to succeed in so difficult an assignment Carol would have to maintain a high level of confidence. She'd be thrown on her own resources for most of the time and, without self-belief, she'd sink like a stone. But it wasn't like her to be blind to the perils of a task so fraught with jeopardy. 'It's obvious that they're right, psychologically speaking,' he said. 'Radecki's bound to be attracted to you. And his emotional investment will make it easier for you to maintain your undercover story. He'll find it hard to be as suspicious of you as he would be of any other stranger. Still, you're really going to be out there on a limb. If your cover does get blown, he's going to be far more dangerous to you than if you were just another undercover cop. It won't be enough to eliminate you. He'll need to make you suffer. You do know that?'

'It crossed my mind, yes. But you know I don't like to brood.'

'You need to be aware of the potential pitfalls. I wouldn't be any use to you if I just sat here uttering anodyne platitudes about how terrific you're going to be at this. Undercover is the hardest job in policing.' He leaned forward, his face earnest. 'You're never off duty. You can't afford to be homesick for who you really are. You have to live it, and it's the loneliest place there is. And you're going to be in a foreign country, which will only compound that feeling of isolation.'

His words hung in the air between them, the intensity speaking of something beyond their superficial meaning. Carol suddenly understood that he was telling her about himself and the way he had chosen to live. 'You sound like you've been there,' she said softly.

Passing for human, he thought. This wasn't the time or the place to get into that one. 'Been there so long I gave the T-shirt to Oxfam,' he said, striving for lightness. 'Academic life is not my natural habitat.' Carol looked disappointed. She had every right, he thought. She deserved better than that from him. 'Nor was Frances,' he added. 'But I didn't come here to talk about me. Will it be possible for us to be in touch?'

'I hope so. Morgan said they'll find a way of getting me secure e-mail access.'

Tony finished his coffee and topped it up from the cafetiere. 'I'd like that. Not that I can be of much practical help, but it'd be good to know you were OK. And you might appreciate a place where you can be Carol Jordan for a few minutes every day. On the other hand, you might find that just disrupts staying in role. So play it as it lays. See how you feel when you're in there.'

Carol put her mug down on the table and got to her feet. She walked over to the window and looked out. He could see her in profile, a series of planes and angles his memory held constantly clear. Some of the creases round her eyes were a little deeper, but that was the only change since he'd first known her. Now, though the line of her mouth was stubborn, determined, her eyes were troubled. 'I'm scared, Tony. I'm trying not to be, because I know fear is a bad emotion to run an operation on. But I'm really, really scared.'

'Don't discount the usefulness of fear,' Tony said. 'You're going to be running on adrenaline for as long as this assignment takes to complete. Fear's a good provider of that. And it keeps complacency at bay. Whatever you think now, you're going to have to get to like Radecki. You'll start off consciously behaving as if you're drawn to him, but the very act of maintaining that for any length of time tends to make it a reality. It's a variation on the Stockholm Syndrome, where hostages start to identify with their captors. Like it or not, you're going to find yourself growing close to him, and probably getting very fond of him. Fear is a good antidote to that.'

Carol rubbed her eyes with finger and thumb. 'I want what this could bring me so badly, I'm scared I'll do whatever it takes. What if I fall for this guy?' She turned back towards him, her face troubled.

'You wouldn't be the first. And there's no easy recipe for avoiding it.' He crossed to her and took her hands in his. 'If he's nice to you – and there's no reason why he wouldn't be – it's going to seem very appealing to go with the flow. What you have to do is hold on to one fact about this guy that you find totally abhorrent. I don't know what that would be for you. But there has to be something in his file that really got to you. Remember what it was, and hold that thought like a mantra.' He squeezed her hands tight, conscious of their coolness against his warm skin, trying not to think what they would feel like on his back.

'That's easy,' she said. 'The callousness. The way he engineers all this without ever getting his hands dirty. I can't get rid of the image of that dead dealer, lying on the steps of the police station with his brains on the pavement. And Radecki sitting in his expensive Charlottenburg apartment, sealed off from all the shit, listening to Verdi or Mozart, as if it wasn't connected to him. That's what gets to me.'

'So every time you feel the tug towards him growing too strong, summon up those two contradictory images. That'll ground you in what you're there for.' He dropped her hands and stepped back. 'You can do this, Carol. You're good enough. You're strong enough. And you've got something to come back to.' He held her gaze. For the first time since they'd met, he was making her a promise he thought he just might be able to keep.

If Dr Margarethe Schilling had known she was experiencing her last afternoon alive, she would probably have chosen to spend it differently. Perhaps a reprise of their favourite woodland walk with her lover. Or perhaps round her kitchen table with her closest friends, good food and wine and conversation flowing freely. Or, most likely, playing a computer game with her eight-year-old son Hartmut. Even her hard-hearted bastard of an ex-husband wouldn't have refused to vary the conditions of Margarethe's contact time with her son if he'd known she was about to die.

Instead, unaware of what lay ahead of her, she considered her hours in the university library well spent. Her main academic interests lay in the psychological effects of religious belief systems, and a recent visit to the Roman museum in Köln had triggered off some ideas relating to the effects on the indigenous population of the imposition of Roman gods following their occupation of Germany. She was also intrigued to see if the collision between two contradictory religious systems had had any modifying influence on the Roman occupiers.

Her research was still at the embryonic stage where she had to accumulate information before she could begin to formulate theories. This was the tiring, tedious part of the process; hours spent in dusty archives, following trails that dead-ended as often as not. She had heard of researchers who had actually been infected with ancient illnesses as a result of poking around among materials that had barely been disturbed for centuries, but so far nothing that dramatic had ever happened to her.

The risks she normally ran from her work were quite different. Margarethe had spent years working with live subjects, probing the intersection between their religious beliefs and their personalities. Part of that had involved attempts to undermine those beliefs, and sometimes the results had been unsettling, to say the least. It had provided little comfort to her subjects to remind them that they had given informed consent to the clinical experiments, and she had on several occasions been subjected to strenuous personal abuse. In spite of her training, Margarethe found such confrontations stressful, and she had to admit to herself that the idea of researching the long dead had definite consolations.

She left the library just after four, when her head started to ache from too much close concentration on obscure materials. Emerging into the overcast afternoon had felt like a blessing, even with the humid promise of rain in the air. She didn't fancy going home to her empty house any sooner than she had to. She still hadn't grown accustomed to living alone; the rooms seemed too large, the echoes too present in the absence of her son.

For Margarethe the most bitter irony of her divorce was that the very thing that had poisoned her marriage was the single factor that had worked against her when it came to gaining full-time custody of her son. His father was a lazy leech, preferring the excuse of childcare to the demands of a job. Never mind that he didn't do a hand's turn in the house, leaving her to fit cooking, cleaning and shopping into the interstices of work and quality time with Hartmut. Never mind that he'd been the one to have an affair while their son was at school. It had left him in the perfect position to argue that he was Hartmut's primary carer and should therefore continue in that role. It wouldn't have been so bad if she'd thought he'd done this out of love for the boy. But she suspected it was more about exerting a last vestige of control over her.

So she preferred not to go home of an evening until she had to. She worked late, she dived into the cultural life of the city, she saw friends, she spent time in her lover's apartment. It was more than a desire not to be at home that took her into the centre of Bremen that day. She always enjoyed strolling in the narrow cobbled streets of the Schnoor, an enclave of gentrified medieval fishermen's houses, admiring the contents of the antiques shops' windows, even though she couldn't afford their prices. While the university where she worked and the suburb where she lived offered little in the way of aesthetic pleasure for the eye, the old town was a significant compensation.

She glanced at her watch. She had a couple of hours to spare before she met the journalist from the new e-zine. It sounded like an interesting venture, and it never hurt to find another outlet for one's work in these days when professional prowess was no longer measured by how well one taught one's students. Margarethe walked through the Schnoor and cut down one of the alleys leading to the swollen Weser, whose mud-coloured waters were flowing fast in spring spate. She walked along the river for a few minutes, then turned into the city's most bizarre street, the Böttcherstrasse, which combined disparate elements of Gothic, Art Nouveau and pure fantasy, a product of the imagination of local artists and architects in the 1920s, funded by the inventor of decaffeinated coffee. It always amused Margarethe to think that such richness of style had come from so bloodless a product.

She turned left at the end of the street and made for her favourite city-centre bar, the Kleiner Ratskeller. A couple of glasses of Bremer Weisse and a steaming plate of their hearty *knipe* and she'd have recovered her strength, ready for whatever her interviewer had to throw at her.

Those of her fellow diners who noticed her could have had no idea that by morning they'd be witnesses in a murder investigation.

17

His hands moved deftly over the controls of the small crane that lifted his Volkswagen from the rear deck of the *Wilhelmina Rosen*. This was the moment when he shifted from one life into the other, when he stopped being the respected skipper of a fine-looking Rhineship and turned into a walking death warrant. Tonight, he would be lit up once more, celebrating his latest triumph between the thighs of some Bremen bitch.

He stretched his arms across his broad chest and hugged himself. If they only knew what they were taking into themselves when they spread their legs for him. He was the one who made light grow out of darkness. He'd transformed his own blackness into something that glowed like a jewel inside him and now he was turning that brightness on the shadowy secrets of the past, making them obvious to the world.

Later rather than sooner, he suspected, someone in law enforcement would realize that all his victims had turned humans into lab rats for their own selfish ends. Once the connection was established, the next step would be inevitable. Police departments were notoriously leaky. It would be all over the media. As soon as people realized the crimes that were being committed in the name of science, the mind fucks would have to stop. There would be a public outcry, things would have to change. He'd be able to stop then.

He wouldn't mind stopping, because his work would be done. He wasn't some thrill killer, murdering for kicks. It was true that his revenge had finally lifted the clouds from his mind and allowed him to take his place in the world as a real man, but that was a lucky bonus. If he stopped, he would still be able to fuck, because it wasn't murder that turned him on. He wasn't a pervert, he was simply a man with a mission. There was no pleasure for him in the deed itself, merely in what it signified. For him, pleasure was what he felt when he plied the waterways in the *Wilhelmina Rosen*. His other life was work, nothing more. The boat was what gave him joy.

They'd arrived at their destination right on schedule, reaching the wharf on the Weser with enough time to unload that afternoon. They didn't have to pick up their next cargo until ten the following morning. It was all going immaculately to plan. They'd moved the *Wilhelmina Rosen* to the railhead where they were due to load up with coal, and now he was leaving Gunther in charge so that he could conduct his personal business ashore.

He gently lowered the car on to the dockside and released the grabs. 'I'm off now,' he said to Gunther.

'Going anywhere interesting?' Gunther said, not even looking up from his dog-eared paperback.

'I need to see a couple of shipping agents. I wouldn't mind a bit more work up this way.'

Gunther made a noncommittal sound. 'We don't get home enough these days.'

'What's in Hamburg that's so special? You're divorced, you never see your kids even when we are in port.'

Gunther looked up from his book. 'My mates are in Hamburg.'

'You've got mates everywhere,' he said, walking off the bridge. He didn't want to lose Gunther, but finding a new crew member wasn't the hardest thing in the world. If Gunther didn't like the routes his mission had thrust upon them, he didn't have to stay. Of course, there weren't that many good jobs on the barges these days. Somehow, he didn't think he'd be looking for a replacement any time soon. But he wished Gunther hadn't started on about Hamburg now. It was too much like a hook pulling him back into the past, when he was so intent on moving forward into his future.

Now, that future lay here in Bremen, a few miles away. His was a good cover story, he had to admit. He had worked long and hard on it. At first, he had thought of posing as a colleague, but realized that he would be too easily found out. Academics were always meeting at conferences and conventions; there was a high risk his victim might actually know the person he was pretending to be. And in these days of easy e-mail communication, it would be too easy to check. But what else would make them agree to a meeting?

Vanity, that was the key. They all loved to talk about themselves and their work. They were so sure of themselves, convinced they knew best about everything. But how to exploit that?

The answer had to lie in the new technology. It was easy to wear a mask there. They already had a computer on board, of course; so many of their consignments and movement orders arrived that way these days. He was intrigued by its potential for assisting him in his mission. So, he'd sent the boys back to Hamburg, laid the barge up for a week, bought a laptop computer and taken a crash course in the internet and website design. He'd registered the domain name of psychodialogue.com and created a website announcing the imminent arrival of *PsychoDialogue*, a new on-line magazine dedicated to the dissemination of current thinking in experimental psychology. He'd culled enough jargon from his own victim research to make it look like the real thing, he thought.

Then he had business cards printed up announcing himself as Hans Hochenstein, managing editor of *PsychoDialogue*. He had e-mailed his victims to arrange appointments to talk about their work, and the rest had fallen beautifully into place. One of the tutors on the computer course, a self-confessed former hacker, had even shown him how to send e-mails containing a logic bomb that would make them automatically erase themselves from the host computer after a pre-determined period of time had elapsed. So even that potential fragment of evidence was gone.

Tonight, Dr Margarethe Schilling would pay for her cruelty and her vanity. He checked the directions she'd given him, savouring the irony of her willing contribution to her own downfall. Then he set off.

The street where she lived was on the outskirts of the city. Here, fingers of countryside clung on to the land with an arthritic grip, a stranded straggle of trees and scrubby grass the only reminders of what used to be there. These last remnants of nature formed divisions between the housing developments, giving their owners an illusion of being country dwellers. They could look out at the darkling woods and imagine themselves lords of all they surveyed, ignoring the fact of their ugly square houses with their two reception rooms, three bedrooms, one and a half bathrooms and a fitted kitchen replicated like some grotesque multiple birth all along the street. He couldn't see the attraction. He'd rather live in a tiny apartment in the heart of the city than reproduce ugliness along with space. Better still, to be cabined on a boat, a moving world that travelled with you and allowed you to change your view on a daily basis.

He drove slowly along the street, lights on against the gloomy drizzle of the evening, checking the house numbers. There was nothing to distinguish Margarethe Schilling's home from those of her neighbours. Although the colours of doors and the patterns of curtains varied, somehow they all merged into one amorphous identikit. Her car was parked in front of the garage door, he noticed. He wondered if his own car would be too conspicuous, left on the street when every other vehicle was garaged or on a drive. There was room for the Golf behind her elderly Audi, so he decided to park there.

He walked up to the front door, bag in hand, hoping suburban eyes would be too busy with their own concerns to notice him. Not that they'd remember someone so insignificant. It was only on the inside that he was remarkable. He rang the doorbell and waited. The door opened to reveal a woman of medium height and build. *Not too heavy to lift,* he thought with satisfaction. Her greying blonde hair was pulled back in a ponytail from a face that looked tired and careworn. Mascara was slightly smudged round her eyes, as if she'd rubbed them without thinking. She wore tailored charcoal slacks and a maroon chenille sweater that effectively disguised her figure. 'Herr Hochenstein?' she said.

He inclined his head. 'Dr Schilling, it's a pleasure to meet you.'

She stepped back and gestured to him to enter. 'Straight ahead,' she said. 'I hope you don't mind us talking in the kitchen, but it's the most comfortable room in the house.'

He'd hoped for her study. But as he walked into the kitchen, he could see it was ideal for his purpose. A scarred pine table stood in the middle of the floor, perfectly positioned for the ceremony that lay ahead. Later, he would find her study and leave his calling card in her files. For now, though, the kitchen would suffice.

He turned as Margarethe followed him, offering a smile. 'This is very comfortable.'

'I spend most of my time in here,' she said, passing him and heading for the stove. 'Now, would you like a drink? Tea, coffee? Something stronger?'

He measured the distances. The fridge would give him the best chance. 'A beer would be good,' he said, knowing this meant she'd have to turn her back on him.

And so it began again. Hands and brain moved in a smooth sequence, following the practised routine without a stutter or stumble. He was bending down to fasten her left ankle to the table leg when the sharp chime of the doorbell made him jerk upright, the cord falling from his startled fingers. His heart thudded in his chest. He felt the choke of panic close his throat. Someone was there, only twenty yards or so away from him. Someone who expected Margarethe Schilling to open the door.

She couldn't have made an arrangement, he reasoned. She knew he was coming, so she wouldn't have invited anyone round. It must be someone selling religion or household goods door to door, he told himself, fighting for calm. Either that or one of the neighbours who'd seen Schilling's car on the drive and expected her to be home. It had to be. Didn't it?

The doorbell pealed out again, this time for longer. He didn't know what to do. He stepped away from the table where Margarethe lay spread-eagled, still fully clothed. What if the caller was persistent enough to come round to the back of the house? All it would take would be one glance in the brightly lit kitchen windows. He scrabbled for the light switch. Just as his fingers closed on it, he heard a sound that chilled him even more than the doorbell. The unmistakable click of a key in a lock.

He froze, dry-mouthed, wondering about escape. The front door opened and a man's voice shouted, 'Margarethe?' The door closing, then footsteps heading for the kitchen. 'It's me,' he heard.

Grabbing a heavy cast-iron pan from the stove, he flattened himself against the wall by the door. It opened without a moment's hesitation and a tall, male shape appeared, crossing the threshold and stopping in his tracks. Enough light spilled in from outside to show the shape of Margarethe's body lying on the table. 'Margarethe?' he said again, reaching for the light switch.

The pan crashed down on the back of his head and the man dropped to his knees like a felled steer. His upper body teetered for a moment then collapsed face down in an untidy heap.

He dropped the pan with a loud clatter and turned the light back on. The interloper was sprawled on the floor, a trickle of blood coming from his nose. Dead or unconscious, he didn't mind which, just so long as it would give him time to finish what he'd started. He kicked him savagely in the ribs. Bastard. Who did he think he was, barging in like that?

Hurrying now, he returned to his task. He finished the bindings, then hastily ripped the tape from her mouth. He had to keep checking the man was still out cold, which slowed him up even more. He didn't bother explaining to the bitch why he was making an example of her. She'd fucked up his routine, ruined his pleasure in a job well done, and she didn't deserve to know that there was good reason for what was happening to her.

It pissed him off more than he would have believed possible that he was having to rush things. He managed to do a neat enough job with the scalping, but it wasn't as precise as he liked. Cursing with the vigour of the boatman he was, he finished up in the kitchen, wiping every surface his hands could possibly have touched, and giving the stranger a brutal kick in the kidneys as he passed, just for good measure.

All that was left was the placing of the file. He ran

upstairs and started checking the rooms, unwilling to turn on the lights in case it drew more attention to him. The first room was clearly hers, dominated by a king-size bed and a wall of fitted wardrobes. The second looked like a kid's room, with its posters of Werder Bremen footballers and the Playstation on the table by the window.

He struck gold with the back bedroom, which was fitted out as a home office. He dragged open the drawer of the old-fashioned wooden filing cabinet and thrust the file into place. He was past caring if it was in the right slot. He just wanted to be done and out of there before things got even worse.

One final check that the stranger was still unconscious, then he warily opened the front door a crack. Nothing moved. He saw a VW Passat parked in front of the house, but thankfully it wasn't blocking the drive. Head down, he hurried out of Margarethe Schilling's house and into the car.

His hands on the wheel were slippery with perspiration, his fingers antsy and trembling. Sweat trickled down his temples and into his hair. He had to force himself to keep his speed down in the quiet suburban streets. His brain kept replaying the terrible sound of the front door opening, and every time his heart constricted in panic again. Fear was staking out its familiar territory inside him, and he struggled against it, moaning as he drove. He was on the dock road before he felt his breathing return to normal. For the first time since he had started his campaign, he had been directly confronted with the dangers of his chosen path. And he didn't like it one bit.

Not that that was any reason to stop, he told

himself. What he needed now was to take his mind off his panic. What he needed was a woman. He slowed down as he approached a row of bars, their dim lights yellow against the night. He'd find what he wanted here. He'd take some bitch and fuck her till the light came back.

Case Notes

Name: Margarethe Schilling

Session Number: 1

Comments: The patient has a god complex. She believes she has the divine right to undermine and destroy the legitimate beliefs of others in the interests of furthering her own status. She lacks all sense of proportion.

Her value system is hopelessly skewed by her erroneous belief in her own infallibility. Nevertheless, she seeks to impose her own world view on others and refuses to accept the possibility that she is wrong.

She is clearly overcompensating for an unacknowledged sense of inferiority. Like many professional females, she fails to recognize her innate weaknesses compared to males and reacts to this by seeking to castrate them psychologically.

Therapeutic Action: Altered state therapy initiated.

18

Tadeusz crossed the pavement and climbed into the back seat of the black Mercedes. If any of his neighbours had seen him, they might have wondered at his appearance. Instead of his usual immaculate and expensive surface, he was dressed in old moleskin trousers, battered work boots, an ex-army parka covering a thick fisherman's sweater. But nobody wore Armani for an afternoon's rough shooting, which was exactly how he planned to spend the rest of the day.

Darko Krasic lounged in the opposite corner of the rear seat. He wore a scarred leather jerkin over a padded plaid shirt whose tails hung over corduroy trousers so old the raised wales were rubbed flat on the surface of the thighs. 'Good day for it,' he said.

'I hope so. I feel like killing someone whose disappearance would make the world a better place,' Tadeusz said. He spoke with the distaste of a man who has bitten into a fruit and found decay at its heart. Apathy and cynicism had been his alternating companions since Katerina's death. Everything he did now was an attempt to break free from their suffocating grip, and everything so far had failed. He had no conviction that this afternoon would bring anything different. 'And since we've no traffic cops to hand,' he continued with a wan attempt at humour, 'I'll have to settle for something small and defenceless. Furry or feathered. You bring the guns?'

'They're in the boot. Where are we headed?'

'A nice bit of forest on the edge of the Schorfheide. That's the great thing about nature reserves. The wildlife doesn't recognize the boundaries. An old friend of mine owns a piece of land that butts right up against the protected area. And the ducks from the wetland don't know any better than to fly over his woodland. We should bag some good stuff. He's lending us a couple of his gun dogs so we can do the thing properly.' Tadeusz reached inside his jacket and pulled out a burnished pewter hip flask. He unscrewed the top and took a swig of Cognac. He held the flask out to Krasic. 'Want some?'

Krasic shook his head. 'You know I always like to keep a clear head round guns.'

'Speaking of guns and clear heads, what's the news on Marlene?'

'Some bitch from Criminal Intelligence has been sniffing around her. She spoke to her in the GeSa, and she's been back to see her in jail. Marlene's playing dumb and keeping her mouth shut, but it's winding her up.'

'You're sure we can trust her?'

Krasic gave a lazy smile. 'As long as we've got the kid, Marlene won't put a foot wrong. Funny how women get about their kids. You'd think they could only have the one, the way they go on about them.

They seem to forget that all they're going to get from them is heartache. Especially someone like Marlene. She should have the sense to realize that any daughter of hers is going to grow up using, or selling herself. But it doesn't seem to matter to her. She still thinks the sun shines out of the kid's arse.'

'Just as well for us,' Tadeusz said. 'Where are we keeping her?'

'I've got a cousin who has a smallholding on the outskirts of Oranienburg. The nearest neighbour is half a mile away. He's got a couple of kids of his own, so he knows how to deal with the little buggers.'

'And Marlene is convinced this isn't just a bluff?'

Krasic curled his lip in a sneer. 'Marlene believes I'm capable of anything. She's not going to play games with her child's life. Don't worry, Tadzio, it's all boxed off.'

'I wish I could say the same about the English end of things. The people who are trying to fill Colin's shoes, they're nothing but a bunch of clowns. They're too small-time to run a competent operation. I don't trust them to deliver. Meanwhile, we've got a bottle-neck in Rotterdam. We can't go on warehousing illegals indefinitely.'

'Can't we just take them over to England and dump them?' Krasic sounded like a petulant child who can't understand why the world doesn't turn to suit him.

'Not in the sort of numbers we've got stockpiled. It'd be far too obvious that something on a large scale was going down. The last thing we want is to attract the attention of the immigration authorities. I've been successful for so long precisely because I haven't done things like that,' Tadeusz pointed out. 'We had such a convenient arrangement with Colin. I can't believe he was stupid enough to get caught in some minor league gangland shoot-out.'

'It should be a warning to you,' Krasic said. 'That's the kind of thing that can happen when you get too close to the action. You shouldn't have made that trip the other week. I don't like it when you're exposed like that.'

Tadeusz glowered out of the window. He knew Krasic was right, but he didn't like being told what to do by anyone, not even his trusted assistant. Now he felt mean. 'It doesn't hurt sometimes to remind people who's in charge,' he said.

'Tadzio, it could have blown up in your face. If they'd got Kamal to talk . . . Well, we might not be so lucky next time.'

'There was no element of luck there. We've got all our bases covered.' He turned and gave Krasic a hard stare. 'We do have all our bases covered, don't we?'

'Of course we do. That's why we keep cops on the payroll.'

'And speaking of the cops on our payroll, why haven't we heard anything more about the investigation into Katerina's accident? This has been going on far too long. I want to know about that fucking motorbike. Lean on them, Darko. Don't let them think they can ignore me on this.'

Krasic nodded. 'I'll chase them up, boss.'

'Do that. And remind them that whoever pays the piper calls the tune. I want the man who killed Katerina. I don't give a fuck about the legal process.

I want to make him pay in a way he'll remember for the rest of his life. So tell those bastards to stop fucking around and produce some results.'

Krasic sighed inwardly. He had a feeling this was one investigation that was going to hit a brick wall sooner or later. He didn't relish the moment when he would have to report that fact to Tadzio. For the time being, he'd just have to keep going through the motions. 'I'll talk to someone tonight,' he promised.

'Good. I'm tired of problems. I could use some solutions. Whatever it takes.' He leaned back against the soft leather and closed his eyes, signalling that the conversation was over. Playing the bully didn't come naturally to him, but he'd found himself slipping into the role depressingly often since Katerina had died. He couldn't bear the thought that the rest of his life was going to be like this, a constant succession of crises and problems. It felt as if her death had taken all the ease from his life, and he wondered if he would ever again feel relaxed and comfortable in his own shoes. Perhaps vengeance would help.

It was the only thing he could think of that might.

It was Petra Becker's first visit to Den Haag, and she was surprised by its lack of flamboyance compared to Amsterdam. The canal houses were models of understated classical demureness, with few of the ornate flourishes that gave a walk in central Amsterdam so much visual richness. This was an expense account city, with none of the bohemian colour that provided Amsterdam with its variety. Here, there was an air of sedate prosperity, speaking of a prim propriety that made Petra's Berliner soul feel stifled. She'd been here less than a day and already she was craving the disreputable.

She wasn't sure how she felt about the day that lay ahead of her. She was due to meet the British cop at eleven. Carol Jordan, a Detective Chief Inspector, whatever that meant. Petra was supposed to tell her everything she knew about Tadeusz Radecki, and it stuck in her throat. It didn't seem fair that she should hand over such hard-won gains to someone who hadn't earned her stripes in the battle. When Hanna Plesch had told her that her new role was to act as liaison for someone else's undercover, she'd felt cheated. Of course, she was too familiar a face in Berlin to go undercover herself, but it pissed her off that her bosses had rolled over and handed the whole affair to the Brits. What did they know about German organized crime? Who did they think they were, muscling in on her territory? And how dare they think they could succeed where her department had failed?

Plesch had read her reaction in her face, in spite of her best efforts to keep it under wraps. She'd told Petra that she only had two choices. She could work with Jordan, or she could walk away from the whole Radecki investigation. Reluctantly, Petra had accepted the assignment. It didn't mean she had to feel happy about it.

She consoled herself with the knowledge that the take-down would have to be carried out by German cops. The Brits wouldn't be prosecuting this one. At the end of the operation, when they put Radecki away, Carol Jordan would be long gone. Petra Becker, on the other hand, would still be here, and she'd be the one who would be remembered as being instrumental in the final dismemberment of Radecki's rackets.

She found a café, bought coffee and a couple of warm rolls and took them over to a table by the window. She pulled a slim file out of her battered leather briefcase and began to read.

Detective Chief Inspector Carol Jordan had graduated from Manchester University and gone straight into the Metropolitan Police. She'd been fast-tracked for promotion and had reached the rank of Detective Sergeant in the shortest possible time. She'd worked in general CID and also done a stint in the specialized major-incident team that dealt with murders and other serious crimes. When she'd passed her inspector's examination, she'd left the Met and moved north to the industrial city of Bradfield. That seemed to be when her career had really taken off.

DI Jordan acted as liaison officer with Dr Tony Hill, a Home Office approved offender profiler, on a series of murders in Bradfield. Her work was instrumental both in uncovering the identity of the perpetrator and also in saving the life of Dr Hill. Petra read the dry words and made a mental note to check out the case on the internet when she had the opportunity. Serial killers always made it big on the world wide web.

She continued reading. *Jordan then moved to East Yorkshire Police, where she was promoted to Detective Chief Inspector and took charge of the CID in the North Sea port of Seaford. While she was stationed at Seaford, she renewed her professional relationship with Dr Hill, taking the lead role in an investigation which led to the eventual capture of the serial killer Jacko Vance. DCI Jordan's work was central in obtaining the conviction of Vance, who is believed to have killed at least eight young girls.* Another serial killer investigation, Petra noted. She'd take a look at the background to this one too. Maybe Carol Jordan could do her career another favour, aside from Radecki. There weren't that many officers around who had experience of tracking serial killers. Perhaps Petra could pick Jordan's brains and come up with a strategy for nailing the killer she believed had already struck in Leiden and Heidelberg. If Jordan was as good a cop as she appeared to be on paper, it was worth considering.

Petra returned to the file. *Two years ago, DCI Jordan returned to the Metropolitan Police, where in addition to operational duties with the serious crimes unit, she has undertaken extensive training in intelligence gathering and analysis. For the purposes of this undercover, she has been temporarily assigned to the National Crime Squad.*

That was the end of the brief. There was nothing in the file to suggest that Jordan had any undercover experience. Maybe they just hadn't gone into details. Petra couldn't believe they would put anyone into an operation this dangerous unless she really knew what she was doing. Radecki was way too smart to take anybody at face value. He'd be deeply suspicious of anyone who turned up with so convenient a proposal for solving his current problems. Jordan would have to be a superb operator to stay alive, let alone get under his guard and uncover anything worth knowing.

There was one more sheet of paper in the file. Petra flipped it over, seeing it was a photocopy of a photograph. She couldn't stifle a gasp of astonishment. If the caption hadn't told her this was Carol Jordan, she would have been convinced that she was looking at a photograph of Tadeusz Radecki's late girlfriend.

What was going on here? The resemblance was so spooky it made the hairs on the back of Petra's neck stand up. Where the hell had they found this cop? With looks like this, no matter what Carol Jordan's background, she'd have been drafted in for this assignment. She could imagine the guys thinking that if anyone was going to make Radecki drop his guard it was this particular British cop. And she supposed they had a point, though it was the kind of coincidence that would freak her out if they'd pulled a stunt like this on her. It would certainly make Radecki's sidekicks suspicious, but the man himself probably wouldn't be able to resist Katerina's *doppelgänger*. She gazed down at the picture and a slow smile spread across her face. For the first time since Plesch had briefed her, she was looking forward to this.

Back at her hotel, with time to spare, Petra decided to check her e-mail. There was nothing particularly interesting or urgent, so she turned to her favourite news site on the web to see what had happened in Germany since she'd left. She browsed the index of the day's stories till something buried far down the list caught her eye. LECTURER BRUTALLY MURDERED IN BREMEN, she read with a sinking feeling.

Hastily she clicked on the link that would bring her the full story.

A psychology lecturer was found brutally murdered in her home on the outskirts of Bremen last night. The victim's boyfriend, who disturbed the killer, was also attacked and left for dead.

Johann Weiss, 46, an architect, was battered uncon-scious by his assailant when he arrived at the home of Dr Margarethe Schilling, 43. He alerted police when he regained consciousness and discovered the murdered body of his partner.

Dr Schilling was a lecturer in experimental psychology at the University of Bremen and the mother of an eight-year-old son from a previous marriage. The boy lives with his father near Worpswede.

Police are refusing to release details of the crime, but a source close to the investigation revealed that Dr Schilling's body was bound and naked. Her body had been mutilated in a ritualistic manner.

A police spokesman said, 'Investigations are contin-uing into the death of Dr Schilling. We are pursuing various lines of inquiry. This was a particularly brutal and callous murder and we are determined to bring Dr Schilling's killer to justice. We would like to appeal for any witnesses who saw anyone in the vicinity of Dr Schilling's home yesterday evening to contact the police immediately. We are particularly keen to speak to the driver of a dark-coloured Volkswagen Golf.'

Petra gazed at the screen, appalled and excited in equal measure. It looked as if the killer had struck again, and on German soil. And this time, there might just be a lead to pursue.

Carol followed Larry Gandle, the British Europol Liaison Officer who had picked her up at the airport, through the corridors of Europol headquarters on the Raamweg. With his sharp suit and his cropped, thin-ning hair, he looked more like a financial services salesman than a police officer. But there was something indefinable that marked him out as English, something beyond his nasal Black Country accent.

He led her to a small conference room on the third floor of the main building. The only window looked out on to a central courtyard, allowing no possibility of being seen from the outside world. As Carol settled herself at one corner of the long bleached wood table, the door opened and a tall, rangy dark-haired woman walked in. She had the loose-limbed stride of an athlete at home in her body. Dressed casually in black jeans, a charcoal sweater and a creased leather jacket, a black satchel promoting the Berlin Film Festival slung over her shoulder, she looked more like a TV producer than a cop. Her hair was cut short and fashionably tousled with wax. She had a triangular face, broad across the forehead and narrowing to a pointed chin beneath a thin-lipped mouth. She looked unnervingly severe until she smiled a greeting, her blue eyes crinkling at the corners and promising compromises her expression in repose flatly denied. 'Hi,' she said. 'I'm Petra Becker.' She crossed the room, ignoring Gandle and making straight for Carol. 'You must be Carol Jordan.' She spoke English with a transatlantic hint overlaying her slight German accent.

Petra held out a hand to Carol, who stood up and shook it. 'Pleased to meet you. This is Larry Gandle, one of the British ELOs.'

Petra nodded acknowledgement and pulled out the chair nearest Carol, so they were sitting at ninety degrees to each other. Gandle was immediately shut out of their communion, though he didn't realize it. He sat down opposite Carol, a large expanse of table separating them. 'Nice to meet you, Petra,' Gandle said with an air of condescension. 'I'm here purely to facilitate this meeting, to answer any questions that might come up that fall into our remit. But essentially, this is a joint operation between the British and the Germans, and it's up to you two to run it in a way that works best for you.'

'Thanks, Larry,' Carol said, not quite dismissing him, but clearly focused now on Petra, the woman who would be her link back into her real life from the chilly wastes of deep cover. Petra would be her first line of defence, but, paradoxically, she would also be the person who could most put her at risk. For Carol, it was vital to establish a bridgehead of respect at the very least. Liking would be a bonus. 'I appreciate you coming up here so we can thrash things out off the territory,' she said. 'I'm sure you're just as busy in Berlin as I used to be in London. It's never easy to get away from the day-to-day case-load.'

Petra raised one corner of her mouth in a crooked smile. 'Tadeusz Radecki has been the most significant element of my case-load for a long time now. This doesn't feel like an escape, believe me.'

'No, I can see that. It's a big weight off my mind that they've assigned me a liaison officer who knows so much about the background to the case. I've come into it cold, and I'm going to need all the help I can get. What I wanted to do, if this is OK with you, is to hammer out the practicalities of how we work this, while Larry's still here to keep us straight on what's possible and what isn't. Then I thought the two of us could go back to the hotel and brainstorm all I need to know about Radecki and his operation. How does that sound to you?'

Gandle looked as if he was about to protest, but Petra caught his movement out of the corner of her eye and cut across him. 'Perfect. These official meeting places are so stifling to the soul, no?'

'Exactly. And I need to understand Radecki with my heart as well as my head. So I'm relying on you to open him up for me.'

Petra raised her eyebrows. 'I'll do my best.' She paused and cocked her head to one side, studying Carol's face. 'You know, they told me you looked like Basler, and it's true, your photograph does resemble her. But in the flesh, it's uncanny. You could be her twin sister. You are going to blow Radecki away. I swear to God, he is going to be freaked out when he sees you.'

'Let's hope it's in a good way,' Carol said, feeling self-conscious under the other woman's appraising gaze.

'Oh, I think so. I don't see how he could resist.' Petra smiled. 'I think this is going to work.'

'It'll work,' Gandle said confidently. 'DCI Jordan is one hell of an operator.'

Petra ignored him and continued to focus on Carol. 'So, we need to establish where you are going to be staying in Berlin, how we feed you into Tadzio's world, and then how you and I maintain contact.'

'For starters, yes.'

Petra opened her satchel and took out a stylish ring-bound notebook, its pages edged in a rainbow of colours, its black plastic covers embossed with a chain-link design. She flipped it open at the green section and tore out a page. 'I think a hotel is not a good idea for you. Too many people have access to the room, and it's too easy for Radecki's people to bribe a chambermaid to let them in. Radecki himself may be bowled over by your resemblance to Katerina, but I think the people around him – especially his lieutenant, Krasic – will be suspicious of you. Krasic will want to check you out as far as he possibly can. What I think is better is this: there is a building on a quiet street between the Ku'damm and Olivaerplatz that used to be a hotel and has been turned into service apartments. They are mostly used by business people, like you are supposed to be. Each has a living room, a bedroom, a bathroom and a small kitchen. You rent them by the week and a maid comes in twice a week to change the linen and to clean the place. It will be more secure, but also you will feel more at home there. It will be more relaxing, no?'

Carol nodded. 'Sounds good to me.'

Petra passed her the sheet of paper, which contained an address and phone number. 'I checked this morning that they have vacancies. I pretended to be a business associate of yours and asked them to hold one for you. They're expecting you to call. You do have credit cards in your alias?'

'I've got everything. Passport, driving licence, credit cards, a couple of old utility bills and bank statements. I don't have any Carol Jordan ID on me at all – I handed it all over to Larry for safekeeping.' She smiled across at him. 'Just don't sell my warrant card on the black market, Larry.'

He raised his eyebrows. 'Don't tempt me.'

'Next is how we stay in contact,' Petra continued.

'Now, I've got something that will help here,' Gandle butted in. 'Carol, you're going to have a laptop with you, right?'

'That's right. The London boys set it up. It's all Caroline Jackson stuff. A shedload of old e-mails, various business-related files and letters. Plenty of stuff to back up my cover story and nothing that shouldn't be there.'

Gandle placed his showy aluminium briefcase on the table and snapped open the locks. He produced a flat black rectangle with a cable protruding from one end. 'This is an auxiliary hard drive that you can plug straight into your laptop. It's preloaded with all the access codes you need to get into TECS.'

'TECS?' Petra asked.

'The Europol dedicated computer system. It incorporates an analysis system like the one you've trained on, Carol, together with an index system. And we've just got the information system up and running, so you can access all we hold on Radecki and his known associates. Everything Petra and her colleagues have passed on to us is in there, at the touch of a key. There's also an encryption system that will allow you to send secure e-mail to anyone who has the key. Petra, we're also going to make that available to you, so Carol can communicate securely with you via e-mail, which will be much safer than phone calls.

'And to keep it out of sight . . .' His hand went back into the briefcase and came out with a blue rubber box with a stubby antenna coming out of one corner. 'The coolest radio in town,' he said. 'You can buy them in all the smartest shops. Only, this one's different. The techies stripped out the guts of it and inserted a miniature radio. It works just like the original, but when you open it up –' he pushed a metal slider on the base of the radio and it fell neatly in half – 'there's a hiding place for your spare hard drive.'

Carol and Petra exchanged a look and burst out laughing. 'Boys and their toys,' Carol spluttered.

Gandle looked offended. 'It does work, you know. Nobody's going to give it a second look.'

'Sorry, Larry, it's very clever,' Carol said, not wanting to alienate her British back-up. 'And you're right, it's entirely unsuspicious.' She reached for the radio and slotted the hard drive into place then closed it up. She pressed a small blue rubber button and static crackled out of the speaker. 'Very good. It's exactly what I need, even if it does make me feel a bit like James Bond.'

'So, that solves your communication problems,' Gandle said, closing his briefcase with a self-satisfied smile.

'Only technically,' Petra said.

'I'm sorry?' Gandle said.

'It's not enough. Undercover is shit. It's the scariest, most isolated place in the world. And then you have the added risk of Zelig's Syndrome.'

'Zelig's Syndrome?' Gandle frowned.

'Like in Woody Allen's film, *Zelig*. Zelig is so insecure that he becomes a human chameleon, taking on not only the style and manner but also the appearance of the people he moves among. It's the big danger for the undercover cop. You spend so much time with these people, alienated from your own culture, that you start to identify with them.'

'You go native,' Carol said.

'Precisely. E-mail is all very well for the exchange of information, but it will not protect you from yourself. For that, we need face-to-face contact.'

Gandle looked dubious. 'You already said that Radecki's people are going to be suspicious around Carol. They're going to be watching her. And, with respect, Petra, you're a Berlin cop. Somebody's bound to recognize you. The last thing we want is to take the risk of regular meetings between the pair of you.'

'I think we can do this at no risk to Carol,' Petra said firmly. 'There is a very upscale women's health club a few blocks away from the apartment. As well as the gym and the swimming pool, they have private sauna suites that members can book for half-hour sessions. This is not a place where Krasic or anyone else in Radecki's inner circle can follow us. Trust me, Larry, I would not make an arrangement that would expose Carol.'

Gandle looked dubious, but Carol nodded. 'I agree. it's important to keep me connected to the real world. Besides, sometimes you need to talk something through face to face. There might be things that I see or hear but don't understand the significance of, things I might leave out of a written report because I don't realize they're important. But Petra will know the right questions to ask to draw the information out of me. I think she's right, Larry. We need that regular contact.'

Gandle fiddled with his silk tie. 'I don't know, Carol. You will be going in and out of Berlin every seven to ten days, we were thinking that you'd get your debriefs then. In London or here.'

'Ten days can be a very long time on the front line,'

Petra said. 'It's up to Carol, of course . . .' She met Carol's eyes, an expectant look on her face.

Carol gave an almost imperceptible nod. 'What you have to remember is that I've never done undercover before. I want all the back-up I can get. If I get burned, I need to be able to get clear in a hurry. With the best will in the world, Larry, you're not going to be much use to me up here in The Hague. If it all goes belly-up, Petra's the one who's going to have to deal with it on the spot. We need an arrangement to cover that eventuality. It's not as if she's going to be sitting glued to her computer twenty-four seven. And if the shit hits the fan, I may not even be able to get back to the apartment to access the computer. I want an insurance policy, Larry, and from where I'm sitting, that's Petra.'

Gandle pursed his lips. 'I'm not happy about this. Maybe it would be better if I came to Berlin too. Then you could liaise directly with me.'

Carol shook her head. 'You don't know the background like Petra does, and you certainly don't know the city like she does.' He still looked mutinous. Time to play her ace. 'Morgan told me I should set up systems that I felt comfortable with. And this works for me. If you're still not happy, I suggest we run it past him.'

Gandle flushed. 'I don't think that will be necessary. If it's what you want, I'm prepared to support you. Though, for the record, I do have my reservations.'

'Thank you,' Carol said prettily. It was good to know that Morgan's name carried as much clout as she had suspected. 'That's settled, then. Petra, you said you wanted to talk about how I infiltrate Radecki's world. What did you have in mind?'

'If you are going to do these things, they should be done in style. I have a plan that I believe is both stylish and also calculated to hit Radecki in his weakest spot,' Petra said.

Carol grinned. 'I can't wait to hear it.'

19

The phone was ringing as Tony walked back into his office after a lecture that he feared had bored his students almost as much as it had him. He grabbed it as he slumped into his chair. 'Tony Hill,' he said, covering his ennui with a coating of brightness.

'Dr Hill? This is Penny Burgess. I don't know if you remember me . . .'

'I remember you,' he said abruptly. Penny Burgess had been the crime correspondent of the *Bradfield Sentinel Times* when Tony had been working with the local police on his first serial killer case. She'd dogged his footsteps and done her best to turn him into a household name.

'The thing is, Tony, I was hoping we might have a little chat. In the light of what happened in the Court of Appeal this afternoon.'

The danger signs were flashing before his eyes. If Vance's appeal had failed, nobody would care what he thought. 'I'm sorry,' he stalled. 'I haven't heard the news today. What are you talking about?'

'Nobody called you?' Penny sounded surprised.

'I've been teaching. I literally just walked through

the door when you rang. What happened in the Court of Appeal?'

'The judges decided that Vance's conviction for the murder of Shaz Bowman was unsafe.'

Tony felt as if a pit had opened at his feet. A spasm of dizziness left him clinging with his free hand to the edge of the desk. Through the buzzing in his ears he could hear Penny Burgess speak. He compelled himself to listen to the words. 'It's not as bad as it seems,' she was saying. 'He was immediately rear-rested and charged with the murder of Barbara Fenwick. He's back behind bars, on remand. According to a police source of mine, there was a witness statement from a market trader in the orig-inal investigation that completely undermined the case and made the CPS decide not to proceed on that charge back then.'

'I remember,' Tony acknowledged.

'Well, apparently, a BBC radio reporter has been investigating the case, and she's managed to get the witness on tape admitting that he only said what he did because Vance asked him to. He's now completely recanted his earlier statement. So there's going to be another trial, and I hear that the CPS are quietly confi-dent. I wondered what your thoughts on the matter were.'

'I've got no comment to make,' he said wearily.

'I'm not asking you to comment on the new charges, obviously that's sub judice. But you must be upset that he's walked free of the murder of someone you were mentoring.'

'Like I said, I've got no comment.' Tony gently replaced the receiver on its cradle. He wanted to slam

227

it down hard enough to break the plastic casing, but the habit of self-control was too deeply ingrained for that. He closed his eyes and let out his breath in a long steady stream. That bastard Vance had once threatened to make his life a misery. It looked as though he was fulfilling his promise. He might well be convicted of other killings now, but he had wriggled out of the one murder conviction that really mattered to Tony. Not only that, but the relative anonymity he'd struggled to find had been shattered with a single phone call.

Before he could do anything else, the phone rang again. This time, he ignored it. He wondered how long he'd be able to carry on doing that before some bright spark from the university press office decided that what they really needed was the sort of high profile that an interview with Tony Hill could bring. He jumped to his feet and made for the door. Time to go into hiding.

Sometimes there were distinct advantages in having a brother who was a computer expert. Carol had learned enough from Michael to recognize what a program file looked like, which meant she'd been able to identify the encryption software on the secondary hard disk that Gandle had given her. It had been the work of a few minutes to transmit the program on to her brother in Manchester, asking him to forward it to Tony, complete with instructions on how to install it. As a result, they were now exchanging e-mails in complete security. Of course, it was all highly irregular – a breach of the Official Secrets Act at the very least. She'd had a moment of doubt, understanding only too well how her apparent cavalier regard for security might be interpreted by someone who didn't know Tony. But it had only been a moment. She knew nobody more committed to confidentiality than Tony, nor anyone who could be more help at the sharp end of a complicated investigation. And Carol had always trusted her maverick streak to do what was best. She had warned Michael on pain of death not to spread the software any further, and she felt sure she could trust him. If it ever came to light, she would plead Morgan's orders that she should do whatever it took to make her feel secure.

This evening, more than ever, she was glad their line of communication was open. For she had something in her possession that might just tempt Tony out of his self-imposed retirement. More than that, it might bring him to her side. Carol frowned at the computer screen. She needed to get this one absolutely right. Impatiently, she pushed the chair back from the desk and paced the room, trying to gather her thoughts.

The apartment in Berlin was everything Petra had promised. Comfortable without attempting opulence, quiet and secure, its anonymity was somehow less impersonal than that of a hotel room. Caroline Jackson would relish those same qualities, she felt sure. The few personal items in the room marked it out as the territory of her alter ego. She'd never have chosen those books, that photograph frame, those extravagantly ostentatious flowers for herself. But for this evening she needed to remind herself that she was Carol Jordan. Caroline Jackson would be no help whatsoever in composing the finely balanced e-mail she needed to send; for that, she needed all her own qualities of mind.

The past few days had been a whirlwind of mental activity. She'd been astonished by how much information Petra Becker had on Tadeusz Radecki, and she could well imagine how frustrated her German contact had become with her team's apparent inability to close down his operations and put him behind bars. He seemed to operate with complete impunity, largely because he had never made the mistake of most criminals, who eventually came to believe in their own invincibility. It was that hubris that brought most of them to disaster, Carol knew from her own experience. But Radecki had never lost the habit of constant caution. His was a recipe for success; he trusted few people, he understood the difference between turning a good profit and greed, and he apparently never breached the firewalls between his deceptively immaculate public persona and the dirty businesses that kept him in style. The icing on this perfect cake was Krasic, a man who had cultivated a reputation for brutal ruthlessness with apparent glee.

But although Radecki had managed to stay beyond the reach of legal sanction, it hadn't rendered him immune from the relentless probing of Petra Becker. The dossier she had assembled on him was remarkable. Everything from his taste in music to the shops where he bought his clothes was documented. Assimilating this had been Carol's first task, and it brought with it a genuine taste of the undercover life. She had to retain as much of this information as she possibly could while simultaneously shunting it to the back of her mind. Caroline Jackson would know almost nothing of Radecki's life and tastes, and Carol found the necessity of splitting her mind in two profoundly dislocating. That was when she had decided, to hell with protocol, she needed a conduit to Tony.

If she'd had any doubts about the wisdom of her course of action, they vanished in the course of the second evening she spent in the company of Petra Becker. They had used the morning to go over everything Petra knew about Radecki's criminal network, and the afternoon had been devoted to working with Carol's cover story, pushing to see where the cracks might appear, trying to identify possible danger zones and letting her explore the personality she would be living inside for the foreseeable future. Finally, Petra had stubbed out the twentieth cigarette of the day and leaned back in her chair. 'I think it's time to unwind a little,' she said. 'We can't be seen out together once we get back to Berlin, so we should make the most of our anonymity and have dinner out somewhere nice to celebrate the successful completion of phase one.'

Carol stretched her cramped back with a groan. 'I'll drink to that.'

Half an hour later, they were sitting in a quiet booth in a dimly lit Indonesian restaurant. In the centre of the room, brightly illuminated under heat lamps, an extensive rice table buffet was laid out. But for now they were happy to sit with their drinks and unwind. Carol took a healthy swig of her gin and tonic and Petra raised her glass. 'It's been a pleasure working with you these past few days, Carol,' she said. 'I must admit, I had some very negative feelings about this operation, but you've reassured me.'

'Why did you feel so negative about it? Did you think I wouldn't be up to it?'

Toying with the stem of her margarita, Petra studied the liquid as it slid up and down the side of the glass. 'That was part of it. But mostly it was because I felt we'd worked our guts out trying to nail Radecki and it wasn't fair to take it away from us.'

'I can understand that. I'd have felt exactly the same in your shoes. When you spend so long on a case, it feels very personal.'

Petra flicked a considering glance up at Carol. Then, coming to a decision, she leaned her elbows on the table and moved closer. 'Was that how you felt about Jacko Vance? And before that, the Queer Killer in Bradfield?'

Carol's relaxed expression was replaced instantly by wariness. 'You've done your homework,' she said, the distance in her voice shattering the intimacy they'd built in the past two days.

Petra held up her hands, palms out towards Carol, in a placatory gesture. 'Of course I've done my homework. I wouldn't be much of an intelligence officer if I hadn't. But I didn't bring up those cases out of some prurient curiosity. I have a genuine reason for mentioning them.'

Carol wasn't so easily mollified. 'I don't talk about those cases,' she said repressively. *Talk about them? I try not to even think about them. I wish I didn't dream about them either.* She drank back the rest of her gin and signalled to the waitress for a refill.

'That's cool. I don't want the gory details. I'm not some sensation seeker. But you are the only cop I've ever met who has so much experience in tracking down serial killers. And I need your advice.'

Carol wondered wearily if she would ever leave that part of her past behind her. She had thought she was coming to a place where all anybody would care about was her performance in the here and now. 'Look, Petra, I'm not an expert. The first time, I just happened to be a CID officer in a city where a serial murderer was operating. And the second time was . . . well, I suppose you'd have to call it a favour to a friend.'

'That would be Dr Tony Hill?' Petra wasn't giving up.

Carol massaged her forehead with thumb and forefinger, shielding her eyes with the rest of her hand. 'That would be Tony Hill, yes,' she said, sounding exasperated. She dropped her hand and gave Petra a cold, defiant stare. It was as if she was challenging the other woman to make something of it.

Petra could sense that her mention of Tony's name had stirred something deep inside Carol, but she had no way of telling whether that was positive or negative. 'I'm sorry, Carol. I don't mean to offend you by asking you about these cases. I realize they must have been tough to work. I really don't mean to bring back bad memories. But if I can explain . . . ?'

Carol shrugged. She was going to have to work with Petra on the toughest assignment of her career. Already, she liked and respected her and she knew she needed that to continue. It wouldn't hurt to hear what she had to say. 'I'm listening,' she said as the waitress arrived with her second drink. 'You might want another drink?'

Petra shook her head. 'Later. OK. First thing is, I'm a dyke.'

233

Carol had wondered, but it wasn't a big enough deal for her to have wondered much. 'Makes no difference to me.'

'I didn't think it would, but that's not why I'm telling you. I'm trying to explain how this all started. I hang out on a private website for gay and lesbian cops in the EU, and that's where I met Marijke. She's a brigadier in the Dutch police, based in Leiden. We talk three or four times a week in a private chat room, and we've got close over a period of time.' Petra's smile was crooked, self-mocking. 'Yes, I know what they say about meeting people over the net, but it's clear that she is who she says she is, not some impostor fishing for information or a cop junkie who gets off on pretending to be one of us. So, me and Marijke, we each found in the other the sounding board we lacked in our everyday lives.'

'Doesn't make you a sad bastard,' Carol said with a smile of reassurance.

'No. Anyway, Marijke and I have the habit of being confidential with each other. Just over a week ago, she had a murder in Leiden. She told me about it because it was such a strange case, with no obvious suspect or line of inquiry. The dead man, Pieter de Groot, was a professor of psychology at the university there. He was found naked, tied across the top of his desk. The killer had forced some sort of tube into his throat and poured water down it until he drowned.'

Carol shivered. 'That's seriously nasty.'

'There's more. The killer also scalped his victim. But not the head. The pubic hair.'

Carol could feel the hair on the back of her neck

bristling erect. She knew enough about psychopaths to recognize the work of a disordered personality when she came up against it. 'Well,' she said, 'it sounds as though it has some of the elements of a sexual homicide. Which means your man has quite possibly killed before and is likely to kill again.'

'Both, I think. When Marijke told me about the case, it rang a distant bell at the back of my mind. And I found the murder of Dr Walter Neumann.' Petra explained briefly what she'd discovered about the Heidelberg case. 'So I began to think that we might be looking at a serial killer operating across national boundaries.' She looked at Carol for a response.

'A reasonable conclusion. From what you've told me, these crimes contain signature elements.' She gave Petra a questioning glance, to see whether she needed to explain herself.

Petra nodded confidently. 'OK, so I figured we had a big problem on our hands. As you know, there's no formal operational liaison between national police forces in the EU, in spite of Europol and Interpol. Oh, we're supposed to swap information and work jointly on transnational crime, and that sometimes works, like with what we're doing against Radecki. But we both know how jealously cops guard their territory. Something as glamorous as a serial killer, nobody is going to want to mount an operation that might take the credit away from them. Getting them to share will be harder than pulling teeth.'

It smacked of cynicism, but Carol knew Petra was right. She also suspected that the greater glory of Petra Becker might be an element in the equation, but that wasn't necessarily a bad thing. She knew herself she tended to be more committed to cases that would make her look good. It wasn't something she was proud of, but she had to acknowledge it as a reality. 'So you decided to sit on it and do some investigating of your own?'

Petra looked slightly uncomfortable. 'I don't know that I'd got as far as making a decision,' she admitted. 'It's true that I wanted to be the one to break the news, and so I asked Marijke to send me the full details of her case. Because, if I was right, he started killing in Germany, which would give us some claim to be the primary investigators.' Petra stopped abruptly and reached for her cigarettes. 'But then, a couple of days ago, there was a third murder. I haven't been able to get much detail yet, but it appears that a Dr Margarethe Schilling from Bremen University has also fallen victim to the same killer.'

'Surely other people are going to pick up on it now?' Carol said.

Petra shrugged. 'Not necessarily. The police forces in the different länder don't have any formal liaison. There's no central clearing house for information on crimes like murder, only for organized crime. We're a big country and, frankly, most cops are too busy with their own workload to be bothered about what's happening in other cities hundreds of miles away. And it's not like America, where serial killing is almost part of the culture. Here, in Europe, we still don't expect it to happen outside books and movies. No, Carol, the only way anybody's going to make this link is if some detective like me picks up on it. And who's going to connect the murder of a man in Heidelberg and a woman in Bremen, just because they were psychology lecturers?'

'So *you're* going to have to make it official now,' Carol said.

'Oh, I know,' Petra said, blowing smoke down her nostrils. 'It's awkward, though. The first German case was never directly mine, and if I submit a report to Europol asking them to help co-ordinate an investigation, I will have to explain that Marijke broke her own duty of confidentiality when she told me about the Leiden case. And that is going to drop her right in the shit with her bosses.'

'I see your point,' Carol said thoughtfully. 'Is there any way you could have read about the Leiden case and noticed similarities to the one you'd seen from Heidelberg, then connected those to Bremen?'

Petra shook her head. 'There wasn't much detail in the media. Not enough to mark it out as something that would have jogged my memory.'

'I don't suppose Marijke put out a search notice through Europol, to see if there were any other similar cases?'

'I doubt it was even considered. Most cops, especially provincial cops, really don't think of Europol as something that affects them. It's not been up and running in an operational sense long enough to have become part of their automatic thought processes. I would think of it, of course, because my work is intelligence-based. But for someone like Marijke's boss, it wouldn't even cross his mind.'

'Well, if you're serious about wanting to protect Marijke, that might be the way to go. Get her to send a search request to The Hague, on the basis that this case has the hallmarks of the kind of killer who is likely to be a repeat offender and may be operating elsewhere in the EU. That would go out with the regular Europol bulletin, which I presume you see routinely?'

Petra nodded. 'I think my team is one of the few departments that actually reads what comes out of Den Haag,' she said wryly.

'Perfect. Then you can weigh in with your recollection of the Heidelberg case. And bring in the Bremen case as a possibility.'

Petra stared off into the middle distance, examining what Carol had suggested from every possible angle. It would play, she thought. She wouldn't make quite as big a splash as she had hoped, but still, she'd get the credit for picking up on the first known case. And she might even end up as the officer in charge of co-ordinating the inquiry, since it could then be claimed as a German case and nobody would want to leave it in the hands of the woodentops in Heidelberg. But though they might not be overly smart in Heidelberg, they weren't completely stupid. 'There's only one problem,' she said.

'Go on.'

'I asked for the Heidelberg case details to be re-sent to me last week. If there's a new investigation opened up, they're likely to remember that.'

'Bugger,' Carol said. 'You're right, they won't have forgotten that. Look, let's get some food and have a think. Maybe a solution will come to us once we've woken up our taste buds.'

They made their way to the buffet and loaded up their plates with an assortment of starters. For a while, they ate in virtual silence, breaking it only to comment on the quality of the food. Halfway through a chicken satay stick, Petra suddenly beamed. 'I've got it, I think. They sent that case to us originally because they thought it might be connected to organized crime. Now, Radecki's network extends as far as the Rhine and the Neckar. I could say that, in preparation for this operation, I was pulling in everything that might have a possible link to Radecki. I'm notoriously obsessed with this case. Nobody will think twice about me grasping at straws.'

Carol thought it over. It was thin, but it wasn't as if it would have to stand up to detailed scrutiny. Once a serial killer investigation was mooted, nobody would be seriously wondering how the show got on the road in the first place. 'It'll do,' she said. One corner of her mouth lifted in a sardonic smile. 'Somehow, I have the sense that you're not bad at blagging your way past your bosses.'

Petra frowned. 'Blagging? I don't understand this word.'

'Talking your way out of a tight spot.'

'I've had lots of practice. Thank you for your help with this.'

Carol shrugged. 'No big deal. You're welcome. You needed a fresh eye on the situation, that's all.'

Petra pushed her empty plate to one side. 'There's one other thing about this killer that is bothering me.'

Smart woman, Carol thought. *In your shoes, I'd be going crazy, not just feeling bothered.* She nodded. 'He's not going to stop. You see this slipping away into some no-man's-land of turf wars and arguments over the chain of command. Meanwhile, this bastard is free to carry on killing.' As she saw recognition on Petra's face, Carol realized with a sense of wonder that she was talking like Tony, stepping inside someone else's head and articulating her fears.

'You have put your finger on it precisely. This killer, he is a planner. He is good at what he does, and there is no reason for him to stop until he is caught. Meanwhile, the bureaucrats will be playing their games and the investigators will have their hands tied. It's frustrating.'

'It's more than frustrating. It goes directly against the grain of what your instincts as a cop tell you needs to be done.'

'Exactly. So, in my shoes, what would *you* do, Carol?'

The million-pound question, with only one possible answer. 'Phone a friend,' she said ironically. Petra frowned. Maybe *Who Wants to be a Millionaire* hadn't travelled to Germany, Carol thought. 'I wouldn't let it go. I'd do everything I could to progress the investigation myself, and to hell with the official channels. And the first thing I'd do would be to get a profile.'

Petra's face cleared. 'Ah,' she said. 'I see. You would call Dr Hill?'

'He's the best. So yes, I'd call him and try to persuade him to come out of retirement and get back into the game.'

'He has retired?' Petra's disappointment was palpable. 'I didn't think he was so old.'

It dawned on Carol that this whole thing had been one long preamble to try and secure Tony's services for an unofficial serial-killer hunt. Sure, Petra had genuinely needed help with the mechanics of bringing it together in the public domain, but the real agenda was to enlist Carol and Tony on her team. Strangely, she didn't feel at all used. She was genuinely amused, because she identified the strategy as one she would have cheerfully attempted herself. 'He's not old. But he's not profiling any more. After the Vance case, he decided he didn't want to be at the sharp end any longer.'

Petra looked dismayed. 'Shit,' she said. 'I thought maybe . . .' She shook her head, clearly angry with herself.

'You thought exactly what I'd have thought in your shoes,' Carol said gently. She felt for Petra, knowing how discouraged she would have been in the same position. On the spur of the moment, she made a decision. 'Look, leave this with me. I saw Tony only a few days ago, and I've a feeling he just might take the bait. He's not enjoying the quiet life as much as he'd hoped. This could intrigue him enough to draw him back into combat. Meanwhile, get Marijke to set the official ball rolling. The sooner the better. And I'll do what I can to help.'

'I think you have enough to be worried about without this,' Petra said, half-hearted.

'It'll give me something to keep me grounded in who I really am,' Carol said. 'Nothing like reality to beat Zelig's Syndrome.'

So now she had to keep her promise to Petra. She had to find the words that would entice Tony to give his help. She had the feeling she was kicking at a half-open door, but it would still take all her powers of persuasion. Carol walked through to the kitchenette and opened a bottle of red wine. Time for a little Dutch courage. First, she had to e-mail Tony. Then she had to prepare for tomorrow, when she would finally come face to face with Tadeusz Radecki.

20

Tony stretched his arms out, feeling the crack of joints in his neck and shoulders. He was getting too old to spend the evening hunched over a computer screen. But it was as good a way as any to escape from the complicated reaction the news about Vance had provoked in him. He'd unplugged the phone and immersed himself in work, avoiding thought and journalists alike.

He closed down the file he'd been reading, the draft dissertation of one of his graduate students. It wasn't a bad piece of work, although the theories ran ahead of the evidence in a couple of crucial places. He'd have to take a stern line with her in their next supervision session. She needed to iron out these problems now, before they became too entrenched to unpick easily.

Before he switched off, he crossed to his communications program and flicked the button to send and receive all mail. It was always worth a late-night mailbox check; he might be heading for bed, but much of America was still in the middle of the working day, and he was in regular touch with several friends and colleagues on the other side of the Atlantic.

Tonight, there was a single message. He activated the encryption software that Carol's brother had sent him and opened her e-mail.

Hi, Tony,

Well, here I am in Berlin. There's a real buzz here, it feels like a place that's doing well for itself. Which, as we know, is always a good breeding ground for the more sophisticated sorts of crime!

I've not made contact with TR yet – that's scheduled for tomorrow night, when we see if Petra's strategy will work or explode in our faces. I know you said you thought it was psychologically sound, but I'm still feeling very nervous about it. Now that it's so imminent, I'm a basket case. I can't eat and I know I'm going to struggle to sleep tonight. I'm having a few glasses of wine to take the edge off, but I'm not convinced that'll make any difference. Petra has been working me intensively, and I suppose that should give me some confidence. I can't say that it has, however. Although I feel I know TR pretty well, I'm not sure I know who Caroline Jackson is . . . Let's hope I don't fall flat on my face at the first hurdle.

Anyway, talking about this is only making me more nervous. And the real reason I'm writing to you tonight is actually nothing to do with my undercover.

When we saw each other recently, you seemed to be suggesting that you would welcome the chance to use your skills in criminal profiling again, if the right opportunity came along. Well, I think I might have the very thing for you.

The basic scenario: definitely two, possibly three murders that we know of. Two males, one female. All the victims have been psychologists working as university academics. They have all been found lying on their backs, bound hand and foot to their desks. Their clothes have been cut away, leaving them naked. The cause of death was drowning – they had a tube forced into their throats and water was poured down it until they died. And there is an interesting postmortem mutilation: the killer scalped their pubic area. No damage to the genitals, just the removal of hair and skin.

The problem: the first murder that we know of took place in Heidelberg in Germany, the second in Leiden in Holland, the third (the possible) in Germany again, in Bremen. The connection was made because by chance Petra had seen details of the first case, and a friend of hers, Marijke, who is a cop in Holland, told her about the second case and Petra spotted the link. Then, when the third murder of a psychology lecturer was reported, it jumped out at her, even though she hasn't got enough detail yet to be certain it fits. So, as you will see, there is a jurisdictional nightmare ahead. What's more, it's not formally out there yet because we've had to work out a way of officially linking the cases without dropping Marijke in the shit for talking out of school. Some time over the next few days, though, it's going to be shunted through Europol, which should start the wheels moving.

But I don't have to tell you how it will get bogged down in the machinery of bureaucracy. Petra thinks it's unlikely that anyone else has made these connections yet, given how little communication there is between German police forces on the ground (sound familiar???). Petra also thinks, and I agree with her, that he's going to take more victims before a properly constituted international task force can get moving. So she wants to try to short circuit that process with an unofficial investigation.

To a large extent they're working in the dark. This killer seems to be very good at covering his tracks. There seems to be almost nothing from forensics in either case.

Why has Petra taken the risk of spilling the beans to me? Well, let's not forget that she's in intelligence. And she'd done her homework on me. Which led her inexorably to you.

Obviously, what the girls want – no, what they NEED – is a profile. And, like the song says, nobody does it better.

And Petra wants the best.

It's a chance to get back into the game, Tony. And it would be a safe environment to do it in. Because it would be entirely unofficial, you'd be working out of the public eye, nobody looking over your shoulder expecting instant results. No stories in the press pressurizing you to come up with the goods. Simply a low-key piece of work that might just save some lives.

Of course, if the girls do manage to pull something off, you'd get the credit, which would maybe open some doors for you in Europe.

Please don't feel you have to say yes on my account. I've told Petra that I don't hold out great hopes. But I'd like you to say yes on your own account, because I don't think what you're doing right now is giving you much sense of satisfaction. And doing what you do best might make you feel happier with yourself.

Think about it.
Take care,

CJ

Tony scrolled back to the top of the message and reread it more slowly, the occasional ironic smile twitching the corners of his mouth. She was good, he had to admit. She'd always been quick, and she'd learned a few neat little tricks along the way. He wondered how long it had taken her to compose something so apparently artless but which was nevertheless clearly calculated to push all his buttons. There was enough information about the cases to whet his appetite, but not enough to allow him to draw the conclusion that they lacked sufficient interest to suck him in.

Oh, and it was very cleverly done. Right down to bait that it would be a black exercise, off the official books, something entirely deniable whether it went right or wrong. 'And it would be a safe environment to do it in.' The subtext being, of course, that there would be nobody to see the egg on his face if his skills had gone rusty and he fucked up. He didn't think Carol believed that would happen, but he understood that she thought he might carry that fear. And she was right, too.

It was tempting. But he wasn't sure if he was drawn to it for the right reasons. The thought that kept butting its way to the front of his mind was that it would provide him with a legitimate excuse for getting on a plane to Berlin, because naturally he'd have to consult in detail with Petra, who seemed to be in the driving seat of this black operation. And Berlin right now meant Carol. Carol, who could benefit from the support he could offer. Carol, who had never been out of his thoughts since he'd left London.

And that was a dishonest reason for snatching this opportunity. If he went to Berlin for Carol's sake, his mind wouldn't be focused on the job he was supposedly there to do. Worse yet, his presence might prove to be the opposite of helpful for Carol. She needed to stay in role as much as possible, and if he kept popping up like a jack-in-the-box, it could damage her ability to maintain Caroline Jackson. Providing insights and reinforcement from a distance was one thing; to be there in person could tempt her to lean too heavily on him. Then if it came to the crunch and she was thrown entirely on her own resources, she might lack the necessary confidence to carry it through.

Still, he thought, *it wouldn't hurt to check it out on the web.* He loaded his search engine and typed in, 'Bremen + murder + psychology + lecturer', going for the most recent one first. Seconds later, he was looking at a German newspaper report. Luckily, he'd learned German at school and had kept it up so he could read scientific papers. But even if he hadn't been able to understand it, one thing would have leapt out like a firework in the night sky.

Tony stared at the screen, scarcely able to believe his eyes. There had to be a mistake. His hands clenched into fists and his face closed in a frown. He rubbed his temples with his knuckles, trying to make sense of what he was reading.

There was, however, no room for doubt. There couldn't be two Margarethe Schillings who were psychologists attached to Bremen University. That was beyond the bounds of credibility. But equally impossible was the idea that Margarethe Schilling was dead at the hands of a serial killer.

He could see her face now. Wide mouth grinning at something someone had said, laughter lines scored in the corners of her eyes. Hard to believe any psychologist could have found enough in the world to laugh at to etch them so deep. Blonde hair loose, impatiently pushed back behind her ears when she was making a point in debate. Lively, intelligent, argumentative to the point of being infuriating.

They had met at a symposium in Hamburg three years before. Tony had been interested in the relationship between religious belief and certain types of serial offender, and Margarethe's experimental work had intrigued him. He'd listened to her paper and found several points he wanted to discuss with her. So they'd gone off to a bar with a few others and missed the official banquet, so wrapped up had they been in their discussion.

They'd found a lot of common ground, him and Margarethe. So much so that she'd persuaded him to change his flight and come back to Bremen with her for a couple of days so he could see her research results at first hand. It had been a fascinating experience, and the vigorous exchange of information and ideas had exhilarated him. She'd even put him up in the spare room of the charming nineteenth-century barn conversion she shared with her husband Kurt and their son Hartmut in a small village near an artists' colony a dozen miles from the city.

He hadn't taken to Kurt, he recalled. He'd made not a virtue but a martyrdom of necessity, complaining about his boring life of childcare following his redundancy from a research post with a pharmaceutical company. 'Of course, having to look after a child all day means it's impossible for me to keep my knowledge current,' he'd moaned over dinner. 'It's all right for Margarethe, she can scale the heights of the academic world, but I'm stuck out here in the backwoods with my brain rotting.'

It had become clear to Tony that Kurt was parenting not out of necessity but out of idleness. According to Margarethe, his parents had left them enough money to buy the house with a little left over. Kurt had seized the chance to take redundancy with the intention of assuming the life of a dilettante. As she told the tale, Margarethe had smiled wickedly. 'The first thing I did when he told me what he'd done was to sack the nanny. He couldn't argue with me, because it would be like saying he didn't want to spend time with his son. But he's never forgiven me for it.'

At the time, Tony had thought it was remarkably bad psychology for someone who made her living out of the labyrinth of the human mind. Unless, of course, she had wanted the marriage to fail. Which had followed with depressing inevitability, as he'd gathered from her Christmas cards and occasional e-mails. What she hadn't expected was for Kurt to hang on to Hartmut, and he could tell, reading between the lines, that the loss of her son had devastated Margarethe.

And now, if this report was to be believed, Margarethe's son had lost her in the most final of ways. Tony still couldn't take it in. There was a terrible element of happenstance in such a death.

It was too late for Margarethe. But it might not be too late for others. Never mind that it suited him to escape the press baying for comments on Jacko Vance. Never mind that he was desperate with boredom in his job. And never mind that he wanted to be near Carol. Saving lives was paramount.

For better or worse, he'd made his choice.

In the half-hour before she could expect to find Marijke in the chat room, Petra browsed the web, dipping in and out of various serial killer sites to see if she could find any correspondences between recorded cases and the particular fetishes of their own killer. But her search proved fruitless. The depraved minds whose activities were recorded in lurid detail hadn't indulged in death by this sort of drowning, nor could she find cases of pubic scalping, though she did discover that it had a name – gynelophism. Not much help there when it came to attempting to extract some motivation for their killer.

As usual when she was surfing, Petra was surprised to see how quickly the time had gone. Already she was four minutes late for her rendezvous with Marijke. Hastily, she made her way to the discussion room, where she found Marijke trying to avoid being drawn into a debate on European human rights legislation with two gay men and a bisexual woman. She signalled her arrival and double-clicked on Marijke's name to bring her into a private space.

P: sorry to keep you waiting, i got lost on the web.

M: No problem. I only just got here myself. So, what is Carol Jordan like?

P: very professional. very smart. she's very quick to pick things up, and i think she has the nerve to carry off this undercover job.

M: Is she easy to get along with?

P: very easy. you can tell she's been a proper street cop, not one of the management who sits behind a desk and forgets what life is like for the rest of us. i think we're going to be a good team. she's not afraid to listen to advice.

M: I have my fingers crossed for you. Did you get the chance to talk to her about the murders?

P: yes, jordan had a good idea about that. she thinks you should persuade your boss to send the details of this murder to europol with a request for any information about similar cases. then europol will circulate all the other member forces, and i can come up with the heidelberg and bremen connections quite legitimately. what do you say?

M: You think it will work?

P: i think it's the only way to cover our backs. once it's out in the open, it'll take them weeks to set up a proper task force because nobody will want to give up jurisdiction, and they'll all be fighting over which country is the lead investigator. meanwhile, we can get on with our own investigation. jordan is going to ask her dr hill to do a profile for us, so we will have a head start. we still have a chance to do ourselves a big favour here, but nobody can point the finger at us for doing anything we shouldn't have.

M: I suppose it makes sense. But it won't be easy to persuade Maartens to look to Europol for help. He has very old-fashioned ideas about organization. He's against anything that takes police work off the streets and into the office.

P: so you have to make it look like there's something in it for him. maybe he'd like the glory of being the first person to spot that there might be a serial killer out there? because it'll be his name on the report, not yours, right?

M: Good idea. He could make it look like a triumph for traditional police work, if I persuade him right. I'll try in the morning.

P: let me know how it goes.

M: Tomorrow night?

P: i'll try. make it late, though. midnight. if everything goes right, jordan will be working late, which means i might have to as well. sleep well, babe.

M: Slaap ze, liefje. Tot ziens.

Tadeusz Radecki excused himself from the restaurant table when he saw that the number calling his mobile phone belonged to Darko Krasic. In the passage

253

leading to the toilets, out of earshot of his respectable companions, he answered its insistent chirrup. 'Yes?'

'When will you be home, boss?' Krasic asked. 'I've got some news for you.'

'Good or bad?'

'It's nothing that needs urgent action.'

'Won't it wait till tomorrow?'

'I think you'll want to know this.'

Tadeusz looked at his watch. 'Meet me there in an hour.'

'OK. See you then.' Krasic ended the call and Tadeusz walked back into the noisy restaurant. They were already at the coffee stage, so the party would be breaking up within the half-hour anyway. And since he had no intention of offering to escort home the single woman his four comfortably coupled friends had invited along for his benefit, there would be no problem in getting back home within the hour. Darko had sounded very enigmatic on the phone. But wondering about something he couldn't guess at was a waste of energy, and Tadeusz had never been inclined to worry about anything before he had to. He joined in the conversation round the table as if his call had been of supreme unimportance, but precisely thirty minutes later, he pushed back his chair and announced that he had an early start in the morning. He dropped a sheaf of banknotes on the table to cover his share of the bill, kissed all three women on both cheeks, hugged his male friends and left.

The familiar black Mercedes was sitting outside his apartment building when he turned the corner into the street. As Tadeusz approached the front door, Krasic emerged from the car and fell into step beside him. 'So, what's this mysterious news?' Tadeusz asked as they entered the lift.

'It'll keep for a few minutes longer,' Krasic said.

Tadeusz laughed. 'You are so cautious, Darko. I promise you, this lift isn't bugged.'

'It's not that. You might want a drink when you hear what I have to tell you.'

Tadeusz raised his eyebrows, but said nothing more until they were both inside his apartment. He poured two glasses of Armagnac and handed one to Krasic. 'Now, tell me what it is that is so terrible I need a brandy before I can hear it.'

Krasic looked less than his usual imperturbable self. 'It's bloody strange, that's what it is.' He walked over to a set of shelves where three photographs of Katerina were displayed in silver frames. 'I finally managed to get some information about the motorbike.'

Tadeusz experienced a convulsion in his stomach, a strange turbulence that seemed to rearrange his internal organs. Whatever he'd been expecting, it wasn't this. 'You have a name?'

'No, nothing that straightforward. Our man went back and talked again to the teenage boy who recognized the bike as a BMW. The kid was really enthusiastic. He kept offering to have hypnosis, to see if he could come up with any more details.'

'And?'

'It took a little while to get the session organized, but eventually, he got some woman to come along and put the boy into a trance. And the kid came up with quite a bit more detail.'

'Such as?' Tadeusz was leaning forward now, eager as a hound with a scent in his nostrils.

'Like, he noticed that you couldn't read the number plate because it was all smudged with mud. He said there was something funny about the number plate. He couldn't be any more clear than that, but he was very definite that there was something wrong.' Krasic turned away from the images of Katerina and sat down on the sofa. 'And he was able to describe the bike much better than he had before. Stuff like the shape of the exhausts, that sort of bollocks. Anyway, our man wrote it all down. Then he got on to BMW and asked what model of bike this matched up with. And this is where it gets very fucking strange.'

Tadeusz drummed his fingers on the wall. 'Strange how?'

'According to BMW, the description our man gave them didn't fit any bike they've ever made for sale in Germany. So, our man thinks it's all been a fucking total waste of time, getting this kid under the influence and picking his brain. Then the man from BMW calls him back.'

'Christ, Darko, get on with it,' Tadeusz growled.

'All right, all right, I'm getting there. The BMW guy had gone and checked with their special projects people and it turns out they did once make a bike that fits the description. It was a limited edition of three hundred and fifty high-performance bikes. Export only. They sold it in the UK and Scandinavia. And get this – almost all the bikes were sold to law enforcement. For traffic cops and special ops.'

Tadeusz looked bewildered. 'What? That doesn't make any sense.'

'That's what our man said. He asked them how come an export-only bike was involved in an accident in Berlin. They didn't have a clue, but they gave him all the details of the bike. And when he ran it through vehicle registration, it turns out there isn't a single fucking bike with this spec registered in Germany.'

'So you're saying that whoever killed Katerina, chances are they did it on a foreign police bike?' Tadeusz took a deep swig of his brandy and paced the floor. 'This is insane. It makes no sense at all.'

Darko shrugged. 'I don't know. I've had longer to think about it than you have, and there is one explanation that sort of fits the facts. You know how these fucking motorbike cowboys get about their machines. It's like they're joined at the hip. You can imagine one of them deciding to take his undercover traffic bike on a little holiday. So, let's say for the sake of argument that it's a Brit. For a split second, he forgets he's driving on the wrong side of the road, he causes a major accident and he goes into total fucking panic and just steps on the gas. I mean, he's not even supposed to have the bike over here, and now he's fucked somebody up big time. Of course he's going to leg it fast as he can.'

'And you think that makes *sense*?' Tadeusz demanded belligerently.

Krasic shifted in his seat, spreading his overcoat wide and splaying his meaty thighs, maximizing his physical impact to cover his uncertainty. 'I can't think of any other explanation.'

'Neither can I. And that's what I don't like.' He slammed the flat of his hand against the wall. 'It's bullshit, however you look at it.'

'Tadzio, it was an accident. They happen all the time. You're just going to have to let it go.'

Tadeusz whirled round, his face a rictus of anger. 'Fuck that. Whether it was an accident or not, somebody should pay.'

'You'll get no argument from me on that. And if there was any chance of finding out who was riding that bike, I'd be the first in there, making the bastard pay. But he's out of our reach.'

Suddenly, all the fight went out of Tadeusz. He crumpled into a chair, head lolling back. A single tear gathered in the corner of one eye and slithered down his temple. Krasic got to his feet, awkward in the face of emotion. 'I'm sorry, Tadzio,' he said gruffly.

Tadeusz rubbed the tear away with the heel of his hand. 'You did your best, Darko,' he said. 'You're right. It's time to let go. Time to move forward.' He managed a faint smile. 'I'll see you tomorrow. It's time I started thinking about the future.'

Though it pained Krasic to see his boss hurting, he walked out of the apartment with a spring in his step. It looked as though they could finally start concentrating on business again. He had one or two ideas of his own, and he guessed that the time would soon be ripe to broach them. If there was a niggle of concern at the back of his mind about the mysterious identity of the bike that had caused Katerina's death, he wasn't going to think about it now. Paranoia was for the weak, and Krasic knew he wasn't one of them.

21

Tony walked through the arrivals gate at Tegel Airport, scanning the meeters and greeters. Over to one side, he saw a tall, slim woman with spiky black hair holding a small placard that read, 'Hill.' He moved towards her, a tentative smile on his face. 'Petra Becker?' he asked.

She extended a hand and they shook. 'Dr Hill. It's a pleasure to meet you.'

'Tony, please,' he said. 'Thanks for coming out here to fetch me.'

'Not a problem. You saved me having to listen to one of my colleagues complaining that I gave him the impossible task of tracking down a missing six-year-old.'

He raised his eyebrows in a question. 'I didn't think that was your kind of case.'

Petra chuckled. 'It's not normally. This particular six-year-old is being held hostage by Carol's friend Radecki against her mother's good behaviour. And I want her mother's co-operation, so I have to find the child. But you don't need to think about that. You've got more important things to deal with. Anything I can do to help, just ask.'

She'd already done plenty, he thought, as he followed her to her car. After reading Carol's e-mail, he'd booked himself on the first flight to Berlin, told his departmental secretary there had been a sudden death in the family and that he was taking compassionate leave as of now. He knew he couldn't call Carol, but he had Petra Becker's name and he knew she worked for Criminal Intelligence. A few phone calls had tracked her down, and she had reacted with delight to the news that he was coming to Germany. He hadn't bothered to explain the reason for his sudden decision; he didn't want her changing her mind about having him on board because he had too close a relationship to one of the victims.

'I'll need somewhere to stay,' he had told Petra. 'It'd be helpful if you can book me into the same place as Carol. I know she's probably being followed, so it's important that there's somewhere we can meet where we're not going to be spotted. If we're in the same building, it should be easier for us both.'

As they left the airport behind, Petra said, 'I managed to get you an apartment in Carol's building. You're a couple of floors below her, but it's easy to come and go without anyone seeing you.'

'Thanks,' he said. 'I understand you two are meeting in a women's health club to do your debriefs?'

'That's right. I'm afraid you won't be able to join us there,' Petra said with a grin.

'No, but I can see Carol in the apartment block, and I can presumably meet you at your office? I'm going to need access to all the case materials that you can get for me, so that would probably be the best place.'

Petra pulled a face. 'That might be a bit of a problem, Tony. You see, officially I'm not supposed to have anything to do with the serial killer cases yet. So if you show up at the office, my boss is going to ask some very difficult questions. How would you feel about working in my apartment? It's quite civilized, really. All the materials I have are there anyway.'

'That's fine by me, as long as you don't mind having me under your feet. I tend to work quite long hours. And I'm eager to get moving on this profile right away.'

'I have the case information from Heidelberg and Leiden. And I've sent Bremen a request for their investigation reports, so we should have some material from them soon. I told them I believed their case might connect to one of our on-going investigations. I think they were quite relieved at the idea of sharing the load. They're a small force, they don't have much experience with anything out of the ordinary.'

'Good. I need as much information as I can get.'

'I'm glad we tempted you out of retirement.'

He gave her a quick sideways glance. If she was sufficiently driven by her ambition to be operating outside the rules, he didn't think she would mind that he too was bringing his own agenda to this case. 'It was more than that. I knew Margarethe Schilling.'

'Shit,' Petra said. 'I'm sorry. Carol didn't tell me.'

'Carol doesn't know. Did you get the chance to tell her I'm on my way?' he added, wanting to move away from the painful subject of Margarethe's death.

'I hope you don't mind, but I didn't tell her yet. She has her first encounter with Radecki this evening, and it's important she stays focused on that.'

'You're right. Hopefully we can link up tomorrow morning.'

'She'll be pleased to see you. She speaks very highly of you.'

'I'll be pleased to see her, too.'

'It's good for her that she has someone around to anchor her into her real life,' Petra said, swerving to avoid someone trying to cut in front of her. 'Asshole,' she muttered.

'As long as I don't pull her out of character too much,' he said.

'I'm more concerned with her getting stuck in Caroline Jackson. Radecki's a charming bastard. That's hard to resist when you're feeling isolated. I think having you around will help her with that.'

'I hope so. And her insights will be valuable to me when it comes to drawing up my profile too. She's got a very unusual mind. She comes at things from odd tangents, sees things I don't always see.'

'When will you start work?'

'As soon as possible. If it's all right with you, I'll drop my bags off and maybe you can take me back to your place?'

'OK. I'll give you a key so you can come and go as you please. Don't worry about disturbing me. I'm hardly ever there and I sleep like the dead.' Petra turned off the Ku'damm into the quiet side street with the apartment complex. 'Here we are. Let me give you a hand.'

He followed Petra into the small concierge office next to the main entrance. She dealt with his registration, then led him through to the entrance hall. 'You're on the first floor. Carol is two floors above you, in 302. I'll wait here for you while you drop your things off.'

Tony nodded and pressed the call button for the lift. He'd burned his bridges this time. For too long, he'd been telling himself he could be a chameleon, taking on the colouring of his surroundings, fitting in with other lives because in truth he had no fixed points in his own life. But it was slowly dawning on him that he'd been lying to himself. There *was* a core that was uniquely Tony Hill. And the harder he tried to escape its clutches, the stronger its grip became. Forget blandness, forget conventionality. This was who he was: the hunter, sniffing the air for the delicate scent of his prey. He was back where he belonged, and it felt wonderful.

Carol was alive to the ironies of the opera she was watching from the back of the stalls at the Berlin Staatsoper. Janácek's *Das Schlaue Füchslein*, *The Cunning Little Vixen*. The drama that might have distracted her if a different opera had been before her served only to hammer home the dangers of her mission. The first act unfolded before her; the gamekeeper's capture of the little vixen; her defence against the dog's sexual advances and the tormenting of the children; her tempting of the hens into her ambit; her slaughter of the hens and her escape before retribution could be visited on her.

I'm the cunning little vixen, Carol thought. She would allow Tadeusz Radecki to think he'd brought her into his camp at his command. She would resist any attempts to bait her into revealing her true nature; she suspected she would have to find a way to keep

Radecki at arm's length. Then she would sneak into his henhouse, bring his chickens home to roost and get out from under before he could make her pay the price.

As the finale of the act approached, bringing its confrontation between the vixen and her human captors, Carol slipped out of her aisle seat and made her way out of the auditorium. Her heart was racing, her stomach a knot of pain. In spite of the lightweight material of the midnight blue silk sheath she was wearing, she could feel sweat gathering in the hollow of her back. Adrenaline coursed through her. Behind her, applause broke out. It was now or never, she told herself as she headed for the stairs that would take her up to the private boxes. Left-hand side, just as Petra had told her.

Petra had done her homework. According to her, Radecki had recently begun to visit the opera again. He was always alone in his box, remaining confined during the intervals, avoiding mixing with any of his friends or contacts in the audience. He never went to the bars, instead preferring to sip champagne delivered ahead of the performance by one of the opera house staff. 'It's a dramatic place to stage your first encounter,' Petra had said. 'He always went to the opera with Katerina, so he will already be focused on her memory.' Tony had agreed that, psychologically, it would be a powerful moment that Carol could exploit. Taken so completely off his guard, Radecki would be more vulnerable to her appearance than in any business context.

Carol climbed the stairs, her steps soft on the heavy carpet. The doors from the auditorium were opening and the audience was spilling out, the air thick with chatter and laughter. She pushed her way up against the tide and carried on into a side corridor. Second on the right, Petra had told her. Carol stared at the door, saying a silent prayer to whatever guardian angel might be listening. She tucked her evening bag under her arm and tapped on the door.

There was no reply. She knocked again, this time harder. A pause, then suddenly the door was yanked open. Tadeusz Radecki stood framed in the doorway, his lean frame a good six inches taller than her. *The photograph didn't do him justice,* Carol thought irrelevantly. Even disfigured by a scowl, in the flesh his dramatic good looks were far more striking. His beautifully cut dinner jacket emphasized broad shoulders, narrow hips and long legs. *'Was ist?'* he demanded, the words spilling out before his eyes had taken her in fully.

Before she could say anything, his brain caught up with his eyes. Carol had never seen anyone physically recoil before, but there was no other word to describe his actions. Tadeusz reared up to his full height, simultaneously taking a step backwards. His eyes widened and his mouth spread in a thin line as he sucked his breath in.

'I'm sorry, I didn't mean to alarm you,' she said in English, assembling puzzlement on her face.

A turbulent series of emotions crossed his face. She could imagine his thought processes. Was he seeing a ghost? No, ghosts didn't speak. Was she a hallucination? No, a hallucination wouldn't talk to him in English. But if she wasn't a ghost or a hallucination, who was she, standing here in the doorway of the opera box he'd shared with Katerina?

Carol took advantage of his confusion to step across the threshold. He took another step backwards, banging into one of the chairs, without even glancing to see what he'd hit. His eyes were fixed on her face, his gaze perplexed, frown lines etched deep between his brows. 'Who *are* you?' he said, his voice a small croak compared to the resonant demand he'd made when he'd first opened the door.

Carol kept the bewilderment in her face as she said, 'You are Tadeusz Radecki? I am in the right place?'

'I know who I am. What I want to know is who *you* are.' Radecki had recovered some of his composure and his words were delivered in a tone that was almost covered by a veneer of civilized manners.

'Caroline Jackson,' she said, extending a hand tentatively towards him.

He reached for her hand and took it gingerly, as if afraid it would disappear under his touch. His fingers were cool and dry, but the handshake was strangely limp, like that of a politician who has to press the flesh more often than is comfortable. He bowed slightly, the familiarity of instilled manners providing him with a space to gather himself. 'Tadeusz Radecki, as you rightly assumed.' He dropped her hand and moved slightly further from her, still frowning, but with caution overlaying the hard-edged features of his face. 'Now, perhaps, you would do me the courtesy of telling me what you are doing in my opera box?'

'I wanted to meet you. I'm sorry to butt in on you like this, but I needed to be sure of getting you on your own. Somewhere private. Do you mind if I sit down?' Carol wanted to be closer to the front of the box, where she could be seen from the tiers of seats in the circle. She knew Petra was out there somewhere, but she also wanted the added security of being visible. If she blew it from the start, she didn't want to be vulnerable to violence. Not that he looked the sort who would need to resort to that.

Tadeusz pulled out a chair for her, but didn't sit himself. Instead, he leaned against the parapet of the box, his back to the auditorium. Behind him, the low buzz of conversation swirled upwards from the stalls. He folded his arms across his chest and studied her as she settled into the velvet upholstery. 'So, Ms Jackson, we are private. Why are you here?'

'I know – that is, I used to know Colin Osborne.'

Radecki raised his eyebrows and his mouth quirked in a 'so what' expression. 'Should that mean something to me?' he asked.

Carol smiled broadly and enjoyed the spasm of reaction across Radecki's eyes that provoked. She had him, she knew. He was seeing Katerina in front of him and, in spite of his attempts to maintain a cool facade, he was unsettled. Which was precisely what she wanted. 'Considering how much business the two of you did together, I think he'd be very hurt that you've forgotten him so quickly.'

'You must be mistaken, Ms Jackson. I don't recall ever having done business with a Mr . . . Osborne, did you say?' He was aiming for genial indulgence, but he wasn't hitting the mark. There was a wariness in his posture that might have escaped many observers. But Carol had learned her lessons, from

Tony and from others, and she recognized his unease. Now she was in the thick of it, she was starting to enjoy herself, feeling the power she had to control this situation.

'Look, I understand why you're being wary here. You know how Colin died, so of course it makes you edgy, having some strange woman walk through the door and start talking about him. But I know that you guys made a lot of money together, and that's what I want to talk to you about.'

He shook his head, a tight smile failing to loosen up his face. 'You must have the wrong person, Ms Jackson. The only business interest I have is a chain of stores that sell and rent videos. Now, your Mr Osborne may well have been one of our suppliers, but I employ staff to deal with people like that. You don't think I conduct the day-to-day purchase of stock myself, do you?' His mild air of condescension was well done; he was recovering control of himself by the second. She couldn't afford to let that happen. Not quite yet.

Carol leaned back in her chair, bidding for the relaxed look. 'You're very good,' she said. 'No, really, you are,' she added as he tried a look of mild surprise. 'If I didn't know better, I'd fall for the "legitimate businessman" line. But I didn't come all the way to Berlin to talk about videos, Tadzio.'

The use of the diminutive form of his first name was another calculated move on Carol's part to wrongfoot him. That it had worked was obvious in the narrowing of his eyes. He was trying to get past his initial reaction, to size her up, but he couldn't escape the power of memory. 'Then you've wasted your time, Ms Jackson,' he said.

She shook her head. 'I don't think so. Look, it's obvious that you must be missing Colin badly. I've come to take up the slack.'

He shrugged. 'You're not making sense.' The five-minute bell rang, signalling the imminent end of the interval. 'Now, if you'll excuse me, I think you should be getting back to your seat.'

'The view from here is much better, you know. I think I'd rather stay.' Carol dropped her bag on the floor and crossed her legs, tilting her head and smiling at him. She could see the war of instinct and interest flickering in his uncertain eyes.

'I don't think so,' he said.

Carol gave an exasperated sigh. 'Look, Tadzio, stop pretending. You need me.'

He looked shocked. His mouth opened, but no words emerged. 'Colin was doing a good job for you,' she continued. 'But Colin's history. You need someone to take your illegals off your hands once they get to the UK. I can do that. Can we stop pussyfooting around and talk straight? Naturally you're nervous about discussing this with a total stranger, but, right now, I suspect I'm the only show in town when it comes to getting you off a very awkward hook. What do I need to do to prove to you that I'm trustworthy?'

'I still don't know what you're talking about.' There was a stubborn set to his jaw now. 'Illegals? What do you mean? We don't sell blue movies in my stores. We certainly don't import them into the UK.'

Carol smiled again, genuinely delighted that she was having to stretch for this. If it had been too easy at the start, she would have had to work harder later on. This way, she was getting into her stride, feeling

269

her way through Caroline Jackson's skin to an argument that would open him up to her. 'Oh please,' she said, injecting a little steel into her voice. 'That line is getting rather tired. Look, I know what you and Colin had going for you. I can give you the addresses of his factories in Essex where the illegal immigrants ended up working for a pittance. I can tell you how many of your imports he handled in the last year. I know where Colin lived, who he drank with, who he was sleeping with – and, before you jump to any conclusions, it wasn't me. I know who killed him and I've got a fair idea why, and luckily it was nothing to do with you or your line of business.'

He started to say something, but she steamrollered over him. 'You'll get your turn. Tadzio, I'm not here to cause you problems, I'm here to help you solve them. If you'd rather keep your problems, if you like things to be difficult, fine. I'm out of here. But I don't think that's what you want. From what I hear, you're desperate to sort something out on my side of the water. So why don't we sit and listen to Act Two while you think about what I've said?'

He looked at her as if he couldn't take in what she'd said. 'Who sent you?' he asked.

Carol frowned. 'Nobody sent me. I don't work for anybody but myself. If we make a deal, I won't be working for you either. We'll be working together. You better be straight about that from the beginning.'

There was a thin sheen of sweat on his forehead. 'Perhaps you would like to stay for Act Two?' he said.

Carol patted the seat next to her and smiled pertly. 'I thought you'd never ask,' she said.

*   *   *

Petra seemed to embody the cliché of German efficiency, Tony thought as he surveyed the neatly labelled boxes on the living-room floor. The three cases were arranged in order, although the amount of material varied enormously, with almost nothing in the third box.

Before he could even contemplate a profile of the killer, he first had to profile the victims. They might apparently be selected at random, but there was rhyme and reason behind their deaths. To the outside world, egged on by hysterical headlines, people who preyed on stranger after stranger were insane maniacs. But Tony knew otherwise. Organized serial killers operated to their own logic, men with a mission marching to a drum only they could hear. It was Tony's job to worm his way inside the victims' lives in the hope that he would then start to hear the faint reverberations of that beat. Only by uncovering that secret rhythm of the killer's progress could he start to understand why these crimes had meaning for the murderer. If he could put himself inside the killer's head and rearrange the world in terms that made sense to him, Tony could hope to reach out and grasp enough key elements of the killer's life to make it possible to track him down.

One of the first things he always did was to give the killer a nickname, to personalize him. It was one step along the road to giving him a human face, behind which there existed a psyche that functioned according to its own particular rules. 'You're killing people who are obsessed with the workings of the mind,' Tony said softly. 'This is about mind games. You're drowning them. Is that literal or metaphorical? You're scalping

271

their pubic area, but leaving their genitals alone. You think this isn't about sex. But of course it is. You're just in denial about it. You think there's some higher purpose here. You're waging a war. You're leading the battle. You're Geronimo, aren't you?' He remembered a curiously apposite echo of a line from Kyd's *Spanish Tragedy*. 'Hieronimo's mad againe.'

'Geronimo it is,' Tony said. Now he had a name, he could build a dialogue between them. He could ease into his target's shoes, working out his steps and learning his gait. He could chart his progress and explore his fantasies. For this type of killing was always about fantasies. Geronimo, like so many others before him, could find no satisfaction in reality. For whatever reason, he had never learned to fit in. He had never matured into a rounded individual, however dysfunctional. He had become stuck at the point where the universe revolved around him and where fantasies could fulfil the desires that the real world refused to.

Tony understood that psychological state only too well. He had spent his own adult life feeling out of place in the world. He had lived with a sense of worthlessness that made it impossible to love, for loving carried implicit within it the conviction that one deserved to be loved in return. And he had never been able to believe that about himself. He had constructed his own series of masks, an empathetic sequence of facades that allowed him to blend in. *Passing for human.* If his circumstances had been different, he had always believed he might have ended up a predator himself, instead of a hunter. It was that awareness that underpinned all he did. It made him supremely good at unpicking the minds of the deranged and depraved.

It also made him supremely bad at forging relationships that penetrated beyond the superficial. Mostly, he had accepted that as a price worth paying for having in his grasp so useful and beneficial a skill. Carol Jordan was the only person who had ever made him feel that this was just another lie he told himself.

He knew he didn't deserve her. But the harder he tried to pull away from her, the stronger the tug towards her grew. One of these days he was going to have to take the chance of losing what he did best in the attempt to become what he had never understood how to be. Being a man instead of acting a part might alter him so profoundly that he could no longer navigate the labyrinth of messy minds.

But that was for another day. Tony gave himself a mental shake and set about reading the trail that Geronimo had left behind him. He began to plough through the contents of the crime files, taking notes as he went. The material from Heidelberg and Leiden was comprehensive, the boxes containing everything from witness statements to crime scene photographs and background reports on the victims. Luckily, the Dutch files had been translated into English for Petra's benefit, so he had no trouble reading them, apart from the odd awkward rendering. There was almost nothing from Bremen, simply because the investigation was still in the early stages and Petra's request hadn't yet borne much fruit.

Petra had made no attempt to engage him in conversation once he began, simply placing a fresh pot of coffee on the dining table where he was working. She poured herself a cup and said, 'I'm going out soon. I have to keep watch over Carol.'

He'd nodded absently, not really taking it in. He was too wrapped up in his study of the victims. It was after midnight when he finished his preliminary read through. He had a stack of paper with scribbled notes at his elbow. He would have to draw up a formal table relating all three cases to each other, but first he needed to know more about the academic specialities of the targets. He stood up and stretched, the muscles in his neck and back protesting at the sudden movement. Time for a change of scene.

He packed up his notes and let himself out of the flat. A short taxi ride brought him back to his apartment block. In the street, he glanced up at the third-floor windows. All was shrouded in darkness. If Carol was home, she was probably in bed. Their meeting could wait.

Upstairs, Tony ignored his still-packed bags and set up his laptop on the small writing table. He connected to the internet and navigated to the metasearch engine that he found most useful for tracking academic references. Within an hour, he had a reasonable overview of the research interests of Walter Neumann, Pieter de Groot and Margarethe Schilling. He scrolled back and forth through the material he'd downloaded, puzzled. He'd expected to find some glaring connection that would link the three dead psychologists. But their areas of specialism ranged from Margarethe's interest in religious belief systems, de Groot's studies of emotional abuse to Neumann's work on the psychological dynamics of sado-masochism.

He went through to the kitchen and brewed himself a fresh pot of coffee while he ran through what he'd learned and compared it against what experience had taught him. Every serial offender had a mental profile of his victims. Usually, the common factors that linked them were purely physical. Whether the victims were all males, all females or a mix of the two, it was almost always possible to draw conclusions about the type he would go for. The elderly female victims of a certain kind of rapist; the vulnerable waifs who appealed to the sort of killer who had been abused himself as a child; the beautiful blondes who had to be wiped out because they would never look twice at the woeful inadequate who preyed on them. Even though the details of the offences could vary widely, the victims were usually as much a physical signature as the actions the offender took to make the crime uniquely his.

With this case, it had been clear from his first glance at the police reports that this wasn't true of Geronimo. Unusually, what remained absolutely constant and inviolable was the ritual. There seemed no sign of escalation or variation caused by a lack of satisfaction with previous efforts. The victims themselves varied widely, from de Groot's trimly muscled frame to Margarethe's neat slenderness to Neumann's comfortable bulk. That meant there had to be another element at play in the selection process, and Tony had been utterly convinced it must lie in a shared professional interest, since this was the one thing that connected the dead. Which only went to show how foolish it was to theorize ahead of the data, he reminded himself as he carried his cup back through to the living room.

'What is it about psychologists that winds you up, Geronimo?' he asked out loud. 'Do you hate them? Did a psychologist make decisions that adversely affected the way your life has turned out? Or do you think they need to be put out of their misery? Is this personal, or do you see yourself as an altruist? Are you doing them a favour or are you doing the world a favour?'

He flicked back through the information he'd garnered from the web. 'If this is about something somebody did to you, why are you going for academics? If you were fucked up by some educational psychologist or some pre-sentence report in the courts, why aren't you going for practitioners? What do academics do that clinicians don't?'

If anyone could answer that question, it should be him. He'd walked on both sides of the wire, after all. He'd started out as a clinician and turned to academe only relatively recently. What was different about his own working life these days, apart from the obvious one – that he didn't see patients? Was that it? 'Are you taking it out on academics because they're not putting their training to proper use, Geronimo?' he asked of the hazy shade who was refusing to take shape in his mind.

'No, I don't think so,' he continued. 'That's too ridiculous. Nobody kills people because they're *not* fucking with people's heads.' He rubbed his tired eyes with his knuckles and leaned back in the chair. What did university staff do? They lectured. They supervised graduate students. They did research.

'Research,' he said softly, jerking upright. Hastily, he looked back through the articles and papers written

276

by the three victims. This time, he saw it. 'Experiments,' Tony exclaimed with satisfaction. The one thing that academics did, that all three of these victims had done, that could remotely be defined as messing with people's heads was to carry out experiments with live human subjects.

'You believe you've suffered as a result of psychological experiments,' he said, confident now. 'Something happened to make your life different from other people's lives, and you blame the psychologists. You see them as vivisectionists of the mind. That's it, Geronimo, isn't it?' He knew at some instinctive level that he'd conjured up the visceral motivation behind this series of killings.

Now he was ready to begin thinking about drafting his profile. But the hour was late, and he knew it would be better left for morning. Reluctantly, he turned off his machine and unzipped his travel bag. He doubted he'd get much sleep, but at least he could go through the motions. And tomorrow not only would he have the chance to do what he did best, he'd see Carol again. The thought made him smile. For once, he was convinced the positive elements of their relationship were starting to outweigh the bitter memories of the past. He might be kidding himself about that, but at least he was willing to put the theory to the test.

22

The second act seemed to last forever. Carol couldn't concentrate on the music; all her mind was capable of was rerunning their conversation and finding fault with what she'd said and how she'd said it. She wished she'd had the chance to role-play the scenario with Tony in advance. At least then she'd have felt more confident that she was pushing the right buttons. It wasn't that she'd expected instant capitulation from Radecki. But she had hoped for something more than his obstinate refusal to acknowledge that he had any idea what she was talking about.

She was aware too of his eyes on her. His seat was set slightly further back than hers, and out of the corner of her peripheral vision, she could sense him studying her for long periods. She couldn't catch his expression, which made her feel exposed and edgy. What was he thinking? What effect was she having on him?

Carol stifled a sigh of relief as the second act reached its climax with the wedding of the vixen and her mate. *No echoes there*, she thought thankfully. Before the house lights could come up, she saw Tadeusz rise from his chair and move to the back wall. She turned to catch him reaching inside the pocket of the over-coat hanging on a hook by the door. His hand came out holding a mobile phone. 'I have some calls to make,' he said loudly, so his voice would carry over the applause. 'I will be back shortly.'

'Yes,' she breathed triumphantly as the door closed behind him. He had decided to check her out. Morgan had told her not to worry about the UK end of her cover story; they had, he assured her, been working on it for a while. Her alias was a name that had been fed on to the streets from two directions. Undercover cops had mentioned her as a player in a quiet but powerful way. And the people brought in for questioning after Colin Osborne's shooting had all been questioned hard about Caroline Jackson. 'We really leaned on them,' Morgan had explained. 'The interviewing officers were all briefed to act as if they couldn't believe it when the suspects said they'd never heard of you. They planted the idea that you were connected to Colin, that you were in the same line of business, and that you and he had big plans for the future. So when Radecki starts to check you out – and he will check you out, make no mistake about that – you'll show up as a name that people have heard of. The fact that nobody knows you face to face is something you can work to your advantage. It makes you look as if you're a completely clean operator, like Radecki himself.'

Morgan had been right about that at least. She was sure Radecki was making those first calls right now. And she had a trump card to play later this evening that should tip the balance and get him as interested in her as a potential business partner as he was clearly intrigued by her as a woman.

Tadeusz was gone for the whole of the second interval, not returning until ten minutes into the third act. Carol deliberately didn't turn round when he came back, pretending to be entirely absorbed in the music. As the opera drew to a close, Carol wondered if Radecki was seeing parallels between the action on stage and what was happening to him this evening. There was the dying vixen, killed more by accident than design. And there was the gamekeeper, confronted with one of the vixen's cubs, which he recognizes as the spitting image of her mother. Was all this provoking resonances for him? She could only hope so. The more her resemblance to Katerina was hammered home, the better her chances of success.

As the audience burst into their final round of applause, he pulled his chair forward so it was in line with hers. He leaned close to her. She smelled the faint tang of cigar smoke and the complex notes of an expensive cologne. 'It has been interesting to meet you. Even though I still don't understand what you were talking about.'

Carol turned her head and met his eyes. 'You take a lot of convincing. I like that in a colleague. People who trust too easily tend to talk too openly, which isn't clever in our line of business. Look, why don't you give me a call tomorrow? We can meet and discuss matters of mutual interest.'

He raised his eyebrows. 'I don't think we have a mutual interest. At least, not in terms of business. But I think I might like to meet you again.'

Carol shook her head. 'This is a business trip for me. I don't have time to waste on social engagements.'

'That's a shame,' he said, his face guarded now.

The applause began to die away and she reached down for her evening bag. 'Look, Colin had problems with his end of your joint operation. He was good at promising but he couldn't always deliver. That's probably why he's dead now. The people you sent to him, they expected him to supply them with documentation. That's what they'd paid through the nose for, after all. But he didn't have a proper source. That's why he was always setting them up to get caught.'

Tadeusz's eyebrows rose slightly. 'Is this supposed to mean something to me?'

'I don't know. I have no idea if you were aware of what he did with the illegals after you passed them on, but he was skating on thin ice. Eventually the immigration service was bound to cotton on to his connection with all these little sweatshops that kept getting raided.' Carol gave him a questioning look. 'Especially since the raids were engineered by Colin himself, whatever he may have said to the contrary.'

She could see she had him now. He might still have a condescending smile on his face, a look of puzzlement in his eyes, but he didn't want her to stop.

'I'm different,' she continued. 'I never promise what I can't deliver.' She opened her evening bag as the opera house lights came up, and took out what she thought of as the ace up her sleeve. It was an Italian passport. When she'd asked Morgan whether it was a fake or the real thing, he'd simply smiled and said, 'It's not going to get you into trouble. Whatever checks Radecki makes, it'll come up clean.'

She held it out to him. 'An act of good faith. I can get hold of as many of these as I need, within reason.

281

You bring me people who can pay the price, and I'll make sure I keep my end of the bargain.'

His curiosity finally overcame his caution. He took the passport from her and flicked it open at the ID page. His own face stared back at him, a faint smile on his lips. The passport said he was Tadeo Radice, born in Trieste. He studied it attentively, moving it back and forward to let the light catch it. Then he turned back to the beginning and looked through it. Finally, he met Carol's eyes, his gaze serious. 'Where did you get the photograph?' he said.

'That was the easy part. A news magazine did an interview with you last year, remember? Part of a series about Berlin businessmen who had seized the opportunity of reunification to build a new empire? I pulled it up out of their on-line archives and scaled down one of the pics. So, tomorrow? Why don't you call me in the morning?' She fished in her bag again and came out with a business card that simply gave her name and mobile phone number. 'I really do think we should talk.' She handed him the card, gave him the full hundred-watt smile and watched the play of emotions in his eyes again.

He held out the passport to her. 'Very interesting.'

Carol shook her head. 'It's no use to me. Keep it. You never know when it might come in handy.' She stood up and straightened her dress, smoothing it down over her hips in a consciously sexual gesture. 'Call me,' she said, heading for the door. She grasped the handle then turned. 'Otherwise, you'll never see me again.'

As she stepped back into the corridor, Carol became conscious of her body once more. The adrenaline that had kept her so firmly in control inside the opera box was starting to bleed away, leaving her weak-kneed and worn out. But she couldn't afford to relax yet. If Radecki was anything like as good as he was supposed to be, he would have arranged for someone to pick her up when she left his box, and to stick with her. She and Petra had discussed how they would handle that. Petra would hang well back, but close enough to make sure Carol got into a cab and to check out who was on her tail. Petra would try to follow the followers, but would take no risks of discovery.

Exhausted though she was, she acted as nonchalant as she could manage and made her way down to the cloakroom to stand in line and collect her coat. Or rather, Caroline Jackson's coat, a luxuriously soft lambskin that managed the trick of fashionable elegance coupled with the kind of warmth that early spring in Berlin demanded. Without looking around to see if she could spot the expected tail, she strolled out of the Staatsoper and stood by the kerb, looking for a passing taxi.

Me and half of Berlin, she thought wearily after five minutes, when her attempts to snag a ride had completely failed. Feeling a hand touch her arm, she whirled round, eyes wide, fight or flight reflexes on full alert. Radecki stood behind her. Whether it was deliberate or not, he maintained the perfect distance to avoid crowding her. Even in her heightened state of anxiety, Carol noted how unusual that was in a man. 'I'm sorry, I startled you,' he said.

She collected herself quickly. 'You did,' she said with a smile. 'Just be grateful I didn't have my pepper spray in my hand.'

He inclined his head with a rueful look. 'I couldn't help noticing when I came out that you were having trouble getting a cab. Perhaps I can help?' He reached for his mobile phone. 'My driver can have the car here inside five minutes. He can take you wherever you want to go.'

So much easier than following me, Carol thought with admiration. 'That would be very kind,' she said. 'My feet are freezing.'

He glanced down at the high-heeled, thin-soled, fuck-me shoes she'd chosen for the occasion. 'I'm not surprised. It's easy to see you're not a Berliner. Come back inside the foyer, it's warmer there.' He took her elbow and steered her towards the opera house, talking rapidly into his phone as they walked. Carol was aware of several curious looks from some of their fellow patrons as they passed. That was hardly surprising; if they were familiar with Tadeusz and Katerina, the sight of her by his side would be worth some serious gossip. She could imagine it now. 'Hey, did you see Tadeusz Radecki at the opera with that woman? She could be Katerina's sister. That's weird. What kind of pervert goes out with a woman who looks that much like his dead girlfriend?'

They stood just inside the doors, slightly apart, saying nothing. She didn't want to break the silence with the wrong words; sometimes it was better to let the fish come to you. A few people nodded a greeting to Tadeusz as they left the building, but no one stopped to speak.

He was true to his word. Only a few minutes passed before he nodded towards a black Mercedes that was drawing up at the kerb. 'My car,' he said. He walked her to the kerb and opened the rear door.

284

'I really appreciate this,' Carol said, climbing in. He leaned in past her and spoke to the driver.

'It's nothing,' he said, withdrawing. 'Just tell him where you want to go.' He began to close the door.

'Wait,' Carol said. 'You're not coming?'

'No.'

'But how will you get home?'

'I live close by. Besides, I prefer to walk.' This time, his smile was apparently uncomplicated. 'I'll call you,' he said, closing the door with a soft thud.

Carol gave her address to the driver and leaned back against the firm leather upholstery. It was a clever move on his part, to place her in his debt without making any kind of move on her. She wanted to shout out loud to release some of the jubilation she felt. But not in front of his driver, who would doubtless report back on every nuance of her behaviour. Instead, she let her head fall back and closed her eyes. Phase one was complete. And it had gone even better than she could have hoped.

Maybe she could do this after all.

Maybe she really could walk inside someone else's skin.

Brigadier Marijke van Hasselt walked into the detective squad room at Regio Leiden headquarters, carrying a carton of coffee and a bag of *smoutebollen*, the deep-fried choux pastry balls dredged with icing sugar that were her one concession to junk food. Carbs, caffeine and sugar; the only way to start the day.

Early as she was, Tom Brucke was ahead of her. He sat frowning over a pile of reports, his curly brown hair

285

already rumpled from his constant fiddling with it. He looked up at the sound of her footsteps. His boyish face looked strained and tired, heavy lines tracking under his eyes. 'Hey, Marijke,' he said. 'Fucked if I know where we're going to find a perp for this case.'

She took an instant decision. Two heads were, as she had already proved, infinitely better than one. 'Oddly enough, Tom, I had an idea about that last night.' She pulled up a chair and sat at the end of his desk, tucking one leg under her.

Tom curled a tendril of hair round his index finger. 'I'm staring at so many dead ends here, I'd seriously consider a clairvoyant,' he said. 'I don't know about you, but this case is doing my head in.'

'I keep waking up at night thinking I'm drowning,' Marijke admitted.

Tom snorted. 'Drowning in a sea of fucking paper,' he said, waving a hand at the piles of reports on his desk. 'Talk about living for your work. De Groot seems to have been on every committee he could get nominated for. He also organized an annual weekend conference for psychologists working in the same area as him. "The psychodynamics of emotional abuse," whatever that means. The upshot of which is that half the bloody world seems to have known him. It's a nightmare. So what's this brilliant idea of yours?'

'I didn't say it was brilliant, but at least it's something fresh to try. We're both agreed that this is a stranger killing, right?'

'There's nothing in his life to indicate anything different. On the other hand, there's no sign of forced entry. Balance of probabilities? He didn't know his killer.'

Marijke lifted the lid on her coffee and took a sip. 'From everything I've read, people who kill like this – no apparent relationship to the victim, sexual elements in the murder – they don't stop at one. Agreed?'

'Oh yes, I think we all know deep down that he's going to do it again. Particularly since we don't seem to be able to do fuck all to stop him,' Tom said pessimistically. 'Are those *smoutebollen* you've got there?' He pointed to her paper bag.

'Help yourself.' She pushed the bag towards him. 'Save me from myself.' Tom unwrapped the bag and pulled out one of the pastries. Icing sugar scattered on his pale blue shirt and he brushed at it impatiently with his free hand. 'But what I was thinking was, what if this isn't the beginning of his series?'

Tom stopped eating in mid-chew, then swallowed hard. 'You mean you think he's done this before?'

Marijke shrugged. 'It didn't look like an amateur job to me. If I had to guess, I'd say he's been doing this, or something very like it, for a while.'

Brucke shook his head doubtfully. 'We'd have heard about it. It's not like pubic scalping is an everyday occurrence, Marijke.'

'We might not have heard about it if it had happened in another jurisdiction. In France, say. Or Germany.'

Tom scratched his head. 'You've got a point. But there's not a lot we can do about it.'

'Yes there is. There's Europol.'

Tom snorted. 'Bunch of fucking desk jockeys.'

'Maybe so, but they do send out those international bulletins.'

'More fucking paper. Who reads that crap?'

Marijke reached for her paper bag and pulled out one of the napkins she'd placed inside at the *smoutebollen* stall. Then she extracted one of the pastries, careful not to spill the sugar on her clothes. 'I do,' she said. 'And I bet I'm not the only one.'

'So you want to pass the case on to the office boys in Den Haag?' he said incredulously.

'No, that's not what I'm talking about. I'm suggesting we send a request to Europol with details of the case, asking them to circulate it to member states, asking if anyone else has had anything comparable on their patch. That way, we can at least find out if he's done it before. And if he has, and if we can pool our information with the investigating team there, we might start to get somewhere.'

Tom gave her a considering look. 'You know, that might not be such a bad idea.'

'So I can count on your support when I run it past Maartens?'

He laughed. 'You're such a fucking politician, Marijke.'

'I'll take that as a yes.' She got to her feet and retrieved the remains of her breakfast. She had just made it as far as her own desk when Hoofdinspecteur Kees Maartens barrelled through the squad-room door, his meaty hand dwarfing the can of Coke that was halfway to his mouth. He took a swig as he strode, tossing the empty can into the next wastepaper bin he passed. Recycling was for people with time on their hands, not for busy men like him, his gesture seemed to say.

'What's new?' he demanded, stopping beside Tom's desk.

'Nothing of any significance,' Tom said.

Maartens turned towards Marijke. 'What about you, Marijke? Anything useful come through from forensics yet?'

She shook her head. 'It's all negatives. Nothing that takes us any further forward.'

Maartens rubbed a hand along his jaw. 'I hate this case,' he muttered. 'It makes us look stupid.'

'Marijke's got a good idea,' Tom volunteered.

Gee, thanks, she thought as Maartens turned back to her, his heavy brows lowering in an interrogative frown. 'What's that, Marijke?' he asked.

'I've been thinking about how meticulous de Groot's killer was. How methodical, how organized. This wasn't a spur of the moment thing. It was planned. What it reminds me of is the work of a serial killer. I know we're all worried about the prospect of him killing again if we can't catch him, but it occurred to me that he might have killed before.'

Maartens nodded, his head to one side. He crossed to her desk and dropped into a chair facing her. 'I can't argue with the theory,' he said heavily. 'But haven't we already checked to see if there's anything similar in the records?'

'We can only check Dutch records, though,' Marijke said. 'What if his previous victims weren't in Holland? What if he's killed in Belgium or Germany or Luxembourg? We'd have no way of knowing.'

'And these days, post-Schengen, we're all citizens of Europe,' Maartens said acidly. 'I see what you mean, Marijke. But how does that take us any further forward?'

'Well, I've noticed in the past few months that the

bulletins coming out of Den Haag from Europol have been a lot more specific. They used to be fairly generic, but now they've taken to circulating much more detailed requests for information about particular areas of concern. I wondered if it might be worth approaching them and asking them to include a request for information about any similar cases elsewhere in the EU?'

Maartens looked deeply sceptical. 'Don't you think it's a bit too near street level for them? They're only interested in the stuff that lets them play with their fancy computer databases. They don't want to get their hands dirty with something as vulgar as murder.'

'But this isn't some run-of-the-mill killing. And murder can be part of their brief. I checked it out on their website. Where there are international implications, they've got a responsibility to act as an intelligence clearing house for murder as well as the organized crime stuff.'

Maartens shifted in his seat. 'They'll think we're too stupid to manage our own cases,' he grunted.

'I don't think so, sir. I reckon they'll respect us for sussing out that we could be looking at a serial killer. It could be a feather in our caps. We'd go down as the ones who had the brains to see the implications of what we were looking at and the courage to say, "We want input from other jurisdictions." They'll be able to hold us up as an example of how cross-border co-operation should work in the new Europe.' Marijke turned on all her charm as she spoke, desperate to persuade Maartens into the course of action that suited the plans she and Petra had already made.

Maartens considered for a moment, then swung round to look at Tom. 'And you think this is a good idea, do you?'

Tom waved a hand over the paperwork on his desk. 'We've exhausted every conventional avenue and we've got fuck all. The way I see it, we've got nothing left to lose. And we might have a lot to gain.'

Maartens shrugged. 'OK, we'll give it a shot. Marijke, put something on paper for me, and I'll see it gets sent off later today.'

'I'll have it on your desk within the hour.'

Maartens got to his feet and lumbered towards his office. 'That doesn't mean we stop working the case,' he growled as he disappeared behind his door.

'Nice one,' Tom said. 'Smooth as butter, you are.'

'Yeah, well. We both know that if it works out, it'll be down to Maartens. But if we end up looking stupid, it'll be thanks to me.'

'It's good to know that in a changing world, some things always remain the same,' Tom said with a smile.

And some things we can force to change, Marijke thought cheerfully as she booted up her computer. This was it. The big chance. And she was determined not to blow it.

Carol felt as excited as a teenager on a first date. He'd come to Berlin after all! She'd woken up after her dramatic night at the opera to an encrypted e-mail from Petra, revealing that Tony was staying in the same apartment building and drawing up a profile of the serial killer. And that he was expecting her this morning. But what more could Petra say? She had no idea of the complex matrix that was the relationship between Carol and Tony. She had no idea how much like salvation his arrival would feel to Carol.

Hastily, she towelled herself dry from the shower and pulled on fresh jeans and a loose shirt, the simplest outfit in Caroline Jackson's wardrobe. She wanted to be as close to Carol Jordan as she could manage. She finger-combed her hair and hastily applied lipstick. No time for more.

Her heart was racing as she waited for the lift. *Calm down,* she told herself. *He's not here for you.* But deep down, she was convinced he was. The murder investigation might be the perfect excuse, but he'd resisted coming back into the game for the past two years. All that had changed was that this was an investigation that offered a chance to bring them together.

She knocked on the door and, suddenly, there he was, his familiar face as dear to her as ever. Impulsively, Carol stepped towards him. Their arms went round each other in a hug, her head on his shoulder, his hand in her hair. 'Thank you for coming,' Carol whispered.

Gently, Tony moved out of their embrace and closed the door behind her. 'I knew Margarethe Schilling,' he blurted out.

It hit her like a glass of wine in the face, taking her breath away and making her eyes smart. 'What?' she said, feeling stupid.

Tony ran a hand through his hair. 'The Bremen victim. I knew her.'

'So you came out of . . . what? A desire for vengeance?' Carol asked, following him and sitting down in the single armchair, taking care to stay well

292

away from the window. Even though she hadn't spotted a tail, that didn't mean there wasn't someone dogging her every move and she didn't want to reveal herself anywhere she wasn't supposed to be.

With his back to her, Tony stared out of the picture window into the street below. 'Partly. Partly because I'm big-headed enough to think I can maybe help to save more lives. And partly because . . .' He paused, searching for the right words. 'Because what happened to Margarethe made me fret about the dangers you're exposed to.' He turned to face her, arms folded across his chest. 'I don't mean to sound presumptuous. I don't know anyone who's better at their job than you. I don't know anyone who's more self-sufficient or stronger.' He looked down at the floor. 'But I'd never forgive myself if anything happened to you that I might have helped prevent.' He gave a short bark of laughter. 'I don't even know what I mean by that, which is a very strange thing for a psychologist to have to admit. I just . . . I don't know. I suppose I wanted to be around in case there was anything I could do to help you.'

His words were more valuable to Carol than gold. Just when she'd thought he was delivering a slap in the face, he'd turned it into a caress. She'd waited years to hear this level of personal concern from him, and it had been worth every minute. The knowledge that he cared this much was almost enough in itself. It held its own guarantee for some sort of future. It promised the chance to take things at their own pace, without any necessity for her to push. 'You have no idea how much it means to me that you're here. Whatever the reason,' she said. 'I've been feeling so isolated on this job. Petra's a star, but she's not part of Carol Jordan's life. She's not going to see if I'm slipping away from myself, because she doesn't really know what that self is. You do. You can be the Carol Jordan benchmark, you can be my sheet anchor. And you can help me decide how to handle Radecki.'

'I can try. How did it go last night?'

Carol took him through her first encounter with her target. Tony sat on the sofa, chin propped on his fists, listening intently and asking the occasional question along the way. 'It sounds to me as if you handled it well. I was afraid he'd be so suspicious of your resemblance to Katerina that he'd refuse to have anything to do with you. But you seem to have got over that hurdle.'

'Maybe. He's still not called, though.'

'He will.'

'Let's hope so. But we shouldn't be spending all this time on me. I don't want to take you away from the work you have to do on your profile. That's what you're here for. That's the most important thing. Because if this bastard isn't stopped, he's going to do it again and again. He's got to be taken down. And if anyone can make that happen, it's you.'

'I hope so. I owe this bastard a death. Or at the very least, the rest of his life behind bars.' Tony shook his head. 'I still can't take in the fact that Margarethe's dead.'

'Were you old friends?'

'I wouldn't really describe it as a friendship. We were colleagues with some common interests. I stayed at her house for a couple of nights once. We talked about collaborating on a paper, but we never got round to it. We e-mailed a few times a year, exchanged cards at Christmas. So, not friends, but more than mere acquaintances. I liked her. I liked her a lot. She was imaginative, intelligent. She was doing good work. And she had a son. She adored him.' He shook his head. 'What does that do to a kid's head? He must be seven, eight, something like that. And he's going to have to grow up knowing somebody treated his mother like a piece of meat.'

'Will you let me help?'

Tony looked surprised. 'Don't you have enough on your plate?'

'I'm probably going to have plenty of free time on my hands. When I'm not with Radecki or writing up my reports, I've got nothing else to do.'

He frowned, considering. 'I'm working at Petra's apartment. Obviously, you can't come there in case you're being watched. But if I can talk through my ideas with you, that would be a big help for me. You're always good at coming up with the off-the-wall idea that nobody else gives house room to.'

'Great.' Carol smiled. 'So when do you start?'

'I made a start last night.' He glanced at his watch. 'Ideally, I should get over to Petra's now so I can start drafting out some ideas.'

'Do you want to get together later?' she asked, rising to her feet.

'We can e-mail securely, right? Let's arrange it that way.' He stood up and crossed to her, tentatively putting his arms round her. 'I'm glad I'm here.'

'Me too.' She turned her face to his. They smiled at each other, then let go. For the first time, Carol thought, it felt as if they had all the time in the world.

23

Tadeusz Radecki was restless. Sleep had eluded him for hours after he'd returned from the opera. The encounter in his private box would have been unsettling under any circumstances, speaking as it did of someone having researched him as thoroughly as he investigated anyone he had dealings with. But beyond the natural discomfort of knowing he'd been studied, this confrontation with so close a simulacrum of what he'd so recently lost had left him feeling that the world had turned upside down.

His first sight of Caroline Jackson had made his heart skip a beat. His chest had constricted, his legs had trembled. He'd doubted the evidence of his eyes, convinced he was having some sort of psychotic episode that had produced this hallucination. But as soon as she'd spoken, he'd realized this was reality, not some pathetic projection of his deepest desire. He'd never have conjured up a Katerina who addressed him in English, that much had penetrated even his bewildered and alarmed state.

Luckily, years of guarding his face and tongue had allowed him to cover the worst of his confusion. At least, he thought it had. Whatever the truth of that view, she had shown no sign of being aware of the effect her appearance had on him. He'd been dry-mouthed and bemused, unnerved by a resemblance that stirred up the morass of memory.

And as if it wasn't enough that he'd come face to face with a woman who could have been the twin sister of the woman he'd adored, the conversation had lurched into the most dangerous of areas almost from the beginning. This woman who made his stomach churn and his skin turn clammy knew who he really was, knew what he really did. Either she had discovered enough about his business to comprehend exactly what he needed right now, or else this was another example of the eccentric serendipity that had brought Katerina's double to his door in the first place. Either way, it was a set of circumstances so strange it turned on its head everything he knew about how the world worked.

He had no idea how he'd managed to hold it together during their subsequent conversation, only that he'd never felt so relieved as he had when that apparently interminable first interval had drawn to a close. He'd sat through the next act oblivious to the music, completely absorbed in the private drama that had unfolded in his immediate ambit. The tension in his body had made his muscles ache, but he hadn't been able to take his eyes off her.

He'd studied every feature in her face, comparing it to the database of images stored in his head. On closer inspection, he had become aware of discrepancies. Of course, the hair was different. The long cornsilk of his lover's hair was far more beautiful than the short, thick blonde crop of this stranger, though it was clearly as natural a shade as Katerina's. Their profiles were subtly distinct in ways he couldn't quite gauge. Katerina's eyes had been a deep hyacinth blue, but even in the dim light of the theatre, he could see that Caroline's were grey-blue. Their mouths were different too. Katerina's lips had been sensuous, full, beautifully shaped, appearing always to be on the point of a kiss. This Englishwoman had thinner lips, her mouth promising far less than Katerina had always delivered. But when Caroline smiled, the contrast had disappeared and the resemblance had become even more profound. Seeing that mouth pronounce the familiar 'Tadzio' had disconcerted him more than almost anything else.

The strangest thing about his scrutiny of her face was that although he could see clearly that she wasn't Katerina, those small variations only served to reinforce this interloper's effect on him. She wasn't Katerina, which was both a disappointment and a relief. But she was a woman who had the power to move him as no one had done since Katerina's death. That was unnerving, but also fraught with strange possibilities. The notion of working with her made him both apprehensive and excited.

But not so excited that he had forgotten the basic rules of the game. As soon as the second act had ended, he had taken the first steps to find out what he could about Caroline Jackson. He remembered a man he'd met a couple of times when he'd been setting up the deal with Colin Osborne. Nick Kramer was another Essex boy who had worked with Colin in the past. He clearly wasn't a lieutenant in the way that Darko was, and Tadeusz reckoned the main reason Colin had brought him along was to make it look as if the teams were even. Tadeusz, always covering the bases, still had Kramer's number stored on his mobile phone.

Kramer had answered on the second ring. 'Yeah?' he grunted.

'This is Colin's German friend,' Tadeusz said. 'We met in London?'

'Oh yeah, right, I remember you. What's happening?'

'I've come across someone who says she was a friend of Colin. I wondered if you knew her.'

'What's her name?'

'Caroline Jackson. She says they were looking to do some business.'

There was a short pause. 'I know the name. But I never met her. I've heard she's in the same line of work as you and Colin. Runs an operation somewhere in East Anglia. Keeps herself to herself, by all accounts. Oh, and I heard that after Colin . . . died, her name came up when people was questioned. That's all I know. Sorry I can't be more help, mate.'

'Do you know anyone who does know her?'

An exhalation of breath. 'There's this geezer out Chelmsford way. A friend of Charlie's, if you get my meaning?'

A cocaine dealer, Tadeusz translated. 'Do you have a number where I can contact him?'

'Hang on a minute . . .' The muffled sound of conversation. When Kramer returned, he reeled off a mobile phone number. 'Tell him I said you were kosher.'

'Thank you.'

'Any time. Listen, you want to do some business – not the kind that breathes, the other kind – you gimme a call. I'm well up for it.'

'I'll bear that in mind.' Tadeusz ended the call. He didn't think he'd be dealing drugs or guns with Nick Kramer any time soon. He hadn't taken to the man, and on the evidence of this last conversation, he lacked discretion. He keyed in the number Kramer had given him and waited to be connected.

He was on the point of giving up when the phone was answered. A cautious voice said, 'Hello?'

Tadeusz made a quick decision. 'My name is Darko Krasic. Nick Kramer gave me your number.'

'Do I know him?'

'Well, he has your phone number.'

'So does my local Indian takeaway.'

'My boss and I used to do business with Colin Osborne.'

A snort of laughter. 'He can't give you much of a reference, now can he? Look, I don't do business over the phone.'

'Sure, I understand. All I'm looking for is a character reference. Somebody has applied to work with us, and Kramer seems to think you know her.'

'I know a lot of people.' The voice was cautious again.

'Her name is Caroline Jackson.'

A long pause. 'I know Caroline. What do you want to know?'

'Whatever you can tell me.'

'Fucking hell, you don't want much, do you? Look, if you're thinking about working with Caroline, all you need to know is that she's a serious player. But she's a loner. She doesn't trust anybody with her business. She's smart, she knows how to keep stumm, and she's very fucking good at what she does. She wants to work with you, you should bite her fucking hand off, because you're getting the opportunity to work with the best. OK?'

'OK.'

'Now you got what you wanted. Good night.' The call ended abruptly, leaving Tadeusz feeling less uneasy than he had ten minutes previously. What he didn't know was that he'd just been talking to one of Morgan's undercover operatives, briefed to give Caroline Jackson as vivid a reality as possible.

Tadeusz had sat through the third act, brooding over his course of action. As *The Cunning Little Vixen* drew to a close, he came to a decision. He had to see the virtual reappearance of Katerina as a good omen. He'd go with his gut reaction and see what she had to offer him.

In the cold light of morning, the decision still felt like a good one. He wished he'd been able to talk it over with Darko, but his right-hand man wasn't due back from Belgrade until that afternoon. And this was too important to entrust to telephones. He'd have to rely on his own intuition. He reached for the phone and dialled the number on the card she'd given him.

'Hello?' Her voice was already familiar.

'Good morning, Caroline. It's Tadeusz here.'

'Good to hear from you.'

She sounded determined not to show any enthusiasm that might not be matched on his side. 'I wondered if you might be free for lunch?' he asked.

'That rather depends.'

'On what?'

'Whether it's business or pleasure on the agenda,' she said coolly.

'I suspect that, with you, business would always be one sort of pleasure or another,' he said, an undertone of amusement in his voice. He was surprised by how at ease he felt flirting gently with her.

'You didn't answer my question.'

'I think we may be able to do business,' he said. 'But first, we have to get to know each other a little better. You see, I only deal with people when my instincts tell me they're reliable.'

'Really?' she asked, sounding incredulous. 'And you still chose Colin?'

His source had been right. She was smart. 'If that was such a bad decision, then by your own admission, the condemnation falls equally on your shoulders, Caroline,' he pointed out.

'Touché,' she said.

'So, will we have lunch?'

'If you can make it earlier rather than later. I have some important calls to make this afternoon.'

'How is noon for you?'

'I can do that.'

'I'll send the car for you at eleven forty-five. I look forward to it.'

'Thanks, but I've got to go out this morning. I don't know where I'll be at eleven forty-five. Just tell me where to be, and I'll get there for noon.'

He named the restaurant and gave her the address. 'I look forward to seeing you,' he added.

'The feeling is mutual. See you later.' The line went

dead. So. To smart and discreet, add independent and wary. Caroline Jackson was beginning to intrigue him. And not just professionally. He found himself looking forward to lunch with an appetite that had nothing to do with food.

Tony stared at the screen. Petra had been as good as her word. The investigation reports from Bremen had been waiting for him when he'd arrived at her apartment, and he'd forced himself to put his feelings for Margarethe to one side and read them as objectively as he could. The fact that the killer had been interrupted had provided a few nuggets of information that might help as he went along, but the most telling details had come from Margarethe's boyfriend, and these could be incorporated right away in his draft profile.

At this stage, it could only be a rough outline. There were things he still needed to do and see. He wanted to go to Bremen, partly to make his peace with Margarethe, but mostly to see the house where she had died, to see if the crime scene could tell him more about his prey. He needed better quality photographs of the crime scenes. But for now, he could make a start.

He loaded his word processing program and called up his personal template for profiles. It began with a standard disclaimer. This might be an informal, unofficial investigation, but that was no reason not to do things properly.

The following offender profile is for guidance only and should not be regarded as an identikit portrait. The offender is unlikely to match the profile in every detail,

*though I would expect there to be a high degree of
congruence between the characteristics outlined below
and the reality. All of the statements in the profile
express probabilities and possibilities, not hard facts.*

*A serial killer produces signals and indicators in
the commission of his crimes. Everything he does is
intended, consciously or not, as part of a pattern.
Uncovering the underlying pattern reveals the killer's
logic. It may not appear logical to us, but to him it is
crucial. Because his logic is so idiosyncratic, straightforward traps will not capture him. As he is unique,
so must be the means of catching him, interviewing
him and reconstructing his acts.*

Tony then gave a brief overview of the three cases,
with particular attention to the nature of the victims'
academic research. Moving on from there, and assimilating his new information, he wrote,

*All academic psychologists who conduct experimental
research on human subjects may be at risk from this
killer. Given that Margarethe Schilling told her
partner she was scheduled to meet a journalist repre-
senting a new psychology e-zine, it may be advisable
to ask psychology lecturers to contact this investigation
if they receive such an approach. However, it is clear
that this poses potential problems. If the killer has
links to the academic community, he may be privy to
any such warning and alter his strategy accordingly.
Furthermore, such a warning may provoke a panic
response among those at risk. There is also the difficulty of the scale of the operation. The killer has
already operated in two EU countries that we are*

*aware of – Germany and Holland. There is no reason
to suppose that this is the limit of his range.*

*What do we know of the killer from his actions so
far?*

*1.   Although there is almost certainly an element of
sexual stimulus in the commission of these crimes, the
motivation is not explicitly sexual. The victims do not
correspond to any physical class and encompass both
genders. It is therefore impossible to predict where he
will strike next based on any superficial description of
appearance. Contingent on this, and on the scalping
of the pubic region (reducing his victims to something
resembling a pre-pubertal state) I would suggest that
the killer's own sexuality is relatively unformed. By
this I mean that he has never successfully established
adult sexual relationships. He may have experienced
sexual humiliation at an early age and decided that
he was not prepared to expose himself to that again.
At some level, he blames this inability to form normal
sexual contacts on his victim group. I believe it is highly
unlikely that he will be either married or in any sort
of long-term relationship. He is most likely to be a
single man with no history of emotional relationships
with either sex.*

So many reasons for the corruption of the sexual
impulse, Tony thought sadly. His own experience of
impotence, and the soul-searching journey that had
taken him on, had given him a unique empathy with
those whose natural desires had been morphed into
something the rest of the world saw as perversion.
There was always an explanation, always a sequence

as unique as DNA that lay beneath these strange surfaces, and it was one of the many paradoxes of Tony's life that what had given him so much personal pain had also given him a professional head start. Maybe, like the killers themselves, he was looking for something that would make him feel less of a failure.

2. His choice of victims gives him a sense of superiority. People like them have always made him feel slow, un-sophisticated. But now he can move into their world, invade their territory and there is nothing they can do to stop him. It is a way of proving to himself that he is not the inadequate he thinks he is. It's extremely unlikely that he has a university-level education. I would doubt he even completed secondary education, although he is clearly far from stupid. Given what I believe to be his strategy in the choice of victims (see below), it is likely that he has educated himself in their field of expertise. He has probably read extensively about psychology and its applications, both in books and on-line. He may even have taken adult education classes in the subject. He probably thinks of himself as an expert in his field, although his knowledge will of necessity be superficial.

3. He is capable of a high degree of self-control and organization. To execute his plan, he has developed a strategy of sufficient finesse to convince victims who are experienced in negotiating with the world. In order to succeed at this, he must be able to disguise his unfamiliarity with their universe.

4. He must have planned this series of attacks well in advance, since the victims require prior research rather than the opportunistic picking at random of a candidate who meets certain physical criteria. It is clear from how close together the last two murders are that he has a pre-set list of victims. The fact that his time-scale is shortening means that he is growing in confidence but also that he needs more kills to satisfy whatever his agenda is.

5. What might that agenda be? The answer to that must lie in his choice of targets. What all three have in common is that they are academic psychologists who have published research based on experiments conducted on (willing) human subjects. I believe he entertains the conviction that his life has been blighted as a result of experiments carried out by one or more psychologists. He may himself have been a direct victim, but I doubt that. If that were the case, he would have a specific object for his revenge and it would probably have been sufficient for him to kill that single practitioner. Perhaps he suffered childhood abuse at the hands of a parent or other adult who had been the victim of psychological torture? Given the abuse of psychology at the hands of, for example, the Stasi, this does not seem as improbable as it might in another time and place.

Tony read over what he had typed so far. It made sense, in the context of what he'd been able to glean from the files. But it didn't take them any closer to who the killer might be. Now he had to start moving away from what he knew and could logically surmise into the realm where he excelled. He had to reason backwards from the crime to the man who had committed it.

What does all this tell us about the killer?

1. He is subject to high stress levels, which will be perceptible to those around him. His behaviour will be more erratic than usual.

2. He is posing as a journalist on an e-zine in order to gain private access to those he has targeted. I believe he will have made the arrangements for his meetings with the victims via e-mail, since he is unlikely to possess the interpersonal skills to set up meetings with such highly socialized victims either face to face or via the telephone. Therefore we can state with some certainty that he possesses his own computer; he would not risk such communications on a system available to others. Furthermore, an expert search of the victims' computers may reveal traces of these communications.

3. He is unlikely to be unemployed; he can afford a computer, he can afford to travel. He is also comfortable moving around in more than one country, suggesting a familiarity with them. In my opinion, he is likely to have a job that involves travelling, but not one that requires people skills. It may well be a job that demands a certain level of intelligence and responsibility, yet one that is not highly regarded by the world at large. Perhaps a long-distance lorry driver, or a maintenance engineer on some specialized equipment. He will drive a well-maintained mid-range car of unassuming appearance. It is unlikely that he uses public transport to go to and from the scenes of the crimes, and this may mean that he is either hiring cars in or near the cities where he has

killed, or that he has local access to company vehicles because of his job.

4. The first crime of serial offenders tends to take place nearest their home. Since the first crime in this series took place in Heidelberg, I believe he is probably based in the central region of Germany.

5. He is most likely to be in his late twenties or early thirties. Typically, serial killers take time to work up to their ambition. If they make it into their late thirties without killing, they're less likely to start because they have found alternative ways to sublimate their desires.

6. It is likely that a member of his immediate family has a history of treatment for mental illness or a record of psychological torture at the hands of officialdom. If the latter is the case, it may well be that the family originated from the former East Germany.

7. If he has a criminal record, I'd suggest that it may include stalking or Peeping Tom offences. Most serial killers exhibit a history of bullying, animal torture, minor vandalism and arson, but in this case, I believe he is more likely to have convictions for violence against the person. Whatever was done to damage his psyche will have produced enormous levels of suppressed rage in him. Until he found an appropriate (for him) target for his anger, he may have been prone to outbursts of violence against anyone who he perceived as laughing at him. He may have assaulted prostitutes or other men who made fun of his lack of a girlfriend.

Tony stared bleakly at the screen. In truth, it wasn't much. As usual, he felt like the conjuror who is expected to produce an elephant from his top hat but only manages the same tired old rabbit. He reminded himself that this was only a raw first draft. He needed more data and he wanted to talk a couple of ideas over with Carol before he committed them to paper.

Tony packed up his laptop and scribbled a note to Petra. *Thanks for your help. I've begun work on the profile but I need to go to Bremen. Can you book me on a train or a plane first thing? And is there any way of arranging things so I can talk to the local cops? Also, it would be helpful if you could put me in touch with someone who can talk to me about the Stasi's use of psychiatry. I'm going back to my apartment – I'll expect your call.*

He let himself out of the front door and wearily descended to the street. It was a beautiful spring day, the air damp and cool, the sky bright with sunshine. *Only a clod could fail to be moved by the possibilities of life on a day like this,* Tony thought. But somewhere out there, rain or shine, a killer was planning his next move. And it was up to Tony to try to make sure it would be the one that ended in checkmate.

The restaurant he had chosen surprised her. She had been expecting somewhere with private nooks and crannies, where they could talk without fear of being overheard. There was nothing intimate about this place, however. High ceilings with steel and tungsten light fittings, the tables and chairs a design statement in themselves. It was smart and noisy, the sort of place where everyone automatically checked out the rest of the clientele to satisfy themselves that the cutting edge hadn't moved somewhere else since they were last there.

He was already seated when she arrived, smoking a small cigar and reading the menu at a table in the middle of the room. Carol noticed she attracted a couple of curious glances as the waiter led her to his table. She was going to have to deal with that, and sooner rather than later.

When she reached the table, Tadeusz got to his feet and gave a small, formal bow. 'Thank you for coming,' he said.

'Thank you for asking me.' The waiter held out her chair and Carol settled herself. 'Tell me, are you some sort of celebrity in Berlin?'

He frowned. 'What do you mean?'

'I noticed last night and again just now. People stare at us. And since nobody in Berlin has a clue who I am, it must be you.'

His cheeks flushed scarlet and he looked down at the table. He fiddled with his fork, then glanced back up at her, his mouth a thin line. She could see he was struggling not to show emotion. 'I'm not a celebrity, though many people know who I am. But that's not why they're staring.'

'No?'

'It's you.'

Carol gave a self-deprecating snort of laughter. 'I'm disappointed. I thought your flattery would be a little more sophisticated than that.'

Tadeusz breathed deeply. 'No, that wasn't flattery. Which is not to say that you're not beautiful enough

311

to turn heads.' He gave a short sharp sigh. 'This is going to sound crazy.'

'Oh yes?' Carol reckoned Caroline Jackson would be suspicious by now and she worked on the matching facial expression.

Tadeusz studied his cigar. Impatient, he stubbed it out in the ashtray. 'You have a remarkable resemblance to someone.'

'What? I have a double who's famous in Germany?'

He shook his head. 'No, not like that.' He shifted awkwardly in his seat. 'You're the spitting image of a woman called Katerina Basler. She was my lover. That's why people are staring.'

Carol raised her eyebrows. 'They think you've replaced Katerina with a lookalike?'

He shrugged. 'I guess.'

'How long ago did you two break up?'

He cleared his throat. She could see the pain in his face, but she couldn't afford to indicate that she knew why he deserved sympathy. So she waited. 'We didn't break up,' he eventually said. He reached for his wine glass and emptied the contents in one long gulp. 'She died, Caroline.'

Carol had known this moment would come, and she had thought long and hard about how to play it. Shock, obviously. She'd have to act astonished. Appalled, even. Affronted would have to come into the equation somewhere along the line too. She let her face go slack, her mouth falling open.

That was the moment the waiter chose to appear, asking what they wanted to drink. Distracted, Tadeusz spread his hands in a gesture of confusion.

'Scotch,' Carol said decisively. 'Large, on the rocks.'

'Cognac,' Tadeusz said, waving the waiter away.

Carol concentrated on keeping the look of pitying horror on her face. 'She died?'

He nodded, eyes downcast again. 'A couple of months ago. A road accident. A stupid, stupid road accident.'

'God, I'm so sorry,' she said. It wasn't an act this time. She'd have needed a harder heart not to have been moved by his obvious grief.

He shook his head. 'It is I who should apologize. I didn't mean to impose this on you.'

Impulsively, she reached out and covered his hand with hers. 'It's not an imposition. I'm glad you told me. I was beginning to feel paranoid. But, Tadzio, that's terrible for you. I can't imagine how I'd feel if that happened to someone I loved.'

'No. It's not imaginable.' He looked at her with a pained smile. 'I think everyone who truly loves another person has terrible guilty fantasies about how they would feel if their lover died. I think that's common, probably even natural. But there is nothing that prepares you for the reality. All your certainties disappear. If this can happen to you, anything can. It's like you lose your anchor to reality.'

'I'm so sorry,' she said. 'And you say I look like Katerina?'

He squeezed his eyes shut. 'Yes. You could be her sister.'

'No wonder you freaked out when you saw me last night,' Carol said, her voice soft. 'I had no idea, Tadzio. You must believe me, I had no idea.'

'Why would you? You had no way of knowing. Colin never met Katerina, he couldn't have told you.'

He took a deep breath and exhaled slowly. 'I'm sorry. When I suggested we get to know each other better, this wasn't what I had in mind.'

'No, I can see that.'

Before she could say more, the waiter arrived with their drinks. Carol wasn't in the habit of drinking Scotch in the middle of the day, but Caroline Jackson would need a stiff pick-me-up after Tadeusz's bombshell, so she took a healthy mouthful right away.

Tadeusz sipped his brandy and gave her a tired smile. 'So, now you know probably the most important thing about me right now. Why don't you tell me something about yourself?'

Carol shrugged. 'I've nothing to say that comes close.'

'I don't want this to be some solemn, grim meeting,' he said. 'As I said, I think we can maybe do business, but I need to have more of a sense of you before I'm prepared to make any kind of commitment. So, tell me about yourself.' He raised one finger. 'But before you do, let's order some food.'

They scrutinized the menus, Carol asking for his recommendations. She settled on a traditional German fish dish, while Tadeusz ordered steak. By the time the waiter left, he was back in total command of himself. 'OK,' he said. 'Tell me about Caroline Jackson.'

She raised her glass and clinked it against the rim of his. 'Once upon a time . . .' she said, a quirky smile lifting one corner of her mouth. After all, she was telling a story. And she needed to make it very convincing indeed.

Petra walked into the health club, gym bag over her shoulder. Setting this place up as a meeting point had been one of her best ideas. The minimum membership period was three months, and she was determined to make the most of it. She had already spent an hour working out in the well-equipped gym first thing that morning. She'd told Plesch she'd dropped by to book the private sauna for that afternoon's debrief, but she'd left herself enough time to take full advantage of the facilities. This liaison job was certainly giving her a taste for the good life. The opera last night, lunch in a restaurant that was well outside her salary bracket, and access to one of the best leisure clubs in the city. All this and the best possible chance to nail Radecki.

Of course, it wasn't all fun and games. When Carol had e-mailed her to pass on the details of her lunch date with Radecki, Petra had had to use all her charms to get a last-minute table somewhere so fashionable. Even worse, she'd had to take The Shark along with her for camouflage. He'd been the only member of the team who wasn't too busy to come out to lunch.

It really was a pity that Marijke wasn't a Berlin cop, she'd thought regretfully, and not for the first time. The Shark had bored her stupid with tales of his attempts at digging up information on Marlene Krebs and her missing daughter, but at least she'd been able to tune him out and keep an eye on Carol. And when he'd suggested he accompany her that afternoon, she'd sent him off to chase his tail again. She reckoned that there weren't many people Darko Krasic would trust to look after Marlene's kid, so she told The Shark to abandon Marlene for now and concentrate on finding out who Krasic might have dumped Tanja with. He wouldn't get anywhere, of course, but at least it would keep him out from under her feet.

Petra collected the sauna key from the front desk and went through to the changing rooms. Carol wasn't due for another twenty minutes, so she reckoned she had time for a quick swim. She ploughed up and down the pool for a dozen lengths, thinking about the serial killer case. There was still nothing from Europol, but, realistically, she couldn't expect anything before tomorrow at the earliest. At least Bremen hadn't questioned her request for copies of their case material. Sometimes there were distinct advantages to working for Criminal Intelligence. It might piss off local officers, but she could always pull the 'need to know' line when she really wanted access. She hoped Tony had found it useful. A profile would give them a head start, she knew.

By the time she returned to the changing rooms, Carol was sitting on a bench, wearing nothing but a bath sheet. There were a couple of other women getting changed, so the two police officers ignored each other. But under cover of opening her locker and heading for the showers, Petra unobtrusively dropped the sauna key in Carol's lap.

Five minutes later, they were side by side on the wooden bench, naked save for the sheen of sweat on their skin. Petra couldn't help admiring the sleek lines of Carol's body, the well-defined shoulders and thighs and the flat stomach. Not that she was tempted, but it would have been perverse not to notice, she told herself. 'Did anyone follow you from the restaurant?' she asked.

'I don't think so,' Carol said. 'I was expecting a tail, but I didn't spot one. You came out behind me, didn't you? Did you see anyone?'

'No. And that surprised me too. I felt sure he'd have you under surveillance by now. He's normally so circumspect, I can't believe he's leaving you alone.'

'Maybe he's still dazzled by my resemblance to Katerina.'

Petra wiped her damp forehead. 'Even if Radecki is walking around in a daze, I can't believe Darko Krasic isn't on the ball.'

Carol shrugged. 'Maybe he hasn't told Krasic about me yet.'

Petra looked sceptical. 'I don't see it. And I don't think Radecki is completely blinded by your looks. I spoke to your man Gandle earlier this afternoon, and he told me that one of your undercover colleagues in the UK got a call from Radecki himself last night. Apparently he claimed he was Krasic, but from the report of how good the guy's English was, it sounds as though it was Radecki himself.'

'That must have been when he left the box at the

second interval.' Carol leaned forward and ladled more water on the hot coals. Steam hissed and the temperature shot up, making her a little light-headed.

Petra nodded. 'Radecki was looking for someone who could vouch for you personally. He was told you were very good at what you do, but that you're also a loner and very cautious about who you work with. I must say, your people have calculated exactly what will appeal to Radecki.'

'We couldn't have done it without help from you, Petra.'

She smirked, pleased at the compliment. 'So, how was lunch?'

Carol told her about Tadeusz's admission that he recognized her resemblance to Katerina. 'I almost felt sorry for him,' she said. 'It's obvious that he absolutely adored her.'

'Even if that's true, it still doesn't stop him dealing in the sort of racket that robs other people of the ones they love.'

'Oh, I know. It's not that I think it excuses anything, just that it's hard not to be touched by someone who's in that much pain. Even if you think almost everything else about them is repellent.'

'So, did you manage to get him to talk about business?'

Carol wiped sweat from her face. 'No. And I didn't push it. He kept saying he wanted to get to know me better before he would consider any professional liaison. That's obviously why he chose such a public place. Nobody in their right mind would try to have a private conversation there. Besides, if he's been briefed that I'm the sort who takes care, he must have known I wouldn't broach anything as sensitive as business arrangements where we could be overheard.'

'You gave him your cover story?'

'I made him work for it. But yes, I made sure he has enough information to check me out. Morgan's people set up a load of false records and planted stuff where it can be found without too much difficulty. If he follows up what I gave him today, Caroline Jackson will check out all over town.'

'Did you arrange to meet him again?'

'He found out that I like messing around on boats. So tomorrow he's taking me out on the Spree. He has a little launch, he says. That probably means a forty-foot gin palace.'

'No, I know his boat. It's quite a fast little motor boat with a small cabin. He'll probably take you round the city ring of the river and canals. We should be able to keep an eye on you from land, because there's a speed limit and a few locks to slow you down.' Petra groaned. 'I bet I have to spend the afternoon on a bike.'

Carol pushed herself off the bench. 'Exercise is good for you. I've got to shower,' she added. 'I'm dying here. Are you coming?'

Petra followed her out of the sauna into the cold showers on the wall opposite. Both women gasped as the stream of freezing water needled their skin, snapping the open pores shut in shock. Carol chickened out first, jumping clear and running back into the sauna, and Petra joined her moments later. 'Bloody hell, that was cold,' Carol said, more in admiration than complaint.

'It's good for the heart.'

'Kill or cure. There's one thing about being on a boat with Tadeusz,' she said, getting straight back to business. 'We'll be private. He'll feel able to talk.'

'It's a pity we can't wire you up,' Petra said.

Carol gave her an odd look. Had she finally found a chink in the German detective's briefing? 'I don't need to be wired.'

'Oh, I know, it's a risk we can't afford to take.'

'No, I mean, there's no need.' Carol took in the puzzlement on Petra's face. 'They didn't tell you, did they?'

'Tell me what?'

Carol rubbed her towel over her damp shoulders and leaned back against the hot wooden wall. 'I have an eidetic memory for speech.'

'I don't understand this word, eidetic.'

'I have total recall of whatever I hear. I can transcribe a conversation verbatim, as long as I do it within a few days of it taking place. I don't need to be wired, because I can remember everything.' Seeing Petra's dubious look, Carol continued. 'It's been scientifically tested. This is no party trick, it's for real.' She closed her eyes. '"You know, they told me you looked like Basler,"' she said in an approximation of Petra's accent, '"and it's true, your photograph does resemble her. But in the flesh, it's uncanny. You could be her twin sister. You are going to blow Radecki away. I swear to God, he is going to be freaked out when he sees you."

'"Let's hope it's in a good way,"' she continued in her own voice. Then back to Petra's tones. '"Oh, I think so. I don't see how he could resist."'

Petra wiped clear the sweat that threatened to

overflow the dam of her eyebrows and frowned. 'How can this be possible?'

Carol shrugged. 'There's some quirk in my brain that lets me replay conversations word for word. I don't know why. No one else in the family can do it. Just me.'

'That's an amazing gift for a cop,' Petra said.

'It does come in handy,' Carol admitted. 'So you see, there's never any fear that I'm going to be exposed wearing a wire. Because I don't need one.'

'I *thought* your written report was very comprehensive,' Petra said.

'Only trouble is, it takes forever to transcribe.' Carol rolled over on to her stomach. 'Thanks for sorting out an apartment for Tony in my building.'

'It was the least I could do after you arranged for him to come over and help us. He doesn't waste any time, does he?'

Carol smiled. 'He's very driven. When he commits to something, he sleeps, eats and breathes it.'

'I just hope that together we can come up with something before he kills again.' Petra clenched her hands into fists. 'I'm starting to take this very personally.'

Krasic walked into the Einstein Café just off Unter den Linden and scanned the room. He saw Tadeusz sitting alone in one of the wooden booths beyond the bar counter. He shouldered his way past staff and customers and slid in opposite his boss. Tadeusz looked up and gave him a preoccupied smile. 'Hi, Darko,' he said. 'How was the trip?'

The noise level in the café was high enough to

make their booth as private as Tadeusz's sitting room. Krasic shrugged out of his overcoat and made a circle with the thumb and forefinger of his right hand. 'Sweet,' he said. 'I don't know, you'd think every fucker in the Balkans who wanted a gun would have half a dozen by now, but their appetite's endless.' The waiter approached and Krasic ordered a black coffee and a large Jack Daniels. 'There are a couple of nutters looking for something more serious. I said I'd see what we could do.'

'We've got that shipment coming in from our friends in the east next week. There should be something there to satisfy them,' Tadeusz said. 'Nice work, Darko.'

'Oh, and I checked with my cousin – Marlene's kid is still tucked up tight. No sign of anyone looking for her out there. Everything quiet at this end?' the Serb asked, wondering what was on his boss's mind, hoping nothing else had gone up in smoke in his absence.

'Yes, no problems at all.' Tadeusz stirred his hot chocolate, the lines between his eyebrows deepening. 'But something very strange happened to me last night.'

Krasic was suddenly on the alert, like a guard dog who senses the air has changed. 'What's that?'

'I was at the opera. And a woman came to my box at the first interval.'

'Most blokes would see that as a welcome distraction from all that screaming.'

'I don't think this is grounds for humour, Darko,' Tadeusz chided him. 'This woman was English. Her name is Caroline Jackson. She claims to have known Colin Osborne. She says she was about to do some

322

business with him when he was killed. She also says she can step into his shoes and do a better job of dealing with our illegals at that end.'

'Sounds like good news to me, if she is who she says she is. Did you get enough details to check her out?'

'I made a couple of calls last night, and she seems to be on the level. And I met her again today and got a lot more out of her. But I want her turned over top to bottom before we even think about doing any business with her.'

'You don't trust her?' Krasic scowled.

'I trust her far too much, Darko. That's the dangerous thing.'

Krasic looked bemused. 'I don't get it.'

Tadeusz opened the silver case sitting in front of him and drew out a cigar. He took his time clipping and lighting it. Krasic waited, the years having taught him that his boss couldn't be budged until he was good and ready. An unreadable expression crossed Tadeusz's face, then he said, 'She's Katerina's double.'

The waiter arrived with Krasic's order, temporarily silencing him. He took a mouthful of Jack Daniels while he wondered how to react. Had his boss finally lost it? 'What do you mean?' he stalled.

'Exactly what I say. She could be Katerina's twin. I nearly had a heart attack when she walked into my box last night. I thought I was seeing a ghost till she opened her mouth and this English voice came out. So you see, Darko, I can't be responsible for making any decisions about whether we trust this woman or not. Because every time I look at her, my heart stops.'

'Shit.' Krasic poured the rest of his drink into his

coffee and drained half of it in one. 'You sure you're not suffering from some kind of delusion?'

'No. That's why I arranged to see her again today, to confirm that I wasn't dreaming. But it's not just me she freaks out. I saw the way people's heads were turning last night outside the Staatsoper and today at lunch. Like they couldn't believe their eyes. It's a complete mind fuck, Darko.'

'So you want me to check her out?'

'Till the pips squeak.' Tadeusz reached into his inside pocket and drew out an envelope. 'Inside here, there's an Italian passport she gave me as proof that she can do the business. Also, her address in Berlin. I got the car to take her home last night. And I've made a note of everything I can remember that she told me about herself. I want you to find out all you can about her. Either this is the weirdest fucking coincidence or else there's something very dangerous going on here. Find out which one it is, Darko.'

'I'm on it already, boss.' Krasic finished his drink and slid to the edge of the booth, gathering his coat as he went. 'If she's dodgy, we'll nail her. Don't you worry about it.'

Tadeusz nodded, satisfied. He watched Krasic leave, butting through the crowd like a bull with a destiny. Darko would sort it out. Either Caroline Jackson was up to something shady. Or else she was possibly, just possibly his salvation.

The Rhine was in spate. The skipper of the *Wilhelmina Rosen* stood on the massive steps of the Deutsches Eck monument at the confluence of the Rhine and the Mosel and glared at the racing brown flood tide, now closed to commercial traffic. If he was honest, he'd been expecting it. These days, it was a regular spring occurrence, not like in his youth. Global warming, he supposed. But it felt like another element in a giant conspiracy to thwart him.

He'd planned to get as far as Köln that afternoon and moor up in the basin just off the main river. Instead they were stuck here at Koblenz. For the first time in his life, he felt oppressed by living at close quarters with two other men. He'd suggested to Manfred and Gunther that they might as well go home for a few days, since the river showed no sign of falling and there was nothing useful for them to do on board. He'd even offered to pay them for the days they were gone. But neither had felt like taking him up on his proposal.

Gunther kept pointing out monotonously that it was a bloody long way from Koblenz to Hamburg and by the time they got there, it would be time to come back, and none of this would have happened if they'd been working the Oder and the Elbe, where they'd have practically been on their own doorstep.

Manfred didn't want to go because he was enjoying himself too much. With so many boats marooned there, he was in his element. He could sit around in bars all day and half the night, swapping stories with other boatmen. His capacity for drink was legendary, and he didn't often get the chance to indulge it like this, his wife being a woman who believed that when her man was in his home port, home was where he should be.

So he was stuck with the pair of them, driving him mad with their conversations as they compared notes about where they'd been, who they'd seen, what gossip they'd picked up and where they were going next. All he wanted was peace and quiet, the chance to restore his equilibrium after Bremen. He wanted to be alone so nobody would ask him why he was buying all the papers every day and scanning their columns for details of one story in particular. With Gunther and Manfred underfoot, the only way he could search the news to see if he'd been seen and described was to read the papers on-line. Once his crewmen had realized he wasn't spending his time on the internet looking at porn, they'd lost all interest.

Even with this access to the news, he still worried. Sometimes stories didn't make it into the on-line editions. Sometimes only an abbreviated version of the story was published electronically. And even if he was getting all that was available in the public domain, it didn't mean that they weren't looking for him. Only that they hadn't made it public. They might be combing the country with his description. At the very least, they must know what car he was driving. He wondered if he should sell the Golf immediately, trade it in for another make and model. But if there was a search out for a black VW Golf with Hamburg plates, he would only be drawing attention to himself by getting rid of it.

He was in a dreadful state. He couldn't sleep for more than half an hour at a time. Food stuck in his throat. The incident in Bremen had been petrifying, not least because he had never seriously considered the prospect of being caught. He had outsmarted those clever bastards with their degrees and diplomas, he had shown them he was master. He couldn't believe he'd so nearly been snared.

He'd been so careful. Everything had been planned, right down to the last detail. After all, if his campaign were to be cut short, his message would be lost and it would all have been wasted. That stupid woman had almost destroyed everything because she hadn't told her boyfriend to stay away. Stupid fucking bitch. Probably wanted to show off the fact that she could still get a man at her age. The cow had nearly ruined everything, and he had no idea whether he was in the clear or not.

In his good moments, he reassured himself that there was nothing the boyfriend could have told the police that would lead them to him. He was sure he hadn't been seen, and there must be hundreds of thousands of black VW Golfs all over Germany, even supposing the boyfriend had remembered what kind of car had been sitting in the whore's drive.

But in his bad moments, he lay on his bunk, his body secreting the rancid sweat of pure fear. It wasn't prison he was afraid of. Nothing that could happen to him there could be worse than what had already happened to him.

What he was afraid of was the things failure would tell him about himself.

And so, in order to combat the terror that was eating him from the inside, he refused to allow himself to use the river as an excuse. He had made an appointment in the usual way with Dr Marie-Thérèse Calvet, flattering her in e-mail and stressing her importance to the reputation of his e-zine: Your work on the manipulation of memory using deep hypnotic suggestion is unrivalled in Europe. Your 1999 study on the alteration of recollection of early sexual experience was groundbreaking. I'd be fascinated to hear about your follow-up studies. It would make a terrific special feature for our launch edition. No, it hadn't taken much persuasion to get her to agree to be interviewed. Like all of them, she was infested with narcissism, a trait he could use as a weapon against her.

But now he had to make a success of tonight's business. Dr Marie-Thérèse Calvet had wanted to meet in a restaurant, perhaps because she was reluctant to allow a strange man into the privacy of her home, or perhaps because she just wanted to screw a free meal out of him, he thought cynically. They had compromised with an agreement to conduct the interview in her office at the university, thanks to his argument that she might want to be in a position to refer to her research materials. It wasn't ideal, but at least in the evening there wouldn't be many people around to notice him.

The one thing he was worried about was the water supply. The chances were that Dr Calvet wouldn't have a sink in her office. And he couldn't really wander through a university department with buckets of water. He knew from experience, however, that it took remarkably little to drown his victims. So he had packed four one-and-a-half-litre bottles of Spa in his holdall. It made it heavy to carry, but years of hard physical labour had made him strong. And he'd asked Dr Calvet about parking. She'd told him that at that time in the evening, he could easily park on either of the streets that flanked the Psychology Institute. It shouldn't be too arduous.

The journey passed more quickly than he would have believed possible. Running over his plans always shrank time, he'd found that out in the past few months. The images of what he would do to Marie-Thérèse Calvet were better distraction by far than any kind of in-car entertainment. Before he knew it, he was on the outskirts of Köln, the main artery from Koblenz delivering him right to the inner ring road, a short distance from the university. He checked his street map and navigated his way to Robert Koch Strasse. From there, it took him only a couple of minutes to reach the institute building. Luckily, Calvet had been efficient with her directions, and he didn't have to stop and ask anyone the way to her office.

The corridor wasn't quite empty. A couple of students were walking towards him, deep in conversation. With the self-absorption of the young, they didn't even glance at him as he passed, his head angled down and away from them to minimize the chances of them being able to describe him afterwards. After Bremen, even so casual an encounter was enough to set his pulse fluttering and quicken his breath.

He counted the doors. Fourth on the left, she'd said. He stopped outside the plain wooden door and read the nameplate: DR M-T CALVET. He took a deep breath and held it, trying to force his previous state of calm to return. He raised his hand and knocked once, firmly. 'Come in,' he heard, the high pitch of the voice slightly muffled.

He opened the door and led with his head, his smile stretched to breaking point. 'Dr Calvet? I'm Hans Hochenstein.' He continued into the room, fixing his eyes on the woman emerging from behind the desk.

She was tiny. She couldn't have been more than five feet tall, with a fine-boned gamine face. Her chestnut hair was cut close to her head, and she wore an outfit of smartly casual top and capri pants, which he recognized from the old movies Gunther loved to watch as an homage to Audrey Hepburn. Unfortunately, he thought, she didn't have the eyes to carry it off. Dr Calvet's dark eyes were small, set close against the narrow bridge of her nose, making her look slightly cross rather than carefree and vulnerable. She held out a slim, bony hand to him, and he took it gently, enveloping it in what suddenly felt like an excess of damp, sweaty flesh.

'I'm pleased to meet you, Mr Hochenstein. Please, take a seat.' She gestured towards a pair of armchairs on either side of a wall-mounted gas fire.

He would have to move fast because there was no knowing how long they would be left alone. In order to get behind her, he stepped to one side and gave a courteous bow. 'After you, doctor.'

Her mouth and eyebrows quirked in an ironic smile and she passed in front of him. His hand flashed in and out of his jacket pocket, emerging with the heavy cosh. She must have registered some movement, for she half-turned as his arm descended in a swift arc towards her head. He had meant to hit her firmly on the back of the head, but caught her on the temple. She staggered and moaned, but didn't go down. Instead, she stumbled towards him. Panicked, he raised the sap again and smashed it down on the crown of her head. This time, she crumpled in an awkward heap at his feet. He gasped in relief, his head swimming. After what had happened with Schilling, even the slightest glitch was enough to provoke the momentary clutch of terror in his chest. But it was fine, he told himself. Everything was fine.

He crossed to the door and flipped the catch, locking them in. Then he hurried to the desk and swept all the books and papers to the floor in an untidy heap. He turned to Dr Calvet and bent to pick her up. She was light as a child in his arms, which was a welcome change from his first three victims. He laid her on her back on the desk and took the cords from his holdall. It was the work of moments to fasten her wrists and ankles tightly to the metal feet. He flicked up an eyelid with his thumb. She was still out cold. No need to gag her. He was back in control.

He took his grandfather's cut-throat razor from its case and painstakingly cut her clothes away. There was scarcely a scrap of flesh on her bones. If he'd felt inclined, he could have run his fingers over her ribs like the beads on an abacus. He stepped back for a moment, savouring her exposed defencelessness.

Suddenly he felt desire well up inside him, a richness in his blood that made him almost dizzy. Until now, he'd always refused to acknowledge that the surge of adrenaline-fuelled urgency that swept through him when confronted with his victims had anything to do with sex. There was no place for carnal desire here. Sex was for afterwards.

But perhaps he'd been wrong. He took a deep breath, noticing the citrus tang of her perfume overlaying the more human scent of her naked flesh. Why settle for low-life whores when he could take what he wanted from his victims? Didn't they deserve that final humiliation, to be fucked over like they'd fucked over their own victims?

His hand crept to his fly, his fingers hesitant on the zip. Suddenly, his grandfather's voice was loud in his head, his taunts blocking every other thought. *'Call yourself a man? What's keeping you, little boy? Scared of a woman who can't even fight back? All you're good for is dockside whores like your mother.'* He bit back a sob. Now his desire was insistent, impossible to ignore. He'd show the old man. He reached inside his jacket and pulled out the packet of condoms he'd been saving for later. Eagerly, he ripped open the foil package. He smoothed the latex over his erection, his craving making him ham-fisted. Then he was on top of her, thrusting clumsily against her dryness.

She stirred. Her eyelids flickered, showing the whites of her eyes. It didn't matter now. He was in control. There was nothing she could do. He gripped her by the throat, gasping as his climax approached more swiftly than he would have believed possible. He could see her oesophagus spasm as she fought for air, but he continued relentlessly.

Now her chest was heaving, the lungs fighting to snatch some oxygen to keep the heart pumping. Her eyes were bulging, tiny pinpricks of red blossoming in the whites. Her animal panic was wonderful to see, because it was all down to him. Suddenly her body went limp, and he came immediately, his spine arching in a violent spasm. The release was like a veil lifting from his mind.

What had he done? He'd blown it. He'd killed her already, and he hadn't completed his task.

Furious with himself, he rolled off the table and

stood leaning on his fists, his breathing ragged. What was he thinking of? He had a plan, a mission, and he'd failed. He'd killed her, but in the wrong way. A wave of despair washed through him. The old man had been right. He was a pathetic failure, a poor excuse for a man.

He stared down at her body, cursing himself for a fucking fool. Then he noticed a tiny flicker of movement in her throat. Was it a pulse? He reached out tentatively. His fingers felt the faint beat of blood. It was going to be all right.

Hastily, he reached into the holdall and raced through his final preparations. After he poured the third bottle down the funnel rammed into her throat, he checked her pulse points. No question about it. She had paid the price.

He picked up the razor again and considered his target area. She had a compact, dark bush, shot through with occasional coarse grey hairs. He'd never cut a woman before Margarethe Schilling and it had taken a little more thought. But now his was a practised hand. He made his first incision across the top, where the pale skin of her flat stomach disappeared under the hair. Then he made two further incisions at an angle down the side of the mound of Venus. Delicately, he teased the edge of the razor under the skin, gently peeling it back from the flesh below. It was easier every time, his movements more assured. Where her body began to curve downwards towards the labia, he made a straight cut across the skin and lifted the scalp on the blade of the razor, leaving a raw scarlet trapezoid oozing blood. He unscrewed the jar he'd brought with him and slid his trophy into the formalin, relishing the swirl of red fading to pink as the blood washed clear of the skin. He smiled beatifically, then fastened the jar. Then he began to clear up. The last act was to take out a handkerchief and rub down everything he had touched, including her skin. Finally, wrapping the handkerchief round his fingers, he took a slim folder from his bag and crossed to the filing cabinets. He slid the file into place under the letter C. His case notes on the bitch were safely in place.

The job was done. And done better than ever before. He was the master now, no question of that.

Case Notes

Name: Marie-Thérèse Calvet

Session Number: 1

Comments: The patient presents with a lack of respect for other human beings. Her self-importance blinds her to the needs and rights of others. She sees herself as the centre of her own universe to whom everyone else should defer. Other people exist purely for the furtherance of her own desires.

That she has attained her position in her chosen field is a tribute to her ruthless pursuit of her own desires to the detriment of others. She attempts to negate her femininity with an approach to her work that is aggressively masculine. She is reluctant to concede the contribution of others to her work, invariably claiming credit for herself. She lacks affect or empathy.

Therapeutic Action: Altered state therapy initiated.

25

Darko Krasic supposed he had better things to do than sit outside an apartment block off the Ku'damm waiting for a woman. On the other hand, time spent preventing his boss from making a fucking fool of himself had to be time well spent. It had been bad enough when Tadzio had wanted to show his face on the front line. Look where that had got them. Krasic had to set up an assassination *and* childcare, and he knew which was harder of those two to manage.

While wanting to be involved at the sharp end of his own business was almost understandable, seeing mirages was the kind of thing that got a man a bad name, especially in their line of business. A little megalomania was fine, some degree of paranoia almost obligatory in the circles where Krasic and his boss made their money. But seeing the features of the dead on the face of a stranger definitely fell into the dangerously demented category. If Krasic didn't nip this in the bud, before he knew it they'd be signing up for séances. They would become a laughing stock. Which he needed right now like he needed a hole in the head, what with those crazy Albanians wanting ground-to-air missiles and the Chinese Snakehead gangs agitating about shipments of illegal immigrants and heroin.

He shifted in the seat of the anonymous Opel he'd chosen for his surveillance. It wasn't designed for anyone with shoulders, he thought. Fine for skinny intellectuals, but not for real men. Half past ten and no sign of anyone answering the description Tadzio had given him. He'd been there since half past seven, and nobody who looked remotely like Katerina had gone in or out.

Shame about Katerina, he thought. She'd been a bit special. Not a brainless bimbo by any means, but, equally, not one of those smart-mouthed tarts who thought it was clever to try to put a man like him in his place. Lovely looking girl, too. Best thing about her, though, was that she'd kept Tadzio happy. And Tadzio happy was Tadzio on the ball. But right now, the boss was very definitely neither happy nor on top of his game. Eventually, he'd have to accept that the accident had been nothing more than that. Until that happened, Krasic saw a lot more wasted time ahead of him.

On that thought, the door of the apartment block opened and Krasic's jaw dropped. If he hadn't seen Katerina's dead body with his own eyes, he'd have sworn that was her emerging on to the street. OK, the hair was different and he thought this woman had a bit more muscle about her than Katerina had ever had, but from this distance, he couldn't have told them apart. 'Fuck,' he said, outraged. That'd teach him to take Tadzio's word for things.

He was so astounded by what he was seeing that he almost forgot what he was there for. She was already well past him before he gathered himself together and clambered out of the car. She was walking at a good clip, long legs in sensible flat pumps covering the ground confidently. Krasic had to shift to keep her in sight as she reached the corner of Olivaerplatz and turned right.

As he reached the corner, he realized she had stopped at a news kiosk. He mingled with the handful of people waiting for the lights to change while she bought an English newspaper. Then she carried on to the café further along the street. Optimistically, the patron had put out a handful of tables on the pavement, but it was still too early in the spring for most Berliners to fancy their chances outside. Like them, Caroline Jackson went inside.

Krasic hesitated. She might be meeting someone, she might be making phone calls. He didn't want to draw attention to himself this early in the game, but he couldn't let it go. He walked briskly past the café, registering that about half the tables were occupied. Enough of a crowd to hide in, probably. He stood moodily staring into a shop window for five minutes by his watch, then walked back to the café. He took a seat at the counter, where he could see the back of her head. He quite liked the idea of not having to see her face. It was too fucking spooky by half to look at somebody who resembled so closely someone you knew to be dead.

She was doing nothing more sinister than reading her newspaper and drinking black coffee. He ordered an espresso and a Jack Daniels and made them last. Thirty-five minutes later, she folded her paper into her bag, paid her bill and walked out. Krasic, who had already settled his tab, was close enough behind her to see which way she went. *Heading for the Ku'damm*, he thought miserably. Women and shops. What was it about them?

Two hours later, he was still on her tail. She'd been in and out of half a dozen clothes shops, thumbing through the designer racks. She'd bought a couple of classical CDs in a record store and spoken to no one except shop assistants. It had done his head in comprehensively. Not to mention making him feel as out of place as a cherry on a dungheap. He was going to have to get somebody else to keep an eye on her, that much was clear. Ideally, a woman. But failing that, one of those lads who were more interested in Armani than Armalites.

He trailed behind her as she turned into the street where she was staying and watched as she went back into the apartment block. Well, that had been a proper waste of a morning. She was due to meet Tadzio in an hour, so he reckoned nothing much was going to happen between now and then. Time enough to get someone else on the case. Krasic got back into the Opel and took out his phone. If there was anything dodgy about Caroline Jackson, he'd find out. But someone else could do the legwork from now on.

Petra Becker was rising in Tony's estimation all the time. She'd rung him at 9.17 to tell him that a car was on its way to take him to Tempelhof for the short flight to Bremen, where he would be met by one of the detectives on the Schilling inquiry. 'How the hell did you swing that?' he said, still groggy from lack of sleep.

'I lied,' she said calmly. 'I said you were a leading

British Home Office profiler who just happened to be doing some work with Europol and that we would be very much obliged if they would extend every courtesy to you.'

'You're an amazing woman, Petra,' he said.

'It's been said before, but not usually by men,' she'd responded dryly.

'Am I right in thinking that nobody in Bremen has made the connection with the earlier murder in Heidelberg yet?'

'The Heidelberg boys were so eager to hand off their unsolved murder to us, they sold it to the local press as a seedy drug-related murder rather than a ritual killing, so it didn't make headlines outside the region. I'd be very surprised if anyone in Bremen had even read a news report about the case.'

'Doesn't it feel weird, being the only cop in the country who's made the connection?' He couldn't resist the chance to probe. He'd never been able to.

'You want the honest truth?'

'Of course.'

'I get a buzz from it. Oh, I know I have to come back inside the rules with these cases, I can't go on acting like somebody in a movie. For now, though, I'm enjoying it. But I don't think we have time for this. You have a plane to catch.'

Tony smiled. It was an obvious evasion, but he didn't mind. 'Thanks for sorting it out.'

'My pleasure. Have a good day. We'll talk soon, yes?'

'I should have something for you before too long, but don't expect a miracle,' he said, guarded.

She laughed. 'I don't believe in miracles.'

The detective who met him at Bremen was a stumpy blond in his early thirties with bad skin and excellent English who announced himself as, 'Berndt Haefs, call me Berndt.' He had the slightly blasé air of someone who is incapable of being shocked. Tony had seen it in cops before. What worried him was that it was generally neither a pose nor a defence mechanism, but rather indicative of a blunting of the sensibilities that destroyed any capacity for empathy.

Certainly Berndt showed no signs of caring much about the woman whose death he was supposed to be resolving, referring to her throughout their drive to Bremen as 'Schilling'. Tony, perversely, made a point of always giving Margarethe her title of Doctor.

They approached the city via a wide bridge over the swollen Weser, which flowed past in a swift torrent the colour of beer slops. 'The river's very high,' Tony said to fill the lull that had grown in the conversation once Berndt had run out of nuggets of largely irrelevant information about the murder.

'It's not as bad as the Rhine or the Oder,' Berndt said. 'I don't think it's going to flood.'

'What about the barges? How do they cope?'

'Well, they can't cope, can they? Haven't got the horsepower to deal with it when it's flowing like that. If it gets any higher, the river will be closed till the water level subsides. That's already happened on the Rhine. The boats are all tied up in basins and back-waters. The skippers will be tearing their hair out at the thought of the money they're losing, and the crews are all getting drunk.'

'Not much fun for the local cops, then.'

Berndt shrugged. 'It keeps them off the street,' he

said with a high-pitched giggle at odds with his squat frame. 'That's the cathedral over there,' he added with a degree of redundancy. It was impossible to miss the twin towers. 'Schilling was in the city centre the afternoon of the day she died. She ate alone in a little bar off the main market square.'

'Are we far from Dr Schilling's house?' Tony asked.

'About ten minutes.'

'Has her partner been able to remember anything about his attacker?'

'The boyfriend? About as much use as a eunuch in a brothel. He didn't see anything, didn't hear anything. All he knows is that there was a strange car on the drive. A VW Golf, either black or dark blue. I mean, he didn't even notice if it was a local registration. Have you any idea how many black or dark blue Golfs there are in Bremen alone?'

'Quite a few, I should imagine.'

Berndt snorted. 'So many we can't even think about pursuing that line of inquiry.' He turned off the main road into a quiet tree-lined street. 'This is the start of the suburb where she lived. Our man would have had to drive in this way, it's the only logical way in and out.'

Tony looked out of the window, imagining the street in darkness. Houses set back behind small, neat lawns. Private lives going on behind closed front doors. No reason why anyone should pay attention to the dark outline of a car making its way to a fateful destination. He wondered if the killer had scouted the area out ahead of his crime. Often they did, staking out their ground, stalking their victim, learning their lives, getting to know the gap that their deaths would leave. But he had a feeling that Geronimo wasn't that kind of killer. His need was of a different order.

Tony pictured him nosing down the darkened streets, making sure he was taking the correct turns. It was a complicated route with lots of potential to end up at the blind end of a cul-de-sac. 'I wonder if he lost his way? Annoyed somebody by turning round in their driveway?'

Bernd looked at him as if he was mad. 'You think we should do a door-to-door to see if he pissed anybody off?'

'Probably pointless,' Tony agreed. 'But you never know. People can be very possessive about their property, especially if strangers make a habit of using their drive as a turning circle.'

Berndt had the expression on his face that Tony had seen from cops before. It was the physical manifestation of the thought that went something like, *Fucking shrinks, haven't got a clue about police work.* He resolved to keep his mouth shut and save his ideas for Petra and Carol.

The car turned into a small road of a dozen houses that dead-ended in a tarmac semi-circle. They pulled into the drive of a house identical to every other in the road, save for the police tapes across the front door. 'This is it.' Berndt got out of the car and headed for the house without waiting to see if Tony was behind him.

Tony stood by the car for a moment, looking at the other houses in the street. Anyone glancing out of any of a dozen windows could have seen him clearly. 'You're not afraid of being seen, are you, Geronimo? You don't mind if somebody catches a glimpse of you.

You think you're so insignificant they won't remember anything about you.' Nodding in satisfaction, he followed Berndt, impatient in the doorway, foot tapping and arms folded.

They walked in, both automatically attempting to wipe their feet on a doormat that wasn't there. 'Forensic took it away. Like they're going to find some rare mud that only exists in a particular quarry somewhere in the Ruhr,' Berndt said sarcastically. 'It happened through here.' He led the way to the kitchen.

Under the film of fingerprint dust, it all looked surprisingly domesticated. Tony even remembered the table. They'd sat around it discussing the possibilities of writing a paper together, drinking endless cups of coffee and glasses of cheap red wine. The thought that it had become the stage for Margarethe's death made him feel queasy. He prowled around the room, taking in its neat order. It didn't look like the scene of a brutal murder. There was no visible sign of blood, nor were there any of the smells associated in his mind with violent death. It was impossible to imagine this mundane kitchen as the location for so deliberately violent an act.

'Nothing much to see,' Berndt said. 'Most murders look like a slaughterhouse. But this? Clean up the print powder and you could do dinner for six.'

'Any indication that he went anywhere else in the house?'

'Nothing was disturbed, according to the boyfriend. So no, he didn't go through her knicker drawer and wank on the bedspread, if that's what you're getting at.'

Tony could think of nothing polite to say in response. Instead, he went to the window and looked down the garden to the woods beyond.

'Nothing there either,' Berndt offered. 'We checked to see if he'd been watching her from the woods, but there was no sign that anybody had been near the back fence.'

'I don't think he stalked her. Not physically, anyway. It was her mind that interested him, not her physical presence,' Tony said, half to himself. He turned back and smiled at Berndt. 'Thanks for bringing me out here. You're right, there's nothing much to see.'

'Detective Becker said you wanted to look at the crime-scene photographs. Is that right?'

Tony nodded. 'If that's possible.'

'They're running an extra set off for you. We'll have to go down to headquarters to collect them. And then, if there's nothing else, I can drive you back to the airport. There's a flight just after two, but if we don't make that, there's another one an hour later.' No offer of lunch, Tony noted. Co-operation with Europol clearly only went so far.

'That would be fine.' He smiled. 'I look forward to being back in Berlin in time for tea.'

Berndt looked at him as if he had just confirmed everything he thought about the eccentric English. Which was exactly what Tony had intended. If Berndt was going to remember anything about this visit, better that than anything else.

Petra bounced into the squad room on the balls of her feet. So far, the operation against Radecki was

346

going to plan. And she had great expectations of what this morning would bring. Even the sight of The Shark staring gloomily into a computer screen wasn't enough to dampen her good spirits.

'What are you doing?' she said, crossing to her desk. 'I thought I told you to check out Krasic's associates?'

He looked up, his narrow pinched face expressing indignation. 'That's what I'm doing,' he said. 'Somebody told me that Krasic has relatives around the city, and I'm trying to track them down through official records. With something like this, Krasic might trust family more than his fellow crims.'

It wasn't a bad idea. Petra was both surprised and impressed. Maybe they were going to make a cop out of him yet. 'Good thinking,' she said. 'Any joy?'

'Not so far. I'm having to cross-check all sorts of stuff, it takes ages. How's your operation going?'

'Fine.' She booted up her computer and headed straight for the Europol section of their database. This was where any bulletins from Den Haag ended up. To her satisfaction, there was a message with that morning's dateline.

'You want a coffee?' The Shark asked.

'Are you making fresh?'

'I suppose so.'

'Then I'll have one.' She opened up the bulletin. There was some boring admin stuff at the beginning. She scrolled through it and halfway down the second page she found what she was looking for. *REQUEST FOR INFORMATION FROM POLICE IN REGIO LEIDEN, HOLLAND*, she read. 'Yes,' she hissed softly.

It was short and straightforward:

*Detectives in Leiden, Holland, investigating a murder
are concerned that the killer may be a possible serial
offender. They have asked us to circulate member forces
with details of the offence with a view to comparing
any similar crimes in other jurisdictions. The victim
was Pieter de Groot, a professor of psychology at the
University of Leiden. His body was found in his home,
bound and naked. He had been tied to the desk in his
study, on his back. His clothes had been cut away from
him. The cause of death was drowning. The method
appears to have been by insertion of a funnel or tube
into the mouth, into which water was poured. There
was post-mortem mutilation, which took the form of
the scalping of the victim's pubic area. The genitals
themselves were undamaged.*

*Member forces of Europol are requested to check
their files of unsolved homicides to see if there are any
similar offences outstanding in their jurisdictions.
Information should be passed directly to Hoofdinspecteur Kees Maartens at Regio Leiden, with a copy
to the Europol Intelligence Section.*

Petra couldn't help smiling in satisfaction. She was
rereading the text when The Shark loomed up at her
elbow. 'What's that, then?' he asked, placing the mug
by her left hand.

'Europol bulletin,' she said.

'You're the only person I know who bothers with
that bumf.'

'That's why I'm the only one around here who's
going places, Shark.'

He leaned over her shoulder, reading the bulletin.
'Wow. That sounds nasty. Typical of the Dutch,

though. Too dumb to solve their own murders so they try to play pass the parcel with them.'

Petra scowled. 'You couldn't be more wrong. It's extremely smart of the Dutch to read the message of this crime and understand that this has all the hall-marks of a potential serial offender. And very coura-geous of them to ask for help.'

'You think?'

She tapped a key to print out the relevant page of the bulletin. 'I don't think, I know. And you know what's most interesting about this murder, Shark?'

'I'm about to find out, right?' He moved to one side and perched on the edge of her desk.

'You should know already. Because we're *all* supposed to read the stuff that is referred to us by our regional colleagues here in Germany. Just like we're *all* supposed to read whatever Europol sends us.'

He rolled his eyes back in his head and groaned. 'Yeah, yeah. Look, I skim it, OK?'

'Sure, we all do that sometimes. But there's stuff in there that we should be paying attention to. Like a murder five weeks ago in Heidelberg? Ring any bells?'

He frowned. 'Some small-time drug dealer, wasn't it?'

'That was their excuse for handing it on to us. But it was obvious that it wasn't a drugs hit.'

'That'd be why I didn't pay much attention,' The Shark interrupted defensively. 'No interest to us.'

'Murder should always interest a cop. I did read it, Shark. And that's what makes me think that the man who killed in Leiden had done it before in Heidelberg.

349

And he's done it since in Bremen.' She got busy with the mouse and pulled up the Leiden report, then sent a command to the printer to make a hard copy of the file. 'Which is why I am going to earn myself some Brownie points by bringing it to the attention of the boss.' She got to her feet, picking up her coffee, and walked across to the common printer. She gathered together the sheets of paper and waved cheerfully to The Shark. 'Don't let me keep you from Krasic,' she offered as a parting shot.

She found Plesch in her office, going through expenses claims. She gave Petra a grateful smile. 'Petra. Bringing me facts, instead of these fictions, I hope?'

She shrugged and dropped into the chair facing Plesch. 'More speculation than hard fact, I'm afraid.'

'Oh well, never mind. It's still a welcome distraction. What's on your mind?'

She placed the print-outs in front of her boss. 'Europol bulletin this morning. The Dutch police are looking for possible connections to a murder they've got in Leiden. It so happens that I was reviewing unsolved murders last week, in the run-up to this undercover operation. Just to see if there were any we might be looking to connect to Radecki and Krasic. I came across a case in Heidelberg that looked vaguely promising, so I asked them to send me a full report. When I went through it, it was clearly not one of ours. But then when I read the details of the Dutch murder, all the bells started ringing. I checked it out, and there are some very striking points of similarity.'

Plesch picked up the papers and read them, her expression deepening to a frown as she noted the common ground between the two cases. 'Jesus Christ,' she said when she got to the end.

'There's more,' Petra continued. 'There's been another murder in Bremen. I pulled the files on it because it reminded me of the case in Heidelberg. The MO is identical.'

Plesch raised her eyebrows. 'The same weird, fucked-up bastard?'

'Looks like it. So what do we do?'

Plesch shrugged. 'We get on to Heidelberg. It looks like that's Case Zero. They probably haven't read their Europol bulletin out there in the sticks. They'll have to liaise with this Dutch cop through Europol. And talk to the people in Bremen.' She blew a breath out through pursed lips. 'Rather them than me. What a nightmare. All that red tape and diplomacy.'

'Couldn't we keep hold of it?' Petra asked.

'On what basis? It's not organized crime, it's not our remit.'

'We made the connection. We're experts in intelligence analysis. We're used to working with Europol.'

'You're kidding me, right? As if you haven't got enough on your plate with Radecki. Come on, Petra, this isn't our kind of thing, and you know it. Let me call the chief investigator on the case in Heidelberg and set the ball rolling. You've done a good job, spotting this. But you've got to let it go now.'

Before Petra could argue further, the door burst open without ceremony and The Shark stood there, pink-faced and bright-eyed. 'Sorry to butt in, ma'am,' he gabbled. 'But this case that Petra showed me the bulletin about – something's just come in on the wire. It looks like there's another one. Only in Köln this time.'

26

Petra had been right about the boat, Carol thought. This was no rich man's party toy. It was a wooden motor launch, perfectly proportioned, with a sloping roofed cabin amidships. Tadeusz told her he'd bought it as a virtual wreck because he'd fallen in love with its sleek clinker-built lines. He'd had it restored to its former glory, and now it was an immaculate museum piece that was as functional as when it had been built in the 1930s. Gleaming brasswork and polished mahogany caught the light wherever Carol looked in the small cabin. No space was wasted; the three-sided bench had slots for the table to drop into it, making a narrow double bed. The bulkheads had stowage space built in, using every nook and cranny without adversely affecting the elegant proportions of the compartment.

Above and behind the cabin, a tall, morose man leaned on the wheel, waiting for the word from Tadeusz to cast off. 'He doesn't speak more than two words of English,' Tadeusz had said as he helped her aboard. 'He's a Pole, like me. We're the best sailors in the world, you know.'

'I think we English might want to dispute that,' Carol said.

He inclined his head in rueful acknowledgement. Today, he looked nothing like the serious businessman she'd seen so far. Dressed in jeans and a thick fisherman's jersey, a woollen cap jammed over his hair, he resembled every other waterman she'd seen on the short walk from the car to the boat. Only his hands were a giveaway, smooth and uncalloused by hard work. 'Let me show you my boat,' he insisted, ushering her below. He stood back, waiting for her to take it in.

'She's a beauty,' Carol said, meaning it.

'I suspect she was built for someone quite high up in the Nazi party,' he admitted. 'But I've never researched it. I think I'd rather not know. It might spoil her for me if I knew too much about her past.'

'A bit like a lover, then,' Carol said, her wry smile taking any flirtatiousness out of the remark. The irony of his comment was not lost on her; that he too made his money from misery seemed blindingly obvious. For Tadeusz to paint himself as higher up the moral totem pole than the boat's putative original owner was, she thought, repugnant. Such ethical blindness would make it easier for her to play her devious game, however.

'I suppose,' he said, his answering glance amused. 'So, a drink? Then we'll go up on deck and I can play at being a tour guide.' He opened one of the wooden hatches and revealed a tiny fridge containing beer and champagne. 'It's too small for full-sized bottles,' he said apologetically, holding up a half-bottle of Perrier-Jouët. 'This OK?'

A few minutes later, they were sitting on the stern bench, champagne glasses in hand as the helmsman cruised gently out of the Rummelsbergersee into the broad reaches of the River Spree. 'Are we talking business today, or just getting to know each other better?' Carol asked.

'A bit of both. I wanted to show you the city from a different perspective, and I thought maybe you could tell me something more of your plans.'

Carol nodded. 'Sounds good to me.'

The boat swung left and turned into the mouth of a lock. As they waited to go through, Tadeusz told her tales of the commercial barges. How they'd shifted twenty thousand tonnes of rubble a day during the reconstruction of Potsdamer Platz. How a routine customs inspection had revealed a bargee's dead wife buried in the coal bunker. How the river police were called the duck police.

'You seem to know a lot about life on the waterways,' Carol said as they sailed on through Kreuzberg towards the Tiergarten. The trees that lined the canal were heavy with blossom, lending an air of romance to what was, after all, a commercial transport route.

'A certain amount of my business depends on the waterways,' he said cautiously. 'As you've discovered for yourself, I like to know who I'm dealing with, so I've talked to many *schippermen* over the years. Having the boat makes it easy for me to be among them for legitimate reasons.'

'Surely you don't cruise all over Europe? It would take ages.'

'Usually I have the boat lifted out of the water and towed to where I want it to be. Then I do a little cruising, and a little business.' He smiled. 'All very unsuspicious, no?'

'Very clever,' she acknowledged, pleased that her masquerade was finally beginning to produce some hard information.

He pointed out various landmarks as they continued along the canal and into the River Spree again. As they turned into the Westhafenkanal, Tadeusz waved his arm towards the right bank. 'This is Moabit. Not always the nicest part of Berlin, I'm afraid. There were some rough turf wars here between the Albanians and the Romanians, fighting over who got to run their prostitutes where. Low-life stuff, not the sort of thing that interests business people like us.'

'What interests me is supply and demand,' Carol said. 'You can supply me with what I need, and I can supply the paperwork they're paying for. For a price, of course.'

'Everything has a price.' Tadeusz stood up. 'Time for more champagne,' he said, disappearing below.

Damn, Carol thought. She was fed up with this. Not that he wasn't a charming and entertaining companion, but if she'd wanted a guided tour of Berlin, she could have climbed aboard an open-topped bus. It wasn't easy to sit back and appreciate the architecture when her survival required her never to let her guard drop. She wanted to cut to the chase, because the sooner they got down to business, the sooner this whole operation would be over and she could return to her own life.

Tadeusz returned with another half-bottle of champagne. 'OK. We have a little way to go before the next really scenic bit. So maybe you can tell me what it is you think I can do for you.'

Carol sat up straight, assuming the body language

of someone engaged in serious discourse. 'It's more what we can do for each other. Are you going to be straight with me this time, or are you still pretending you don't know what I'm talking about?'

He smiled. 'I'll be honest with you. I did make some preliminary inquiries to see if you were who you claimed to be.'

'As I did with you,' Carol interrupted. 'I wouldn't have made an approach to you if I hadn't taken a long, hard look at your professional pedigree. So, am I the woman I say I am?'

'So far, things have checked out. My associates are still asking around, but I'm someone who sets great store by gut reactions. And I have a good reaction to you, Caroline. You're clearly smart, you're cautious but you can be bold when that is what will get results.'

Carol made a mock salute with her glass. 'Thank you, kind sir. I'm glad to see we operate in the same way. Because, in spite of all the good things I'd heard about you, if I hadn't taken to you on that first meeting, I'd have disappeared into the night and you'd never have seen me again.'

He draped his arm along the stern rail, not quite touching her, but making a statement of physical closeness nevertheless. 'That would have been a pity.'

'It would have cost you a lot of hassle that I can save you,' she said, firmly bringing the conversation back to the purely professional. It didn't hurt her campaign if Radecki started to fall for her, but she had to play hard to get, to keep him at arm's length. She couldn't afford to let romance blossom to a point where it would start to seem odd that she wasn't sleeping with him. Even if she wanted to, which she reminded herself forcibly she did not, it would destroy her mission, devaluing everything she had found out about him and his business. If Radecki could demonstrate that they'd been to bed together, it would be a gift to a defence lawyer, turning her testimony from the reliable evidence of a respected police officer into the bitter revenge of a woman scorned. Besides, it would be utterly unprofessional. And Carol didn't do unprofessional.

'You think so?'

'I know so. You were delivering between twenty and thirty illegal immigrants a month to Colin Osborne. The only trouble was that Colin bullshitted you about what he could actually supply. He didn't have access to the kind of paperwork your customers were paying for. That's why he had to double-cross them before they realized he was bluffing.'

'I didn't know about this,' Tadeusz said.

'I don't suppose you did. This isn't a business where dissatisfied customers turn up at the Customer Services desk asking for their money back,' Carol said acidly. 'Once they were in the hands of the immigration people, they were either deported or stuck in detention centres. There was no way for them to contact whoever they'd paid their money to in the first place. And Colin was always clever enough to make sure the businesses they were working in couldn't be tracked back to his door. He used fake names to rent the premises, he always made sure any stock was cleared out before the raids happened. He didn't even lose the sewing machines. It was a shitty way of doing business.'

Tadeusz shrugged. 'I suppose he thought he was doing what he had to to survive.'

'You think so? That's not how I do business. If you're going to work outside the law, you need to be more honest than the straight people.'

He frowned. 'What do you mean?'

'If you operate in the straight world and you don't deliver what you promise, you maybe lose your job or your marriage, but mostly nothing truly terrible happens to you. But if you operate in our world and you let people down, sooner or later it costs you more than you're willing to pay. You sell fake drugs on street corners and you're going to take a beating, either from ripped-off customers or from other dealers. You double-cross your mates on a bank job and you're looking over your shoulder for the rest of your life.

'Take Colin. If he did the dirty on one deal, chances are he did it on others too. And look what happened to him. Head blown off on a dirt track in the middle of the Essex marshes. Now, I don't want that to happen to me, so when I do business with people, I do it honestly. And I expect the same from them.'

Tadeusz had drawn his arm back halfway through her speech. He was looking at her with a strange intensity, as if she was giving voice to his most deeply held beliefs. 'You've obviously thought a lot about this,' he said.

'I'm a survivor,' she said simply.

'I can see that.'

'Look, Tadzio, I'm a smart woman. I could have made a reasonable living in the straight world. But I didn't want to make a reasonable living. I wanted to make a lot of money. Enough money to stop when I was young enough to enjoy it. So I found a way to work outside the system. And I'm bloody good at it.

I try not to mix with other criminals unless I have to, I cover my tracks and I deliver on my promises. Now, are we going to do business?'

He shrugged. 'That depends.'

'On what?'

'On who killed Colin Osborne.' He raised his eyebrows.

She hadn't expected that, and she was afraid her face showed how startled she was by the question. 'What do you mean?'

'Colin's death was very opportune for you. And nobody seems to know what exactly happened to him. No one has claimed responsibility. Usually, when one villain takes out another, they're eager to capitalize on it. Respect, fear. You know how it works. So, Caroline, did you kill Colin?'

She didn't know what the right answer was. He could be bluffing. He could know more than he was letting on, and this was a test to see how far she'd go to earn his good opinion. He might want her to be the killer, as evidence that she was prepared to be ruthless. Or he might be put off dealing with her if she claimed the kill, uneasy that her way of dealing with the competition might rebound on him in the worst way. 'Why would I do that?' she stalled.

'To muscle in on his trade.'

She shrugged. 'Why would I need to take that route? All I'd have to do would be to come to you with a better deal. I suspect you could supply enough bodies to keep us both happy.'

'You didn't, though, did you? You didn't come near me till Colin was well out of the way.' There was a hard edge to his voice now, and his eyes had lost their warmth. 'That makes me suspicious, Caroline. That, and the fact you look so like Katerina. OK, Colin never met Katerina. But if he was halfway good at what he did, he would have checked me out. He would have seen photographs of Katerina at least. And then, when she died, maybe he thought this was the chance to set up some kind of sting using you to get to me. Only, you decided to eliminate the middle man.'

Carol was unnerved. He was wrong in almost every detail, but he was wrong in the right sort of way. Suddenly, they'd shifted from easy companionship to the edgy realm of suspicion. She didn't know what to do.

She set her glass down and stepped away from him, folding her arms across her chest. 'Let me off this boat.'

He frowned. 'What?'

'I don't have to listen to this shit. I came here in good faith to do business. I'm not going to stand here and take accusations of murder and conspiracy from you. Tell your man to let me off this boat, now. Unless you want me to start screaming?'

Tadeusz looked amused. 'You're overreacting.'

Carol let the flare of anger show in her face. 'Don't you dare patronize me. You're just another gangster, Tadzio. You've got no right to come the moral high ground with me. I don't have to account for anything to you. And I certainly don't want to do business with somebody who thinks I do. This is a waste of my precious time. Now let me off the boat, please.'

He took a step back, clearly unsettled by the vehemence of her reaction. He said something to the helmsman, and the boat veered towards a narrow wharf where a couple of launches were moored.

'Caroline, I didn't mean to offend you,' he said as she moved to the side of the boat nearest the wharf.

'And that's supposed to make me feel better?' The boat pulled alongside and, without waiting for the helmsman to tie up, Carol jumped ashore. 'Don't call,' she threw over her shoulder as she marched up the wharf towards a flight of stone steps. Her whole body was trembling as she reached street level. She checked that he wasn't following her, then stepped to the kerb to hail a cab.

She hoped she hadn't wrecked the operation. But she hadn't been able to think of anything else to do. His suspicions had come out of a blue sky, and she'd allowed herself to sink into complacency, so she hadn't been quick enough on her feet to talk him round. She sank back into the cab seat and prayed she'd got it right.

The small plane from Bremen to Berlin was configured with a single seat on one side of the aisle, which meant Tony could look with impunity at the crime scene pictures Berndt had handed him at police headquarters in Bremen. He took them out of the envelope with some trepidation. He wasn't looking forward to seeing the mutilated corpse of a woman he had been acquainted with. There was always something bizarrely intimate about poring over photographs of the dead, and he didn't want such familiarity with someone he had known in life.

In the event, it wasn't as bad as he had anticipated. The harsh glare of the flash had made the images of Margarethe's body impossible to connect with the lively woman he remembered. He studied the photos in detail, wishing he had brought a magnifying lens with him. To the naked eye, there seemed to be no significant differences between the body of Margarethe and Geronimo's other victims. They were all laid out in similar fashion, their clothes cut away to form an improbable table cover beneath them, the incongruous wound left by the scalping almost identical.

He was about to give up his perusal of the photographs when something caught his eye. There was something odd about one of the ligatures that bound Margarethe's limbs to the table legs. He peered harder, trying to make out the details. The knot looked different from the others.

Tony felt a faint surge of excitement. It might not seem much but, at this stage of an investigation, any deviation from the pattern carried potentially huge significance. And in this instance, it could be all the more important because this was the crime that had been interrupted. Under the stress provoked by that intrusion, Geronimo might have let his guard slip enough to provide a chink in his boilerplate security system.

He was in a fever of impatience to pick up his laptop and get back to Petra's. Of course, the taxi from Tempelhof seemed to take forever, finding every traffic hold-up in central Berlin. He let himself into the empty flat and made straight for the study and Petra's scanner. While he was waiting for his computer to ready itself, he took out the magnifying glass from his laptop case and studied the picture more closely. He went back through to the dining area and pulled out the other crime scene photographs. A few minutes with the magnifying glass and his heart rejoiced. He'd been right. All the knots on the ligatures appeared to be straightforward, common or garden reef knots, apart from the single exception in that one crucial Bremen photograph.

He returned to the study and plugged the scanner into his laptop's USB port. Minutes later, he was looking at an enlarged and enhanced section of the key picture. Tony knew nothing about knots, only that this one was different from the others. He connected to the internet and linked to a search engine, typing in <knots>. Within seconds, he had a list of websites devoted to the craft of knot-tying. The first site he tried offered him a link to an on-line newsgroup of knot enthusiasts. Tony logged on to the newsgroup and posted a message:

I'm a knot ignoramus, and I need some help in identifying a knot from a photograph, also info on where
it's likely to be used and by whom. Is there anyone
out there that I can send the pic to as a JPEG file?

It would take at least a few minutes to get a response, always supposing there was a knot anorak on-line at this precise moment. To calm his urgent excitement, Tony went through to the kitchen and made himself a pot of coffee. For the first time in hours, he wondered how Carol was getting on. He remembered their tentative arrangement to meet at some point, but he didn't know when he would be able to get away now he had the bit between his teeth.

When he got back to the desk, he sent her an e-mail, suggesting they meet later that evening. There was a message in his in-box from someone who signed himself Monkey's Fist. Tony knew enough to recognize the name of a particular knot, and he opened the message with a glimmer of hope.

> Hi, Knot Newbie. Send me your JPEG and I'll see what I can do.

Within ten minutes, Tony was looking at a second message from his new correspondent.

> Easy peasy, Newbie. It's not a common knot, but it's not really outré. This is a Buntline Hitch. It was traditionally used by sailors to tie a line to the bottom of a square sail. It's basically a clove hitch tied around itself. It's more secure than the more common two half hitches, but it has a tendency to jam under pressure. You wanted to know what sort of person would use it, right? Well, like I said, it's a sailor's knot. So I guess they're the most likely people to use one . . .
> Tie one on for me.
> Monkey's Fist.

Tony sat back and stared at the screen, his eyebrows lowered in concentration. After a few minutes, he got to his feet and scanned the bookshelves that lined one wall of Petra's study. He found what he was looking for on the bottom shelf, along with other oversized volumes. Tony opened the atlas and thumbed through the pages. But there wasn't enough detail for what he wanted.

Impatient, he turned back to the computer and the search engine. First, he looked at city plans of all the murder sites. Then he studied various physical maps of the countries where the murders had taken place. Finally, he disconnected from the internet and returned to his profile.

8. *There is one crucial variation in the murder of Margarethe Schilling. We know the killer was interrupted in the commission of this crime, and any such variations therefore assume great significance since, under stress, we revert to what comes most naturally to us. In this instance, the deviation from pattern takes the form of the knot on the ligature binding the left ankle to the table. All other knots are simple reef knots, involving no specialist knowledge. But the odd one out is a buntline hitch, a relatively uncommon sailor's knot.*

It is worth noting that all the cities where the murders were committed have significant access to waterways. Heidelberg and Köln are on major commercial navigable rivers – the Neckar and the Rhine. Although Leiden is no longer a commercial port, it has an extensive canal network at its heart and is close to the convergence of several major routes at Rotterdam. Given my earlier conclusion that our killer can move around Europe with ease, and given his use of a knot that most lay people would have no knowledge of, I'm prepared to go out on a limb here and suggest that it is a strong possibility that the killer is a commercial sailor, perhaps a crew member on a barge. Of course, he may simply be someone with a nautical background who is employed in another area, but I think the combination of factors gives us a strong likelihood of him being a waterman.

Suggested action: I have no idea what records are

kept of barge traffic, but I would recommend, if it is
possible, that an attempt be made to ascertain whether
any particular vessels were in the general area of all
of these murders on the relevant dates.

Tony indulged in a moment of satisfaction. He had
a good feeling about this. It was, he thought, finally
getting somewhere. He didn't know how far Petra and
her Dutch friend would be able to take the case, given
their limited resources. But at least he felt confident
that he was pointing them in the right direction. He
glanced at his watch. He had no idea when she'd be
back, and he was feeling tired and grimy from his
day's travelling. He decided to head back to his own
apartment, leaving a note for Petra asking her to call
him when she had the chance. With luck, they could
sit down later and thrash out what he'd gleaned so
far. And if the gods were really smiling, she might
have news for him too, if the Europol scheme had
borne fruit.

Marijke frowned at the notes she'd made. Hartmut
Karpf, the detective from Köln, had decided to call
her directly as well as sending his initial notes via
Europol because there were discrepancies between
their two cases that he wanted to discuss. 'I've spoken
to my colleagues in Heidelberg and Bremen, and it's
not that I doubt we're dealing with the same man,'
he'd said. 'But I thought you should know that I think
we're looking at a serious escalation here.'

'I appreciate you calling,' she'd said. 'So, what
exactly do you have?'

'You want the whole story?'

'Everything you have, from the beginning.'

The rustle of paper down the phone, then he spoke. 'OK. Dr Marie-Thérèse Calvet, aged forty-six. Senior lecturer in experimental psychology at the University of Köln. She didn't turn up for work this morning, and her secretary couldn't get a reply from her home number. She was due to give a seminar, so one of her colleagues was enlisted to stand in for her. But the slides that accompanied the seminar were locked in Dr Calvet's office. So the colleague borrowed the master key from the janitor and let himself into her office. Dr Calvet was lying naked and dead, tied to her desk.' Karpf cleared his throat. 'Her colleague was not exactly helpful. He threw up all over the crime scene.'

'If it's any consolation to you, it probably made no difference. This killer doesn't leave us anything to work with in forensic terms,' Marijke said consolingly.

'I gathered as much. Our scene-of-crime officers were very disgruntled. Anyway, for the record, Dr Calvet's body was on its back, arms and legs spread out, each tied to a leg of the desk near the floor. Four standard reef knots, incidentally. Her clothes were underneath her, they'd been cut away once she was tied down. And it was obvious that her pubic hair had been cut away, along with the skin.'

'So far, this is all according to his pattern,' Marijke said.

'Except of course that this is the first time he has killed someone inside their university,' Karpf corrected her. 'All the other victims were found in their homes.'

'That's true,' Marijke said, mentally kicking herself

for her stupidity. But at least now she knew she was dealing with a detective who was as sharp as this inquiry needed. 'What else did you find?'

'I demanded an urgent postmortem. Dr Calvet sustained two blunt trauma head wounds, at least one of which would have been enough to knock her out for a while. There were bruises to her throat consistent with manual strangulation.'

'That's new,' Marijke confirmed.

'The cause of death, however, was drowning. A tube of some sort had been forced into her throat and water poured down it. As with the other cases, I believe. But the really significant difference here is that Dr Calvet was raped vaginally before she was killed.'

'Oh shit,' Marijke breathed. 'That's bad. That's very bad.'

'I agree. Killing's no longer enough for him.'

There had been little more to say. Marijke had promised to send Karpf a full report on the murder of Pieter de Groot, and he had assured her that all the relevant material from his case would be sent immediately via Europol. The one thing Marijke hadn't shared was what she was going to do next. She opened up her e-mail program and began to compose a message. Escalation could change a profile dramatically. Dr Hill needed to know what she had learned as soon as possible. Marijke might not know much about serial killers, but she did know that when anyone as controlled as this killer appeared to be losing it, life could become very cheap indeed.

27

The private room looked as if it had been modelled on a nineteenth-century hunting lodge. Wood panelling covered the walls, relieved only by heavy oils of rural landscapes. A stag's head was mounted on one wall, a wild boar's on another, the glass eyes glittering in the candlelight. A log fire blazed at the centre of an inglenook fireplace flanked by a pair of leather club chairs. In the middle of the room was a small circular table, blazing brilliant with crystal and silver and dazzling white napery. But it was all an elegant fake.

A bit like me, Carol couldn't help thinking. She hadn't expected to see Tadeusz again so soon after her abrupt departure from his boat. But within an hour of her return to the apartment, she'd opened her door to a bouquet of flowers so large it completely obscured the delivery woman. The card read, *I'm sorry. My manners are atrocious. I'll call you soon – please don't hang up. Tadzio.*

The relief was physical. Her shoulders dropped and her back muscles unclenched. She hadn't blown it after all. Luckily, the reaction she'd invented had proved to be the correct one to disarm him. When he called, he managed to be graciously apologetic without grovelling. And so she'd agreed to his dinner invitation. She'd have liked to have talked strategy with Tony, but he was out of reach. She'd have to make do with a late-night debrief.

To reach the private room, they'd taken a lift to the seventeenth floor of one of the modern skyscrapers in Potsdamer Platz and walked through the reception area of a modern restaurant. Crossing the threshold had been an entry into another world. Carol couldn't help a bubble of laughter escaping her lips. 'It's absurd,' she said.

Tadeusz beamed with delight. 'I hoped you'd think so. I can't take it seriously, but the food is exceptional, and I think it's an experience one should have at least once.'

They sat by the fire, supplied with champagne by their personal waiter, who left them in peace, pointing out that he could be summoned by pressing a buzzer when they were ready to order dinner. 'I really am sorry about this afternoon. I think your resemblance to Katerina unsettles me. It stops me thinking straight. And of course, in our line of business, paranoia is never far from the surface,' Tadeusz said.

'I won't deny I was angry. I'm not accustomed to being accused of murder,' Carol said, allowing a little acid into her tone.

He inclined his head in a regretful nod. 'It's not a good basis for building trust. I feel ashamed of myself, if that's any consolation.'

'Let's try and put it behind us. I promise not to

walk out if you promise not to ask if I assassinate my business associates.' She smiled.

'I promise. Perhaps I can demonstrate my good intentions by listening to the details of your proposal?' Tadeusz said.

Carol felt butterflies tumbling in her guts. This was one of the many testing points of the operation, she knew. She took a deep breath and outlined her fictitious business in East Anglia once more. 'In exchange for a roof over their heads and food, they work for me without wages for a year. At the end of that time, they get an Italian passport and their freedom. And that's the deal,' she concluded firmly.

He raised his eyebrows. 'A sort of slavery, then?'

'I prefer to think of it as indentured labour,' she said. 'Obviously, I only want adults. I don't want families – kids are no use to me.' Carol marvelled at how easily she was playing the role of the tough businesswoman she was supposed to be. She seemed to be getting in touch with a side of herself that she hadn't realized existed. She wasn't sure how much she liked this cold and calculating person, but it took surprisingly little effort to slip into the personality she'd fixed on for Caroline Jackson.

'I don't traffic in kids.'

Carol raised her eyebrows. 'I had no idea you had such a sentimental streak.'

'It's not out of sentimentality or squeamishness,' he said. 'Kids are harder to control. They're noisy. They cry. And they provoke stupid heroics from the parents. It's better to avoid them. So, if we do make a deal, you can rest assured you won't be getting any kids from me.'

He was talking explicitly now, Carol realized with quiet delight. Somehow, she'd penetrated his defences. It never occurred to her that part of the reason for his candour was that she was on his turf; if she proved to be dangerous, she could be closed down permanently without a trace. Had she thought of this possible consequence, she would never have had the courage to up the stakes as she did. 'I'm glad we understand each other. But before we talk terms and details, I want to see how you operate. You can sacrifice me any time it suits you with a call to the British authorities. So I need to be sure that I'm linking up with an outfit that is every bit as professional as mine.'

It was a challenge, a gauntlet thrown down between them. Tadeusz stared at her long and hard, watching the changing light from the fire play across those features at once both strange and yet as familiar as his own. 'How do I know I can trust you?'

'Like I said. You'll have something on me. I show you mine, you show me yours. Take your time. Don't decide now. Think about it. Sleep on it. Do what you have to do to satisfy yourself that I'm on the level. But if you're not prepared to let me see for myself that you can run a serious operation, I'm not taking a chance on you.'

He looked at her, his face unreadable. Carol wondered if she'd pushed too hard, too fast. Had she lost him before she even had him on the hook? Eventually, his lips curled upwards in a smile. 'I'll see what can be arranged. But for now, let's concentrate on paying our debt to pleasure.'

A surge of pure exhilaration swept through Carol.

She was really getting somewhere, and it was a great feeling. She tucked her feet under her in the big leather chair and opened the menu. 'Why not?' she said.

The worst thing about profiling, Tony thought as he read the detailed message from Marijke, was the deaths that he couldn't prevent. His way of working was intense, burrowing under the skin of the perpetrator, finding a meaning in behaviour the rest of the world condemned as monstrous or perverse. It was as if he was conducting a dialogue with the dead that made it possible for him to have some sort of intercourse with the mind of the living killer. That, theoretically, should provide the police with a signpost they could place on their own map of the information they had gathered, a signpost that would point them in the right direction. And so, when another name was added to the roll call of victims, it was impossible not to take it as a measure of personal failure.

It was important, he knew, not to let this profound disappointment erode his confidence in what he had already achieved. There was nothing in what Marijke had told him that undermined any of his previous conclusions. What he had to do now was to analyse the new material and incorporate it into his profile. This was simply an accumulation of more data, not an implicit criticism of his performance nor a marker of failure, he insisted to himself.

He could almost believe it, but not quite. He reread what had happened to Dr Calvet, his mouth tightening as his imagination conjured the scene before his eyes. This tiny, fragile woman, completely unsuspecting, an easy target for Geronimo. Odd, he thought. Most killers would have gone for such an easy target first. But this killer had so much confidence in his abilities that he'd started with much greater challenges. Tony wondered if having been disturbed in Bremen had shaken that confidence enough for him to have deliberately chosen a weaker victim in an attempt to shore up his belief in himself. 'It must have been a shock to you, to have someone walk in on you in the middle of your moment of glory,' he said softly. 'You dealt with it, but it must be preying on your mind. Is that why you killed this one in her office? Did you think there was less chance of being disturbed there in the evening, after everyone had gone home?'

Whatever the answer to that question, the change of venue demonstrated that Geronimo was flexible in certain elements of his crimes. But the rape and the attempted strangulation weren't markers of adaptability. They indicated something quite different. He pulled the laptop towards him and began to type.

Following the murder of Dr Calvet in Köln, he will be in a state of considerable agitation. The first three murders are apparently lacking in any obvious element of sexuality. However, there is invariably a link between serial homicide with ritualistic elements and erotic satisfaction for the killer. That there was no overt indicator of this in the earlier crimes would suggest to me that he was in denial about the sexual component in his actions. The rape of Dr Calvet should not, strictly speaking, be seen as an escalation in his activities. In practical terms, it represents the surfacing of a motivation that has been there from the beginning, albeit suppressed.

What is more significant is that he has allowed this breach in his self-control to occur. I believe this may have come about in part because he was disturbed mid-murder in Bremen. This must have unsettled him to a considerable degree, making him much more nervous when approaching Dr Calvet. I believe he will have shocked himself with his actions in Köln. To maintain his earlier level of denial about the erotic nature of what he was doing, he probably convinced himself he had some kind of altruistic mission. But now he has descended to rape, it will be harder for him to maintain the integrity of that delusion.

What does this mean for detection and prevention?

I believe he will try to kill again very soon, perhaps within a matter of days. He has to restore his vision of himself as some sort of avenging angel or righter of wrongs, to erase this momentary lapse into the behaviour of what he may well see as an 'ordinary' criminal.

If I am right that he is somehow connected to the waterways, then his options may be limited to quite a small geographical area. I believe the time has come when his potential targets should be informed of the risks. I would urge that this be done in a low-key manner to avoid alerting the killer. Officers should identify university departments with an experimental psychology specialism and make personal visits to the campuses. They should stress the importance of maintaining confidentiality if they are to have the best chance of capturing the killer, and they should invite co-operation. Lecturers who have been contacted about interviews for a new on-line magazine should be identified. This could allow a sting to be set up. If this is done quickly, it may prevent a fifth killing.

Tony read over what he'd written, then sent it to Marijke and Petra, with a copy to Carol. From what Marijke had told him, it looked as if the cases were already getting bogged down in red tape, with everything being routed through a secure area in the Europol computing centre at Den Haag. He hoped that, between them, they could inject a sense of urgency into the investigation. Otherwise, they were all going to end up with more blood on their hands.

Tadeusz walked Carol to the door of the apartment block. 'Thanks,' she said. 'It's been an interesting evening.'

He took her hand and bowed deeply over it, planting a kiss on the back of her hand. 'Thank you for coming. I'll call you, yes?'

Relieved that he wasn't angling to come up for coffee, Carol nodded. 'I'll look forward to it. Good night.'

She took the lift to the third floor and let herself into her apartment. If he was standing in the street below watching, he'd see that she'd gone straight home. As she walked through to the bedroom, Carol unzipped her dress and let it fall to the floor. She wanted to see Tony, but she didn't want to go to him in Caroline Jackson's clothes that held a whisper of Tadeusz's cigar smoke. She grabbed a clean T-shirt and a pair of jeans and hastily dressed, then walked down the two flights of stairs to his apartment, taking care to check the hallway was empty before she stepped out of the stairwell.

He looked strained, she thought, as he opened the door. But then, he had spent the day probing the murder of a friend. It would have been more strange if he'd greeted her with a cheerful grin. She stepped towards him and kissed him on the cheek. He responded with a tight hug. 'It's good to see you,' he said. 'How did it go today?'

'Interesting,' Carol said. 'As in, "May you live in interesting times."'

Tony led the way back through to the living room where the curtains were already drawn, and they settled down at opposite ends of the sofa, both still more than a little tentative about the new shape of their relationship. 'Tell me about it,' he said, pouring her a glass of red wine from the open bottle on the table.

Carol filled him in on the events of the day. He listened attentively, head cocked to one side. Finally, he said, 'It had to happen. There had to come a moment where he suddenly freaked about the resemblance between you and Katerina and got suspicious.'

'Well, even though it wasn't entirely unexpected, it still threw me. For a moment, I couldn't think how I should react.'

'You ran with your instincts, which in your case is always a good way to go. You've got good gut reactions, Carol, and they worked to your advantage this afternoon. You didn't cave in, you turned it around on to him, which was the best possible way to distract him from what was niggling away at him. But don't be surprised if something like this comes up again.'

'So what do I do next time? Take umbrage again?'

Tony ran a hand through his hair. 'I don't have all the answers, Carol. Tell you the truth, I've seldom felt less infallible than I do tonight.'

Carol's eyebrows rose. 'Hey, you were the one who said you wanted to help me with this,' she protested.

'I know, but I'm not sure I want to feel accountable if I suggest something that turns sour,' Tony said with a weary smile.

Carol unconsciously drew away from him. 'You could give guilt seminars to Catholics, you know. Look, Tony, I'm just asking for advice here. I take responsibility for my own actions.'

He cursed himself silently for striking the wrong note yet again. 'You want advice?' he said sharply. 'OK, entirely without prejudice, I'd say that if Radecki asks you again, you should tell him you didn't kill Osborne and that you don't know who did. And that you're as uncomfortable with the resemblance to Katerina as he is. That you don't want people thinking you're the sort of person who would exploit his private grief for business advantage. And frankly, it would be easier for you to walk away from this whole deal, because it's not like it's hard to find a source of illegal labour.'

Carol nodded. 'Thank you. I'll give it some thought,' she said formally.

Tony shook his head. 'Shall I go out and come in again? Then we can start fresh? Look, we're both tired and scratchy, let's not take it out on each other.' He reached for her hand and laced her warm fingers through his. 'Tell me how you're feeling.'

Carol shrugged. 'It's hard to describe. A mixture of

378

exhilaration, because I feel like I'm doing better than I had any right to hope, and absolute terror because I know I don't have a safety net if I screw up. I'm living on adrenaline, and it's exhausting. So take my mind off me and tell me about your day.'

'It's not exactly uplifting material. There's been a fourth murder.'

Her eyes widened in shock. 'So soon? That's very close.'

'And he's losing control.' Briefly, he outlined what he'd learned from Marijke earlier that evening. 'Do you want to see my draft profile?'

'If you don't mind letting me see it.'

He got up, crossed to his briefcase, and extracted a few sheets of paper. 'Here you go,' he said, passing it to her. 'Would you like some coffee?'

'Mmm, please,' Carol said, already reading the familiar opening disclaimer. While he brewed up, she gave her attention to the short report. Tony kept out of the way until she'd finished, then returned with the coffee.

'So, what do you think?' he asked. 'I think it's a bit thin, myself. I don't feel that I've come up with anything that really moves the investigation much further forward.'

'Given how little you had to work with, I'd say you've done a good job,' Carol said reassuringly. 'The most important thing is obviously your theory that he's a boatman.'

'Yes, but have you any idea how much commercial traffic there is on the waterways of Holland and Germany? There must be thousands of craft on the rivers, and our man could be on any of them. I don't even know if there's any record kept of their movements. I spoke to Marijke briefly this evening, and she seemed to think that boats have to register when they go through locks or tie up at wharves, but that still doesn't narrow it down much, and ploughing through all that material could take months. We haven't got months, Carol.'

'And even if they warn potential victims, it might not be any help in catching him,' Carol said.

'That's right. It's possible he might just go to ground temporarily and resurface with a new strategy for cornering his victims.'

'If he's on-line, might there be any mileage in checking with the internet booksellers to see who's bought a wide range of psychology textbooks?' Carol asked.

Tony shrugged. 'If he lives on a boat, it would be easier for him to buy his books in a shop rather than have them sent to an address he might not get to for a few weeks.'

'I suppose,' she said, trying not to sound too dejected. 'What about the Stasi angle?'

'Petra has arranged for me to talk to a historian tomorrow. But again, I think we're going to be doing needle-in-a-haystack stuff.'

'I'm interested in what he thinks he's doing here,' Carol mused. 'If you're right, and he thinks his life has been screwed up because somebody close to him was a victim of mental torture, what's his goal here? Is it vengeance, pure and simple? Or is he trying to send a wider message?'

'Well, it depends on whether we're talking conscious or subconscious motives here,' Tony said.

'I'd say that subconsciously he's trying to get his own back. But that's too personal, too petty for him to acknowledge as his primary motive. I think he sees himself as cleaning the Augean stables of psychology. He's sending a message out – if you mess with people's heads directly, you deserve to die.'

Carol frowned and fiddled with her coffee cup. 'I know this is going to sound off the wall, but do you think he sees what he's doing as a kind of cure? A form of ultimate therapy? Now you won't indulge your horrible destructive habit any more?'

This was what Tony loved about working with Carol. Her mind sloped off laterally and came up with ideas that he would either never have or would have dismissed as too improbable for consideration. She'd done it before, and she'd been right when he'd been wrong. 'You know, that's not a bad idea,' he said slowly. 'But where are you going with this?'

'I'm not sure . . .' Carol stared at the wall opposite her, trying to put into words the idea that was lurking at the corner of her mind. 'If he sees himself as an instrument of vengeance, couldn't it be that he chooses to humiliate them further, using the tools of their trade? What if he's written to academic journals denouncing them or criticizing their work? It might be an idea to do an on-line trawl as well, given that he's apparently posing as an e-zine journalist.'

Tony nodded. 'It's possible. Worth looking at, anyway.'

'Or maybe writing to their departments complaining about their academic failings?' Carol had a faraway look in her eyes now. 'Maybe he sees their final encounter as a sort of therapeutic session?'

381

'You mean, he thinks they're the patients and he's the one with the cure?'

'Exactly. What do you think?'

'It's possible. And?' Tony added, pushing to see where Carol might take this idea.

She slid along the sofa and leaned into him. 'And nothing. Sorry, that's my lot.'

'Never mind. Inspiration doesn't always arrive on cue. I'll suggest to Petra and Marijke that they have a look for public or professional criticism of the victims' work.' He put his arm round her.

'Oh, this is so comfortable,' Carol sighed. 'I wish I didn't have to drag myself back upstairs.'

Tony swallowed hard. 'You don't have to.'

'I think I do. We've waited so long to get here. I don't want our first time to have the shadow of Radecki hanging over it. I want it to be just you and me, to be special.' She turned her face up to his. 'I can wait a little bit longer.'

He leaned down and gave her a soft kiss on the lips. 'You're determined to give me no excuse for failure, huh?' he said, hiding his anxiety behind a jokey smile.

'Stop right there,' she said, putting a warning finger to his lips. 'I'm not worried, and neither should you be.' She disentangled herself. 'And now I'm going to bed. We both have too much responsibility to miss out on our sleep right now.' She got to her feet. 'I'll see myself out. And I'll see you soon.'

He watched her walk across the room, amazed at the warm glow of contentment he felt. Maybe, just maybe they could make it work.

*   *   *

Krasic arrived at Tadeusz's apartment shortly after eight with a bag of fresh pastries from the Turkish bakery on the corner of Karl Marx Allee nearest to his apartment. While his boss brewed the coffee, he tipped the contents of the bag on to a plate and absently picked up the crumbs on the tip of a licked forefinger. 'She's a dark horse, this Caroline Jackson,' he said. 'Nobody seems to know much about her. They've heard the name, but not many people have ever met her face to face. I talked again to that dealer that Kramer put you on to. He says he met her first about six years ago, when she was doing some dodgy property dealing in Norwich.'

'What sort of dodgy property dealing?' Tadeusz poured the coffee into cups and carried them across to the table. 'Stop eating the crumbs, Darko, you're not a peasant any more,' he added affectionately.

Krasic sat down and took a gulp of the scalding coffee. The heat didn't seem to bother him. 'She got a tip about a planned supermarket development that involved knocking down some old houses. Some of the owners didn't want to sell to her at the rock-bottom prices she was offering, so she used the traditional methods to persuade them.'

'Violence?' Tadeusz asked, reaching for a crescent studded with toasted sesame seeds.

'Only as a last resort. More general domestic terrorism. You know. Break the car windows. Dogshit through the letter box. Funeral wreaths on the doorstep. Taxis arriving every twenty minutes all through the night. She was extremely imaginative, by all accounts. Anyway, they all sold in the end except for one old lady who was adamant that she'd been born there and she was going to die there. Well, she was adamant until she came home from the shops one day and found her cat nailed to the front door.'

Tadeusz sucked his breath in through his teeth. 'Ruthless. I like that in a woman,' he said, grinning. 'I take it she made a killing selling the land to the supermarket?'

'Kramer's mate reckons she must have cleared about a quarter of a mil. She used it as seed money for more property deals. She always keeps her own hands clean, though. Does everything at one remove, he says. And she's not involved in the drugs trade at all. He offered to cut her in on a deal once, but she said she didn't like being in hock to the kind of gangsters he was hanging with. He's heard she's got something going up on an old American base out in the middle of nowhere, but he's got no idea what it is.'

'Well, that checks out.' Tadeusz brushed the crumbs from his mouth with a linen napkin and reached across the table for his cigar case. 'What about personally? What's her background?'

'The stuff you told me looks kosher. You remember that geezer we paid to hack into the Customs' computer last year? Hansi the hacker? Well, I slipped him a bundle of readies to check out all he could about Jackson. She was born where she said, when she said. Went to university in Warwick. She's lived at the same place, some fucking manor house in Suffolk, for the last three years. Pays her taxes. The taxman thinks she's a freelance planning consultant, whatever the hell that is. Looks a citizen on paper. Got no criminal record, though she was charged once with conspiracy to pervert the course of justice. But they never got it to court.'

'What about boyfriends? Husband? Lover?'

'Nothing. Kramer's mate calls her the Ice Queen. He's never seen her with anybody. Could be a lesbian for all he knows.'

Tadeusz shook his head, a knowing smile on his face. 'She's not a lesbian, Darko.'

Krasic looked momentarily panicked. 'You've not shagged her?' he demanded, outrage mixing with incredulity.

Tadeusz closed his eyes and breathed out smoke. 'Do you always have to be so crude?' he said sharply.

Krasic shrugged. 'She's not Katerina, Tadzio. She's another villain, just like us.'

Tadeusz glared at him. 'I'm perfectly aware that she's not Katerina. But you treat her with respect all the same, Darko. It's twice as hard for a woman to make it on our side of the law, and she's proved herself. So you don't talk about her as if she's some street-corner slag. Is that clear?'

Krasic knew better than to argue with the suppressed anger in his boss's tone. 'Whatever you say,' he muttered.

'For the record, there is nothing between me and Caroline,' Tadeusz continued, his voice tight and distant. 'I enjoy her company. Being with her, I feel more like myself than I have for a while now. I'd have thought you would welcome that, since you seem to have been concerned about my focus recently.' He pushed his chair back and stood up dismissively. 'Is everything secure with Marlene's kid, by the way?'

'Yeah, I called my cousin last night. He's not seen any strangers around the place. He says the kid whinges about being bored all the time, but what can you expect when she's shut up in the house all day?'

'At least she's safely out of the way. Now, why don't you go and talk to your Chinese friends and see when they want to send us another shipment? We should be set up to deal with it by the end of the month.'

'You're going to do business with her?'

'I think so. She wants to see something of the way we do things before she commits herself. So make sure everything is running smoothly, OK?'

Krasic tried to hide the dismay he felt. 'You're going to let an outsider into our business?'

'She's not going to be an outsider, is she? She's going to be on the inside. We've been checking her out, haven't we? Well, now she wants to check us out. And at least she's doing it up front, not being underhand like us.'

Krasic shook his head dubiously. 'I don't know, we've always kept things tight, and it's worked for us.'

Tadeusz put a hand on his arm. 'Look, Darko, I know you're uneasy about her. But I've spent a lot of time with her in the past couple of days. And my instincts say she's one of us. She can be trusted. So now you have to trust me. OK?'

Krasic pretended to accept the olive branch. 'If you say so, boss. I better be on my way. I've got things to see to.'

Tadeusz watched him leave, a speculative look on his face. Having Darko so mistrustful around Caroline was no bad thing, he thought. He was well aware that she had crawled under his defences. Who knew what might be going on in his blind spot? Just as well Darko was there to keep an eye on things. Because, if Tadeusz was wrong, someone would have to clear up the mess.

Carol lay back on the sauna bench and felt the sweat trickle down her temples and tickle the skin above her ears. 'This has got to be the best meeting venue ever,' she groaned.

Petra grinned. Her eyes were on a level with Carol's breasts. 'It has its good points, I have to admit.'

Carol arched her spine, feeling the satisfying crunch of vertebrae realigning themselves. 'Oh God, I am so out of condition,' she complained. 'By the way, I think Radecki's got someone on my tail. I noticed a young guy outside the apartment this morning, and I thought I spotted him yesterday. So, on my way here, I did a double-take as I passed a shop window. You know the kind of thing? Walk past, then turn back as if you've just realized what caught your eye?'

'Sure. The kind of thing us empty-headed girls do all the time.'

'Exactly. Anyway, I caught him out of the corner of my peripheral vision. Dodging behind a car, trying to look as if he was crossing the road. Fairly professional, but not good enough to fool anyone who's looking for a tail.'

'Are you worried about it?'

'Not really. They'd be sloppy if they weren't keeping an eye on me. It's not as if I'm doing anything to make them worry. At least I know now what my tail looks like if the occasion arises when I do need to shake him.'

Petra nodded approvingly. 'Good thinking. By the way, I read your overnight report. I have to say, you handled Radecki well on the boat. You seem to be making real progress.'

'I'm cautiously pleased myself. But yesterday afternoon was a real warning to me not to get over-confident.'

Petra stood up and dripped some citrus oil on the coals. The sharp intensity of the fumes seemed to shift her brain up a gear. 'It's working because you look like Katerina. However much his conscious mind wants to distrust you, his emotions are dragging him in the opposite direction. I'm surprised he hasn't made a move on you yet.'

'Are you? I'm not. He had Katerina on a pedestal. She was his angel, his goddess. He's not going to jump on someone who reminds him that strongly of her. He's going to court me,' she said. 'Tony and I talked about this beforehand, and he reckoned that was what would happen. And, speaking of Tony, he told me about the murder in Köln.'

Petra groaned. 'It's terrible. I get so angry because it feels like the whole investigation is snarled up in bureaucratic nonsense. Apparently, Heidelberg have got on their high horse. They're insisting on being the lead investigators because theirs was the first case. This is the same bunch of fuckwits who tried to hand it off to my unit because they couldn't solve it.'

'I thought everything was going through Europol?'

'They're exchanging information, but there's a mountain of case notes and nobody really to take an overview except Tony. It's very frustrating. But I thought his profile came up with some interesting leads. At least the lead detective in Köln seems to have half a brain. He cottoned on right away to the idea of having a computer expert look at the victim's hard drive, just like Marijke's doing. But that could take days, weeks even, to produce results. Marijke has also asked the German teams to check out your idea about a campaign of academic criticism.'

Carol shook her head. 'It's not my finest idea. I hope they don't waste too much time on it.'

'It might just be the lead they need,' Petra said. 'God, I hate not being able to be involved in the investigation.' She stood up. 'Time for a shower. Then I better get back to the office.'

Carol groaned. 'And I have to tour Radecki's video shops and try to look interested.'

'Rather you than me,' Petra said as she walked out of the sauna cabin. 'You take care, Carol.'

Yeah, right. Like that's an option, Carol thought wryly. If taking care was her first priority, she'd never have accepted this assignment. Taking risks was the name of the game. That and survival. And she was determined to survive.

28

Mostly, Darko Krasic enjoyed his work. He had a taste for power and a profound disregard for suffering. He understood his limitations and had no ambitions to take over Tadeusz Radecki's empire for himself. Why should he? He was already making more money than he could spend, and he wasn't so vain as to think he was smarter than his boss.

But even Krasic occasionally found elements of his work distasteful. Take this, for example. Pawing through a woman's underwear was no job for a man like him. A pervert might get off on it, but Krasic was no pervert. If he ever reached the point where the only way he could get off was by fumbling with lingerie, he thought he would simply pick up one of his handguns and blow his brains out.

Still, it had to be done. Tadzio was carrying his brains in his boxer shorts right now, and somebody had to take care of business. When he'd left the apartment, Krasic had called Rado, his second cousin and the young man he'd assigned to keep an eye on Caroline Jackson. 'Where is she?' he'd asked.

'She's just gone into that fancy women's health

club on Giesebrechtstrasse,' Rado told him. 'She was carrying a gym bag.'

If Caroline Jackson could afford temporary membership there, Krasic thought, she was clearly not short of cash, nor was she afraid to spend it. She'd be at least an hour, he reckoned. 'Call me when she leaves,' he told Rado.

He'd stopped off at a florist and bought a bouquet of flowers. Getting in to the block then had been a piece of cake. He'd simply rung bells until he got a reply, then said he had a delivery for that apartment number. In the lift, he'd scribbled something illegible on the card and handed them over to a slightly bemused Dutch businessman. He knew Caroline Jackson's apartment number, because the car had picked her up there for dinner the previous evening. The lock was pathetic, in his opinion. It took him less than five minutes to pick it, and then he was inside.

Krasic made a quick sortie before he began his search. Bedroom, bathroom, kitchen, living room. No serious hiding places. Not even a safe for valuables.

He began with the living room. There was a laptop on a small escritoire by the window. He switched it on and left it to boot up while he looked around. A handful of paperbacks sat on a shelf beside a blue rubber radio. He flicked through the books. Nothing. A stack of English newspapers on the coffee table revealed nothing more than that Jackson liked to do the crosswords and was good at them. The notepad by the phone contained nothing except a note of her arrangement to meet Tadzio at the boat. A briefcase held surprisingly little; estate agent's details of a couple of properties in Ipswich with some scribbled notes in the margins relating to their suitability; a printer's proof copy of a catalogue of hand-made wooden toys with a post office box in Norwich as the ordering address; a sheet of paper with what looked like a series of financial calculations; and a statement for a current account at a bank in Bury St Edmunds. Krasic copied down the details of the account then replaced everything as he had found it.

He turned his attention to the laptop. She didn't even have it password protected, he noted contemptuously. He opened up her comms program, his heart sinking as he saw a couple of hundred e-mails in the in-box. He opened a few at random and found nothing of any significance. They seemed mostly to be from friends or business contacts, generally concerning arrangements for meetings or the exchange of gossip. Ideally, he could use a few hours alone with it to go through everything in more detail, but that wasn't going to happen.

Next, Krasic opened her word processing software. There was a folder of letters, many of which seemed to be concerned with the lease of a former US airbase in East Anglia and applications for its change of use to light industrial units and residential accommodation for the workforce. Other letters dealt with property sales and purchases, none of which meant anything to him. He opened another folder called 'project EA'. His heart leapt when he saw among the file list one labelled 'Radecki'. Eagerly, he opened it.

Tadeusz Radecki. 38. Polish background, based in Berlin. Supplied migrant workers to Colin Osborne. According to J, Radecki has extensive business interests

*with Charlie and Horse. Key player in central
Germany, with substantial export element. Also deals
in live product. Apparently started out dealing in hard-
ware in the Balkans. Owns a chain of video stores.
Said to be scrupulous in delivery but takes no shit.
Second in command, according to CO, 'ruthless mad
bastard Serb' Darko Krasic, muscle who lets TR keep
his hands clean. TR lives in expensive apartment in
Charlottenburg. Is driven around in a big black Merc.
Likes to travel, mostly to European cities. Interests:
opera, hunting, eating out, making money, photog-
raphy. Has a box at the Staatsoper, goes there alone.
Best chance to make initial contact away from possible
interference from the Serb?*

She'd done her homework, though she hadn't left
many clues as to where her information came from.
He didn't like it that an outsider could know even
this much about them. And now she wanted to probe
further into their business. He didn't like it one little
bit. Not from someone this smart.

He closed the word processing software and tried
to open the accounts program. This time, he came up
against the brick wall of a demand for a password.
He didn't blame her; he'd have done the same in her
shoes. It showed she understood what was really
dangerous and what wasn't.

Krasic glanced at his watch. He'd been inside for
thirty-five minutes. He'd better close down the laptop
now. He wasn't going to learn anything more from
it, and it wouldn't do for Jackson to come back and
find it still warm from use.

He turned his attention to the bedroom. Clothes

hung in the wardrobe; an Armani business suit; a couple of evening dresses with designer names he'd never heard of; a couple of pairs of Armani jeans; a pair of Paul Costello trousers; half a dozen tops with more designer labels. Three pairs of shoes were sprawled on the floor – Bally, Fly and Manolo Blahnik, he noticed. They all looked fairly new; he could still easily read the manufacturers' names inside them. *Another Imelda Marcos,* he thought negligently.

Finally, the drawers. Her underwear was nothing special. She obviously preferred to spend on what could be seen and stick to the chain stores for what went unnoticed. It was an interesting insight into the way her mind worked, but it didn't take him any further in his attempts to find out if she really was who she claimed to be. Irritated by the fruitlessness of his search, he slammed the drawer shut and headed for the bathroom. He had just opened the cabinet above the washbasin when his mobile rang.

'Hello?'

'It's me, Rado. She's leaving now. Looks like she's heading back to the apartment.'

'Thanks. I'll talk to you soon.' Krasic stuffed his phone back into his pocket and closed the cabinet. Time to get out.

Luckily, he didn't have to fiddle about with his picks, for the door locked automatically when it was closed. He didn't want to risk the lift, so he headed for the fire stairs at the end of the corridor. Within two minutes he was back outside, ducking into a bar on the other side of the street. He was halfway down a glass of pilsner when he saw her walk into the apartment building. Rado was a comfortable thirty yards or so behind her. Krasic glared through the window at Caroline Jackson's retreating back. Even though he hadn't found any reason not to, he still didn't trust her.

Emil Wolf looked as if he spent most of his life in dusty archives, Tony thought as he sat opposite him in the small café in Prenzlauer Berg. Thin as a whip, his untidy steel grey hair hung over a forehead the colour of parchment. His brown eyes behind oblong glasses were pink-rimmed, his cheeks pale. His mouth was a grim little line, his lips almost invisible until he opened his mouth to speak.

'I appreciate you giving me some of your time,' Tony said.

Wolf's mouth turned down at one corner. 'Petra can be very persuasive. Did she tell you I used to be married to her sister?'

Tony shook his head. 'No.'

Wolf shrugged. 'Petra thinks this still means we're family. So I have to jump to her orders. So, how can I help you, Dr Hill?'

'I don't know how much Petra has told you?'

'I understand it is a confidential matter relating to a serious crime. And that you think it possible that the perpetrator or someone in his family has suffered abuse at the hands of the psychiatric profession?'

'That's right.'

'I'm presuming because you are talking to me and this is my area of expertise that you think this may have happened at the hands of the Stasi?'

'It crossed my mind, yes.'

Wolf lit a cigarette and frowned. 'In the West,

people tend to lump the Stasi in with the Soviet Union when it comes to the abuse of psychiatry for political purposes. But really, the dynamic was very different in Germany. The Stasi had huge resources at their disposal, and they used them to build an unparalleled network of informers. It's been estimated that one in fifty of the population was directly connected to the Stasi in this way.

'They relied on what they called the "decomposition" of people. Decomposition meant making people feel they had no power to act. They were paralysed as citizens because they were convinced that everything was controlled. One of my colleagues has called this "the relentless application of a quiet coercion leading to compliance."

'Stasi oppression was subtle; people were persuaded that a throwaway remark in a bar could ruin any chances of career advancement. Children were taught that any adolescent rebellion could deny them a university place. Co-operation, on the other hand, was the route to a better life. So you had the twin methods of bribery and blackmail.

'The Stasi controllers targeted people they thought had a predisposition to collaborate then motivated them into believing they were doing something worthwhile. When you live in a culture where you have been conditioned to believe you have no power, it's very seductive to be offered the chance to do something active. And, of course, because they believed they were doing the right thing, it's very difficult to confront or punish them afterwards. The aftermath of the fall of communism has poisoned many people's lives, because the opening up of their files has forced them to acknowledge how much they were betrayed by wives, husbands, children, parents, friends and teachers.

'So you see, there was seldom any need for the state to abuse psychiatry. The population was cowed into submission already.'

Tony looked sceptical. 'But there was still dissidence. People were imprisoned and tortured. I've read that some activists were incarcerated in psychiatric units for short periods of time to prevent them taking part in planned actions against the state. It's disingenuous to say that there was no abuse of the medical system, surely?'

Wolf nodded. 'Oh, you're right. There were cases, but they were relatively rare. And most of them have been documented since. Some thirty psychiatrists have been discredited because they allowed themselves to be used for this purpose, but they were a small minority. And their names are known. If your criminal had an axe to grind from the Stasi years, he wouldn't have to look too hard to find people to blame. Really, in the great scheme of things, their crimes were insignificant. You see, the Stasi had a unique way of dealing with dissidents. They sold them to the West.'

'What?'

'That's right. Every year, the Federal Republic bought the freedom of East German citizens who were imprisoned for expressing views or taking action against the state. I'm not just talking about high-profile people like writers and artists. I'm talking about people from all levels of life. So there was no real need to exploit the possibilities of subverting the psychiatric profession.'

This wasn't what Tony had expected to hear from a West German historian. 'You're certainly undermining my prejudices here,' he said wryly.

'You don't have to take my word for it. There have been studies done both by academics and government institutes. They all say the same thing. A few isolated incidences of people having their spirit broken by psychological torture, but very little abuse of the process. If you want details of documented cases, I have a colleague who could probably supply them. Also, you should bear in mind that the medical profession in general was resistant to the controlling efforts of the Stasi. They had a very low percentage of internal informers, they did all they could to maintain the right of patient confidentiality, and the state really didn't trust them to be reliable administrators of government policy.'

Tony couldn't help feeling disappointed at Wolf's words. He'd been convinced he'd been right in his supposition. But it looked as if he'd been mistaken. Since the guilty practitioners from the old Communist regime had been publicly identified, if the killer believed his troubles had originated under the Stasi regime, those individuals would have been the obvious targets, not academics from the West.

'You look depressed, Dr Hill. I'm sorry I haven't been able to tell you what you wanted to hear. But if you're looking for serious and widespread abuse of psychiatry and psychology in this country, you're going to have to go back to the Nazi era.'

'That all seems very remote now,' Tony said.

Wolf stubbed out his cigarette. 'Not necessarily. Don't forget, they destroyed many children's lives with their eugenics policies. Some of those children survived. They would only be in their seventies now. That's still well within living memory. It's certainly possible they will have told their stories to their children and grandchildren. And, of course, the people responsible for what was done to them are long dead, so they're not available as targets.'

Tony perked up as the implications of what Wolf was saying sank in. 'Are there records from that period of admissions to psychiatric units?'

Wolf nodded. 'The Nazis were obsessive record keepers. It's one of the more depressing things about them, I've always thought. They had to find a justification for what they were doing that went beyond the service of Hitler's desire to create a master race, so they convinced themselves that they were carrying out proper scientific research. There are records of admissions, records of deaths, and records of a lot of the experiments they conducted.'

Tony felt a quickening of his pulse. 'So where are these records held?'

'There is a castle on the Rhine – Schloss Hochenstein. They called it the Institute of Developmental Psychology. The reality was that it was a euthanasia factory that also conducted radical psychological experiments. After the war, it became the record centre for the euthanasia programme. It has also been turned into a tourist attraction, though they don't mention that particular element of the castle's history,' Wolf said, an ironic twist to his mouth. 'Our reconciliation with our past only goes so far. We really don't like to admit that we stood by and let our own children be slaughtered.'

'No, I can see how that might be a bit hard for the

national psyche to cope with,' Tony said. 'So, is it possible for me to gain access to these records?'

Wolf smiled, his thin lips spreading over yellowed teeth. 'Normally, it would take time to obtain the necessary permissions. But I'm sure Petra can cut through all the red tape for you. She's very good at getting her own way.'

Tony pulled a face. 'So I've discovered.' He pushed his half-drunk coffee away from him. 'You've been a great help, Dr Wolf.'

The other man gave a self-deprecating shrug. 'Any excuse to get away from campus for an hour.'

'I know the feeling,' Tony said, realizing as he spoke that he had already mentally left that life far behind him. 'I'll tell Petra she owes you a drink.'

Wolf snorted with laughter. 'I won't hold my breath. Good luck at the schloss.'

Luck was exactly what Tony felt he had on his side. The tide was slowly turning, allowing him to replace vague notions with real possibilities. It wasn't a moment too soon. Given the escalation into overt sexuality that was evident in the Köln case, they needed to stop this killer before he lost even more of his self-control. Tony could easily imagine him turning into a spree killer, cutting a swathe through a university campus with a machine gun before turning his gun on himself. It was time to put a stop to it. He could feel his blood rising in anticipation. *I'm coming for you, Geronimo*, he thought as he walked out of the café into the clean spring day.

Carol tossed her gym bag through the bedroom door and walked on into the living room. Her nostrils twitched. She could swear she was picking up the faintest aroma of cigars. Either the occupant of the apartment below was puffing his way through an entire humidor of Havanas, or someone had been in here. She smiled. She'd expected them to search the place, just as she'd expected the tail she'd spotted this morning on the way to the gym. She'd have been more concerned if nothing like this had happened. That would have meant that while Radecki might be taking her seriously as a woman, he wasn't taking her seriously as a possible business partner.

What was interesting, though, was that the search had taken place now, while she was out at the gym. If she'd been responsible for organizing it, she would have chosen a very different time. While she was on the river with Radecki, for example. Then the searchers would have known they were sure of at least three hours in her empty apartment. The timing, coupled with the slight scent on the air, made her wonder if Radecki had been determined to do the search himself. If he had, it was indicative of how far he had succumbed to her charms. A man who was really smitten wouldn't have wanted one of his minions nosing into her knicker drawer.

Carol crossed to the bookshelf and took the radio down. She slid the panel open and smiled with satisfaction as the hard drive dropped into her hand. They'd never have left that behind if they'd found it. Better double-check, however. She plugged it into the laptop and turned it on. She opened the special security program that recorded all user sessions and noted happily that nobody had used the drive since she had last logged off. Then she launched the encryption program and sent e-mails to Morgan and Gandle, alerting them to the fact that she was being followed and telling them about the search. She read an e-mail from Morgan, congratulating her on her success so far and warning her that Krasic had been making inquiries into her background. He assured her that her cover was holding up well under the spotlight. *Like you'd know if it wasn't,* she thought cynically.

She wondered how Tony was faring. She knew that, whatever he was doing, it would take its toll. The one thing that had always moved Tony was the victims of violent criminals. The killers fascinated him, it was true. But profiling had never been an arid academic exercise with him. He cared about the dead; like her, he believed that the investigators were the living representatives of the murdered and mutilated. Their role was not to seek an Old Testament vengeance, but rather to give some kind of closure to those left behind. That, and to save the lives of the potential victims.

Part of her wished she was out there in the field with him, but her own operation was sufficiently demanding and exciting to make that no more than a mild nag. For now, she was happy to leave him to his own devices, secure in the knowledge that when the decks were cleared, the world would be a different place for both of them.

Marijke had escaped from the mountain of paperwork in the office and headed over to Pieter de Groot's canalside house. She was responding to a call from Hartmut Karpf in Köln, whose search team had found something curious when they'd combed Marie-

Thérèse Calvet's filing cabinet. It didn't actually take the investigation much further forward, but she had a feeling Tony would be very, very interested.

It also had the advantage of getting her away from the glowering scowls of her team, whom she'd set the task of trying to establish every inland shipping vessel that had been within a fifty-kilometre radius of Leiden on the day of de Groot's murder. She hoped her German colleagues were being as assiduous, so they could compare results. Otherwise, the exercise would be a complete waste of time. If they found any correlations, then the Germans could see if any of the bargees also owned a dark-coloured Golf. With a lot of luck and persistence, they might just come up with enough suspects for Tony's profile to be genuinely useful.

She'd also sent one of her detectives off to the university library to see if he could find any letters or articles critical of the work of Pieter de Groot and the other victims. She had even less confidence that this wild idea of Carol's would produce a worthwhile result, but she was determined to leave no avenue unexplored, no theory unexamined.

Marijke had to admit she felt disappointed with what they'd achieved so far. Sure, she knew profilers weren't miracle workers, but she'd hoped for something more concrete than Tony had been able to give them. Maybe they'd been hoping for too much. It looked as if the only way these cases were ever going to be solved was by traditional, plodding police work. It wasn't glamorous, but it sometimes got results.

It felt strange to be back in Pieter de Groot's study. There were few traces of what had happened there.

Just a watermark on the polished surface of the desk and a few traces of fingerprint powder where the technicians hadn't cleared up properly after themselves. Maartens wouldn't like that, she thought irrelevantly. He hated it when the SOCOs left a crime scene in a worse mess than they'd found it.

Now a thin layer of dust lay on the room's surfaces. She couldn't imagine that the cleaner would be back any time soon. And, so far, there were no signs that the ex-wife had turned up to claim her children's inheritance. She probably had little appetite for returning to the former family home in these circumstances.

Marijke turned to the filing cabinet. She might as well try the obvious and look under de Groot first. She snapped on a pair of latex gloves and pulled open the relevant drawer, ticking through the files with her long fingers.

And miraculously, there it was. Exactly as Karpf had predicted it would be. A standard suspension file, distinguishable from the others only because it was a paler shade of manila. There was no identifying tab on the top of the file, but an ordinary white adhesive label on the front was printed with 'Pieter de Groot. Case notes'.

Marijke gingerly lifted the file out of the drawer. She took it over to the window, the better to read the contents. First, she studied the outside of the file, noticing with a small surge of excitement that there was a faint smear of something dark that gleamed like oil along the bottom corner on the back. She sniffed, but caught nothing from it. Then she opened it. There was a single sheet of paper inside.

Case Notes

Name: Pieter de Groot

Session Number: 1

Comments: The patient's lack of affect is notable. He is unwilling to engage and shows a disturbing level of passivity. Nevertheless, he has a high opinion of his own capabilities. The only subject on which he seems willing to discourse is his own intellectual superiority. His self-image is grandiose in the extreme.

His demeanour is not justified by his achievement, which seems best described as mediocre. However, his view of his capacities has been bolstered by a nexus of colleagues who, for unspecified reasons, have demonstrated a lack of willingness to question his own valuation of himself . . .

Marijke read on with a growing sense of disbelief. It was a bizarre and distorted view of de Groot's personality, if any credence was to be given to the evidence of his friends and colleagues. But the language was clearly an approximation of that used by therapists, justifying Tony's conclusion that the killer had read and assimilated at least the basics of psychobabble.

She couldn't wait to let forensics loose on this. From the look of it, it had originated from a computer printer, but beyond that anonymity, there might be traces that could provide a positive lead. The smear on the jacket, for example. For the first time in days, Marijke felt she had a concrete piece of evidence in her hands.

As she hurried down to the car, Marijke quietly cursed herself. She should have had the files searched before now. She'd had someone go through his personal papers, but because de Groot hadn't been a practising therapist, it hadn't occurred to her that his professional files would contain anything relevant to his murder. If this oversight proved anything, it was the value of sharing information.

She couldn't help wishing she'd made the discovery herself. But at least she'd finally found something that might give Tony a unique insight into the killer's mind. It was, she supposed, better than nothing.

Darko Krasic sat in the driver's seat of his Mercedes, working his way steadily through a large bucket of salted and buttered popcorn and staring out through the rain at a small lake on the outskirts of Potsdam. The passenger door opened and a tall man folded himself into the seat, taking off a cloth cap and shaking the raindrops from it. He was neatly dressed in chinos and a windbreaker with the logo of a designer sportswear brand over the left breast. He had the lugubrious face of a man who is convinced the world holds only the prospect of disappointment. 'Fucking awful weather,' he said.

'It's always fucking awful weather in Potsdam,' Krasic said. 'The sun can be shining in Berlin, and down here, it's grey and miserable. So, what have you got for me, Karl?'

KriPo detective Karl Hauser gave a sardonic smile. 'So much for small talk, eh, Darko?'

'Karl, we're not friends. We're never going to be friends. You're on the payroll, that's all. So what's the point in pretending?' Krasic lowered the window and tipped the remains of the popcorn on the ground. Even through the rain, the waterfowl spotted the bonanza and headed for the car.

'Since you mention money, I think what I have for your boss is worth a bonus payment.'

'You do, huh?' *Greedy bastard,* Krasic thought. 'Let me be the judge of that.'

'That BMW bike? I've been doing some digging.'

'That's what us taxpayers pay you for.'

Karl scowled. 'Listen, Darko, what I've been doing for you goes way beyond the call of duty. Katerina Basler's death was written off as an unfortunate accident. We've got more important stuff than that to deal with.'

'OK, OK, Karl, we appreciate what you're doing. And you know you've always been well rewarded in the past. So, you've been doing some digging . . . ?'

'That's right. It occurred to me that the bike might have taken a bit of damage itself. A couple of the witnesses said they thought it might have caught the wing of the car. And it occurred to me that, if the biker wasn't supposed to be tooling around Berlin on his machine, he might have got it repaired here. So I've been checking all the little back-street garages that specialize in motorbikes. And a balls-acher of a job it's been too.' He paused, like a child waiting for praise.

'You got a result?' Krasic demanded, unwilling to indulge him further. Useful though Karl Hauser was, at the end of the day he was a dirty cop, and Krasic had no time for people who couldn't manage loyalty.

'Eventually. I found a couple of mechanics out at Lichtenberg who replaced the front forks on a bike answering this description. They remembered it for two reasons. It took them a week to get the spare part from BMW for one, and for another, the driver was a Brit. They reckoned the bike had fake plates, but they made a note of the engine number, just to be on the safe side.'

'Why didn't they come forward at the time?' Krasic asked suspiciously.

'They say they didn't know about the accident. They don't read the papers and they never watch the local TV news.'

'Arseholes,' Krasic muttered. 'I don't suppose this biker paid for the repairs with a credit card?'

'Nothing so convenient,' Hauser admitted. 'Cash on the nail.'

'We're no further forward, then.' Krasic lowered

the window again and lit a cigar without offering one to Hauser.

Hauser smirked. 'That's where you're wrong, Darko. With the engine number, I was able to find out from BMW who the bike was sold to. And this is where it gets very strange.' He paused expectantly.

'Strange how?'

'The bike was sold to the National Crime Squad in the UK. And, according to the British licensing authorities, that's who owns it still.' Hauser shifted in his seat to gauge the impact of his words on Krasic.

The Serb's expression didn't change. He put the cigar in his mouth, inhaled, then turned his head to let the smoke trickle out of the gap between the window and the frame. He didn't want Hauser to have any idea how disturbing he found this information. There was altogether too much British shit flying around right now. Krasic didn't believe in coincidences. Katerina's death caused by a British bike; the British business going pear-shaped after another nasty and mysterious death; and now a British stranger charming the socks off his boss. It made him very, very uneasy. 'That's strange, right enough,' he finally acknowledged. 'Any way of finding out who was riding it?'

Hauser smacked the palms of his hands on his knees. 'It's never enough with you, is it? I sweated blood to get this much, and you want more.'

Krasic slid a hand inside his jacket and produced his wallet. 'I'm not the only one, am I?' He peeled off some notes. 'Here's your bonus. There'll be a lot more if you come up with a name.'

Hauser took the money between finger and thumb,

as if he'd suddenly remembered this should feel dirty and distasteful. 'I'm taking a big risk here,' he complained.

'You want to try living on a cop's pay cheque, it's up to you,' Krasic said, not bothering to hide his contempt. 'Is there anything else we should know?'

Hauser replaced his cap on his greying hair. 'I heard a whisper that one of the Arjouni brothers is trying to move in on some of Kamal's street dealers. You're going to have to plug that gap or you'll lose your distribution.'

'Thanks for the advice, Karl,' Krasic said sarcastically. 'Arjouni's working for me. So you can leave him alone.'

'Like Marlene Krebs, eh?' he sneered. 'You tied that one up tight, Darko. I hear the daughter's gone missing too. Very neat piece of work.'

'It's called sending a message, Karl. One you should pay attention to.'

Hauser opened the car door. 'There's no need to be like that. I'll be in touch.'

Krasic was gunning the engine before the door was even closed. As he swept the car round in a broad arc and headed for the exit, he muttered under his breath, 'I can hardly fucking wait.'

29

He stood under the shower and let the scalding water pour over him. Please God, he would finally feel clean again after this. At least this harbour had decent, private shower rooms. He'd felt dirty ever since he'd fucked that bitch Calvet, and the facilities on board the *Wilhelmina Rosen* were too primitive to cleanse a man as defiled as she had left him. He had to get rid of the filth before it ate through his skin and poisoned his very soul.

At first, he'd been proud of himself. Taking the bitch like that had showed his grandfather's shade who was in charge now. But afterwards, with the whore he'd picked up in Köln, he'd lost it. Couldn't get it up, then when he finally managed it, couldn't come. Fucking Calvet was supposed to make him stronger, fill him with light and power, but instead her image kept blazing across his tightly squeezed eyes, distracting him, turning him off. He'd felt as useless and pathetic with that Köln hooker as he had in the days before he'd comprehended what he should be doing with his life.

Driving back afterwards, the blackness had invaded

him, filling the pit of his stomach with cold bile. What if he'd been wrong? What if the old man's taunts had driven him the wrong way? Face it, any drunken sailor would have done what he had. He'd given in to the most basic instinct, he'd become as much of an animal as those bastards he was sworn to kill. His mission had been pure in his mind before he fucked that bitch, but now it felt cluttered and confused. Women, they were always the treacherous ones, dragging men like him down into the shit. Calvet didn't deserve him, but he'd been weak enough to fall into the trap she'd laid for him with the old man.

The whores didn't deserve him either, but at least their corruption was honest. They didn't pretend to be anything other than what they presented to the world, unlike his chosen victims.

He had been pathetic. He had been carried away, let down by his body. He'd betrayed the purity of his cause, and it must never happen again. He had to make the light come back. Only by returning to his mission and carrying it out correctly could he really cleanse himself, he realized as the water streamed over skin rubbed red raw with washing.

Let it be soon.

It felt strange to have Radecki standing in the middle of her living room, looking around him as if he'd never been there before. He'd arrived ten minutes early and she hadn't quite finished her make-up. It seemed churlish to leave him drumming his heels on the pavement, so Carol had invited him up. It was, she thought, what Caroline would have done.

Now she leaned in towards the bathroom mirror,

applying eyeliner. The least convenient thing so far about being Caroline was having to wear much more elaborate make-up than she normally bothered with. Life, in Carol's opinion, was too short for full slap every day. But Caroline would care too much about how she was perceived to skimp on that.

'These places are really rather pleasant,' Tadeusz called from the living room. 'More spacious than I imagined.'

'The furnishings aren't bad either.'

'No. A bit bland, but rather that than in your face.'

'It's a lot better than a hotel,' Carol said. 'Much more room and much more privacy. You don't have housekeeping battering the door down every five minutes wanting to change the towels or check the minibar.'

'How did you find it?' he asked.

Careful, Carol, she cautioned herself. 'My friendly travel agent told me about it. She got someone local to check it out and make the booking for me. She knows the kind of thing I prefer.' Satisfied with the eyeliner, she reached for the mascara.

'You travel a lot, then?'

'I wouldn't say a lot, but fairly regularly. And I like to feel at home when I do. What about you? Do you travel much?'

His voice came closer. He was too polite to peer in through the open door, but it sounded as if he was in the living-room doorway. That meant he wasn't investigating her possessions, which tended to confirm her theory that he had been the searcher. 'I do move around quite a bit within Europe, but it's mostly connected to the business.'

'You deal with things on the front line yourself, then?' she asked.

'I like to know who I'm dealing with. But I leave most of the day-to-day stuff to my right-hand man, Darko Krasic. I hope you'll meet him soon. He's a crazy Serb, but he's easy to underestimate. He looks like nothing more than a thug, but he's actually a very smart operator.'

Not the one who's following me, then, Carol thought. Her tail certainly couldn't be described as thuggish. Willowy, more like. 'I look forward to that,' she said. 'Just got my lippie to do and then I'm ready. Sorry to keep you waiting.'

'Not at all. I'm glad I've had the chance to see where you're living. Now I can picture you when we're not together. Perhaps I can return the compliment? Maybe we could dine in my apartment tomorrow?'

Carol chuckled. 'You can cook too?'

He laughed. 'Not very well. But I can pick up a phone and order a delivery from the best restaurant in Berlin.'

Carol emerged from the bathroom. 'There. All ready.'

He smiled, tilting his head appreciatively. 'Well worth the wait.'

To her surprise, when they left the apartment, the car wasn't waiting at the kerb. 'My flagship store is only a fifteen-minute walk from here, and I thought that since the rain had stopped, we could walk. If you don't mind? If it's a problem, I can call the car.'

'It'll be a pleasure. I need the fresh air,' she said.

He held out his elbow, crooked in offer, and she

414

slipped her arm through his. *Nicely done*, she thought. She wasn't the only one upping the stakes.

The next few hours required little from her but admiration and the occasional question. He was like a small boy showing off the finer points of his favourite train set. By the end of the afternoon, she knew more about the retail and rental of videos than she would ever have believed there was to know. But along the way, she had also picked up useful nuggets of information about the methods Tadeusz had adopted to launder his illegal proceeds through his legitimate businesses. Financial details had never particularly interested her, but even she could see how cunning his set-up was. She knew she was learning things that would help forensic accountants to unpick the financial morass of Tadeusz's empire once he'd finally been arrested.

What was almost as important as the facts and figures that she'd garnered was the way their inter-action was developing. Tadeusz found excuses to touch her at every opportunity; nothing overtly sexual, but something more than casual contact. Handing her a cup of coffee, his fingers would brush against hers. Showing her round the stores, he would place a hand in the small of her back or steer her by the elbow towards something of particular interest. Getting into the car, his knee would brush against hers.

Their conversation too was becoming more relaxed. Carol was surprised by how entertaining he could be. Funny and serious by turns, he made interesting what could otherwise have been brain-numbing. As they drove round Berlin, he amused her with anecdotes and fascinated her with gobbets of fact about the sights he pointed out. For minutes together, she forgot that she was working undercover, that this relationship had nowhere to go except betrayal, and actually found herself enjoying his company. It took an encounter with a video to ground her again in the reality of what she was doing. In one of the stores, Tadeusz showed her a special display. 'Woody Allen films are big in this part of town, so we always make sure we have the full set available for rental and purchase,' he'd said, gesturing towards the shelves. *Zelig* seemed to jump out at her, reminding her forcefully not to succumb to his charisma, to hold on to the memory of the viciousness that lay behind his easy charm and his sophisticated lifestyle.

At the end of the tour, he directed the driver to take them back to her apartment. As usual, he walked her to the door. But this time, instead of a courtly farewell, he gazed down at her and took a step closer. Carol had to make an instant decision. Break the moment and walk away or draw him further into complicity with her. It was, she knew, a key moment. She stood on tiptoe and brushed a kiss against the corner of his mouth. 'I've had a lovely afternoon,' she said softly.

He leaned forward, an arm round her waist, and kissed her, lips slightly parted. The heat of his body provoked a surprising surge of desire in Carol, and she had to make a conscious effort not to let herself go in his embrace. 'Can I see you this evening?' he asked, his voice husky and deep.

Needing some distance between them, she put her hand on his chest, feeling the thud of his heart under her fingers. 'I can't tonight, I'm sorry,' she said. 'I have to work.'

Tadeusz gave a rueful pout. 'Can't it wait till tomorrow?'

Carol stepped away from him. 'I need to send some stuff overnight to my lawyer. We're in the middle of a property deal and he's got a meeting in the morning. I should have done it this afternoon, but you tempted me away.'

He shrugged. 'Never mind. Tomorrow night, then? You'll come to my place for dinner?'

'OK,' she said. 'But you're still planning on showing me the more interesting side of the business tomorrow, aren't you?'

'Of course. I've got a couple of things to sort out first thing in the morning, but after that, I'm all yours.'

'Great. Give me a call with the arrangements. Thanks again, Tadzio, I've really enjoyed your company.'

'And I yours,' he said, moving back towards the car at the kerb. 'I can't remember the last time I laughed this much.'

Carol couldn't help a smile sneaking across her face as she walked into the lift. It might not last, it was true, but for now he was playing the game as if he was following Morgan's script. She hoped it would continue that way.

Tadeusz didn't bother waiting for the lift. Instead he ran up the three flights of stairs two at a time, feeling a surge of energy that he'd forgotten could possess him. As Darko never tired of reminding him, Caroline was not Katerina. It was only their looks that were

417

similar. But, different as their personalities were, they seemed to have a similar effect on him. For the first time since Katerina's death, he felt like a human being when he was with Caroline.

He knew he should be wary. Not for the reasons Darko was mistrustful, but because he understood the mechanics of emotional rebound. It would be depressingly predictable to fall for the first interesting woman he met as a sort of bandage for the heart. But he believed that whenever, wherever, however he had encountered Caroline Jackson, he would have been attracted to her. Had Katerina still been alive, he would have acknowledged it to himself but not acted upon it. With Katerina dead, there was no reason not to allow himself to care. To attempt to ignore how he had started to feel was doubtless the safest course of action. But a man who thrived on risk as he did could no more adopt a safety-first policy with women than he could turn his back on the edgy and lucrative world that gave him so delightful a life.

Tadeusz pushed open the fire door and emerged in the vestibule that led to his apartment. He wasn't alone. Darko Krasic sat on the deep window sill, short legs stretched out in front of him, cigar smoke hazing the air. Tadeusz didn't break stride, heading straight for his front door. 'I didn't expect to see you here,' he said, key in the lock.

'I've got something that won't keep,' Krasic said, following his boss indoors. Tadeusz took off his overcoat and hung it in a cloakroom in the hallway. Krasic carried on into the sitting room and threw his leather jacket over the back of the sofa. 'I could use a drink,' he called.

'Help yourself, you know where it's kept.'

Krasic poured himself a slug of Jack Daniels and swallowed most of it at a single gulp. He topped up the glass and settled into a modernist chair that was far more comfortable than it looked. He crushed out his cigar in the deep crystal ashtray on the end table, then drummed his fingers on his knee.

Tadeusz walked in, a visible bounce in his step. 'It must be a desperate piece of news that has you camping out on my doorstep, Darko.' He looked as if there was nothing in the world that could touch him as he threw himself down on the sofa and stretched out full length, feet crossed elegantly at the ankles.

'I had a meeting with Hauser this afternoon.'

Tadeusz groaned and rolled his eyes back. 'Rather you than me. So what did Happy Hauser have to say for himself? No, wait. Let me guess. He thought he'd bring you the worrying news that Arjouni is moving in on Kamal's business?' He grinned.

Krasic couldn't help returning the smile. Say what you liked about Tadzio, he could generally size people up accurately. Well, men, anyway. 'He did. But that was dessert. The main course was a lot more interesting.'

'Do I have to guess, or are you going to tell me?' Tadeusz's voice was still light and cheerful. However grim Krasic looked, it wasn't enough to dispel the warm glow of his afternoon with Caroline.

'He's been doing some more digging into the bike.' Krasic didn't have to specify which bike. They both knew exactly what he was talking about. 'And what he's come up with is very fucking dodgy, Tadzio.'

Tadeusz swung his feet on to the floor, sitting up

in one smooth motion. 'I'm listening,' he said, suddenly solemn, suddenly catapulted from the pleasant haze of the afternoon into what felt horribly like inescapable reality.

'It was British. Registered to the National Crime Squad, whatever that is.'

'Organized crime,' Tadeusz said automatically, his brain racing ahead of his mouth. 'But the rider can't have been here officially, otherwise Hauser would have been able to find out, surely?'

'I don't know,' Krasic said. 'If they were working with the Berlin criminal intelligence lot, Hauser wouldn't have a fucking clue. You know how hard we've tried to get a mole in that squad, and we've never managed it.'

Tadeusz clenched his fist in a gesture of frustration. 'And we still don't know who was on the bike?'

'No,' Krasic admitted. 'But, Tadzio, I really don't like this. There are too many British connections hitting us right now.' He enumerated on his short, square fingers. 'First, Katerina gets killed by a British cop bike. Second, Colin Osborne fucks up our British connection by getting blown away in what looks more and more like a very moody shooting. I mean, nobody really seems to know what happened to Colin. It looked like a gangland execution and that's what the cops put out. But nobody's admitting to it, which is dodgy, in my book. And now, this British woman turns up, the spitting image of Katerina, and she just happens to be the missing link that solves all our problems. It's too good to be true,' he concluded with an air of incontrovertible certainty.

'Everything you say is true,' Tadzio admitted. 'But

what you make of it is equally open to another interpretation. As you suggested when this first came up, the biker could have been a British cop on holiday and he had to disappear because he wasn't supposed to have his bike in Berlin. Colin's killer is keeping his head down because Colin has business associates who would want to avenge his death and prove they weren't to be crossed. People like Caroline, for example. Unless of course it was Caroline who had Colin killed to eliminate sloppy competition. I think she could be a dangerous woman, but not for the same reasons you do, Darko. I think she's one of us. She acts like a successful criminal. She looks at the world like a successful criminal. And women who make it in our business have to be twice as ruthless as the men.'

He stood up and crossed to the drinks cupboard, where he poured himself a small glass of apple schnapps. 'Darko, I know you think she's not to be trusted, but that's only because of the accident of her resemblance to Katerina. If she looked like the back end of a bus, you'd be a lot less suspicious.'

'Well, that goes without saying. But don't you think the way she looks is reasonable grounds for suspicion?' Krasic sounded incredulous.

'No. I think it's one of the horrible tricks fate plays on us. I would trust her more easily if she looked differently, I think,' he said, knowing in his heart it wasn't true, but refusing to give Krasic any kind of leverage. Then he had a moment's inspiration, based on years of experience. 'But, Darko, you're the one who's been watching her.'

Krasic looked startled. 'How did you know? Has she noticed? Did she say something?'

Tadeusz laughed out loud. 'No, she hasn't said a thing. I guessed. So, has she done anything suspicious?'

Krasic gave him a sheepish glance. 'Some shopping. And she goes to that ritzy women's health club on Giesebrechtstrasse every day.'

'Oh, that's really something to worry about, a woman who wants to keep in shape. So, she's not been hanging out in cop bars or deliberately giving your man the slip?'

Krasic shook his head. 'Nothing like that. But then, if she was dodgy, she'd expect us to be watching her.'

'Now you're being too devious.' Tadeusz crossed the room and clapped Krasic on the shoulder. 'You're a good friend, Darko. But I think this time you're letting your concern for me run away with your imagination. I really don't believe Caroline is part of some Machiavellian plot against me involving motorbikes and dead gangsters.'

'That doesn't mean I'm going to stop keeping an eye on her,' the Serb said stubbornly.

'No reason why you should.' Tadeusz drained his glass and turned to face Krasic. 'Just don't take the costs out of my budget, OK?' There was iron in his voice now.

Knowing when he was beaten, Krasic got to his feet. 'Watch your back, boss,' he said wearily, reaching for his jacket and walking out.

The Shark hated the fact that nobody at work took him seriously. Most of his male colleagues made it clear that they despised him. Petra, for whom he would have walked barefoot on hot coals, patronized him, which sometimes felt worse than contempt. He'd been so excited about his transfer to intelligence, but it had turned out to be a lot less fun than he'd expected. All he ever got to do was the shit work that everybody else thought was beneath their dignity. He understood enough about psychology to realize that, in order for any group to function properly, there had to be a focus for their scorn. He just wished it wasn't him.

He longed to score some remarkable coup that would win their respect. But that wasn't going to happen while he was stuck in the dogsbody role. Take this latest job that Petra had dumped him with. How was he supposed to find out who Darko Krasic would trust to look after a child? He'd checked out the known associates in Krasic's files, but most of them were the type of person you wouldn't trust to hold the dog while you went for a piss, never mind leave in charge of a child. Then he'd had the brainwave of trying to find out if Krasic had any relatives in the area. He had this image of a Balkan stereotype who, like the Italians, would trust family ahead of anyone.

So for what felt like half a lifetime he'd been trawling public records, trying to find anyone with blood ties to Krasic. Immigration lists, tax rosters, property registers had all drawn a blank. Now he was reduced to phoning local police offices and asking if they knew anything. He'd worked his way round Berlin and now he was edging out into the Brandenburg countryside.

He crossed the last number off his list and dialled the next one, a substation on the northern outskirts of Oranienburg, near the former Sachsenhausen concentration camp. When the phone was answered, he went into his spiel. 'I'm calling from the criminal intelligence unit here in Berlin. I know this is a long shot, but I'm trying to trace anyone who might be related to a Serb we've got operating here in Berlin. A guy by the name of Darko Krasic.'

'Hang on, I'll put you through to someone who can help you.'

Silence, then the phone was picked up. 'Detective Schümann,' a voice said. It sounded as if he was talking through a mouthful of crunchy biscuits.

The Shark recited his speech again over the sounds of mastication.

'That'd be Rado's uncle, right?' Schümann miraculously said. 'Or cousin, or something, who knows with those Serbs?'

'You know who I'm talking about?' the Shark asked eagerly.

'Sure, I know. It's my business to know who's connected on my patch, isn't it?'

'So who's this Rado?'

'Radovan Matic. Fourth division criminal, premier league arsehole. I nailed him about four years ago when he was still a juvenile for possession with intent to supply heroin. The usual rap on the knuckles. Then he buggered off to Berlin. We don't see much of him these days.'

'And he's Darko Krasic's nephew, yeah?' The Shark was struggling not to sound too excited.

'I think his old man and Darko are cousins.'

'His father, does he still live in Oranienburg?'

'Arkady? Yeah, he's got a smallholding about six miles from here. Keeps pigs, I think. He's a decent enough bloke. Never been in any kind of trouble. He beat the crap out of Rado after his arrest, so I heard.'

'Does he have other kids, this Arkady Matic?'

'There's a grown-up daughter, I think. But she's not living at home.'

'Where exactly is this farm?'

'You want the address or directions?'

'Both, please, if you don't mind.' The Shark could hear the obsequiousness in his voice, but he didn't care if he was crawling. He just wanted the information.

Schümann gave him a detailed description of how to find the Matic family farm. 'What do you want with them anyway?' he asked.

'I don't really know. I'm making inquiries on behalf of one of the other detectives here,' The Shark said apologetically. 'You know how it is. You clear your own case and somebody thinks you've got time on your hands . . .'

'Tell me about it,' Schümann complained. 'Do me a favour, though. If your colleague is thinking about coming on to my patch, get him to call me first.'

'He's a she,' The Shark said. 'I'll pass the message on. Thanks for your help.' *Bollocks to that*, he thought. He wasn't going to ask Detective Schümann's permission to check out Matic's farm. He wasn't sharing his moment of glory with some provincial plod.

He jumped to his feet and practically ran out of the squad room, grabbing his jacket on the way. He had a good feeling about this. A smallholding in the middle of nowhere was the perfect place to stash Marlene Krebs' daughter. He was on to something here. He'd show Petra he was worthy of her respect.

425

30

The hire car was waiting for Tony at Frankfurt, just as Petra had promised. He was grateful that she'd found the time to organize his trip; it would have been so much harder if he'd had to make his own arrangements. On the passenger seat was an internet-generated route plan to get him from the airport to Schloss Hochenstein in time for the appointment she'd arranged with the curator of the castle's grisly records. He didn't imagine he was going to find the ultimate answer to his quest this morning, but at least he might be able to leave with a list of names that could be used as a cross-reference if Marijke and her German colleagues managed to come up with possible candidates from the shipping community.

Even on a sunny spring morning, Schloss Hochenstein was a grim sight. The winding road that led up from the valley floor to the castle sitting on its bluff offered occasional glimpses of its forbidding grey walls and turrets. This was no fairytale Rhineland castle, he realized, as he rounded the final bend and came face to face with the looming edifice. There was nothing graceful about the schloss. It hunkered on top of the tor like a fat toad, everything about it heavy and overbearing. The towers on each corner were squat and ugly, the crenellated battlements threatening. This was a place to strike fear into the heart of your enemies, Tony thought, gazing up at the facade.

He parked in the visitor car park to one side of the castle and walked across the lowered drawbridge. Instead of a water-filled moat, there was a deep stone-lined ditch with savage iron spikes festooning the sides and bottom. Above the gateway were elaborate stone carvings of mythical beasts engaged in combat. A griffin crouched on the back of a unicorn, its claws buried in the unicorn's neck. A strange serpent had its fangs plunged into the throat of a wyvern. As symbolic greetings went, Tony thought they might as well have carved, 'Abandon hope all ye who enter here,' and have done.

In the gatehouse, there was a ticket office. Tony walked up to it and told the attendant he had an appointment with Dr Marie Wertheimer. The man nodded gloomily and picked up the phone. 'She will be with you now,' he said, indicating to Tony that he should proceed into the courtyard of the keep. High walls towered over him, their narrow windows suggesting an army of hostile eyes. He imagined how this must have appeared to the frightened children herded here and shivered in spite of himself.

A rotund figure approached across the courtyard, swathed in a maroon woollen wrap. The woman looked like an autumn berry on legs, her greying hair twisted on top of her head in a neat bun. 'Dr Hill? I'm Marie Wertheimer, curator of the records here at

Schloss Hochenstein. Welcome.' Her English was almost without accent.

'Thank you for making the time to see me,' Tony said, shaking her tiny plump hand.

'It's my pleasure. It's always interesting to have a break from routine. So, why don't we have a coffee and you can tell me exactly what it is that interests you.'

He followed her through a small studded wooden door at the base of the keep and down a flight of worn stone steps. 'Mind your step,' she cautioned him. 'These stairs can be treacherous. Best to keep close to the handrail.'

They turned into a low corridor, lit with glaring fluorescent strips. 'We have the least attractive quarters in the castle,' Dr Wertheimer said. 'The part the tourists never get to see.' She turned abruptly into a doorway that opened into a large room lined with utilitarian metal shelving. To his surprise, it had narrow lancet windows along one wall. 'Not a very enticing view,' she said, noting his glance. 'We look out on to the ditch. Still, at least I have some natural light, which is more than most of my colleagues. Please, take a seat, make yourself comfortable.'

Tony sat in one of a pair of battered armchairs set in a corner of the office while Dr Wertheimer fussed with kettle and coffee pot. She brought him a mug of startlingly viscous coffee and settled herself in the chair opposite him. 'I'm very curious,' she said. 'When I spoke to your colleague from Berlin, she was reluctant to give me any details of the nature of your inquiries.'

Tony sipped cautiously. There was enough caffeine

in the brew to keep a narcolept awake for days. 'It's a very sensitive matter,' he said.

'We're accustomed to sensitive matters here,' Dr Wertheimer said tartly. 'Our archive contains material that is still extremely uncomfortable for my fellow countrymen to contemplate. So, I need to be clear about the purpose of your visit. You can speak confidentially to me, Dr Hill. It won't go any further.'

He sized up the placid face with its sharp eyes. He was inclined to trust this woman, and he suspected that, unless he opened up to her, she would be reluctant to do the same for him. 'I'm an offender profiler,' he said. 'I was brought in to help with an investigation into a series of murders that we believe have been committed by the same person.'

Dr Wertheimer frowned. 'The university lecturers?' she said sharply. Astonished, Tony simply gaped at her. 'You have not seen the newspapers this morning?' She got up and rummaged in a large shopping bag at the side of her desk. She produced a copy of that morning's *Die Welt* and turned to an inside page. 'You read German?' she asked.

He nodded, still not trusting speech. She handed him the newspaper and settled down in her chair while he read it. The headline was straightforward. Three murders – Are they linked? The text went on to point out that within the past two months, three university psychology lecturers had been found dead in suspicious circumstances. In each case, the police had been reluctant to divulge details of the deaths, except to say that each was being treated as murder. The writer went on to speculate as to whether this might be the work of a serial killer, although he had been unable to find a police source who would confirm the theory.

'I imagine that there will be other stories in the press,' Dr Wertheimer said as he finished. 'I doubt they will be so restrained. So, is this what brings you to our records here?'

Tony nodded. 'I'm sorry I wasn't more candid with you, but we have been trying to keep this out of the public arena.'

'I can imagine. No police officer is comfortable working in the glare of the TV lights. So, what is it you hope to accomplish here?'

'We need to narrow down our field of suspects. Dull, boring police work involving cross-referencing various lists. It's tedious and time-consuming for the officers involved, but it could produce a result that will save lives. My analysis of the crimes leads me to think that it's likely someone in our killer's immediate family was the victim of psychological torture. I was told that you hold the archives relating to children who were either euthanased or experimented on by Nazi doctors. I'm hoping that somewhere in your archives there is a list of survivors.'

Dr Wertheimer raised her eyebrows. 'This was a long time ago, Dr Hill.'

'I know. But I believe our killer is probably in his mid-twenties. It's possible that his father may have been a survivor. Or he may have been brought up by a grandparent who suffered at the hands of the people who operated institutions such as this.'

She nodded acquiescence. 'It seems far-fetched to me, but I can see that you would want to clutch at any straw when you are trying to bring such a killer to justice. Well, we have no master list such as you speak of.'

Tony couldn't help showing his disappointment on his face. 'So I'm wasting your time as well as my own?'

She shook her head. 'No, of course not. What we do have is individual lists for each of the institutions involved in this programme. There were six main centres where the euthanasia was carried out, but for each of those there were several feeder institutions. We hold records for all of these.' She saw his look of dismay and smiled. 'Please don't despair. The good news is that all our data has been computerized, and so it is relatively easy to access. Normally, I would insist that you carried out any study here on the premises, but I can see that these are special circumstances. Perhaps you would like to contact Ms Becker and ask her to fax me a warrant that would allow me to provide you with hard copies of our data under a confidentiality agreement?'

Tony couldn't believe his luck. For once, he'd found a bureaucrat who didn't want to put obstacles in his way. 'That would be extraordinarily helpful,' he said. 'Is there a phone I can use?'

Dr Wertheimer pointed to her desk. 'Be my guest.' He followed her across the room and waited while she scribbled down the fax number. 'I expect it will take a little time for her to obtain the necessary warrant, but we may as well make a start. I'll go and ask one of my colleagues to print out the appropriate data. I'll be back shortly.'

She bustled out of the room, leaving Tony to call Petra. When she answered her mobile, he explained what he needed. 'Shit, that's not going to be easy,' she muttered.

'What's the problem?'

'I'm not supposed to be working on this, remember? I can hardly make a formal request for a warrant for a case that's nothing to do with me. Have you seen the papers?'

'I've seen *Die Welt*.'

'Believe me, that's the least of our worries. But now that everybody knows there's a serial killer out there, of course, they also know it's really nothing to do with me.'

'Ah,' Tony said. He'd wondered when the woman who got things done would finally hit a brick wall. It was just a pity that it had happened now.

'Let me think . . .' Petra said slowly. 'There's a guy in KriPo who really wants to work in intelligence. I know he's got the right people in his pocket. Maybe I could persuade him that it would help him get a move on to my team if he pulled some strings for me on this.'

'Is there anything that's beyond you, Petra?'

'This might be. Depends how sensitive this guy's bullshit detector is. Keep your fingers crossed for me. Oh, and something very interesting came up in the Köln investigation. Marijke just e-mailed me about it. They found a colleague of Dr Calvet's who remembered her saying something about a meeting with a journalist from a new e-zine, though she couldn't swear to when they were supposed to get together.'

'That confirms what Margarethe told her partner.'

'More than that, Tony. It tells us we're on the right track.'

He could hear a note of excitement in her voice. 'What do you mean?'

'The colleague remembered the alias the journalist was using.' She paused expectantly.

'And?'

'Hochenstein.'

'You're kidding.' He knew she wasn't.

'The colleague remembered it because it isn't exactly a common name and, of course, Hochenstein has particular resonances for experimental psychologists in Germany.'

'I bet it does. Well, at least that tells us I'm fishing in the right river.'

'Happy hunting. I'll talk to you later.'

He replaced the phone and walked over to the window. Dr Wertheimer had been right. This wasn't a view for anyone who had depressive tendencies, he thought. He imagined the children cooped up behind these high walls, their lives narrowed to the prospect of death or torture. He supposed some of them were too profoundly handicapped to have been conscious either of their surroundings or their imminent fates. But for the others, those incarcerated because of their supposed anti-social behaviour or minor physical defects, the anguish must have been unbearable. To be wrested from their families and dumped here would have traumatized the best-adjusted of children. For those already damaged, it must have been disastrous.

His reverie was broken by the return of Dr Wertheimer. 'The material you need is being printed out,' she said. 'We have lists of names and addresses, and in many cases there are also brief digests of some of the so-called treatments they endured.'

'It's amazing that the records survived,' Tony said.

She shrugged. 'Not really. They never thought for a moment they would ever be called to account. The idea that the Third Reich might collapse so spectacularly and thoroughly was unimaginable for those who were part of the establishment. By the time the truth dawned on them, it was too late to think of anything else except immediate personal survival. And it soon became clear that there were far too many guilty men and women for any but the most senior to face retribution. We began archiving records in the early 1980s and, after reunification, we were able to track down most of the old ones from the East too. I'm glad we have them. We should never forget what was once done in the name of the German *Volk*.'

'And what exactly was done to these children?' he asked.

Dr Wertheimer's eyes lost their sparkle. 'The ones who survived? They were treated like lab rats. Mostly they were kept down here, in a series of cells and dormitories. The staff called it the U-Boot – the submarine. No natural light, no sense of night and day. They did various experiments with sleep deprivation, altering the length of the perceived days and nights. They would allow a child to sleep for three hours, then wake it and say, "It's morning, here's your breakfast." Two hours later, they would serve lunch. Two hours later, dinner. Then they would be told it was night and the lights would be turned off. Or else the days would be stretched out.'

'This was supposed to be research, right?' Tony asked, the tang of disgust in his throat. It never failed to appal him that members of his own profession could move so far from the avowed duty to help those entrusted to their care. There was something frighteningly personal about this case, summoning as it did the images of a nightmare that had been created by men and women who must at some point have believed in the therapeutic possibilities of their work. That they could have been so readily corrupted from that ideal was frightening because it was a stark reminder of how thin the veneer of civilization truly was.

'This was indeed supposed to be research,' Dr Wertheimer agreed sadly. 'It was supposed to help the generals decide how hard troops could be driven. Of course, it had no practical application whatsoever. It was simply the exercise of power over the weak. Doctors indulged their own whims, tested their own notions to destruction. We had a water torture cell here where they performed acts of unspeakable cruelty both physical and mental.'

'Water torture?' Tony's interest was pricked.

'We weren't the only institution to have such a facility. Notoriously there was also one at the Hohenschönhausen prison in Berlin, but that was for adults. Here, the subjects were children and the intent was supposedly experiment rather than punishment or interrogation.'

'Did they force water down the children's throats at all?' Tony asked.

Dr Wertheimer frowned at the floor. 'Yes. They conducted several series of experiments to test physical resistance to this. Of course, many of the children died. It takes a surprisingly small amount of water to drown a child if you force water into their airway.' She shook her head, as if willing the images away. 'They also used it in psychological experiments. I don't have the details of those, but they will be in the records somewhere.'

'Would you be able to find them for me?'

'Probably not today, but I can have someone make a search.' Before Tony could respond, the fax phone rang. Dr Wertheimer crossed the room and watched as the paper spewed out. 'It looks as if your colleague has been successful,' she said. 'It'll take a while for everything to be printed out. Would you like to take a tour of the castle while you wait?'

He shook his head. 'I don't feel much like a tourist experience right now.'

Dr Wertheimer nodded. 'I quite understand. We have a cafeteria in the main courtyard. Perhaps you would like to wait there, and I'll bring the material to you?'

Three hours later, he was back on the road, a thick bundle of papers in a padded envelope next to him. He wasn't looking forward to reading the contents. But, with luck, it might take them a small step closer to a killer.

The wind tumbled Carol's hair and dredged the stale city air from the depths of her lungs. She could imagine how easily Caroline Jackson might have succumbed to the delights of being whisked off into the spring sunshine in a BMW ragtop roadster. What woman wouldn't? But although part of her was enjoying the sensation of racing down an autobahn at a speed far in excess of anything she could legitimately have experienced in the UK, there was nothing

436

unalloyed about her reactions. Carol was subsumed in Caroline, but she knew who was firmly in control.

Tadeusz had called for her at half past ten, having phoned to instruct her to dress warmly but casually while teasingly refusing to tell her why. When she'd emerged on the street to find him at the wheel of a black Z8 with the top down, he'd taken one look at the thin jacket covering her sweater and pursed his lips. 'I was afraid of this,' he said, going round to the boot. He produced a heavy sheepskin bomber jacket and handed it to her. 'This should fit you, I think.'

Carol took the coat gingerly. It wasn't new. There were creases at the elbow that proved that. She took off her own jacket and slipped her arms into the sleeves of the sheepskin. He was right. It fit as snugly as anything in her own wardrobe. She detected the faint musk of a heavy perfume she would never have worn. She looked up at Tadeusz with a wry smile. 'Was this Katerina's?' she asked.

'You don't mind?' he said anxiously.

'As long as you don't.' Carol hid her unease with a smile. There was something unnervingly creepy about wearing Katerina's clothes. It felt as if somewhere in Radecki's head, the boundaries were starting to blur. And that almost certainly spelled danger for her in one way or another.

He shook his head and opened the passenger door for her. 'I cleared out most of her clothes, but I kept one or two things that I loved to see her in. I didn't want you to be cold today, and it seemed somehow less presumptuous than going out and buying something for you.'

She stood on tiptoe and kissed his cheek. 'That was

437

very thoughtful. But, Tadzio, you don't have to take responsibility for me. I'm a grown-up with my own platinum card. You don't have to second-guess my needs. I'm used to meeting them myself.'

He took the gentle rebuke well. 'I never doubted it,' he said, handing her into the car. 'But sometimes, Caroline, you have to give in to being pampered a little.' He winked and walked round to the driver's seat.

'Where are we off to, then?' she asked as they turned left down the Ku'damm towards the ring road.

'You said you wanted to see how things work in my business,' Tadeusz said. 'Yesterday, you saw the legitimate side. Today, I'm going to show you how we move our commodities. We're going towards Magdeburg.'

'What's at Magdeburg?'

'You'll see.'

Eventually Tadeusz pulled off the autobahn and, without pausing to consult a map, he took several turns that finally brought them to a quiet country road meandering among farms. After ten minutes or so, the road ended on the banks of a river. He turned off the engine and said, 'Here we are.'

'Where is here?'

'The banks of the River Elbe.' He gestured to his left. 'Just up there is the junction with the Mittelland Kanal.' He opened the door and climbed out. 'Let's walk.'

She followed him along a path by the river, which was busy with commercial craft ranging in size from long barges loaded down with containers to small boats carrying a few crates or sacks. 'It's a busy waterway,' she commented, falling into step beside him.

'Precisely. You know, when people think of moving illegal goods around, whether that's arms or drugs or human beings, they always think of the fastest ways of doing it. Planes, lorries, cars. But there's no reason for speed. You're not carrying perishable cargo. And smuggling really started on the water,' Tadeusz said. As the canal came into view, he reached out and took her hand in his.

'This is one of the crossroads of the European waterways,' he said. 'From here, you can go to Berlin or Hamburg. But you can go much, much further. You can use the Havel and the Oder to take you to the Baltic or into the heart of Poland and the Czech Republic. In the other direction, there's Rotterdam, Antwerp, Ostende, Paris, Le Havre. Or you can go down the Rhine and the Danube all the way to the Black Sea. And nobody really takes much notice. As long as you have the proper seals on your containers and the appropriate documents, there's nothing to worry about.'

'This is how you move your merchandise?' Carol said, sounding bemused.

He nodded. 'The Romanians are extremely corruptible. The drugs come across the Black Sea, or else from the Chinese as payment for their travel. The guns come from the Crimea. The illegals come into Budapest or Bucharest on tourist visas. And they all get packed into containers with official customs seals and end up where I want them to be.'

'You pack people into containers? For weeks at a time?'

439

He smiled. 'It's not so bad. We have containers with special air filters. Chemical toilets. Plenty of water and enough food so they don't starve. Frankly, they don't care how bad the conditions are as long as they end up in some nice EU country with a welfare system and a lousy procedure for getting rid of asylum seekers. One of the reasons they love your country so much,' he added, giving her fingers a gentle squeeze.

'So you load them all up in the docks on the Black Sea? And everybody turns a blind eye?' Even with corruptible officials, Carol thought this was a rather chancy operation.

He laughed. 'Hardly. No, when the containers leave Agigea, they're full of perfectly legitimate merchandise. But I own a small boatyard about fifty kilometres from Bucharest. Near Giurgiu. The barges pull in there and the loads are . . . how can I put it? Rectified. The legitimate cargoes are transferred to lorries. And our tame customs officials replace the seals so everything is exactly as it should be.' He dropped her hand and put an arm round her shoulders. 'You see how much I trust you, that I tell you all this?'

'I appreciate it,' Carol said, trying not to show how overjoyed she was at the precious intelligence she had gained. 'So how many containers do you have in operation at any given time?' she asked. It was, she felt, the sort of thing a businesswoman like Caroline would want to know.

'Between thirty and forty,' he said. 'Sometimes there's only a small amount of heroin on board, but it still means you need access to a whole container.'

'That's a big investment,' Carol said.

'Believe me, Caroline, every container pays for itself many times over every year. This is a very lucrative business. Maybe if things work out for us with the illegals, we could move some other merchandise?'

'I don't think so,' she said firmly. 'I don't get involved in drugs. It's too dodgy. Too many stupid people thinking it's easy money. You have to deal with such shitty, unreliable toerags. People you wouldn't want in your town, never mind in your house. Besides, the police pay far too much attention to drugs.'

He shrugged. 'It's up to you. Me, I let Darko deal with the scum. I only talk to the people at the top of the tree. What about guns? How do you feel about them?'

'I don't use them and I don't like them.'

Tadeusz laughed in pure delight. 'I feel the same about drugs. But it's just business, Caroline. You can't afford to be sentimental in business.'

'I'm not sentimental. I've got a very good and very profitable business and I don't want to have to deal with gangsters.'

'Everybody needs a second profit centre.'

'That's why I bought the airbase. That's why I'm here now. You supply the workforce, that's all I need.'

He pulled her closer to him. 'You shall have them.' He turned and kissed her lips. 'Sealed with a kiss.'

Carol allowed herself to lean into him, aware she mustn't reveal the repugnance his revelations had engendered in her. 'We'll make good partners,' she said softly.

'I'm looking forward to it,' he said, his voice heavy with secondary meaning.

She chuckled as she pulled free of his embrace. 'Me too. But remember, I don't mix business with pleasure. First, we do the business. Then . . . who knows?' She skipped away from him and ran back down the path towards the car.

He caught up with her halfway along the river bank, grabbing her round the waist and pulling her close. 'OK, business before pleasure,' he said. 'Let's go back to Berlin and make some plans. I'll call Darko and get him to meet us. We've got a quiet little office in Kreuzberg where we can sit down and make some firm plans and talk money. Then tonight we can relax.'

Oh shit, Carol thought. This was all moving faster than she really wanted. How was she going to get out of this in one piece?

31

Petra looked up gratefully from her computer as The Shark barged into the squad room. Her head was a slow throb of red-eyed pain from too many hours staring at the screen. Her only break had been arranging the warrant for Tony. Late-night reading of the murder files followed by a morning of assimilating Carol's reports and cross-referencing them with the existing files on Radecki had left her convinced she could no longer avoid a visit to the optician. This was it, then. The end of youth. First it would be reading glasses, then contact lenses, then she'd probably need a hip replacement. It all felt too grim to think about, so even The Shark was a welcome distraction.

'Got any codeine?' she demanded before he could open his mouth.

'I've got better than codeine,' he said. 'I know where Marlene's kid is.' He stood there grinning, an overgrown child who knew he'd done the one thing that his mother would approve of.

Petra couldn't stop her mouth falling open. 'You're kidding,' she said.

The Shark was literally bouncing on the balls of

his feet. 'No way, Petra. I'm telling you, I've found Tanja.'

'Jesus, Shark, that's amazing.'

'It was your idea,' he said, his words tumbling over each other. 'You remember? You set me looking for Krasic's contacts? Well, I eventually found this cousin, he's got a pig farm on the outskirts of Oranienburg, his son Rado is one of Krasic's gophers, apparently. So I went over there to check it out. Lo and behold, they've got the girl!'

'You didn't go near the house, did you?' Petra felt a moment's panic. He wasn't that much of a liability, was he?

'No, of course I didn't. I was going to go out there last night, then I thought it'd make more sense to wait till morning. Daylight, you know? Anyway, I got up before dawn, put on my oldest clothes and went across the fields. I found a place where I could see the back of the house and I crawled under a hedge and staked it out. God, it was horrible. Cold and muddy, and I had no idea how much pigs fart. The bastards seemed to know I was there, kept walking right up to me and farting in my face.'

'Never mind the fucking pigs, Shark. What did you see?'

'Well, it's a lovely day, right? Perfect spring weather? Anyway, around seven, this middle-aged guy built like a brick shithouse comes out on a little quad bike and feeds the pigs. Nothing much happens for a while, then the back door opens and a woman comes out. Looks like she's in her late forties. She walks around the yard, taking a good look around her. There's a lane runs along the side of the yard and she sticks her head over the fence, like she's checking if it's all clear. Then she goes back in the house and comes out with this little girl. I had my binoculars with me, and I could see straight off it was Marlene's kid. I couldn't believe my luck. Anyway, the woman is holding Tanja by the hand, then she lets her go, and I can see she's got a rope tied round the little girl's waist. The kid tries to run off, but she gets yanked off her feet before she's gone a dozen yards. The woman walks her round the yard for ten minutes like a dog on a lead, then picks her up and carries her back indoors.'

'You're sure this was Tanja?'

The Shark nodded like a man with palsy. 'I'm telling you, Petra, no mistaking her. I had her photo with me, just to be on the safe side. It was Tanja. No messing.' He gave her an eager grin.

Petra shook her head, hardly able to believe that the bone she'd thrown to keep him quiet had given them so much to chew on. Much as she had come to respect Carol Jordan and the quality of the work she was doing, she still wanted to nail Radecki herself. And it looked as if she might finally have her hand on the lever that would deliver him to her. 'That's terrific, Sharkster.'

'So what do we do now?' he demanded.

'We go and see Plesch and decide how we're going to liberate the kid and take care of Marlene so Krasic and Radecki can't reach out for her. Well done, kid. I'm impressed.'

It was all he wanted to hear. A grin split his face from ear to ear. 'It was your idea, Petra.'

'Maybe. But it was your hard work that made it happen. Come on, Shark. Let's make Plesch's day.'

*   *   *

445

When Tadeusz had told her his was a small office, he hadn't been joking, Carol thought. There was barely enough room for the table and four chairs in the room above the amusement arcade. However, in spite of the scruffy stairway that led upstairs, the office itself was as plush as she would have expected. It reeked of stale cigar smoke, but the furnishings were expensive leather executive desk chairs and the table was a solid piece of limed oak. A bottle of marc de champagne and one of Jack Daniels sat on a small side table beside four crystal tumblers, and the ashtrays were four pieces of hand-crafted glass. The walls and ceiling were lined with sound-absorbing tiles so that none of the electronic cacophony from below penetrated this quiet sanctum.

'Very choice,' Carol said, spinning one of the chairs on its swivel. 'I see you like to impress those you do business with.'

Tadeusz shrugged. 'Why be uncomfortable?' He glanced at his watch. 'Make yourself at home. Darko will be here any time now. Would you like a drink?'

She shook her head. 'A bit early in the day for me to hit the brandy.' She settled down in the chair facing the door.

Tadeusz raised his eyebrows. 'The bodyguard's seat, huh?'

'What?'

'Bodyguards always sit where they can see the door.'

Carol laughed. 'And women over thirty always sit with their backs to the window, Tadzio.'

'Not something you have to worry about, Caroline.'

Before she could respond to the compliment, the

door opened. *Fuck me, it's a Centurion tank with legs,* Carol thought.

Krasic stood on the threshold, shoulders almost as broad as the doorway itself. His eyes were shadowed under frowning brows as he took in the scene. *Turn on the charm, Carol,* she told herself, jumping to her feet. She crossed the short distance between them, hand extended, smile masking the deep unease this man's physical presence provoked in her. 'You must be Darko,' she said cheerfully. 'It's a pleasure to meet you.'

He took her hand in a surprisingly gentle grip. 'Mine is pleasure,' he said in heavily accented English, his brooding stare giving the lie to his words. He looked over her shoulder and said something in rapid German.

Tadeusz snorted with laughter. 'He says you're every bit as beautiful as I said. Darko, you are such a smooth-talking bastard with the ladies. Come on, sit down, have a drink.'

Krasic pulled out a chair for Carol, poured himself a Jack Daniels and sat down opposite her, his eyes fixed on her face. 'So, you are to answer our English problem?' he said, his voice a challenge.

'I think we can be of mutual assistance, yes.'

'Caroline needs workers and she has a source of paperwork that's far better than anything Colin Osborne ever came up with. All we need to do now is to arrange a schedule for delivery and payment,' Tadeusz said, his manner businesslike as he sat down and lit a cigar.

'Tadeusz has shown me how your operation works. I'm impressed with how well organized the system is.' She gave Krasic an encouraging smile. 'I only work with people once I'm satisfied they can deliver what they promise, and I've seen enough now to know that's true of you guys.'

'We also work only with trust,' Krasic said. 'Do we trust you?'

'Come on, Darko, stop being such a hard-nosed bastard. We've checked Caroline's credentials, we know she's one of us. Now, how soon can we deliver her first load?'

Krasic shrugged. 'Three week?'

'It's going to take that long?' Carol asked. 'I thought you had a pretty streamlined operation going.'

'Things are difficult after Osborne has died,' Krasic said.

'What about the ones we're warehousing in Rotterdam?' Tadeusz butted in. 'Can't we move some of them into England sooner than that?'

Krasic frowned. 'I suppose so. You are in hurry?'

'I'll take delivery whenever you can arrange it. But if you've been warehousing the goods, I want to check them for myself before they leave. I don't want a container-load of corpses on my hands.'

Krasic darted a look at his boss. Tadeusz spread his hands. 'Of course, Caroline. Darko, why don't you set up a trip for the beginning of next week. Caroline and I will meet you in Rotterdam at the weekend before you load, and she can check it out for herself.'

Krasic stared at Tadeusz in disbelief, then spoke in German. Carol wished she knew the language better. Her verbal memory only worked in English; there was no way she could reproduce conversation in a foreign language. Tadeusz replied in a tone of rebuke, then returned to English. 'I apologize, we shouldn't exclude you from our discussion, but Darko's English isn't as good as mine. He's simply being over-protective. He's always anxious when I step out of my administrative role and get involved in the action. But sometimes I like to see things for myself. So, are you able to come to Rotterdam at the weekend to inspect your goods?'

She nodded. 'I'd like that. And that gives me enough time to have things in place at my end. I need to make sure my people have everything ready.'

'How many can you take?' Tadeusz asked.

'Thirty, to begin with,' she said. It was a figure she'd agreed with Morgan. Not too many for safe passage in a container, not so few that it wouldn't be worth Tadeusz's while. 'Then, after that, twenty a month.'

'That's not so many,' Krasic objected. 'We can supply many more.'

'Maybe so, but that's all I need. If this goes as well as I expect, it's entirely possible that I will expand my operation. A lot depends on my source for the paper-work. I'm getting top-class documentation, and I don't want to risk that by taking the pitcher to the well too often. So, for now, it's twenty bodies a month. Take it or leave it, Mr Krasic.' Carol had no difficulty in sounding tough. She'd spent enough hours in inter-view rooms with hard cases to have honed her skills in that area. She accompanied her words with a level gaze and unsmiling expression.

'Those numbers will be fine,' Tadeusz said. 'Thirty in the first shipment followed by twenty a month. Yes, we could use an outlet for more than that, but frankly I'd rather ship twenty knowing it wasn't going to backfire than send sixty with no certainties. Now all we have to settle is the financial arrangements.'

Carol smiled. She'd done it. And in record time. She wished she could see Morgan's face when he got her next e-mail. Everything was in place. This weekend in Rotterdam they would finally nab Tadeusz Radecki and bring his empire crashing down around his ears. 'Yes,' she said cheerfully. 'Let's talk money.'

Tony had encountered plenty of clinical psychologists – and cops too – who had built walls between themselves and the distressing experiences their work exposed them to. He couldn't find it in his heart to blame them for imposing that distance. No sane person would seek out the sights they had to see, the verbal torrents of pain and anger they had to hear, the fractured remnants of human beings they had to deal with. However he had promised himself at the start of his clinical career that he would never shy away from empathy, whatever the cost. If the price became too high, he could always do something else for a living. But to lose the capacity to comprehend the pain of others, perpetrators as well as victims, was a kind of dishonesty, he believed.

The sheaf of papers he had brought back from Schloss Hochenstein stretched that credo almost to breaking point. The dispassionate lists of names, diagnoses and so-called treatments conjured up such a vision of hell that he found himself wishing he could assimilate the material with calm scientific objectivity. Instead, he felt harrowed to his very core. Simply being in possession of this information was enough to steal sleep from his nights for a long time to come, he knew only too well.

Dr Wertheimer had been right about the obsessive record keeping of the Nazi medical establishment. There were hundreds of names, spread out across the whole country. Every child had its accompanying set of vital statistics – name, age, address, names and occupations of parents. The reason for their hospitalization came next. Most common was 'mental retardation', closely followed by 'physical handicap'. But some of the explanations for removing children from their families were profoundly chilling. 'Congenital laziness.' 'Anti-social behaviour.' 'Racially contaminated.'

What must it have been like for the parents of such children, having to stand by while their offspring were dragged from them, knowing that to protest would be to bring retribution crashing down on their own heads without any prospect of saving their child? They must, he thought, have entered a state of denial that would have destroyed them emotionally and psychologically. No wonder post-war generations of Germans didn't want to be confronted with what had been done to their own children with their apparent consent.

At least the profoundly handicapped among the children would have been spared any real understanding of what was happening to them. But for the others, watching as their fellow inmates perished around them, daily life must have shrunk to the pinprick of relief when another day dawned and their eyes were open to see it.

The fate of many of the children was listed very

simply. 'Treated with injections of experimental drugs. Failed to respond.' Followed by the date and time of death. It was code for euthanasia, that much was obvious. This was a rare example of a point where the arrogance of the regime had faltered. Even though they were convinced they would never be called to account for what had been done to these children in the name of Aryan purity, they'd felt the need for euphemism here.

That didn't mean there was much residual respect for the innocence of their victims, however. The destiny of other children was catalogued in brief terms that left Tony feeling ashamed to belong to the medical profession. Some had died in agony after being injected in the eyes in a series of experiments relating to eye colour. Others had been subjected to research into sleep cycles that had driven them mad. The list went on, sometimes with references to scientific papers where the results could be seen.

And no one had been punished for this. Worse, there were cases where a tacit deal had been done between the Allies and the defeated Nazis. Research conclusions would become the property of the victors in return for the silence of the perpetrators.

If Geronimo had paid some terrible personal price for what had been done in the name of science sixty years before, it didn't surprise Tony that he would be consumed by rage and bitterness. All those victims, and not a single person called to account. He was a rational man, and it enraged him. How much worse would it feel to be a second or third generation victim of such viciousness?

Geronimo was going for the wrong targets, it was true. He might deplore its end result, but Tony couldn't find it in his heart to condemn unequivocally the desire for vengeance that fuelled him.

. . .P: you're right, the case notes are very chilling. are there any forensic traces on the file?

M: Too early to say. It's with the document examiner now. And I had an idea myself this afternoon. So many of our major traffic intersections are covered by CCTV now, I've asked for all the tapes from the day of de Groot's murder and I'm going to get my team to go through them all to see if they can spot a dark-coloured VW Golf with German plates.

P: great idea.

M: Maybe. It will really only be any use if we can cross-match it with one of the other lists. It's going to take ages to get anything comprehensive about the boats.

P: tony's been pursuing the idea of victims of psychological torture. today he picked up lists of child victims of the nazis. he's spending this evening scanning in all the names on to a master list, so he'll be able to let you have that as well. another possible list for cross-matching of names.

M: It's hard to feel that we're moving forward, all the same.

P: the stories in the papers this morning haven't helped either.

M: At least they don't seem to have picked up on the connection to our case, so we're being left in peace. Has it provoked more co-operation among the German forces?

P: i don't really know. i'm too far out of the loop. you'll probably hear before i will. but the tv news this evening ran a piece about university lecturers living in fear of a serial killer. i'm afraid he's going to go to ground.

M: Either that or take more risks. If he can't rely on his usual method of setting up his victims, he'll find some other way. It's all very depressing. Cheer me up. How are things with your other undercover operation?

P: it looks like we've located marlene krebs' daughter. what we're going to do is simultaneously raid the place where the daughter is being kept AND put marlene in protective custody out of radecki's reach. once we have him behind bars, we'll get everything else we need. clever, no?

M: As long as you don't compromise Jordan in the process.

P: trust me, it's all sorted. or it will be, anyway. i'm thinking we can organize it all for the same time. the sting goes off with jordan and we do our stuff, so nobody compromises anybody else.

M: Congratulations! I know how hard you've worked for this!

P: i think we need to celebrate in person, marijke. will you come to berlin?

M: I'd love to. But right now I'm too wrapped up in this case. Why don't you take some days' leave after you take Radecki down and come to Leiden?

P: i don't know, it'll be crazy here after we nail him. let's just leave it that we'll crack open the champagne in one city or other once we've both got our cases out of the way.

M: OK. But I want you to know that I feel confident about meeting face to face at last.

P: me too. scared, but confident too.

M: I need to go now, I'm actually still at work and there is more stuff I need to do.

P: ok. the harder you work, the sooner the case will be solved and we can plan getting together.

M: You think so?

P: i know it.

32

Under different circumstances, Carol would have found it hard to fault the evening. An attentive, handsome host, gourmet food, an array of remarkable wines, and surroundings that would have been the envy of the production editor of any interior design magazine. Not to mention conversation that had ranged across politics, music and foreign travel before taking roost in the more intimate territory of past relationships.

But these were not consolations enough to overcome Carol's underlying feeling of unease. She could never afford to let her guard slip for a moment, never forget that she was wearing another woman's past instead of her own, never react to any comment of Tadeusz's without weighing and measuring her response. She was so close now, and a single slip could undo everything.

And at the back of her mind was the constant disturbance created by the resurfacing of Tony in her life. It made this elegantly controlled flirtation with Tadeusz feel doubly duplicitous. Knowing she would end the evening with Tony and not the man who was

456

trying so hard to woo her gave everything strange undertones and layered meanings.

Now, he returned from another trip to the kitchen with a laden tray. He stood in the doorway of the dining room and smiled at her. 'I thought we could take our coffee in the living room. It's more comfortable, and the view is prettier.'

Good pitch, she thought. What he meant, of course, was that it would be easier to pounce there than across a table littered with the detritus of a five-course dinner. 'That sounds nice,' she said, rising and following him.

Carol checked out the room as she entered. Two sofas in an obvious conversational grouping and an armchair set off to one side. Taking the armchair would be a statement that put distance between them, and while she didn't want to offer too much encouragement, she was still a long way from home and dry with this sting. Until they had Radecki and Krasic in the bag, she needed to keep him feeling close to her.

Tadeusz had placed the tray on a low sculpted steel and glass table that sat in the angle between the two sofas. He glanced up at her, his eyes lingering over the close-fitting lines of the cocktail dress. 'Make yourself comfortable,' he said, bending over to pour the coffee into paper-thin bone china cups.

Carol sat down on the sofa nearest the coffee, crossing her legs in the hope that it would send out the right signals, but failing to realize how it emphasized the smooth curve of her calf and the neatness of her ankle. Tadeusz leaned across the table, one hand on the top to balance himself as he handed over her coffee. 'Brandy?' he asked. 'It can't be too early now.'

With a slight nod and smile, she acknowledged his reference to their earlier meeting, the first time he'd hinted at business all evening. 'I'd prefer Grand Marnier, if you have it.'

'Your wish is my command.' He crossed to the drinks tray and returned with a balloon of brandy for himself and a liberal Grand Marnier for her. As she'd feared, he took the chance to sit next to her. She was effectively trapped between him and the arm of the sofa. *They're so predictable*, she thought wearily.

She hung on to her coffee cup. Nobody would be crazy enough to lunge at a woman clutching hot coffee. 'That was a beautiful meal,' she said. 'I feel completely spoiled. Thank you for going to so much trouble.'

He put his drink down, leaving himself unencumbered. 'It really was no trouble. A phone call, then the simple adherence to instructions. Turn on the oven at such a temperature. Insert dish A. Wait ten minutes. Insert dish B. That sort of thing.'

Carol shook her head. 'I'd have been just as happy with a takeaway pizza, you know.'

'That dress deserves much more than a takeaway pizza.' His hand strayed to her thigh, his fingertips brushing the delicate linen and silk mixture.

Oh shit, here we go, she thought. 'Both the dress and its owner are honoured,' she said.

He shifted so he was facing her. Gently, he took the cup from her hands and placed it on the table. 'The least I could do for the woman who has reminded me that it's possible to laugh.' He leaned forward and kissed her.

Carol tried to find the appropriate response. She could taste brandy on his breath and it revolted her. But she dared not show that. Equally, she dared not allow herself the luxury of relaxing into an embrace that she found hard to resist. Her body's response to him was automatic, animal. In spite of herself, she found him attractive, and her hormones were responding independently of her brain. She was kissing him with as much heat as he was kissing her.

His hands were on her body now, pulling her closer. She didn't resist, running her fingers over the long muscles of his back. Still they were kissing, tongues flickering in and out of each other's mouths, breath coming harder and faster. Now he was moving on top of her, his hand moving under her dress, a burn against her skin. She didn't want him to stop, she realized with a shock.

Her reason staged a rearguard action against her body's desire. Images flashed across her brain. The corpses spilling out of a shipping container. Morgan's mouth telling her Radecki's human trafficking had to be stopped. The assassinated man on the steps of the GeSa. Then Tony's face, the eyes reproachful, the mouth rueful. Suddenly, Carol Jordan was back in control of Caroline Jackson. She pulled away from Tadeusz's eager mouth. 'No, wait,' she gasped.

He froze, his hand halfway up her thigh. 'What's wrong?' he panted.

She closed her eyes. 'I can't. I'm sorry. I just can't.'

He leaned into her more closely, his fingers pressing more firmly into her flesh. 'You want to, I know you do.'

Carol squirmed as far as she could get from him,

thrusting his hand away from her leg. 'I did. I mean, I do. It's just . . . I'm sorry, Tadzio, it's all too fast. Too sudden.'

He smacked the palms of his hands hard on his thighs. 'I don't understand. You kissed me like you wanted me.' His voice was raised, his eyebrows lowering over narrowed eyes.

'It's not that I don't. Please don't think that. But . . . this is very strange for me. I've never had a relationship with someone I'm doing business with. I'm not sure if I can handle it. I need time to figure this out.'

'Jesus Christ.' He jumped to his feet and took a cigar from the humidor. He fussed over lighting it, as if making an opportunity to collect himself. 'I've never wanted to do this with anyone I was doing business with,' he said, his words far more reasonable than his tone. 'But I don't see why it should interfere with our professional relationship. It could make it stronger. Working as a team. We'd be great, Caroline.'

She reached for her drink and took a sip. 'That's what I'd like too. But I need a little more time to get used to the idea. I'm not saying never, I'm just saying not tonight.' She looked away. 'And there's another thing too.'

'Oh? What might that be?' He glared mutinously at her.

'Katerina,' she said softly.

His face closed down in the tight mask she'd seen the first time they'd met. 'What about Katerina?' he eventually said.

'You're the one who said how much I look like her.' Carol tried for a pleading expression. 'I need to be sure it's really me you want to sleep with, not another version of Katerina.'

His eyes clouded and his shoulders drooped. 'You think I haven't asked myself the same question?'

'I don't know.' Realizing she'd found the button to push that had turned his anger to vulnerability, Carol let herself relax a fraction.

'The first time I saw you, once I got over the shock, I told myself I would never lay a finger on you because it would be sick. But the more I've got to know you, the more I've got to like you. Now when I look at you, I see Caroline, not Katerina. You have to believe that.'

'I want to believe it, Tadzio. But I think I need a little more time.'

He folded his arms across his chest. 'I understand. Take the time you need. It's not like there's any rush. I'm sorry if I came on too strong.'

She shook her head. 'There's nothing to apologize for. At least it's made us clear the air. Find out where we stand.'

He managed a faint smile. 'I have a good feeling about this, Caroline.'

'Me too, Tadzio. But I want to be sure.' She straightened her dress and stood up. 'And now I think I should go home.'

His light was still burning, the curtains wide open. It had been the first thing Carol had checked as she stepped out of Tadeusz's Mercedes and said good night to his driver. She felt dishevelled and faintly dirty from her scramble on the sofa, but she didn't care. The need to see Tony was too strong for her to want to waste time restoring herself to a pristine state.

The door opened so swiftly she could almost have believed he was waiting for her knock. Tony smiled appreciatively at the sight of her. 'You look stunning,' he said, ushering her through to the living room. 'How did it go?' he asked as he followed her through. They stood inches away from each other. She looked breathtaking, he thought, her hair gleaming against the darkness of the window, her lips slightly parted in a tentative smile. There was an air of arousal about her that gave him a pang of distress. He recognized it as jealousy. He wanted her to feel that way about him, not a creep like Radecki who was nothing more than a gangster with a veneer of sophistication.

'It couldn't have gone better earlier in the day. He took me out into the country and showed me how he runs his trafficking operations on the waterways. And this afternoon, we had a meeting with his side-kick, Darko Krasic. God, he looks a total brute. Now there's a man who would make a girl think twice about breaking her cover. And he hates me. He'd snap my neck as soon as look at me if he thought I was going to do anything to damage his precious Tadzio.'

'God preserve us from male bonding. That must have been scary,' Tony said.

'It was. But it helped me concentrate on being Caroline. And it worked, Tony, it really worked. We've got a deal. We're off to Rotterdam at the weekend to check out the illegal immigrants he's going to supply me with and we can nail him in the act. Morgan will be like a dog with two tails when he gets my report!'

Tony nodded. 'You've done really well.'

She shrugged. 'I couldn't have done it without your help.'

'Don't be daft, of course you could. So how did this evening go? Were you celebrating your new business relationship?' He couldn't keep an edge of bitterness out of his voice.

'He tried to jump me,' she said, with a moue of distaste. 'But I managed to fend him off. It's tricky, making sure I give him enough rope to hang himself without me getting entangled in it too.'

'It can't be easy,' Tony agreed, the words dragging out of him.

She took a step forward. 'He's an attractive man. My body seems to find that harder to resist than my head does. And that's very confusing.'

Tony stared at the floor. He was afraid to look at her. 'Just as well you're so thoroughly professional,' he muttered.

Carol put a hand on his arm. 'It wasn't my professionalism that got me out of it. It was because I kept thinking of you.'

'You couldn't stand my disapproval, huh?' His familiar lop-sided smile crept out of hiding.

She shook her head. 'Not exactly. It was more about reminding myself what I really want.' She moved closer to him. He could feel the heat rising from her body. Without thinking, he opened his arms and she stepped into their circle. They stood together, hugging so tight they could feel the thud of each other's blood. He buried his face in her hair, inhaling the sweet smell of her. For the first time since his visit to Schloss Hochenstein, his mind was freed from the images of horror it had generated.

The reprieve didn't last for long. Carol ran her fingers through the hair on the back of his head and spoke softly. 'I'm sorry. All I think about is me. How has your day been?'

His body stiffened in her embrace, and he gently moved away from her. 'You don't want to hear this stuff,' he said, crossing to the table and picking up the bottle of Scotch sitting there. He raised his eyebrows at her and Carol shook her head. He poured a stiff drink and dropped into the upright chair by his laptop. He sipped at the whisky and shook his head. 'Trust me, you really don't.'

Carol perched on the end of the sofa, only a few inches separating their knees. 'I'm not exactly a horror-story virgin,' she reminded him. 'You know how this stuff eats away at you. So come on, share the burden.'

He stared down into his drink. 'Kids. They were just kids. It's not like I don't know in graphic detail what gets done to children.' He frowned. 'But that's individuals. One sick bastard preying on kids. So that's manageable, because they're beyond the pale. They're not like us. That's what you reassure yourself with.' He swallowed more whisky.

'But the terrible thing about this, Carol, the thing that makes me feel like I've swallowed some corrosive poison just by knowing about this stuff, is that it was a collaborative effort. Dozens, probably hundreds of people were involved in what was done to those children. Their parents hid behind their own sense of powerlessness and let those bastards take their kids away. And for what? Because they were physically handicapped. Or because they were mentally deficient. Or just because they were difficult little buggers who didn't stick to the rules.' He ran a hand through his hair, his face revealing his troubled bewilderment. Carol put a hand on his knee and he covered it with his own.

'And then the doctors and nurses. Not ignorant peasants, educated people. People like you and me. People who went into this line of work presumably because they had some desire to heal the sick. But an edict went out from on high and suddenly they stopped being healers and started being torturers and murderers. I mean, how can you get your head round that? I've never had a problem understanding the self-deception involved in being a concentration camp guard. When you feel vulnerable, demonizing some outsider grouping like Jews or gypsies or communists isn't such a big step for most of us. But these were *German* children. Most of the people who destroyed their lives were probably parents themselves. How could they dissociate what they were doing for a living from their own domestic lives? For some of them at least, it must have wrecked their heads.'

He shook his head. 'I'm good at empathy. I'm good at feeling the pain of people who can only function by transferring their own pain on to other people. But I'm damned if I can find a shred of pity for anybody who was involved in committing the acts I've read about today.'

'I'm so sorry,' Carol said. 'I shouldn't have brought you into this.'

He forced a tired smile. 'No need to apologize. But, if I'm right, and our killer is a victim at one remove from what happened in those so-called hospitals, then I've got to say, he's not the only one who's to blame. The people who really carry the responsibility for these murders are way beyond the reach of our justice.'

In the street below, Radovan Matic couldn't believe his eyes. He'd spent a boring evening outside Tadeusz Radecki's apartment block, fully expecting to be there till the early hours at least. No red-blooded male would let a woman like that leave his apartment without giving her one. And from everything his Uncle Darko had said about Radecki, the man was no monk. He'd been mildly surprised when Radecki's familiar black Mercedes had pulled up outside the building just after ten o'clock, and astonished when Caroline Jackson had emerged alone a few minutes later.

He'd followed the Merc back to her place, and been lucky enough to find a parking space directly opposite as she walked inside. He decided to wait until he saw her light come on, then call his uncle in the hope he'd be allowed to go home to bed. Rado got out of his car and moved into the shadows of a florist's doorway so he could better see the apartment block.

Minutes ticked past, and no light appeared at the windows he knew to be hers. What was going on? He knew from watching her previously that as soon as she walked in, a glow from the hall could be seen at the living-room window. Yet the rooms remained in darkness. Had he made a mistake? Was he watching the wrong window? He counted them off from the first-floor corner window, just to be sure.

That was when he saw her. Unmistakably. But she was in the wrong place. Instead of being on the third floor, she was on the first. And she was with a man who definitely wasn't Tadeusz Radecki. As he watched, they moved closer together, clearly having some sort of intense conversation. Then they were in each other's arms.

The bitch had come straight from Radecki's apartment to this other man's embrace. Rado reached for his phone. This was something his uncle needed to know about. And fast.

Krasic was there inside twenty minutes. He'd run every amber light the length of the Ku'damm in his eagerness to discover Caroline Jackson doing something she shouldn't be doing. He parked across somebody's garage entrance and barrelled up the street to his nephew's vantage point. 'What's happening?' he demanded.

Rado pointed up to the oblong of light on the first floor. 'That's where she was. Her and this bloke. Tadeusz's driver dropped her off and her lights didn't go on. Next thing was, I spotted her in the first-floor window with him. They were talking, then they were snogging. Then they disappeared. So I'd say at a rough guess that they're shagging, wouldn't you?'

'I told him not to trust her,' Krasic growled. 'So what number is this apartment?'

'It's two floors below hers. If she's 302, he must be in 102.' As he spoke, the man came into view again. 'That's him, Uncle. That's the man she was with,' he exclaimed excitedly, pointing up to the window as Tony crossed from one side to the other before disappearing again.

Krasic chopped Rado's arm to his side with a savage blow. 'For fuck's sake, Rado, do you want the whole street to see us?'

Rado clutched his aching arm and squirmed with the pain. 'Sorry, Uncle.'

'Never mind. You did a good job, spotting the bitch. Now I need to find out who her fancy man is. It'll have to wait till morning.' He was speaking to himself more than to his nephew. Krasic stared up at the window like a moonstruck hare, an intent frown on his face.

Time passed. Rado fidgeted, but Krasic stood immobile as stone. His military training had taught him the importance of being able to watch without being seen. Then, his life had depended on it. He wondered if that might be the case again.

At last, his patience was rewarded. There was no mistaking Caroline Jackson with her poignant echo of Katerina Basler's beauty. She stood near the window, her mouth moving in silent speech. Then, right next to her, the man popped up again. His hands came up to the side of her head, holding her as they kissed. It wasn't, he thought, the sort of casual good night kiss friends might share. As they parted, Caroline rumpled his hair in a gesture of easy affection. Then they both moved out of Krasic's line of sight.

A couple of minutes later, the man reappeared. He walked across to the window and stared out. Krasic shoved Rado even further back into the dark recess, crushing him against the shop door. But the man showed no signs of noticing their presence as he gazed up at the sky.

Peering over his uncle's shoulder, Rado said, 'Look, she's back home.' A light had gone on two floors above. As they watched, the woman they knew as Caroline Jackson drew the curtains.

Five minutes later, the man on the first floor turned his back on the street and his light went out. 'Go home, Rado,' Krasic instructed him. 'There'll be work for you in the morning. I'll call you when I know what it is.'

He watched the boy leave, glad that he'd had the presence of mind to keep a tail on the two-faced bitch. Whatever she was up to with the man on the first floor, it wasn't something she had chosen to mention to Tadzio. In his book, that meant it had to be something she didn't want them to know.

Krasic didn't like other people's secrets. In his experience, they spelled danger. Before too long, he was going to uncover whatever skeletons Caroline Jackson was keeping hidden in Apartment 102.

33

The Shark hadn't been exaggerating about the pigs, Petra thought grimly as she shuffled along on her stomach in a muddy ditch beneath a thorn hedge. The stink was overpowering, and they definitely did seem to head deliberately in her direction before delivering up their wind with a satisfied grunt. What he hadn't mentioned was the rats. She'd already come eye to beady eye with one, and she could swear she felt them running over her lower legs. Just the thought of it made her flesh crawl.

Before Plesch would authorize a full-scale liberation operation to rescue Tanja Krebs, she had insisted on corroboration of The Shark's sighting. 'It's not that I doubt your abilities,' she'd lied. 'But it's easy to make a mistake, to see what you want to see rather than what is actually the case. So before we make a big song and dance about this, I want Petra to go out there and confirm that the girl is being held there. If you're right, we'll mount a formal surveillance and prepare a hostage release strategy.'

She'd never seen Plesch in such a good mood. She'd even agreed without quibble to Petra's suggestion about putting Marlene into a witness protection programme, and that they should move fast and aim to co-ordinate their raid with Radecki's arrest in Rotterdam. Even the rats and pigs couldn't dissipate Petra's feeling of imminent triumph.

And in spite of Marijke's pessimism, she couldn't help but feel they were making some progress on the serial killer front, thanks in part to Tony Hill. He was a strange guy, she thought. There was obviously some kind of history between him and Carol. They both had that slight awkwardness when they talked about each other, and Carol had been much more relaxed since he'd arrived in Berlin. Well, good luck to them. She knew what a difference it made to have a relationship with someone who spoke the same professional language.

She adjusted her position, making sure she could get her binoculars to her eyes with the minimum of movement. She'd been here for hours, and the only thing that had happened was that old man Matic had fed the pigs. She glared at a heavy old sow who was lumbering towards her in a purposeful way, and held her breath.

At least it wasn't raining.

Yet.

Tony lay on the comfortable bed, enjoying the feel of the cool white cotton on his body. He couldn't remember the last time he'd felt so genuinely at peace. Certainly never in the middle of a serial killer investigation. But this morning, he felt like a swimmer who has finally arrived at the shore after an interminable battle with the waves. Ever since he'd first met Carol, he'd been struggling to make sense of the feelings she provoked in him. At first, he'd tried denial, since he knew he was incapable of giving her the sexual satisfaction she deserved. Then he'd tried to force it into the box marked 'friendship' because he feared the work they'd done together had laid too great a burden of emotional baggage on them. Finally, he'd opted for distance on the basis that what the eye doesn't see, the heart can't grieve over.

Each of these strategies had failed. But now the combination of a little blue pill and his experience with Frances had overcome that first objection. The second objection had fallen to the realization that what they had endured together could make them stronger rather than damage their intimacy. And now the distance had been shattered, and the world hadn't ended.

In all his working life, he had never found it possible to talk openly to another human being about his feelings when confronted with the appalling things one person could do to another. Yet the night before, he'd spilled out the anguish in his heart to Carol without a second thought. Even as he'd spoken, there had been an admonitory voice in the back of his head, warning that he was saying far too much. But he'd ignored it and, instead of revulsion, he'd found compassion. After the horrors of the Nazi records, he'd feared a succession of sleepless nights, afraid to close his eyes because of what dreams could do to him. Somehow Carol had acted as balm, releasing him from the terrible power of his imagination.

For the first time in years, he had something to look forward to beyond the closure of the case that currently occupied his mind. It was a tantalizing prospect. But before then, he had work to do. Tony pushed himself into a sitting position. Something was niggling at the back of his mind and he couldn't quite put his finger on it. It was something he'd seen or heard in Bremen, a detail that hadn't seemed relevant at the time but which should mean something to him now. 'Where are you, Geronimo?' he said softly. 'Are you planning the next one? Where is it going to be next? Where is the water going to take you next?

'Water's your element, that's why you drown them. And, somehow, water ties in to what was done to you. Maybe whoever made you their victim also suffered from it. Maybe your father or your grandfather endured the water torture room at Hochenstein. Is this the symbolic connection that establishes your superiority over your victims? A way of asserting that your magic is more powerful than theirs?' This realization reinforced Tony's conviction that they were looking for someone with links to the European waterway network. Water was the key, he thought.

Then, because the brain works in ways that nobody comprehends, the thought he had been seeking slipped into the front of his mind. 'The river,' he exclaimed. He jumped out of bed, reaching for last night's crumpled shirt and thrusting his arms into the sleeves. A brief waft of the fragrance of Carol's hair hit his nostrils and he smiled.

His laptop sat open on the escritoire. He brought it back to life from snooze mode and started to compose an e-mail to Carol, Petra and Marijke.

473

Good morning, ladies.

Insights for today. The fact he chooses such an unusual method of murder must have some significance for him. I think it must have played a substantial role in whatever childhood experiences shaped his psyche. I now know that similar methods were used in psychological torture by the Nazis, certainly at Hochenstein. That he is using Hochenstein as an alias reinforces this connection. If, as I surmise, he works on a boat, this has tremendous resonance. He is a waterman, water is his world, and by using it to kill them, he's saying that his power is stronger than theirs. So, I really think we should forget lorry drivers and concentrate on bargees.

Now, when I was in Bremen, the cop who was showing me round told me that, because the Rhine was in spate, it was closed to commercial traffic. If our man is on a barge, then surely that means he's not been able to get away? He must still be where he was when he killed Dr Calvet. Therefore he's got to be either in Köln itself or within easy striking distance of it. I realize that's a big area, but if you can start to narrow down the possible boats that were in the areas of the other crimes, it might just make it easier for you to put your hands on him.

I'm sorry this is coming at you in bits and pieces, but I'm conscious that he's working to a short-gap timetable and that the media attention is probably putting pressure on the investigation so I'm throwing stuff at you as it comes to me.

I'm going over to Petra's now to take another

look at the case files. But I'll be checking my e-mail
if any of you need to get hold of me.
    Tony

Rado was bored. He'd been sitting outside the apartment block since dawn, and neither Caroline Jackson
nor the man from 102 had appeared. Caroline's
curtains were still drawn, even though it was past
nine o'clock, and nothing was happening. It was all
right for his uncle Darko, holed up in a café round
the corner. He was warm, coffee'd up and with access
to a toilet. Being stuck in a parked car was a long
way off comfortable.

He was considering a foray to the corner kiosk for
a paper when the door to the apartment block opened
and the man from 102 walked out, a laptop case slung
over his shoulder. He hit the speed-dial button for his
uncle's mobile. 'Hi, it's Rado,' he gabbled. 'The man's
on the move. He's walking down towards the
Ku'damm. Looks as if he's trying to hail a taxi.'

'Stay with him. If he starts heading back to the
apartment, call me right away,' Krasic said. He ended
the call, swallowed the dregs of his coffee and tossed
a twenty-mark note on the table to cover what he'd
consumed. Heading purposefully out of the café, he
made straight for the apartment block, keeping an eye
out for Caroline Jackson. The last thing he wanted
was to bump into her.

Luck was with him as he headed for the door. A
harried-looking middle-aged man was rushing out
into the street, briefcase under his arm, a sheaf of
papers in his hand. Krasic caught the door before it
clicked shut. He was in. He ran up the stairs to the

first floor and got through the lock of 102 inside three minutes.

This time, he started with the bedroom. On the floor lay one of those leather travel bags with a dozen different compartments and pockets. Krasic began going through it methodically. In a zipped inside pocket, he found a passport. He pulled out a crumpled receipt from his pocket and scribbled down the details. Dr Anthony Hill, whoever he was. Date and place of birth. Entry and exit stamps from the USA, Canada, Australia and Russia. There was nothing else of interest in the bag.

Krasic quickly checked the clothes in the wardrobe. In the inside pocket of a battered tweed jacket he found a photo ID for the University of St Andrews Staff Club. Again, he jotted down the details. He headed through to the living room, which showed very little sign of occupancy. There was a pad of paper on the escritoire, but the top sheet was blank.

When his phone rang, he almost jumped out of his skin. 'What is it, Rado?' he growled.

'I just thought I'd let you know that he took a cab to an apartment opposite Kreuzberg Park. He let himself in with a key.'

'OK. Make a note of the address and keep an eye on him. Like I said, phone me when he heads back this way.' He stuffed the phone into his pocket and carried on searching. The only other thing of interest he found was a battered paperback copy of the poetry of T. S. Eliot. An inscription on the flyleaf read, 'To Tony, from Carol, *La Figlia Che Piange*'. Krasic looked up the poem with that title and felt none the wiser

476

after he'd read it. Something about a statue of a weeping girl.

Never mind. He had what he needed. He knew exactly where to go to find out all there was to know about Dr Anthony Hill.

Marijke emerged blinking into the daylight of the police station car park. She'd reached the point where she'd scream if she didn't get some fresh air. It felt like weeks since she'd breathed anything that hadn't already been through twenty other pairs of lungs. She shook her hands from the wrists, then rotated her shoulders. Intellectually, she knew they were making progress, but emotionally she felt mired in a bog of paperwork and electronic communications. The sheer volume of the material that was coming in meant she could scarcely stay up to speed, never mind have the time to process it and make considered decisions. Added to that, she'd had to feed into the investigation the suggestions that Tony had made, as if they came from her alone. All morning she'd been firing off actions for the rest of the team to get on with till she'd lost track of what she'd asked for and what was still to be done. And any minute now, Maartens would swan in and demand an update.

She was leaning against the wall feeling sorry for herself when one of the civilian clerks walked out of the police station looking tentative. He peered around him and, when his eyes lit on her, smiled and headed towards her. 'You're Brigadier van Hasselt, right?'

Marijke nodded. 'That's right.'

'I'm Daan Claessens? I process the traffic tickets?'

477

He had the irritating habit of making every statement sound like a question.

'Pleased to meet you, Daan,' she said wearily.

'Only, I was in the canteen this morning? And we were sitting with some of your detectives, and they were talking about the de Groot murder and the other killings? And they said you'd told them to look at all the CCTV film from the traffic cameras on the day of the murder? To try and spot a Golf with German plates?'

'That's right. It's a line of inquiry we're pursuing.'

'So, I thought it might be worth looking at traffic tickets?' He stood waiting for encouragement.

'Yes?' She was too weary to manage more than polite interest.

'So I went back and checked? And I found this –' With a flourish, he produced a sheet of paper from the folder he was carrying. He handed it over with the pride of a dog delivering a very slobbery stick.

It was a speeding ticket generated by one of the automatic cameras on the outskirts of the town. The date and time corresponded to Pieter de Groot's murder. The photograph showed a black Volkswagen Golf with German plates. Like the one Margarethe Schilling's partner had seen on her drive. Marijke felt her palms sweating as she read the details. The car was registered to Wilhelm Albert Mann. Twenty-six years old. His address was given as the *Wilhelmina Rosen*, care of a Hamburg shipping company. 'Unbelievable,' she breathed. It looked as if Tony had been right all along.

'Does this help?' Daan asked eagerly.

'Oh yes,' she said, amazed that she could still sound

calm. 'Yes, this helps a great deal. Thanks, Daan. Oh, and can you keep quiet about this for now? Confidentiality, and all that . . .'

He nodded. 'No problem, Brigadier.' He scuttled off, turning back at the door to give her a little wave.

The question was, what should she do now? Somehow, she had the feeling that the German detectives might be reluctant to see this as a high-priority solid lead. For one thing, it appeared to be nothing more than a combination of hunch and coincidence. There were plenty of innocent reasons why a German barge skipper's car might have been in Leiden. There wasn't even any proof that Mann himself had been driving it. More importantly, she understood only too well the politics of policing. No matter how eager the detectives were to clear their cases, there would be a reluctance on the part of their bosses to accept guidance from the Dutch police. They'd want the murders solved, sure, but they'd want the cases cracked by their own people. So while they might be glad of a lead on such a tough case, she didn't think it would be treated with the urgency she thought it deserved. Besides, this had been her case from the beginning. If it hadn't been for her and Petra, the German police would be a lot further behind than they were now. If anyone deserved the credit for solving these murders, it was them. She wasn't ready to give it away yet.

What she needed was for one of her unofficial allies to track down the *Wilhelmina Rosen* and check out Wilhelm Albert Mann. If Tony was right about the killer's boat being trapped by the floodwaters, it couldn't be too hard to search the Köln area for Mann's barge.

479

She walked back inside, mentally composing the e-mail.

Krasic looked down at the chubby young man who loomed over his keyboard like a miniature Jabba the Hutt. 'What do you think? Can you find out about this Dr Anthony Hill for me?'

Hansi the hacker smirked. 'Piece of piss. The public stuff I can get in minutes, but the private stuff, like address, bank details, that'll take me a bit longer. Leave it with me, I'll get you everything that's out there in a matter of hours.'

'Good. Oh, and while you're at it . . .' He read out the address Tony had taken a cab to that morning. 'I want to know who lives there. And what they do. OK?'

'And I get paid when?'

Krasic patted him on his greasy head. 'When I see the results.'

'I've never let you down yet,' the hacker said, his mouse pointer already moving across the screen.

'Now would not be a good time to start.' Before Krasic could say more, his phone rang. He stepped to the other side of the high-ceilinged room of the apartment in Prenzlauer Berg, where counter-culture wannabes rubbed shoulders with the real thing like his man in the corner. 'Hello?' he grunted.

'Darko, it's Arjouni.' The heavy Turkish accent was unmistakable, Krasic thought, wishing his new middle man would remember not to use names on the phone.

'What can I do for you?'

'We're short. The supplies that were due, they've not come in.'

'I know that. Don't you have enough to be going on with?'

'I'm nearly out. There's no way I can make it through the weekend.'

'Shit.' Krasic muttered. 'OK, leave it with me.' He ended the call then dialled Tadeusz. 'Boss? We've got a problem with supplies. With the river being closed, there's a shipment still en route.'

'Is it far from home?'

'Köln. I can get there in four, five hours,' Krasic said.

'I'll come with you.'

'There's no need. I can manage.'

'I know you can manage, but I'd like to come along. The last couple of days have given me a taste for seeing what goes on in my business.'

'I thought you were doing a live TV interview tonight on *Business Berlin*?' Krasic objected.

'That's not till ten o' clock. We'll have plenty of time to get there and back, the way you drive.'

'What about your new business partner? Aren't you supposed to have a meeting today?' Krasic said, trying to keep the sneer out of his voice.

'She could come too. She likes to see how things work.'

'No way. This is too close to the bone. Telling her is one thing, showing her is another. You come, if you must. But she stays away.'

He heard Tadeusz sigh. 'Oh, all right. Pick me up in half an hour, OK?'

Krasic replaced the phone in his pocket and headed for the door. 'Let me know when you have what I need. Call me, OK?'

'OK, Darko.' The hacker looked up from his screen. 'I love working for you. It's never the same thing twice.'

Tony clicked on his e-mail in-box again. He'd been checking every fifteen minutes or so, trying to fool himself that he was pursuing the investigation. The truth was he wanted to hear from Carol. But still there was nothing from her. He wondered what she was doing. She'd said nothing about her plans for the day, other than that she was waiting to hear from Radecki about the arrangements for their Rotterdam trip. Oh well, at least Marijke had got back to him.

Hi, Tony

I have some very interesting news. No point in copying it to Petra, because she's on surveillance today, and Carol is of course involved in her undercover. But I wanted to talk to you about this.

We have a speeding ticket issued to Wilhelm Albert Mann on the date of de Groot's murder, just after nine in the evening. It was a camera that caught him, not a cop, and we have a photo of the car, a black Volkswagen Golf with Hamburg plates. Mann's address is a boat. The *Wilhelmina Rosen*. I checked with someone in a shipping registry and this is a big Rhineship, they go all over Europe. What do you think? Is this worth checking out? I am reluctant to call the police in Köln, they will think it's crazy. If you agree it is worth checking out, I have a list of possible places in and around Köln where a Rhineship could be waiting for the river to subside. You can call me, I think.

She was right, he should call her, but first he needed to check something. He reached into his bag and pulled out the papers from Schloss Hochenstein. Of course, if Mann was their killer, it was possible that the person who had made him suffer didn't share his surname. His maternal grandfather, for example, would probably be called something completely different. But if his luck was running, there might be an illuminating correlation in there somewhere.

He hastily looked down the alphabetized lists. It was a fairly common name, and he found eight children whose surname was Mann. Five he dismissed at once. They had been euthanased on the grounds of either mental or physical handicap. A sixth, Klaus, had died of pneumonia within a couple of weeks of being admitted to one of the feeder hospitals in Bavaria. Gretel, the seventh, had been admitted to Hohenschönhausen, but the records said nothing about her. The eighth name was the one that leapt out. Albert Mann, from Bamberg, had been taken to Schloss Hochenstein aged eight, diagnosed with chronic anti-social behaviour. The only comment under his treatment regime was *Wasserraum*.

Tony grabbed the phone and rang the number Marijke had given him. 'Marijke?'

'Ja?'

'It's Tony Hill here. I got your e-mail.'

'You think it is something?'

'I think it's a huge something. It ties in very neatly to a discovery I've just made in the Schloss Hochenstein records. Can you send me a list of places where I should be looking in Köln? I'm going to see if I can get on a flight and I'll hire a car at the other end.'

'OK, I will e-mail you the directions immediately.'

'Don't you think you should get your German colleagues on to this now?' he asked.

'I want to be more certain. And it's still my case. If it wasn't for me and Petra – and you, of course – there would be no leads to follow. I think we have the right to chase this ourselves. And I want to thank you for all you are doing for us,' she said, her English competent but slightly stilted.

There was, Tony thought, little that was more powerful than naked self-interest. But he didn't have a problem with that. In his experience of nailing serial killers, when it came to the endgame, it was always better to keep the team as tight as possible. 'Listen, I haven't felt so alive for ages. It's me who should be thanking you. I'll keep you posted.'

Within fifteen minutes, he was running out of the apartment, laptop swinging from his shoulder. He had forty minutes to get to the airport for a flight to Bonn. Luckily, he got a taxi almost immediately.

He was so excited it never occurred to him to check if he was being followed.

Carol couldn't remember the last time she'd slept so long. She'd crawled into bed just before midnight, emotionally drained but still buzzing with excitement that she thought would keep her awake for hours. In spite of that, she'd crashed out as soon as her head hit the pillow, and when she'd opened her eyes it had been after ten.

As soon as she realized the clock hadn't stopped

the night before, she'd leapt out of bed and raced to the shower. She hadn't written a single word of her reports from the previous day, and that was going to take hours. At this rate, Morgan and Gandle would be convinced she was either dead or fucking Radecki. She'd better send them a quick holding e-mail to warn them what was coming.

'Bugger, bugger, bugger,' she shouted as the water cascaded over her. She wanted to laze in bed, hugging last night's encounter with Tony to her heart, replaying his every word. Instead, she was going to be stuck in front of a keyboard all afternoon, hammering out the details of her meetings with Radecki and Krasic.

She was barely out of the shower when the apartment phone rang. It could only be Radecki, she thought. Petra would never call her here, nor would Tony. And nobody else knew where she was. She dashed naked and dripping across the living room and grabbed it on the fifth ring. 'Hello?'

'Caroline, how are you today?' His familiar voice sounded formal.

'Very well, thanks. And you?'

'I have to chase off on some urgent business that's come up. I'm going to be out of town all day.'

'You sound pissed off with me, Tadzio,' Carol said, keeping her own tone cool.

'Not at all.' His voice softened a little. 'I'm only sorry because I'd hoped we could get together, maybe talk things over, but it's just impossible. Please believe me, this is nothing to do with last night. Darko and I really do have to deal with something very important.'

'That's fine, Tadzio. Business is important, we both know that. And I've got plenty of work to keep me occupied here.'

'OK, I didn't want you to think I was being funny with you after what happened last night.'

Carol smiled to herself. She could almost believe she really did have him right where she wanted him. Always leave them wanting more, that was obviously how it was done. 'I wouldn't want us to be uncomfortable with each other,' she said.

'Good. Oh, and if you want to borrow the Z8, just come round to the apartment. It's in the underground garage. The attendant has the keys. I'll tell him you might show up, yes?'

'Thanks. I don't think I'll have the time to go out gallivanting, but it's nice to know the offer's there if I need it. Give me a call when you get back, OK?'

'I will. And when I get back, we'll sort out our unfinished business, no?'

'I hope so. Bye, Tadzio.' She replaced the handset and smiled. It couldn't have worked out better. With Tadeusz out of the way, she wouldn't have to find an excuse to buy the time to write her report. And even better, she might be able to spend the evening with Tony. Life was going to be very good from now on. She felt it in her bones.

34

If it carried on raining like this, there wasn't much prospect of anything moving on the Rhine for a very long time, Tony thought as he peered through the windscreen of the hired Opel into the gloomy afternoon. According to the maps spread out over the passenger seat, he should be approaching a small canal basin up ahead. He'd already covered half a dozen sites around Köln without any luck, and he was growing tired of alternately soaking in the rain and steaming in the car.

He spotted the narrow opening on the right just in time to turn, though he had no opportunity to signal. He was concentrating too hard to notice the VW that swerved hastily into the turning behind him, Rado Matic at the wheel. The lane was almost a tunnel, with high hedges looming on either side, and Rado hung well back. After about a quarter of a mile, it opened out on to a wharf where half a dozen laden Rhineships were moored three deep.

Tony parked the car and climbed out again into the downpour, oblivious to the VW that carried on past his parking spot and disappeared behind a dilapidated building beyond. He scuttled across to the edge of the wharf where he could see the names of the first three boats across their sterns. No *Wilhelmina Rosen*. He ran down the quayside and checked the other three barges. No luck again. Back at the car, he called Marijke on his mobile. 'You can cross number seven off the list,' he said wearily as soon as she picked up the phone.

'I'm sorry, Tony,' she said. 'You've been wasting your time.'

'It had to be done.'

'No, listen, you *have* been wasting your time. I got one of my boys to phone the bigger canal basins in the area, the ones where you have to pay fees. And he just came up with a location for the *Wilhelmina Rosen*.'

'You're kidding?'

'No, it's right. The *Wilhelmina Rosen* is tied up in the Marina Widenfeld. It's on the Mosel, on the left bank, just outside Koblenz.'

'Where's that?' he asked, shuffling through the large-scale local maps till he found a regional one.

'Back the way you came from Bonn, down the Rhine to where it joins the Mosel. I think it's maybe an hour or so, to look at the map here.'

'Fine,' he groaned. 'Just about long enough to dry off before I have to get wet all over again.'

'Good luck,' she said. 'You won't approach him, will you?'

'No. I'll just watch. I promise.' He hung up and started the engine. To his amazement, the rain suddenly stopped as he emerged from the lane on to the main road. Tony smiled. 'That's better,' he said.

'If it's not raining, I can walk past and tell you what a beautiful boat you have. Hang on to your hat, Geronimo, I'm coming.'

Petra glared at Hanna Plesch across her desk. 'You agreed it would make sense to co-ordinate this with Carol Jordan's sting in Rotterdam. That's not going to happen for a couple of days yet. If we put pressure on Radecki and Krasic now, they might call the Dutch trip off, and we could lose the chance to roll up their whole network.'

'There's a child's life at stake here. I'm not prepared to take any chances. We can have Krebs moved out of the prison population tonight. We'll say she's been taken to hospital with acute appendicitis. That should give us some leeway in case we get into a hostage situation out at the farm. I want to move in on them as soon as it's dark.'

Petra was puce with fury. 'You were the one who was so adamant that we had to give way to Europol and the Brits on this operation. Now you want to grab the glory back.'

Plesch glared at her coldly. 'I'd have thought that would have appealed to someone as ambitious as you, Petra.'

She felt her hands bunch into fists. 'I admit I wanted to be the one to close Radecki down. But not at the risk of someone else's operation. Someone else's life.'

'Jordan is at no risk from our operation. However we don't know if that's the case where Tanja Krebs is concerned. For all you know, Krasic may have left instructions to dispose of the kid if anything happens to him and Radecki.'

'Why would he do that?' Petra raged. 'If they're locked up, all the more reason why they need an insurance policy. You're using anything you can to justify what you want to do.'

Plesch slammed the flat of her hand down on the desk. 'Enough! You're forgetting yourself, Becker. I'm in charge of this unit. If you want to stay a part of it, you have to learn where discussion ends and insubordination begins.'

Petra bit down hard on her anger. Giving way to her murderous fury now wouldn't solve anything. 'Yes, ma'am,' she forced out.

They glowered at each other across the desk. When Plesch spoke, she had miraculously managed to find a conversational tone again. 'I take it you want to be part of this operation?'

'Yes, ma'am.'

'OK. I've got a team coming in from Special Ops to lead the assault on the farmhouse. You'll be in joint command on the ground. I also want you to go and see Krebs and tell her what's happening. We need her co-operation, and I think you're the person to make sure we get it. So, have a briefing with the Special Ops guys, then get yourself over to the jail to talk to Krebs. They're moving her to the hospital wing in an hour.'

'Very good, ma'am.' Petra turned on her heel and walked to the door.

'Petra?' Plesch said as she turned the handle.

Petra swung back to face her. 'Yes?'

'Trust me, this makes sense.'

The look she gave Plesch said she didn't believe a word of it. But all Petra said was, 'If you say so, ma'am.' Then she was gone.

The Shark found her five minutes later standing in the pouring rain in the car park, a half-brick in her hand, pounding it into the wall. He had the sense to say nothing but simply wait until, exhausted, she let it fall to the ground. They stood looking at each other, water dripping down their faces. 'It's OK, Shark,' she said.

'You think so?'

'We'll make it so.' She put her arm round his shoulders and together they walked back inside the police station.

The Mercedes swept imperiously down the outside lane of the autobahn, Krasic at the wheel. 'Bloody weather,' he grumbled as the wipers struggled to cope with the spray as they passed an articulated lorry. The countryside was a misty green blur streaked with rain.

'As my grandmother used to say, if you cannot cure it, you must learn to endure it,' Tadeusz said, looking up from the shooting magazine he was reading.

'Fine. But I bet she never had to drive to fucking Köln in the rain because a shipment of heroin was trapped by a Rhine flood,' Krasic grumbled.

'Come on, Darko, it's only a bit of inconvenience. And look at it this way: the police like this weather about as much as we do. It makes it safer for us.'

Krasic grunted noncommittally. 'I hope it's better than this when we go up to Rotterdam.'

'Why don't we fly up? It's not as if we're going to be carrying anything suspicious.'

'I don't like flying places unless we have to,' Krasic said. 'Names on passenger lists leave a trail, you know that.'

'Well, what about the train? It's more comfortable than the car.'

'It's too public. You can't talk on a train. Too many nosy old women going to visit their grandchildren.'

'God, you really are in a cheerful mood today. What's eating you?'

Krasic debated whether to say anything about Caroline Jackson and Anthony Hill. Better to wait till he had more information, he decided. It was hard to see how there could be an innocent explanation for what he had witnessed the previous night, but given how besotted his boss was with this mysterious woman, he wanted as much ammunition as he could garner before he said a word against her. 'I just don't like the rain,' he said.

They continued in silence, Tadeusz returning to his magazine. Nearly three hours into the journey, more than two-thirds of the miles covered, Krasic's phone rang. He reached into his pocket and answered, while Tadeusz tutted at his failure to use the hands-free kit. 'Hello?' Krasic said.

'I've done that search,' the person on the other end said, distorted to a low alto by some sort of electronic voice changer.

'And?'

'You need to see the results for yourself. There's no way I'm talking about this over the phone.'

Krasic didn't like the sound of this one bit. He knew hackers tended to be fully paid-up members of the paranoid tendency, but that didn't mean they were always wrong. 'I can't come round now. I'm four hundred kilometres from Berlin.' Out of the corner of his eye, he could see Tadeusz looking interested.

'Can you get yourself to an internet café?'

'What?'

'An internet café. A place that rents out computers with internet access.'

'I know what an internet café is. How does that help me?'

'I'll set up an account and send the stuff to you. I'll use hotmail.com. You type in www.hotmail.com then your account name. I'll set it up with your own first name and surname. The password is the street where I live. OK? Can you remember that?'

'Of course I can bloody remember it – www.hotmail.com, then my name and the street where you live. Are you sure this is secure?'

'It's a lot more secure than talking on the phone. And, if I were you, I wouldn't hang about. You need to see this, and fast.' The caller hung up.

'Shit,' Krasic muttered, tossing the phone on to the dashboard. 'Where the fuck am I going to find an internet café?'

'What's going on, Darko?' Tadeusz asked. 'Who was that?'

Krasic swore under his breath in Serbo-Croat. 'Hansi the hacker. He's been doing something for me that turns out to be urgent. I need to find an internet café.'

'Well, take the next exit. Every little town and village has internet access these days. What's it all about?'

Krasic scowled. 'You're not going to like this.'

'I'm not going to like it any better if you make me wait.'

'After she left you last night, Caroline Jackson met another man.'

Tadeusz looked shocked. 'You were still following her?'

'I was still having her followed. You think I'm going to take a stranger on trust? I've had someone on her tail since you told me about her. And this is the first time she's done anything at all except shopping and working out.'

'So who was this man? Where did she meet him?' Tadeusz was trying to sound casual, but Krasic could hear the underlying tension in his voice.

'He has an apartment in the same block where she's staying. When she got home, she went straight to his apartment. Rado saw them in the window. She was kissing him.'

Tadeusz shook his head. 'He must have been mistaken. You know Rado. He's not the sharpest knife in the drawer. They'll have been greeting each other.'

Krasic shook his head. 'No. I saw them myself. They were kissing each other like they meant it. And it looked like it wasn't the first time, either. She was in his apartment for the best part of an hour and a half.'

Tadeusz clenched his fists. 'But she didn't spend the night?'

'No. She wouldn't be that stupid, would she? Not when you might be calling her on the phone,' Krasic pointed out brutally. 'She's stringing you along, boss.'

'So what has Hansi the hacker been doing?'

'When the man went out this morning, I tossed his apartment. Got his name and details. I told Hansi to find out all he could about him. I guess that's what he's been doing.'

'Who is he, this man?'

494

'He's called Dr Anthony Hill. He's on the staff at St Andrews University, I think. That's in England, right?'

'Scotland, actually.' Tadeusz's voice was tight and clipped. 'There's an exit coming up. Let's go and find out what Hansi the hacker can tell us about this Dr Anthony Hill. And then we'll decide what we do about Ms Jackson.'

Krasic glanced at his boss. His profile was grim, the muscles in his jaw bunched tightly. He wouldn't like to be in Caroline Jackson's shoes the next time they met. *Serves the bitch right,* he thought self-righteously as he flicked the turn signal to change lanes. You could never trust a woman.

He'd spent all night tossing in a fever, his berth soaked with sour sweat. His head pounded, waves of blackness pulsing between his temples. All evening, the boat had felt like a trap closing in on him. The forced inactivity was driving him crazy. He had nothing to occupy him except mechanical tasks that did nothing to take his mind off the arguments that raged constantly inside his head. Even Gunther and Manfred had noticed that something was wrong. He'd ended up yelling at them to leave him alone when they'd expressed their concern for the umpteenth time. The look of shock on their faces had been a terrible warning to him about the possible consequences of losing control.

He couldn't afford mistakes, or everything he had worked for so painstakingly would be lost. He had a long way to go before he could be sure that the world would understand what he was doing, and he needed to remember that every waking minute.

But it was hard to keep a grip on himself when his head was splitting with contradictory messages. Every time he thought he'd got things straight, another insidious notion crept into his mind, throwing things into confusion again. First he'd convinced himself that he'd broken faith with his mission by listening to his grandfather's voice and fucking Calvet. Then he persuaded himself that he'd done the right thing by making her so completely his. Then the pendulum would swing again and he'd be as bewildered as before.

On top of this, there had been the shock of reading the news stories that had identified his work. Although he'd known this moment would come, and had thought he was prepared for it, the actuality had thrown him into confusion. They were calling him a monster, which he'd expected. But he'd thought at least one of them would have realized that there was a solid, sensible reason for what had happened to those arrogant bastards. Instead, nobody had had a word of criticism for his victims. They'd been portrayed as innocents, as if it was inconceivable that they might have deserved to die at his hands.

Sure, there had been speculation about possible motives. A couple of the papers had even suggested he might be an insane animal rights activist making a statement against vivisection. Unbelievable. The answer was staring them in the face and they were too stupid to see it.

The more he read, the more angry he had felt. He began to think he would have to spell out to them what was really going on. But he didn't want to do anything yet that might expose him. He still had work to do, and now it was going to be a lot harder. One of the newspapers had broken the story that the police were warning academic psychologists to report any contact from unfamiliar media personnel. He didn't know how they'd uncovered his way of making contact, but he was blown now. Every one of the bastards would be on their guard. He wouldn't be able to use his cover story to lure them into his power again. Not in Germany, at least.

The next one he had planned was due to be in Holland anyway. Those dirty collaborators were as guilty as the German psychologists, he knew that. Maybe he would be safe there one more time, since the single European market still didn't seem to apply to news. He'd have to be, because he hadn't thought up an alternative yet, and he couldn't afford to wait. He needed to blur the memory of Calvet and prove to himself that he wasn't a failure. He'd just have to be extra careful. But after that, he was going to have to come up with another way to capture his victims.

It was all too much. By the time he'd gone to bed, his head was swimming. Then his body had proved as treacherous as his brain, depriving him of sleep and sending his temperature on a rollercoaster ride of fever and chill.

It had been dawn when he'd finally fallen into a deep and nourishing sleep. And when he'd woken, it was to find that a miracle had happened. The fog and confusion had lifted, leaving him as clear-headed as he had been on the day he first understood that he needed to provide a blood sacrifice.

He was smart. He would manage to come up with another ruse to trap his victims. He might even wait a while after the next one. Let the fuss die down, let them all forget that they could be on his list. It was going to be OK.

Now all he needed was for the river to subside.

Tadeusz had been right. Even in the small town just off the motorway junction, it was possible to gain access to cyberspace. It didn't actually run to an internet café, but a local newsagent had been enterprising enough to turn over part of his shop to what was proudly labelled the Net Zone. It consisted of three tables, each with a PC, and a Coke machine. Naturally, all three machines were occupied. Two teenage boys and an elderly woman stared fixedly at the screens.

Krasic snorted in exasperation. 'Shit,' he muttered through clenched teeth.

'Behave, Darko,' Tadeusz said tightly. He stepped forward and cleared his throat. 'I have a hundred marks for the first person to show they have the hospitality to give up their terminal to the stranger in town.'

The woman glanced up and giggled. The two youths looked at each other, confused. Then one jumped to his feet. 'For a hundred marks, it's all yours.'

Tadeusz took a couple of notes from his wallet and waved Krasic to the seat. 'Let's do it.' He leaned over the Serb's shoulder, gazing intently at the screen.

Krasic typed in the url for the free mail site. As he input what Hansi had told him to, the shopkeeper appeared in front of them. 'You need to pay for your time on the machine.'

'Fine,' Tadeusz said, waving another fifty-mark note at him. 'Keep the change. Now leave us alone.'

'Nothing like drawing attention to yourself,' Krasic muttered as he waited for the system to let him in.

'Like they know who we are. Come on, Darko, get this stuff on the screen.'

Krasic opened the mailbox and clicked on the promised message from Hansi. There were half a dozen file attachments and he went straight to the first one. It contained the basic details of Tony's life, from his university degree to his present post. 'Reader in psychology?' Krasic said. 'They give you a job just for being able to read?'

'It's a rank. Like professor, only not so senior,' Tadeusz said impatiently. 'Never mind that. What's all this stuff about consultant to the Home Office on offender profiling? This guy's a profiler?'

'Looks like he used to be, anyway.'

'Which means he works with cops,' Tadeusz said heavily. 'Carry on, Darko.'

Hansi had done a good job. Tony's address, phone number and bank details followed the CV. 'He's not exactly rolling in it, is he?' Krasic said. It didn't say much for Caroline Jackson's taste, he thought. The guy wasn't even good looking. Any woman who passed up his boss for this sad fucker wasn't someone whose judgement he'd be inclined to trust, that was for sure.

He opened the next attachment. It was a newspaper article about the trial of a serial killer called Jacko Vance. It focused on the role in his capture played by psychological profiler Tony Hill, the founder of the National Offender Profiling Task Force. 'Works with cops,' Tadeusz repeated, his eyes dark with anger. 'What's next?'

It was another newspaper article, this time about a serial killer who had claimed four victims in the northern English city of Bradfield. The writer described how psychologist Tony Hill had worked with the police to develop a profile that had led them to the murderer, but that it had almost cost him his life. 'What the fuck is Caroline Jackson doing with him?' Tadeusz demanded. 'You said she checked out, that people knew she was one of us.'

Krasic shrugged. 'Maybe she's the reason he isn't working with the cops any more. If your girlfriend's a criminal, you can't keep running with the hounds, can you?' He didn't really believe what he was saying, but he knew he had a better chance of convincing Tadeusz that Jackson was trouble if he didn't appear to be completely negative about her.

His words tailed off into silence as he opened the next file. It was a news photograph. Tony was in the foreground, three-quarters profile. He looked as if he was saying something to the woman behind him. Even though her face was slightly out of focus, there was no mistaking Caroline Jackson. Krasic kept his hand on the mouse motionless. He wanted to scroll down to the caption, but he had a cold feeling in the pit of his stomach. This was going to be very bad indeed.

He clicked on the <down> arrow and the words came into sight: *Dr Tony Hill, Home Office profiler, with Detective Inspector Carol Jordan at the scene of Damien Connolly's murder.*

'She's a fucking cop,' Krasic said with quiet venom. 'She's a fucking snake in the grass.'

Tadeusz had turned white. He had to grip the edge of the table to stop his hands shaking. This was the woman he had wanted to sleep with the night before. This was the woman he had taken inside his business. This was the woman he had allowed to heal his heart. And she was a traitor. 'We're going back to Berlin,' he said, turning on his heel and storming out of the shop, oblivious to the fact that everyone else was staring at him open-mouthed.

Krasic cast a glance over his shoulder. There was still one attachment to open. He read the text, his heart sinking even further. 'Fuck,' he said under his breath, then quickly exited from the e-mail program and turned off the computer. He jumped up and hurried after his boss, ignoring the shopkeeper's angry shout of, 'Hey, you're not supposed to switch them off like that.'

He found Tadeusz leaning against the locked car, the rain streaming down his face like tears. 'I'm going to kill the bitch,' he said as Krasic approached. 'I'm going to fucking kill the treacherous lying bitch.' He pushed himself upright. 'Come on, let's go.'

'Hang on, Tadzio. Look, we've come this far. Another hour will see us in Köln, we can pick up the drugs and head back then. It's not like she's going anywhere. She doesn't know we've rumbled her. And neither does that bastard she's shagging.'

'I want to go back now.'

'We need to think about this. Because there's more.'

'What do you mean, there's more?'

'Hill went to an apartment this morning. I got Hansi the hacker to check that out too. It belongs to a woman called Petra Becker. She's a cop. She works for the criminal intelligence unit. The bastards who have been trying to get something on us for years.'

Tadeusz smacked the flat of his hand against the side of the car. 'Let's go back. We pick him up, then we kill the bitch.'

'He's not in Berlin any more. Rado called me from Tempelhof, Hill was catching a flight to Bonn and Rado was trying to get on it.' Krasic pulled out his phone and dialled Rado's number. 'Where are you?' He listened intently, then said, 'Fine. Call me with an update every fifteen minutes.'

He turned back to Tadeusz. 'He's been driving around boatyards in Köln. Now he's heading down towards Koblenz. We're a lot nearer him than her. And she's going to be waiting for you to come back. If you want to pick him up, we can do it. And we can send Rado on to Köln to pick up the heroin.'

Tadeusz slumped against the car again. 'I suppose.'

Krasic unlocked the car and opened the passenger door. All the fight had gone out of Tadeusz. He collapsed into the seat. Krasic settled in behind the wheel and put the car in gear. They hit the autobahn at 120kph and the needle kept rising. Tadeusz stared straight ahead, his expression unreadable. After about twenty minutes, he finally spoke. 'You know what this means, don't you, Darko?' There was an agonized note in his voice that Krasic had last heard after Katerina's funeral.

'It means we could be fucked,' Krasic said.

Tadeusz ignored his response. 'If she's a cop, it's no coincidence that she is Katerina's double. They've been planning this for a long time, Darko. They didn't just happen to have a convenient lookalike to step into Katerina's shoes. They thought this whole thing up *because* they had a cop who could have been her sister.' His even tone cracked into a sound like a sob. 'They killed her, Darko. They wiped out the woman I loved so they could set me up. Now I know who to blame for Katerina's death. Not some stupid fucking careless biker, Darko. Carol Jordan, that's who.'

35

Petra leaned back in the comfortless chair and propped her feet up on the narrow prison hospital bed. Marlene was looking as rough as anxiety and prison could make a woman who hadn't started out with that many advantages. There were bags under her eyes, signalling lack of sleep and maybe even a few tears. *All the better for my purposes*, Petra thought. In spite of her ambivalence about the timing of the operation, she couldn't be anything less than whole-hearted in her commitment. She tossed a packet of cigarettes and a lighter to Marlene, who looked at them suspiciously, then shrugged and lit up. 'What am I doing in here?' she demanded. 'There's nothing the matter with me.'

'You've got acute appendicitis,' Petra said. 'Well, we think you have. If we're right, you'll have to be transferred to a civilian hospital for treatment.'

Marlene took a long drag on the cigarette, looking blissed out as the nicotine hit her bloodstream. 'What's your game?' she said, affecting boredom.

'I know where Tanja is.'

Marlene crossed her legs and gave Petra an appraising look. 'And your point would be?'

'Children should be with their mothers.'

'Yeah, but you bastards don't let us have them with us in here, do you?' Marlene blew a thin stream of smoke in Petra's direction.

'Marlene, I've had a hard day. I really can't be bothered going all round the houses with you. Here's the deal. I know Krasic is using Tanja as a bargaining chip. You keep your mouth shut and nothing bad happens to your daughter. Personally, I'd consider being tied up like a dog in a farmyard on the bad side, but I'm not you.'

'What the fuck are you talking about, tied up like a dog?'

Petra cut straight across the interruption. 'What I'm offering you is this. We liberate Tanja from her keepers, we get you out of here, and we put the pair of you into the witness protection programme. New city, new identity, new life. In exchange, you testify against Krasic and Radecki.'

Marlene stared at her, open-mouthed. She even forgot to smoke momentarily. 'Why should I believe you?' she said at last.

Petra fished a sheet of paper from her pocket and handed it to Marlene. 'I took it myself this morning with a digital camera.'

Marlene unfolded it to reveal a colour print of a small child straining on the end of a rope. The photograph had been doctored to remove any identifying features. She let out a small gasp, her hand flying to her mouth.

'Sorry it's a bit blurred, I was using a long lens.'

'Is she OK?'

Petra shrugged. 'As far as I can tell. But, hey, if I

had a kid, I wouldn't be too thrilled at the thought of Darko Krasic's cousin the pig farmer taking care of her. So, Marlene. What do you think? Might we have a deal?'

'You don't know who you're up against here,' Marlene said apprehensively. 'Krasic is an animal.'

'Marlene, I'll let you into a little secret here. You are not the only lever we have into Krasic and Radecki. In a few days' time, what you have to offer may well be strictly academic. Those guys are going away, and they're going to be gone for a very long time. But I would very much like to tie Kamal's murder round their neck along with everything else. Yes, you'll be sticking your neck out, but it's going to feel like a flea bite to those two compared with what we have lined up for them. I promise you, we'll keep you and Tanja safe. You have my personal guarantee of that.'

'A cop's guarantee?' Marlene snorted. Her fingers plucked at the blanket and she stared at the wall for what felt like forever to Petra, though it was probably less than a minute. She forced herself to keep quiet, to let Marlene calculate the odds for herself. Eventually, Marlene gave an impatient shrug. 'Fuck it, what have I got to lose?' she muttered bitterly. 'OK, we've got a deal.'

Petra gave a silent cheer. Now she could go back to the Special Ops Neanderthals cluttering up her squad room and let them release their testosterone in action. 'You made the right choice. For you and for Tanja. You'll be moved from here directly to a safe house, though everybody will be told you're going to hospital. And as soon as we've got Tanja, she'll be brought to you.'

She swung her feet on to the floor. 'Hang in there, Marlene. Between us, we're going to take these bastards down.'

Marlene snorted. 'Listen to little miss gung-ho. You've no idea what you're up against here, have you? I just hope you do the business as well as you talk it.'

So do I, Petra thought as she walked out. *For all our sakes, so do I.*

By the time Tony had navigated his way to the Marina Widenfeld a watery sun was burning off the last of the clouds. The marina was packed with boats, ranging from Rhineships lying low in the water to small pleasure craft with their cockpits covered in tarpaulins. A few people were on deck, swabbing down after the rain or doing the small maintenance jobs that were easily overlooked during the normal working of the river. There were a couple of bars and cafés set back from the wharves, and a large chandlers that announced diesel at competitive prices.

Tony found a space at the far end of the car park and sat for a few moments, lost in thought. 'You're out there,' he said under his breath. 'I know it. We're going to meet today, Geronimo. And you're going to have no idea who I am. I'll be one more nosy tourist, filling an hour before dinner, admiring your boat. Because I've got a hunch it'll be worth admiring. You kill so neatly, you won't live sloppily.'

He got out of the car and started a slow meander around the commercial area of the marina. The working barges were remarkable, he thought. Each was different, each spoke of the character of its owner

507

and crew. There were immaculately kept boats, with troughs of herbs and plants anywhere that wasn't in the way of work. There were scruffy coal barges with wheelhouses seamed with rust and blistered with old paint. Some had neat lace curtains at the windows, while others were adorned with elaborate flounces and ruching. Bright, fresh paintwork sat alongside varnished wood. Several had bikes chained to the safety rails, while others had cars squatting incongruously on the stern roofs. There was endless variety, right down to the pennants and flags that hung limp in the damp air.

Tony sauntered along, camera round his neck, occasionally pretending to take photographs of some of the finer specimens. He had passed a score of barges and Rhineships without success when he rounded a corner of the marina and almost walked into a black Golf. Right next to it was a magnificent wooden ship, its woodwork glistening with yacht varnish. Across the stern, in flowing cursive, he read *Wilhelmina Rosen, Hamburg.*

His heart leapt and he stepped back to take in the full majesty of the boat. He walked her entire length, then turned back to take a photograph. Finally he strolled back to the stern, giving the boat admiring looks all the way. As he drew parallel to the wheelhouse, a young man with dark hair tied back in a ponytail stepped out on to the deck. Even under a shapeless sweater, he was obviously broad-shouldered, his long legs clad in tight jeans, heavy work boots on his feet. He was clearly physically strong enough to be this killer, Tony thought. He pulled a baseball cap on as he emerged, obscuring his eyes.

'You've got a beautiful boat,' Tony called up to him.

The young man nodded. '*Ja*,' he said laconically. He made his way round to the gangplank, a few feet away from where Tony was standing.

'You don't often see older boats in such good condition,' Tony continued as the man came ashore.

'It takes hard work.' He continued towards the car.

'I couldn't help noticing that rather unusual pennant you've got there,' Tony tried, desperate to engage his putative killer in conversation.

The man frowned. 'What? My English is not good.'

Tony pointed to the triangular pennant hanging from a short flagstaff at the stern. It was black with a white fringe. Embroidered in the centre of it was a delicate weeping willow. 'The flag,' he said. 'I've never seen one like that before.'

The young man nodded, a smile of comprehension fleeting across his nondescript features. 'It is for death,' he said in a matter-of-fact tone. Tony felt his flesh crawl. 'My grandfather was skipper before me. But he is dead since two years.' He pointed to the pennant. 'We have flag to remember.'

'I'm sorry to hear it,' Tony said. 'So you're the skipper now?'

The young man opened the car and took a road atlas out of the door pocket, then headed back for the boat. '*Ja*. She is mine.'

'It must be hard for you, not being able to work because of the river.'

The young man stopped on the gangplank and turned back to face Tony. He shrugged. 'The river gives and the river takes. You get used to it. Thank you for liking my boat.' He sketched a wave and went back on board.

509

So much for your people skills, Tony thought wryly. He didn't expect his killer to be over-endowed with the social graces, but he'd hoped to draw him out a little more. There was nothing to confirm or refute their suspicion of the skipper of the *Wilhelmina Rosen*. Unless you counted that slightly morbid mourning pennant, which Tony was inclined very much to do. It was interesting that Mann had claimed his grandfather had died two years before. The sinister flag didn't look nearly bedraggled enough to have been hanging there for weeks, never mind months. If Mann had changed the pennant regularly, it might be a way of keeping his grandfather's death fresh in his mind. But there might be a more sinister explanation. Perhaps the pennant wasn't for the old man. Perhaps it was for Marie-Thérèse Calvet. He had a feeling in his bones that he had just exchanged pleasantries with a serial murderer. Certainly Mann exhibited some of the characteristics he would have expected to find in a personality-disordered killer – the reluctance to engage, the refusal to meet his eyes, the social awkwardness. But these could simply be the marks of a shy man. Bottom line? They had barely a shred of evidence to support his gut instinct.

Probably the only thing they could do now was to keep Mann under surveillance until he targeted his next victim. It was time for Marijke to put ambition to one side and whistle up the cavalry. He'd better call her, he realized. First, however, he had to finish making his stroll round the marina look innocent. Tony turned away from the *Wilhelmina Rosen* and walked on along the quayside, occasionally pausing to study one or other of the barges. It was boring, but necessary. Like so much in the profiler's life, he thought with a smile. But what was a dose of tedium compared to the high of saving lives?

Krasic swung the big Mercedes into the marina and cruised slowly along the perimeter. 'I know this place,' Krasic said. 'We've kept barges here before.' Suddenly, he pointed over to the side of the quay where a man with a camera was pottering along studying the boats. 'There he is. That fucking bastard Hill,' he said.

'That's him?' Tadeusz sounded incredulous. 'The little guy in the stupid tweed jacket?'

'That's him, I swear.'

'Give me your gun.'

'What?' Krasic was wrong-footed. He was the enforcer, not Tadzio.

'Give me your gun.' Tadeusz held out his hand impatiently.

'You're not going to shoot him in broad daylight?' Krasic asked. The mood his boss was in, anything was possible.

'Of course I'm not going to shoot him. Just give me the gun. When I get next to him, bring the car alongside.'

Krasic reached round to the small of his back where a subcompact Glock G27 nestled in a padded leather holster. He drew the gun and handed it to Tadeusz. 'Nine in the magazine,' he said abruptly.

'I don't plan on using it. At least, not yet,' Tadeusz said coldly, putting the gun in his raincoat pocket. He got out of the car and walked briskly over to the man Krasic had pointed out. As he came up behind Tony, he closed his hand round the comforting grip of the pistol. Drawing level, he jammed the muzzle of the gun into Tony's ribs. 'Don't move, Dr Hill,' he said, his voice brutal, his free hand gripping Tony's arm. To a distant observer, it would have looked like two friends meeting and greeting. 'That's a gun.'

Tony froze. 'Who are you?' he croaked, unable to see his assailant.

'My name is Tadeusz Radecki.'

Tony couldn't help the spasm of shock that gripped his muscles. He twitched violently in Tadeusz's grip. 'I don't understand,' he said. 'Who are you?'

Tadeusz jabbed the gun viciously against Tony's ribcage. 'Don't act stupid.' He heard the purr of the Mercedes engine as it came up behind him. The car stopped and Krasic got out. 'Get the back door, Darko.'

Krasic opened the door and Tadeusz pushed Tony inside, taking the gun out of his pocket as he did so. He climbed in beside him, holding the gun pointed at his stomach. 'A gut shot is the worst way to die,' he said conversationally.

'Look, there's been some mistake,' Tony protested feebly. 'I have no idea who you guys are and you're obviously mistaking me for someone else. Just let me go and we can forget all about this.' *Pathetic,* he thought. *Where's your training now? Where's that famous empathy now?*

'Bullshit,' Tadeusz said, his tone curt. 'You're not only fucking Carol Jordan, you're working with her. Darko, find us somewhere we can talk.'

Tony's brain raced into overdrive. They knew who Carol was. Her cover was blown. They knew who he was, and they wrongly assumed he was here because of them. What were they doing here though? How

512

could someone have followed him? He must surely have noticed, so haphazard had his travels been. But then, he hadn't been looking for a tail.

He pushed that thought to one side. Nothing could be more irrelevant than how Radecki came to be here. What mattered now was finding a way to protect Carol. He was under no illusions about what he was dealing with here. These men were killers. If he had to buy Carol's life at the expense of his own, so be it. Saving her was what mattered. If ever he had needed all his ingenuity, he needed it now. He made himself hold Radecki's stare without flinching.

He was surprised when the car suddenly came to a stop again. He hadn't been paying attention to anything other than the man in front of him. Now, he glanced over Radecki's shoulder through the window. They were in a more remote part of the marina, a much smaller dock with room for only half a dozen vessels. There wasn't another person in sight. The Mercedes had stopped alongside a steel barge painted battleship grey. 'Give me a minute, boss,' Krasic said, climbing out of the car. The boot lid rose, and Krasic disappeared behind it. He re-emerged, tucking a crowbar inside his jacket.

Tony watched with mounting anxiety as Krasic looked around him, then ran nimbly up the gang-plank to the barge. He climbed on to the hatch cover and swiftly popped the hasp of the padlock holding it shut. He slid it open and peered inside. Then he hurried back to the car, giving Tadeusz the thumbs-up signal.

'We're going to get out of the car and we're going to board this barge. If you try to run, I will shoot you

513

in the legs. I am a very good shot, Dr Hill,' Tadeusz said calmly. 'There's no point in shouting either. This place is deserted.'

Krasic opened the door and Tadeusz backed out, never taking his eyes off Tony, who slid across the seat and out of the car. Krasic grabbed him by the shoulder and swung him around. The gun was in his back again. He stumbled forward, almost tripping over the edge of the gangplank.

Once on board, he was marched up to the open hatch. Krasic clambered on to the ladder with surprising ease for so bulky a man. He descended into the gloom below. There was the hollow sound of footsteps on metal in an empty space, then a dim glow appeared in the hold.

'Get down there,' Tadeusz ordered him.

Gingerly, Tony turned to face him and negotiated his way on to the ladder. He was a couple of rungs down when he felt an excruciating pain in his hand, so sudden and severe he had to let go. His feet went from under him, scrabbling in mid-air for purchase, and for a terrifying moment he swung by one hand. He looked up in panic, seeing Tadeusz's hand swinging the gun butt towards his clenched fingers. Sweating with fear, he threw his injured arm round the ladder and managed to get one foot on a rung, pulling his undamaged hand out of the way at the last instant. He would never know how he managed it, but somehow he swarmed down the ladder fast enough to avoid any further attrition from above.

His shaking legs had barely reached solid ground when Krasic was on him, delivering a punch to the solar plexus that doubled him over in agony, his lungs screaming for breath, his muscles in spasm. Tony lay curled on the cold steel floor of the hold, a trickle of vomit escaping from the corner of his mouth. When he was next aware of anything outside his body, he saw Radecki towering above him in a distorted perspective that made him look huge and terrifying.

Krasic yanked him up by the collar of his jacket, practically throttling him. He threw Tony on to a pile of folded tarpaulins. 'Sit up, you useless twat,' he growled. Tony managed to prop himself up against the cold bulkhead. 'Now, strip off,' Krasic shouted.

Numbed with fear, Tony struggled to undress. It was made more difficult by the pain in his left hand. He thought at least two of his fingers were broken. The two men circled him like wolves tormenting their prey as his clumsy fingers worked his clothes off. Finally, he sat naked on the tarpaulins, breathing as hard as if he'd just run a mile. *They're doing this to humiliate you, to make you feel vulnerable. Don't let them take control of your head. Keep thinking, keep your brain moving.* The voice in his head seemed ridiculously reassuring, given the extremity of his situation. But it was all he had.

'You're working with that bitch against us, aren't you?' Tadeusz demanded.

'No, you've got it wrong. I'm working on a serial killer case for Europol. That's what I do, I profile serial killers.' Tony said, steeling himself for whatever was coming next. Krasic delivered a brutal kick to his shins that made him whimper in spite of himself.

'Wrong answer.' Tadeusz shifted his grip on the gun, holding it by the barrel. 'She's a cop and you're working with her to bring me down.'

Tony wiped a drizzle of spit from his chin and shook his head. 'Please, listen to me. I'm telling you the truth. Carol used to be a cop, it's true. But she's not any more. She went rogue. She changed sides. I knew her when she was a cop, I've been trying to talk her out of what she's doing now.'

He saw the gun butt coming but he was powerless to do anything more than swerve helplessly. It still caught him, and he heard as well as felt the splintering as his cheekbone shattered. This time, he threw up properly, a stream of hot vomit pouring over his thighs.

'Stop lying,' Tadeusz said, his voice gentle and sad. 'I know the truth. What is it they call it? A black operation. The sort of devious shit that never becomes public. I know what you people did. You killed the woman I loved because she looked like Carol Jordan. And then Carol Jordan moved in on me. Advised, no doubt, by your psychological expertise.'

Fuck, Tony thought. *If that's what they believe, there's no way out of this.* But he had to keep trying. 'No, please. That's not how it was. Look, Carol isn't a cop any more, but she still has friends who are. One of them showed her a photograph of Katerina, after she died, not before. Because he thought it was amazing how alike they were.' He paused to draw breath. The fact that nobody had hit him again gave him hope. 'She decided off her own bat to take advantage of that. She decided she was going to get into bed with you. Literally and metaphorically.' *Big words for a battered man*, he couldn't help thinking irrelevantly. 'I had to come to Germany for this murder investigation. The killer who's targeting psychologists. You must have seen it on the news?'

Tadeusz and Krasic exchanged a quick look. Tony thought he saw a trace of uncertainty in their eyes. 'I'm telling the truth,' he said, almost sobbing. 'I thought I could talk Carol out of what she was doing, get her back on track somehow. I love her. I don't want her to be on the opposite side of the fence.' He forced himself to cry, racking sobs that made his ribs scream in pain.

'So what were you doing here, checking out the barges?' Krasic demanded, his fist crashing into Tony's ribs, smashing his opposite shoulder into the cold steel bulkhead.

Tony screamed with the pain, folding his arms across his chest. This time, the tears were real. 'We've got a suspect,' he gasped. 'For the murders. We think he's a bargee. His boat's here. The *Wilhelmina Rosen*. Please, you've got to believe me,' Tony begged. He wiped the strings of snot from his nose, trying not to think about the blood streaking them.

'It's a good story,' Tadeusz said. Krasic looked at him as if he'd gone mad. 'It's a really good story. It's almost good enough to be true.'

'Boss,' Krasic protested.

Tadeusz raised one finger. 'It's OK, Darko. There's a very simple way to prove whether it's true or not. We're going to take our good friend Dr Hill back to Berlin with us. We've got a warehouse we can store him in temporarily. And then we run our little test.'

'What test?' Krasic said suspiciously.

'If he's telling the truth, then Carol Jordan won't have any compunction about fucking me, will she?'

The cold hand of panic constricted Tony's heart. What had he done?

36

Marijke put the phone down, struggling with mixed feelings. When Tony hadn't called her back, she hadn't known whether to be worried or pissed off. Either way, it left her hanging in mid-air, not knowing what was happening to her one semi-solid lead after weeks of chasing dead ends on the de Groot case. She also found, to her surprise, that she was feeling guilty about keeping her ideas from her colleagues. Reluctantly, she had to admit to herself that she was neither ruthless nor self-confident enough to put her own ambition ahead of the need to put a stop to these killings.

She'd pushed her paperwork to one side and drawn up a brief report of her reasons for suspecting Wilhelm Albert Mann. Of course, without being able to attach Tony's name to the theory, it didn't have the advantage of the weight of expertise, but she considered she'd done a good job of making it sound convincing. She'd concluded with the suggestion that, in the absence of any hard evidence, Mann should be put under surveillance.

Then she'd gone in search of Maartens, eventually

tracking him down in the bar across the street where he'd stopped for a quick beer on his way home. 'I want to send this to the cops in Köln,' she'd said, thrusting it under his nose.

He'd read it carefully, sipping at his Oranjeboom with an expression of vague distrust. 'Nice work, Marijke,' he said when he got to the end of it. 'I'm impressed with your knowledge of nautical knots.'

'The internet,' she said. 'Great research tool. What do you think? Should I send it to them, or is it going to make me look like a crazy woman running on intuition rather than evidence?'

Maartens spluttered a mouthful of beer over his hand. 'Marijke, if the guys in Köln are looking at as little as we are, they're going to give you the keys to the city. If nothing else, it gives them something to do that feels like action. Sure, it might just be coincidence, but what you're saying looks a lot like sense to me. It's not as if this guy has any legitimate professional reason for being here in Leiden, since we don't have commercial traffic on our canals. If this landed on my desk tonight, I'd have a team on the bugger by midnight. And I'd keep them on him till either he made a move or somebody else got killed at the other end of the country. Come on, let me buy you a drink to celebrate the first bit of forward movement we've had since de Groot got killed.'

She shook her head. 'Thanks, boss, but I'll take one in the pump for later. I want to get this on the fax to Köln right away.'

Hartmut Karpf in Köln hadn't wasted any time. Within fifteen minutes of her sending the fax, he'd called her back. 'This is really interesting material,' he'd said enthusiastically. 'Look, I want to move on this fast. But it's going to take a lot of manpower to do it properly. Is there any chance that you can come to Köln tomorrow? It would help me to convince my boss that it's worth doing if you were here to make the case in person.'

'I need to clear it with my commander, but I don't think he'll have any objection. Let me get back to you on that, OK?'

Half an hour later, she had made the arrangements. She needed to be in Köln by noon the following day. Which offered some interesting possibilities. Marijke checked her watch. Before she made any decisions, she had to check out flights.

It was turning into a very good day indeed. If only Tony would call, then it could get close to perfect.

The lane that ran past Matic's farm was as black as an underground cavern. High hedges cut out any light from the farmhouse, and cloud obscured the thin sliver of the crescent moon. It was hard to believe they were only a couple of miles from the edge of town, so still and dark was the spring evening. Petra peered at a green and black world through night-vision goggles, courtesy of the Special Ops commander. She felt as if she were underwater, men swimming in and out of her field of sight like strange aquatic creatures, their faces obscured with goggles and masks to protect against the smoke and tear gas they'd be using when they stormed the place.

The laconic tough guys who had been strutting their stuff all afternoon, crowding out her office, lolling in chairs and sprawling on the floor, had been transformed as night had fallen. They'd become a disciplined team, economic of movement and stealthy as shades. As soon as it had grown dark, a couple of them had flitted across the yard, silently planting microphones in the walls of the farmhouse and diverting the phone line via their own communications system. No incoming calls would be able to get through, and if Matic or his wife tried to make a call, all they would hear would be an unanswered ringing tone.

Now the team had the farmhouse encircled. When the word was given, they would rush the place, breaking the door down with a hydraulic ram. Petra had the plan off by heart. First the smoke, then the tear gas, then the men would pour in. The primary objective was to secure the child, the secondary objective to capture Arkady Matic and his wife. Petra was to wait in the lane with the commander of the unit, only approaching once those objectives had been secured.

The commander was standing over his communications specialist. 'Where are we up to?' he asked.

'They're talking in the kitchen. One adult male, one adult female. The child is there too. The woman just told her to sit at the table. They're about to eat dinner.'

'Good. We'll wait till they're sitting down, then we'll move in.' He turned to Petra. 'We want the minimum of fuss, so we'll go in when they're occupied with their food.'

She nodded agreement. 'The last thing we want is a hostage situation.'

'Quite,' he said briskly, the fingers of one hand

beating a tattoo against his thigh. 'God, I hate the waiting game.'

They stood in tense silence for a long couple of minutes, then the comms specialist gave the thumbs-up sign. 'The woman's dishing up dinner . . . She's sitting down and joining them. Yes, they're all there.'

The commander grabbed his radio. 'This is K-one to all units. Move in. Repeat, move in.' He gestured to Petra to follow him and they jogged the twenty yards to the farm gate. Moving shadows flickered around the house, caught in the soft light from curtained windows. Suddenly the night was split open by the crash of the ram against the solid wooden door, and cries of, 'Armed police, freeze!' filled the air.

The crunch of splintering wood reached them on the faint night breeze, then the soft crump of smoke grenades and the rattle of gas canisters against a hard surface. Muffled shouts followed, then the sound that Petra had dreaded. The boom of a single gunshot rang out. Horrified, she turned to the commander.

'Shotgun,' he said laconically.

There followed the sudden chatter of automatic fire. Then silence. 'What's going on?' Petra cried.

'I'd guess the farmer got a shot off before one of ours took him down. Don't worry, it's not turning into a fire fight.' His radio crackled and he raised it to his ear. Petra couldn't distinguish the words, only an excited jabber. 'I'll be right there,' he said. He clapped her on the shoulder. 'Come on, it's all over. They've got the girl.'

She followed him up the track. Tendrils of smoke drifted out of the open door, which sagged from a single hinge. As they reached the farmhouse, one of the Special Ops men walked out with a wailing child in his arms. Petra ran up and took his burden from him. 'It's all right, Tanja,' she said, stroking the girl's lank, unwashed hair. 'I'm taking you back to your mum.'

The commander was nowhere in sight. 'What happened?' Petra asked the officer who had brought Tanja out.

'Stupid bastard went for his shotgun,' he said. 'We've got one guy with flesh wounds to the arm and thigh. Nothing serious, I don't think.'

'What about Matic?' she asked, rocking the whimpering Tanja in her arms.

The officer made the traditional throat-cutting gesture. 'We had no choice. It's a bugger, though. The come-back we get from something like this, you'd think we went around shooting people for the hell of it.'

'You don't have any option when somebody's pointing a gun at you,' Petra agreed. 'Look, I want to get Tanja out of here. Will you tell your boss I've gone? We'll need to have a proper debrief, but that can wait for morning.'

He nodded. 'I'll pass it on.'

Petra walked away from the farm, wishing her car was parked closer. Tanja was growing heavier with every step, and she didn't know if she could carry her all the way. *What a day,* she thought, plodding onwards. She wondered momentarily how Carol was coping. She presumed there would be a report of yesterday's meeting with Radecki waiting in her mailbox, but there was no way she was going to get to that for the next couple of hours. She had to get Tanja off to the safe house and make sure all the security was in place. Tomorrow, she would organize the first of a series of interviews with Marlene that she hoped would give them enough to make sure Radecki stood trial in Germany, not in liberal Holland.

There was so much to be done. But it would all be worth it when she sat in court and watched Radecki go down for a very long time. She grinned in spite of her aching back. God, she loved this job.

Carol was finally managing to enjoy herself. Marijke had kept her posted about everyone else's activities, and she'd been frustrated at her inability to lend a hand. But there was no point in fretting, she scolded herself. So she'd taken a long luxurious bath, which had left her feeling more relaxed than she had since she first arrived in Berlin. She'd discovered that her apartment TV had a cable channel showing English films in the evenings, and she was sprawled on the sofa in Caroline Jackson's silk kimono, savouring the black humour of *Shallow Grave* and a bottle of Sancerre.

The film had just reached the point where Christopher Ecclestone was holed up in the loft with the money when the entryphone buzzed. Surprised, she hit the mute button, rolled languidly to her feet and went through to the hallway. The only person it was likely to be was Radecki, she thought. She wasn't in the mood for his company, nor was she dressed for it, but she could probably put him off.

Carol picked up the handset. 'Who is it?'

'It's me, Tadeusz. Can I come up?'

'I'm in the middle of some work, Tadzio. Can't we meet tomorrow?'

'I really need to see you. I can't stay long, I have to be at the TV studios in an hour.'

She could manage an hour, she thought, pressing the door-release button and hurrying through to the bedroom. A silk kimono was far too suggestive for Radecki right now, she knew. She pulled on some loose linen trousers, hastily fastened her bra and grabbed a shirt, then he was knocking at her door. She dragged the shirt over her head as she walked back into the hall and let him in.

He gave her no time to greet him, simply hauling her into his arms and kissing her hard and fierce on the mouth. He moved into the apartment, taking her with him, kicking the door shut as they went. Carol managed to free her lips from his, rearing back and laughing nervously. 'Hey, whoa! This is all a bit sudden,' she said.

'I've been thinking about you all day,' he said. There was an intensity to his voice that she had never heard before. 'I know you wanted time to think, but this is driving me crazy. I want you so bad, I can't eat, I can't sleep.' His hands were all over her, strong and urgent, giving her no opportunity to break free. He nuzzled her neck, nibbling at her ear with sharp little bites.

Carol started to feel nervous. This wasn't in her mental script of how things would go. She had been in control, but now she felt the situation running away from her. 'Tadzio, wait,' she said plaintively.

'Why?' he demanded. 'Last night, you wanted me as much as I wanted you. I know, I felt it. Why do we need to wait?'

'I'm not ready for this,' she said, trying to slip out of his embrace. But he was too strong, his encircling arms too tight around her.

'You know you are,' he said, his voice softer now. 'I didn't mean to scare you.' He raised a hand to the back of her neck, his long fingers caressing the soft skin there.

In spite of herself, Carol began to feel the sheer animal pleasure of his body against hers. There was a thrill in the power of his desire for her, no escaping it. But there was no way she could afford to yield. She was a cop, she reminded herself. Everything would be wasted if she let him seduce her. Besides, she wasn't about to do anything she would be ashamed of telling Tony. 'I'm not scared,' she said. 'I'm just not sure.'

'I'll make you sure,' he said, backing her into the living room and running both hands down her back to her buttocks.

Carol saw her chance and managed to slip out from under his grasp. She took a couple of swift steps away from him. 'This is too sudden,' she protested. Tadeusz stared wildly at her, his hair awry. *God, he's gorgeous.* The very thought felt like treachery.

'Please, Caroline,' he said, his voice cracking. 'I know you want me. We were both hot for each other last night. But if you won't trust yourself to make love with me when you want to, why should I believe you're someone I can trust in business? What's the big deal? We're both adults. We want to fuck each other's brains out. It's not like either of us has anybody else, is it? There's no question of infidelity. Just two people going crazy with desire.'

What was the right answer? Carol struggled to find something that would make sense to him, that would keep the deal alive while preserving her position. 'I can't explain,' she said. 'I just need some time, that's all.' He took a step towards her and she retreated. 'Please, Tadzio,' she added, trying for her most appealing smile.

He closed in on her, and suddenly she had nowhere left to go. Backed up against the wall, she was in his arms again. Again he was kissing her, the weight of his body keeping her pinned in place. He ran a hand over her breast, gently squeezing her nipple. She felt it harden involuntarily. 'You see?' he gasped. 'Your body knows the answer.' His hand moved downwards, sliding over her stomach.

Carol summoned up all her strength and pushed, catching him off balance enough to escape again. She backed into the middle of the room. 'This really isn't the time, Tadzio.'

He turned to face her. Now there was no tenderness in his expression. His eyes had darkened, his brows lowered. 'There's never going to be a right time, is there, *Carol?*' He delivered her name with a snarl.

Until then, she had felt no real sense of threat. He had seemed nothing more than an importunate wannabe lover; she had believed she could appeal to his innate good manners to protect herself. But that one word shattered the illusion. It hit her with the force of a physical blow. He knew her real name. She struggled to keep her composure but couldn't keep her eyes from widening in shock.

'Yes, that's right, I know who you are,' he said, advancing on her again.

She tried to circle away from him, but the loose material of her trousers caught in a chair leg, slowing her down enough for him to grab her wrist. 'Of course you know who I am,' she said, trying to sound reasonable. 'You checked me out.'

'I checked out Caroline Jackson,' he said, his voice low and dangerous. 'And I also checked out Carol Jordan.'

It was too late for bluff, she realized. There was nothing left to say. The only weapon she had now was silence. She held his gaze, trying for strength and defiance.

'Your precious boyfriend's been telling tales, Carol. Dr Hill spun me a story about how you weren't really a cop any more. How you'd crossed the line, seen your chance and taken it. But if that had been true, you would have slept with me. You would have let me fuck you seven different ways last night and again tonight. Anything to get what you wanted. Only a cop would hold out. I'm right, aren't I? You're still a cop?'

Still she said nothing, forcing her face not to give away the terror she'd felt as soon as he mentioned Tony. How had he found Tony? Where was he? What had they done to him?

Suddenly, he yanked her arm hard, pulling her off balance. As she staggered, he slapped her face with his free hand. 'You wouldn't fuck me, but you came straight back here and fucked him, didn't you, bitch?'

Carol steadied herself and looked at him with contempt. 'Is that what this is about? Male ego?' As soon as the words were out, she realized her mistake. Faster than she would have believed possible, he threw himself on her, his momentum bringing them both crashing to the floor. Now he had both hands free, and he slapped her face from side to side, her head jerking back and forth till she felt the room spin.

Then she was mercifully, unexpectedly free of him. She rolled on to her side and struggled to her knees, the world a dizzying kaleidoscope around her. She felt herself being jerked backwards and upwards. Her feet scrabbled for purchase on the floor, but before she could support herself, he slammed her into the wall with a sickening crunch. She felt her nose crumple as it hit, tasted the sharp coppery bite of blood at the back of her throat. Her knees failed her, and she collapsed to the floor again.

'I don't care if you fuck every man in Berlin,' he growled. 'What I care about is that you had my Katerina killed so you could play out your shitty little game.'

Carol rolled groggily into a sitting position. He knew what he was doing, fucking her head up like this. She could barely string two thoughts together, so stunned was she. What she did know, however, was that his words made no sense. 'No,' she groaned. 'That's not true. We just . . . took advantage.'

He leaned forward and grabbed a handful of her shirt front, pulling her up again. 'You think I'm stupid? You still think there's any point in lying to me?'

'I'm not . . . lying,' Carol managed to squeeze out through bruised lips. 'We didn't kill Katerina.'

'Don't fucking lie to me,' he screamed, flecks of spittle flying from his mouth and spattering her face. 'The motorbike that caused the accident is registered to your fucking National Crime Squad. You killed Katerina. And then you killed Colin Osborne so there would be two nice little vacancies for you to fill.'

'I had nothing to do with Katerina's death,' she protested weakly. 'I'd never heard your name till a couple of weeks ago.' Now he was dragging her across the room. Dazed, Carol couldn't work out what was going on. He was clearly going to kill her, so why not just get on with it?

When she registered that he was hauling her into the bedroom, her befuddled brain found the answer to that question. The panic that hit her then cut straight through her confused state. *Oh, no,* she thought. *There is no way this is going to happen to me.* Carol let her body flop, turning herself into a dead weight in a bid to slow him down. But he was in the grip of a rage of primeval proportions, a berserker fury that gave him a strength beyond his normal means.

She began to twist and flail, hoping he'd have to loosen his grip to contain her. He stopped heaving her across the floor for a moment and stooped over her. 'You know what's coming, don't you, bitch? I'm not going to kill you. I'm going to make you live with what you've done to me.' Then he slapped her again, so hard she thought her neck would snap. This time, she faded into unconsciousness.

When she came to, she couldn't remember where she was or why her head was a solid throb of pain. Nor could she understand why her hands wouldn't move when she tried to pull them out from under her back. Then he moved into her line of sight and everything clicked back into focus. She was naked on her bed, hands bound beneath her. And Radecki was hell-bent on revenge.

'You've destroyed my life,' he said. 'You killed Katerina, and you've obviously done enough to destroy my business. Well, now it's my turn. You'll get what's coming to you. And then I'm going back to kill your boyfriend. So you'll have to live with the knowledge that you are responsible for the death of someone you loved. Just like you've forced me to do. And then I'm going to walk away.'

'You . . . won't . . . get . . .' she mumbled.

'I won't get away with it? Of course I will. You think I haven't planned for this? You can't get my money. By morning, I'll be somewhere you and your bosses can't touch me, even if you could find me. So you see, all of this has been for nothing.' As he spoke, he was stripping off, placing shirt and trousers delicately over a chair, dropping his socks into his shoes. At last he stood naked before her. His erection was the ugliest thing she'd ever seen.

He walked towards the bed. Desperately, Carol tried to writhe away from him. But her hands were useless and her head wasn't working any more. He kneeled on the bed, forcing her legs apart. 'Come on, struggle a bit more. Make it more fun for me,' he taunted her.

Carol summoned up the last of her courage and spat in his face. He didn't even bother to wipe it clean. He simply smiled and said, 'I'm going to enjoy this, bitch.'

Then he was on top of her and she wanted to die.

37

Darko Krasic sat behind the wheel of the Mercedes smoking a cigar. He didn't want to think about what was happening three floors up. He hadn't believed a word of that stupid tale that Hill had tried to fob them off with. But Tadeusz had it bad for the woman, bad enough to clutch at a straw that thin. If it had been up to him, they would have finished Hill off in Koblenz and left him to rot on the barge. Because if he was right and Carol Jordan was a cop, they were finished, and instead of fucking around they should be activating their long-established escape plans.

After he'd dropped Tadeusz off at the apartment, he'd driven Tony to a small industrial unit they occasionally used for temporary storage. He'd driven the car right inside, then dragged the tarpaulin-wrapped bundle out of the boot and dumped it on the floor. He hadn't even bothered to check if he was alive. Krasic couldn't have cared less.

When he got back behind the wheel, he'd been tempted to cut and run. But loyalty had overcome his primal instincts and he'd driven back to collect Tadeusz as they'd arranged. Still, he couldn't help thinking he was acting like a fool. He tapped the cigar against the open window glass and glanced at the dashboard clock. They were cutting it fine. If Tadeusz was going to be live on air in three-quarters of an hour, he'd better get a move on.

He really didn't want to think about what was taking so much time.

At last, the door of the apartment block opened and Tadeusz emerged, his coat flapping around him as he hurried to the car. He flung open the door and jumped in. The smell of sweat and sex penetrated even the fug of Krasic's cigar, and the Serb's heart sank as he put the car in gear. 'What happened?' he asked, his heart sinking at the thought that the bitch had managed to pull the wool over his boss's eyes.

'She's a cop,' Tadeusz said. A jittery energy seemed to flow from him, filling the car with restless, pent-up edginess.

'We're fucked, then?'

He gave a harsh laugh. 'Well, somebody is.' He rubbed his eyes with his knuckles. 'Yes, Darko, basically, we're fucked.'

'So we're getting out, yeah?'

'Yes. Tonight. As soon as I've done what I have to do. We'll go to the TV station, I'll do my piece to camera, then we have to finish our business with Dr Hill. And then we pull out. We'll be in Belgrade for lunch.'

Krasic frowned. He didn't like this. In his experience, when things needed to be done, you cracked on and did them. You didn't piss about with the frills. 'Why don't we go now?'

'Because I don't want to set any alarm bells ringing. If Jordan has told the local cops what she knows and

I don't show up for the TV show when I'm supposed to, they might realize that I'm leaving town. And we might not make it out of the country.'

'Fine. Do the TV. But leave that asshole Hill alone.'

'No way. He's going to die.'

'Tadzio, he's going to die anyway. He's tied up like a Christmas parcel, he's got his own underpants stuffed in his mouth for a gag. He's got broken bones and no clothes on. And nobody knows where he is. He's going to die a very slow and painful death.'

Tadeusz shook his head. 'Not good enough. I want to see him die. I'm not taking any chances with that.'

'Did you kill her?' Krasic finally found the nerve to ask.

Tadeusz looked out of the window. 'No. That's why I've got to kill him. Let her live with what it feels like to lose the person you love when they've done nothing to deserve it. But don't worry, Darko. She's not in any fit state to set the dogs on us. I left her trussed like a chicken.'

There really was no answer to that, Krasic thought. Tadzio was out of control, and there was no arguing with him when he was in this frame of mind. He remembered it too well from the period after Katerina's death. All he could do was try to exercise some damage limitation.

'OK,' he said. 'But we make it quick and clean. I want to be on the road by midnight.'

'Don't worry, we will be.'

Krasic slowed down as he approached the barrier in front of the TV station car park. He sincerely hoped he wasn't hearing famous last words.

*   *   *

In the end, she had pretended to pass out. It hadn't been much of a stretch, for by then Carol had only been clinging to consciousness by a thread. She listened to him moving around the bedroom, getting dressed, heard his footsteps in the hall and then the merciful slam of the apartment door.

Only then did she let the tears come. Hot and heavy, they dripped from her lids, sliding down her temples to mingle with the sweat that plastered her hair to her head. She hadn't let him see her cry. It was the tiniest shred of victory, but it was enough to save her from feeling utterly destroyed.

Not that she was feeling anything much right then. It was as if by invading her Radecki had simultaneously hollowed her out. And the physical pain helped. It was something to focus on. Her raped, sodomized, and battered body provided plenty to keep her occupied.

But even through the haze of agony and grief and the overwhelming knowledge of degradation, Carol knew she couldn't just lie there and endure her suffering. He was going to kill Tony. It was probably already too late to do anything to stop him, but she had to try.

She tested the bonds on her wrists again. It was no use. Whatever he had used to pinion her had no give. She tried to move her legs, then realized they too were bound. A sob of despair caught in her throat. Somehow, she was going to have to manage.

Carol dug her heels into the bed, wincing at the fresh waves of suffering that pulsed from her lower abdomen and spread through her body. Gradually, inch by excruciating inch, she dragged herself to the bottom of the bed. She wriggled forward and managed to get her feet on the floor. Her muscles screamed their objections as she struggled into a sitting position. The effort left her gasping for breath.

Gingerly, she tried to stand. At the first effort, her knees wobbled disastrously and she collapsed back on the bed. Bile rose in her throat and she spat it out, past caring as it dribbled down her chest. On the second attempt, she coped better. She was swaying like a reed bed in a sea breeze, but she was upright.

Upright but incapable of forward movement. She could no more jump with her feet tied than she could have swung from the ceiling with her bound wrists. There was nothing else for it. She was going to have to roll. Almost weeping with the distress, she let herself fall to the floor. With a mixture of rolling and convulsive crawling, she made it through to the living room, bouncing painfully off the door jambs as she went. The phone on the desk seemed an impossible distance away, but she knew she had to get there. All that kept her going was the knowledge that Tony's life might depend on what fragile strength she had left in her. She couldn't afford to dwell on what had been done to her; there was more at stake than that.

In a blur of anguish, she crossed the room and banged into the desk. She squirmed round so she could grip the phone cable in her teeth and, with a backward jerk of her head, yanked it to the floor, the handset bouncing a foot away from her head. Through eyes puffed with tears and bruising, she peered at the push buttons. She knew she had memorized Petra's mobile number in what felt like a past life and prayed she could remember it now.

Digit by digit, Carol pressed her chin against the keys, hoping she would be quick enough to avoid the electronic switchboard system giving up on her and cutting the line before she reached the end. Finally, she twisted round so she could lean her head against the receiver. She heard the blessed sound of a phone ringing. It stopped abruptly, then she heard the electronic beep of an answering machine. Petra's voice chattered cheerfully in German, then there was another beep.

Carol tried to speak and could only croak. She cleared her throat painfully. 'Petra. It's Carol. I need you now. Come to the apartment. Please.' It was all she could manage. With her last ounce of energy, she terminated the call by rolling over on to the receiver rest.

Her immediate mission accomplished, Carol gave in and let unconsciousness claim her.

Tony had never been so cold in his life. It had been bad enough in the boot of the car, but at least there he'd been lying on carpet. He had no idea where he was now, but it felt as if he was lying on concrete or stone. He'd begun shivering uncontrollably a while ago, but his body seemed to be beyond that effort now. His muscles ached with cramp and, whenever he breathed, he could feel the broken tips of his ribs protest as they grated against each other. Was this how it had been for the children in Schloss Hochenstein? Freezing, in pain, alone and waiting for death?

Physical discomfort, however, ranked a poor second behind the mental torture. He didn't understand how it had happened, but Radecki had found him in Koblenz, and had known exactly who he was. He'd thought he was so smart, coming up with his idea of a plausible story on the spur of the moment. But all he had achieved was to leave Carol in more danger than she had been before.

The worst thing about his gift for worming his way inside other people's heads was that it left him with no illusions about the extremes of evil that human beings were capable of. Someone with less insight would not have understood the psychological message that Radecki had sent out loud and clear. One way or another, he was going to have sex with Carol. Tony knew that could never be consensual; what he had provoked by his futile attempts to save Carol was to deliver her up to rape.

He had heard all the arguments about rape not being the worst thing that could happen to a woman, but he had never found them convincing. For a woman like Carol, whose sense of identity was bound up in her perception of herself as strong and ultimately inviolable, rape brought havoc to the personality. It made the glue that integrated the person come unstuck. It left her with nothing but fragments of the life she thought she had owned. It undermined everything she thought she knew about herself.

And he had not only let that happen to Carol, he had made it happen. To have said nothing at all would have been better than what he had actually done. Even to have admitted the whole truth would probably have given her more chance of survival.

Oh come on, the voice in his head berated him. *Stop making a meal of this. You're using guilt to make yourself*

538

important. As soon as Radecki decided that Carol was part of
a black operation that killed his girlfriend, he was going to
take that kind of revenge. Stop wallowing and start thinking.

The trouble was, there was nothing about his situation that thinking would help. Like those children whose fate had been an abiding presence since he had entered the grim fastness of the schloss, he was powerless. He was bound and gagged, wrapped in smelly tarpaulin, his body too weak to put up any kind of resistance. One way or another, he was going to die here. Either Radecki would kill him, or else they'd simply leave him here to a slow, grim death. And all because some megalomaniac bastard had put Carol in the middle of a black operation.

For, strangely enough, he didn't doubt what Radecki had told him. It made sense of what had seemed the extraordinary coincidence of Carol's resemblance to Katerina. That Morgan and his team had happened to stumble across Carol after Katerina's death had always been hard for him to swallow. But it had been easier to think that ridiculous quirks of fate happened than to contemplate the arrogant brutality that killed an innocent woman simply to set up a snare to entrap her lover.

It would all be deniable, of course. If Carol survived, which was probably no more than a fifty-fifty chance right now, nobody would ever admit the way she'd been set up by her own side. She'd be bought off with whatever professional sop she asked for, but she'd always have Katerina's death hanging round her neck like an albatross. Every time she looked in the mirror, she would be reminded of the accident of genetics that had cost another woman her life.

Whatever the outcome for Carol tonight, he knew she would never be whole again. And while he knew it would be almost unbearable to see that disintegration happen to her, he bitterly regretted that he wouldn't be there to offer what small help he could. He'd never been one for regrets, believing that the choices people make are invariably the only possible ones for them at that point in their lives. But now he was about to die, he realized that they did have some value after all. Regret for things done and undone could provoke change in the future.

Only those with no future left could see that clearly.

Petra walked out of the safe house with a deep sense of fulfilment. Mother and daughter had had a satisfyingly emotional reunion, and Marlene was acting as if Petra were her new best friend. For the first time, she had actually volunteered information, revealing that she knew far more about Darko Krasic's activities than Petra had suspected. 'Tanja's father used to work for Radecki and Krasic,' she had admitted. 'His brother's a shipping agent, and Rudi was the go-between who helped set up their transport arrangements in the early days.'

'Where's Rudi now?'

'Feeding the fishes. His body turned up in the Spree a couple of years ago. It was supposed to have been an accident. He was pissed and they said he'd fallen in and drowned. We'd split up by then, but I always wondered. Radecki and Krasic don't like anybody knowing their business.'

It was yet another angle to go at. But that could wait till morning. Exhausted, Petra walked to her car, taking out her mobile and switching it back on. She'd turned it off while she'd been in the safe house, wanting no interruptions while she talked to Marlene. Immediately it rang, telling her she had a message. She dialled in to her message service and retrieved it. At first, she couldn't make out what was being said, only recognizing the voice as Carol's because she was speaking English. Hastily, she played it again, finger in her other ear to drown out the background traffic noise.

This time, there was no mistaking the words, or the desperation behind them. What the hell had happened? Petra ran the last few yards and drove like a traffic cop to Carol's street. She abandoned the car in a disabled bay and raced back up the street to the apartment block, groping in her bag for the spare set of keys to the apartment, congratulating herself on the foresight that had made her take a copy of Carol's keys. Luckily the lift was standing at the ground floor, so she didn't need to waste her energy running up the stairs.

She was about to put the key in the lock when she had a momentary flash of concern. What if this was a trap? What if Radecki or Krasic had forced Carol to make the call?

Petra pushed the thought away. Carol wouldn't put another officer at risk like that. If she'd been coerced, she would have found a form of words that would have given Petra warning. She unlocked the door and stepped inside. The apartment was silent, though she could see the flicker of the TV screen from the hallway. She picked up the smells of sex and blood and froze where she stood. 'Carol?' she called out.

Nothing. Petra slipped her hand into her bag, where her standard-issue Walther PPK nestled in an easily accessible inside pocket. Cautiously, she drew the gun and slipped off the safety. Gently placing her bag on the floor, she held the gun in a two-handed grip as she inched forward towards the living-room doorway, her back to the wall.

She turned swiftly into the room, straight into a firing stance. What confronted her was far, far worse than she could have imagined. Carol lay in a crumpled heap, wrists and ankles bound behind her back with leather belts. Her face was a streaked mess of blood, saliva, mucus and tears. Her nose was swollen and angled improbably. Her eyes were invisible in the puffy purpling of bruised flesh. Smudged trails of blood and shit were visible on her thighs. There was no room for doubt about what had happened here.

'Jesus Christ,' Petra moaned. She crossed the room in rapid strides, sticking her gun in her waistband. Tears of anger and grief swelled inside her as she sought frantically for a pulse in Carol's neck. Relief hit her as her fingers felt the slow beat of blood in the carotid artery.

What to do first? Petra hurried through to the kitchen and yanked out the drawers, looking for a sharp knife. She grabbed a dishtowel and ran it under the cold tap.

Gingerly she cut the belts away from Carol's hands and feet, swearing as she took in the deep welts they left. Carol's arms fell to her sides and a groan escaped from her lips. Petra sat down behind her and manoeuvred her into a more comfortable position, tenderly cradling her. She wiped the damp towel across Carol's forehead, constantly repeating, 'It's Petra, Carol. I'm here for you.'

Within a minute, Carol's swollen eyelids flickered, a thin gap appearing between them. 'Petra?' she whispered.

'I'm here, Carol. You're safe now.'

Carol struggled in her arms. 'Tony. They've got Tony,' she cried.

'Radecki?' Petra asked, no doubt in her mind who was responsible for this nightmare.

'He's got Tony. He's going to kill him. He told me. He knows who I am. I'm blown. And he's going to kill Tony because we killed Katerina.'

Petra's mind tried to grapple with Carol's words and make sense of them. What was all this about killing Katerina? She shook her head. She couldn't process this stuff now, and it was clear that there were more urgent matters on hand. She had no idea how long had passed since the attack on Carol. She had no idea where Radecki and Krasic were. She headed straight for the salient question. 'Where have they got him? Do you know?'

'No, I don't know. But you've got to find them. Stop them. You can't let them kill Tony.' Carol's voice was desperate. Tears leaked from the corners of her eyes as she clung on to Petra like a terrified child.

'Radecki did this to you?' She needed confirmation.

'Yes.'

'We need to get you to police headquarters, to the rape suite. You've got to see a doctor.'

'That's not important now. I'm alive. Tony might

not be for much longer. You've got to do something, Petra.'

Before Petra could say anything, she heard the distinctive ring of her mobile. 'Let me get that,' she said, gently extricating herself from Carol's grasp. She got to her feet and retrieved her bag.

'Hi, babe.' The voice was familiar, its cheerfulness dislocating in the context of the apartment.

'Marijke?'

'That's right. Guess where I am.'

'What?'

'Guess where I am.'

'I have no idea,' Petra said impatiently.

'I'm nearly at Zoo Station. In a cab. So, where do you want me to meet you?'

'What? You're in Berlin?' Petra wondered if she was losing her mind. This was insane. What the hell was Marijke doing in Berlin?

'I have to go to Köln tomorrow, so I decided I'd make a detour and stay with you. I thought you'd be pleased.' Marijke had realized that Petra was less than delighted and couldn't keep the disappointment from her voice.

'Jesus, Marijke, this is the worst possible moment . . . No, hang on, you can help me here. I've no time to explain, but I need you to come to Carol's apartment. Can you do that?'

'Of course. Where is it?'

Petra gave her the address. 'I'll see you soon. I'll explain. I've got to go, I'm sorry,' she added, glancing over her shoulder to see Carol hauling herself upright using the chair for support.

'Petra, you've got to find them,' she said urgently.

'I will, I will.' She crossed back to the desk and

grabbed the phone. 'Marijke's on her way. She'll take you to the police station.'

'What's Marijke doing in Berlin?' Carol asked, sounding as confused as Petra felt.

'Fuck knows.' Petra punched in a number and waited impatiently for an answer. 'Hello? Shark, is that you? Thank God you're still there. Listen, I need you to do something. I haven't got time to explain, but Radecki and Krasic have to be brought in right now. I want you to talk to KriPo, SchuPo, traffic, everybody. I want every cop in the city looking for them and I want them now.'

For some unfathomable reason, The Shark was laughing. 'Hey, Petra, it's not often I get the jump on you,' he spluttered.

'What? You mean they're already in custody?'

'No, but I can see Radecki from where I'm sitting,' he said.

'What?'

'He's on TV – *Business Berlin.* You know, that live studio programme where they get smart suits to talk to the politicos.'

'He's at the TV studios now?' She couldn't believe her luck.

'Well, yeah. I mean, like I said, it's live.'

'Thank you, God,' Petra breathed. 'Shark, who's around?'

'Well, there's just me from the squad. There's still three of the Special Ops guys here with their boss; they're typing up their reports about the raid on the farm. I wish I'd been there, it sounds wild. Oh, and there's a couple of Brits here too, looking for you actually.'

545

'Brits?'

'Some top man called Morgan and one of the desk jockeys from Den Haag, Gander or something.'

Suddenly, Berlin was the only place to be. 'Never mind them. Tell them to talk to Plesch. Can you put the Special Ops commander on? Now, Shark.' While she waited impatiently, Petra covered the mouthpiece and spoke to Carol. 'I can't believe this. Radecki's doing a live TV show right now. We can put a tail on him, hopefully he'll take us straight to Tony.'

'Oh God, that's right. I forgot. When he got here, he said he had to go to the TV studios. Jesus, I'm such a fucking fool,' Carol moaned.

'No, you're not, you're traumatized.' She looked at her watch. 'The show's only been on air for seven minutes. It's a forty-five-minute programme. The studios are only five minutes from here. It's going to be OK.' She heard a voice in her ear and held a hand up to indicate to Carol that she was back on the phone.

'Hello? It's me, Becker. Listen, I need your help. We've been mounting a major operation against a guy called Tadeusz Radecki. He's just raped and beaten one of our officers, and we believe he's planning to kill one of her associates. I haven't got time to go through the proper channels, but there's a man's life on the line here. Can you get mobile and meet me outside Channel Five in twenty minutes? We can tail Radecki from the studios, maybe manage to stop this going down?'

'Can't you get KriPo to handle this?'

Petra gave it everything she had. 'We haven't got time. Look, I wouldn't ask if it wasn't vital. Radecki and his sidekick Krasic are the worst. Drugs, guns,

546

illegals – they move them all. And they're killers. They know they're blown and, if we don't get them now, we could lose more than a life.'

'Oh, fuck it. Why not? OK. We'll see you outside Channel Five in twenty.'

'I owe you,' she said.

'Fucking right you do. See you there.'

She replaced the phone with an enormous sense of relief. 'I think we've got him,' she said quietly. 'We know where he is. We can tail him and pray he takes us to Tony in time.'

Carol was on her feet and wobbling towards the bathroom. 'He must have gone straight to the TV from here. Tony must still be alive.'

'Where are you going?' Petra demanded.

'I'm going for a shower. You're not leaving me behind.'

'Don't be crazy. You need to see a police doctor, we need to take evidence of what he did to you.'

Carol continued on her way, undaunted. 'This doesn't matter. We've got enough on Radecki to put him away forever. I need to be with you. I need to be sure Tony's OK.'

'No way,' Petra protested. 'You're in no fit state to go anywhere. That's why Marijke's coming here, to take care of you.'

'I'm coming with you,' Carol said stubbornly.

'There's no time. I'm leaving now.' Petra picked up her bag and made for the door.

'You can't do this to me, Petra,' Carol shouted.

'Yes, I can. Because it's the right thing. I need to concentrate on catching Radecki and saving Tony's life. I don't want to have to worry about you as well.

You stay here. I'll call you as soon as there's any news.' She was about to open the door when the intercom buzzed. Petra grabbed the handset. '*Ja?*' She listened for a moment, then pressed the door-release button. 'Marijke is on her way up. I'll call you. I promise, I'll call you.'

Petra opened the door and walked down the hall to the lift. Not in her wildest imaginings could she have come up with this scenario for her first meeting with Marijke. It was hard to picture anything less romantic than leaving her to comfort a rape victim while Petra went in search of a killer.

The doors opened and the two women faced each other. Petra couldn't stop the smile. Taller than she'd imagined, but far more attractive in the flesh than in the photographs Marijke had sent her. 'Hey,' she said. 'Your timing is terrible.'

'I thought you'd be pleased,' Marijke said huffily.

'Christ, Marijke! Carol's been raped, Radecki's taken Tony prisoner and he's going to kill him. I can't think about anything else right now.'

Marijke's face crumpled in shock. 'How is this?'

Petra pushed past her into the lift, gabbling all the while. 'Somehow, Carol's cover has been blown. I don't know how, I haven't had the chance to ask her. Radecki raped her, beat her. She's in a hell of a mess. I need to try and stop him killing Tony. You have to look after Carol, she shouldn't be alone.' She gave Marijke a quick kiss on the lips and gently steered her out of the lift. 'I'll call.' As the lift doors slid closed, she shouted, 'I'm really pleased you're here, Marijke.'

Stunned, Marijke stood staring at the brushed steel doors. This wasn't the encounter she'd fantasized about. She wasn't sure if her English was to blame, but she thought Petra had told her Carol had been raped and Tony was about to be killed. It was hard to take in. Only a few hours had passed since she had talked to them both on the phone. She raised her eyebrows, shrugged her backpack more firmly on to her shoulder and started looking for 302.

The door was ajar, and she could hear the sound of running water. Marijke stepped inside, closing the door behind her. Now she could hear that it was a shower cascading from behind a door on her left. She put down her backpack and knocked hard enough to be heard over the downpour. 'Hello?' she called tentatively.

The water stopped. 'Marijke?' a voice said.

'It's Marijke, yes.'

'Come in, it's not locked.' The shower resumed. Marijke entered to find a woman she presumed was Carol Jordan leaning against the wall of the shower cubicle, scrubbing herself with a bar of soap. Her face was a mess. The soft tissue had ballooned, her nose was clearly broken and her eyes were shrouded in bruises. That her wet hair was plastered to her head only made it look worse.

'I'm so sorry,' Marijke said.

'I'm doing OK,' Carol said. 'Really, I am.'

'I think you should not be washing yourself like this?' Marijke said.

'I've been through this once with Petra. This isn't important. Tony's what matters now.' Carol reached up and turned off the water again. 'Could you pass me a towel? And maybe help me out of here?'

Marijke leapt to her aid, wrapping her in one of

the fluffy bath sheets that hung on the rail. 'I don't understand what's happening.'

Carol closed her eyes, exhausted with the effort of standing in the shower. 'I need to sit down,' she said. Marijke steered her to the toilet. 'Get me some clothes from the bedroom, would you? I can't face going in there just yet. It's across the hall. Jeans and a sweater, underwear, whatever. I'll explain, I promise.'

While Marijke was gone, Carol managed to make a reasonable job of drying herself. She could hardly bear the pain when she tried to towel between her legs. She didn't want to think about the damage Radecki had done to her. There would be the rest of her life to contemplate that.

Marijke came back with an armful of clothes. 'You don't just want a dressing gown?' she said.

'I'm going out,' Carol said wearily.

'I don't think so,' Marijke said. 'You don't stand properly.'

'I need to be there,' Carol said. 'Will you help me dress?'

'OK. But you tell me what's going on, please.'

Carol groaned. 'It's a long story. And I don't know all of it.'

Marijke squatted down and started to put Carol's socks on. 'So make a start with what you do know.'

38

The TV company had clearly devoted all their lighting budget to their studios, Petra thought. If any public car park had been this badly lit at night, the customers would have complained it was a mugger's paradise. Still, she supposed, it was safe enough, given how hard she'd found it to get past the security guards on the gate. If Kamal had been heading for a live TV appearance and not the GeSa, Marlene would never have got to him.

She pushed the search button on the radio, irritated by the inane phone-in that had just started. What was keeping Radecki? The programme must have finished a good fifteen minutes ago. Surely he hadn't stopped to have a drink with the presenter and his fellow guests? He couldn't have left already; at night, the only way out of the building was via the back entrance and the car park. Besides, from where she was sitting, she could see Radecki's black Mercedes with the unmistakable profile of Darko Krasic behind the wheel.

God, she hoped they were going to lead her to Tony. And that he was still alive. For all she knew, Radecki could have been lying to Carol. Tony could have been murdered before that Polish bastard turned up at the apartment. What she couldn't work out was how Carol's cover had been blown. They'd been so circumspect. How had Radecki connected Tony and Carol? And why had he kidnapped Tony? How had something that was in perfect shape this morning turned into a pile of crap by evening?

Well, maybe they'd get some answers by the end of the night. She had confidence in the arrangements she'd made. There were three other cars out there besides hers. The Shark was driving one of the Special Ops guys. There were two others in an unmarked police car. And the Special Ops commander was driving his own SUV. She hadn't been best pleased to discover he had Larry Gandle and some other British cop called Morgan on board, but she wasn't in any position to tell them to fuck off and leave this to the locals. At least all the drivers knew the drill about swapping the tail car at regular intervals. She didn't think there was any way that Krasic could lose them.

The rear entrance of the studio complex opened and three men walked out, clearly in conversation. She spotted Radecki at once. Normally, she would have alerted the rest of the team, but they'd agreed to keep radio silence. With a pair of villains as sophisticated as Radecki and Krasic, it paid to keep risk to a minimum. And even then, as recent events had proved, they could still wreak havoc.

Radecki shook hands with the other two men and walked briskly to his car. Krasic had the lights on and the engine running before he got there. Petra started her engine as the Merc glided out of its bay and headed for the exit. She followed at a discreet distance, catching up as the barrier rose. The Mercedes turned left, and, as agreed, she turned right, flashing her lights at the other cars. They set off in a staggered convoy while she did a three-point turn in the middle of the street and tagged along behind the SUV.

None of them noticed the black BMW Z8 that fell in behind Petra's car.

'That's them,' Carol said excitedly as the Mercedes pulled out of the car park. 'Go, Marijke, go!'

'Wait a minute. We know Petra and her people will follow. We must make sure we don't get in the way. If she sees you, she'll send you home.' Marijke watched intently, noting the car that had followed the Mercedes was turning round to tuck in behind the three vehicles that had already formed a tail.

'Now?' Carol demanded.

Marijke nodded and pulled out. 'Now is good.'

'Thanks,' Carol said again, leaning back in the seat and wishing the pain in her head would subside. She'd swallowed four paracetamol before they came out, but they hadn't made even a dent in her suffering.

Arguing with Marijke hadn't helped. The Dutch detective had been adamant that they were staying put, Carol equally adamant that they didn't have a moment to lose. After a couple of minutes of getting nowhere, Carol had staggered off towards the door. 'You can't keep me here against my will,' she'd said. 'It's not your jurisdiction,' she'd added with a sardonic edge.

'What are you going to do? Follow him in a taxi?' Marijke had protested, snatching up her backpack and following Carol out of the apartment.

'I know where I can get a car.' She looked at her

watch. 'They're still on air for another fifteen minutes. A cab to the car, then drive to the studios. I might just be in time.'

'You're not thinking about driving?' Marijke protested.

'How else am I going to get there?'

'You've got a head injury. You lost consciousness. You could pass out. You could kill yourself.'

Carol shrugged, wincing. 'Well, there's one way to avoid that. You drive.'

Marijke had never met anyone more stubborn. She threw her hands in the air. 'OK. You win. Where's this car?'

'Radecki's apartment. He left the keys for me in case I wanted to use it.'

They were lucky. A cruising taxi passed within a minute of them reaching the street and soon they were standing on the pavement outside Radecki's building. 'You'd better get the car,' Carol said. 'I look like I've already been in a road traffic accident. Just tell the security man you're me and that Herr Radecki left the keys for his BMW.'

Marijke ran off, leaving Carol propped up against the wall. Left alone, with no action to distract her, there was nothing to keep the nightmare at bay. Her mind's eye betrayed her, flashing up the defiling images she wanted permanently erased from inside her head. Radecki's face above hers, the tearing invasion of her body, the transformation of something previously enjoyable into an excursion into brutality. The terrible sense of loss that left her feeling bleached and split open. And the tears that leaked from her eyes in spite of her best intentions.

There was nowhere to go to wrench her mind away from it. It was as if her past had been sprayed with defoliant, withering before her eyes to a shrivelled meaningless husk. And the future was something she dare not think about, since a future that didn't contain Tony promised nothing but sempiternal guilt.

Rescue came in the unlikely form of a BMW roadster roaring up the ramp from the underground garage. Carol limped across the pavement and gingerly lowered herself into the passenger seat. 'I don't know the way,' she said, feeling herself on the point of tears yet again.

Marijke smiled. 'I do. I asked the car park man. It's very near, he says. Just a couple of minutes away.'

Carol looked at her watch. 'We're going to be too late. The programme finished ten minutes ago.'

'Well, we better hurry.' Marijke put her foot down and the car leapt forward.

The car park attendant had been right. The studio was only a few streets away. 'I bet we've missed him,' Carol said morosely as they parked twenty yards away from the gate.

'I don't think so,' Marijke said. 'Two of the cars we passed on the way in had a driver sitting inside. And a passenger too, I think.'

Carol closed her eyes and let herself believe. 'The tag team. Thank you, Petra.'

They hadn't had long to wait. And now they were part of the convoy that might, just might save Tony's life.

They had been driving for about twenty minutes, doing exactly what they were supposed to. Every few minutes, the lead vehicle in the tail would turn off down a side street then double back and pick up the rear, leaving a fresh set of headlights in Krasic's mirror. Petra had no idea where they were headed. The one good thing was that they clearly weren't making for Radecki's apartment. That had to increase the chances that they were going to wherever Tony was being held captive.

They'd headed out east along Karl Marx Allee, and now they were on the fringes of Lichtenberg. Petra was second in line, behind the SUV. Suddenly, the Mercedes swung right into a small industrial estate near the railway marshalling yards. The SUV carried straight on, and Petra switched off her lights before she made the turn. She hung well back, keeping the Merc's tail lights in view. The brake lights burned bright for a moment, then it went dark. Petra turned off her ignition, fearing they might notice her engine, and coasted to a halt. She could see the outline of The Shark's car in her rear-view mirror, black against the outline of a warehouse. Petra switched off the interior light and got out of the car, avoiding the reflex of slamming it shut. She palmed her Walther and dropped her bag into the driver's footwell.

Seven shadows loomed up behind her. 'They've stopped just ahead. About fifty yards,' Petra said in a low voice. 'We need to check it out. Let's fan out and come at it front and side. If we're sure they've got Tony in there, I go in first. Special Ops behind me. Shark, you stay outside, cover our backs. Is everybody cool with that?'

The Special Ops commander grinned, his teeth flashing white. 'Sounds solid. I'll take the front with you. You two, come up on the left. And you, go with The Shark round on the right. We'll link up at the front if it's all clear.'

'We're coming with you,' Morgan said.

'I don't think so,' Petra said firmly.

'Look, I don't know what the fuck Tony Hill is doing in the middle of my operation, but he's a British citizen, and I am not taking a back seat here. I'd stake my pension that I've done a lot more operations like this than you have, Detective Becker.'

'Have you got a gun?' Petra demanded.

'No.'

'Then you're a liability.'

'I'll stay well back.'

'We're wasting time here,' the Special Ops commander muttered. 'Let him come. If he gets shot, it's not our responsibility.'

Petra threw her hands up in the air. 'Fine. You come with us, but the desk jockey' – she pointed at Gandle – 'goes with The Shark.'

Morgan nodded. 'OK. So let's do it.'

Someone yanked one end of the tarpaulin, spilling Tony on to the hard concrete floor. He felt his skin abrade as he skidded off the tarp, but he lay still, apart from his eyes blinking in the sudden light. He didn't have the energy for more. Radecki was standing in front of him, arms folded, legs apart.

'You lied to me,' he said conversationally. 'Please take that rag out of his mouth, Darko.'

Krasic leaned down and jerked Tony's underpants from his mouth. He'd become so dehydrated that he felt pieces of skin rip off with them. His tongue felt like a giant salami lying dead in his mouth. Even if he'd had anything to say, he doubted he could manage it.

'It was a good lie,' Radecki continued. 'Part of me almost believed it. I admit, I wanted to believe it. She's a beautiful woman. Well, I should say, she used to be a beautiful woman. I don't think her looks are going to work so well for her in the future.'

Tony tried not to show the pain Radecki's words gave him. He kept his gaze level, his eyes unflinchingly on the other man's face.

'I set her a little test, you see. I knew she was hot to fuck me last night, but she held back. If you were telling the truth, I knew she'd come across if she thought that playing hard to get was going to cost her our little deal. But if you were lying, she could never fuck me, could she? Because then all her evidence would be tainted. If it ever came to court, my lawyer would destroy her.' He unfolded his arms and thrust his hands in the pockets of his trousers. It was a strut, and Tony recognized it as such.

'And so, I demonstrated to my own satisfaction that you were indeed lying.' His mouth curved in a humourless smile. 'But I fucked her anyway. I fucked her mouth, I fucked her cunt, I fucked her ass. You should be grateful that I'm going to kill you, because after what I did to her, you'd never want to go near her again.'

There was a sort of relief in the confirmation of his imminent death, Tony thought. At least he wouldn't have to live with the guilt. He tried to speak, but nothing came out.

'I think our guest needs some lubrication, Darko.'

Krasic disappeared, returning with a bottle of mineral water. He crouched down and grabbed Tony by the hair, pouring the freezing water over his face and into his open mouth. Tony spluttered and gagged, but his mouth was no longer agonizingly dry.

'You were about to say something, Dr Hill?' Radecki said politely.

'You're boring me,' Tony croaked. 'Just finish the job.'

Radecki pouted. 'What is it with you Brits? You've got no sense of fun. That bitch Carol wouldn't even put up a fight. But then, maybe she was enjoying it?'

Tony wasn't going to rise to such transparent bait. He said nothing.

'You know why I'm going to kill you? It's not because you lied to me. It's because your people killed Katerina. She had done nothing wrong except to love me. Oh, and of course she had the misfortune to look like a convenient detective. So, I have to live with that.' For the first time, his face showed an emotion other than triumph or contempt. 'Just as Carol Jordan will have to live with the fact that what she is has cost you your life.' He pulled a gun out of the waistband of his trousers.

Tony closed his eyes and waited.

Carol reached for the door handle. 'Hold on,' Marijke said.

'Why? Petra's crew are all out of sight. We've come this far, I want to be there.'

'Think about it,' Marijke said, reaching to take Carol's hand in hers. 'It may be this is not the place. If Petra will see you, she will be angry. She will make us go away. You know this is the first time we have met? I don't want her to think I am a fool. Anyway,' she carried on over Carol's objection, 'you cannot walk so far, I think. We wait and see, and if they go in, we drive down and you can see it all for yourself.'

'I'm sorry, Marijke. I'm not thinking straight. You're right.'

'I know this is hard. You love him, yes?'

'Yes. I love him.' She'd never admitted it to another living soul. It was rather late to be starting now, but Carol felt she owed Tony that affirmation at least. 'But I don't think he's ever believed it.'

'You are lovers, yes?'

Carol shook her head. 'It's a complicated story. The circumstances were never right. Or so we thought.' She sighed. 'I wish now it had been different.'

'Don't despair. He's probably still alive. Petra will get him out.'

Carol squeezed the other woman's hand. 'Marijke, even if he gets out of this alive, there's not a chance in hell that we can be together. Not after what Radecki did to me tonight. Besides, it was me who brought him here, remember? If I hadn't asked him to come, he'd be home now. Safe and well.'

There was nothing more to be said, Marijke thought. At least, not now. She had seen too many rape victims over the years to offer platitudes now.

Petra took a deep breath and set off, walking fast but stealthily towards the spot where she'd seen the lights die. The empty Mercedes was parked outside a small building with corrugated metal walls and roof. There was a big roller door in the middle of the frontage, with a small wooden door set to one side. There was no cover between them and the door, but equally there were no windows to reveal their approach.

She put her head down and ran for it, her trainers almost silent on the asphalt. She flattened herself against the wall on one side of the door, Morgan and the Special Ops commander lined up on the other. Petra inched sideways, putting her ear to the door. Nothing. She shook her head. He winked at her and took a small hand drill from one of his many pockets. He placed it against the door and delicately turned the brace. Even standing next to him, Petra couldn't hear a thing.

Once the hole was made, he inserted a small microphone, then handed her a single earphone. Radecki's voice echoed loud and clear in her head as if someone had flicked a switch. '. . . oing to kill you? It's not because you lied to me. It's because your people killed Katerina. She had done nothing wrong except to love –' Petra ripped the earphone out.

'He's in there. Tony's in there. Radecki's threatening him. We need to go in now.'

He nodded. 'Stand clear.'

Petra jumped back as he drew his semi-automatic machine pistol and blew the lock out of the door in a single burst of fire. He kicked the door open and raced inside. She was at his heels, gun drawn for the second time that night. She had no idea where Morgan was, nor did she care.

She took it all in instantaneously, brain processing the scene. Radecki swinging round to face them, gun in hand. Krasic over to one side, reaching towards his back, then looking baffled and horrified. Tony's white body naked and bound between Radecki and them. 'Armed police, drop your weapons!' a voice roared. She realized with a shock that it was hers.

Radecki's face showed panic. He let off a loose shot that came nowhere near them. Petra took aim, her world narrowing to a tight focus. But before she could squeeze the trigger, there was another burst of automatic fire. Scarlet sprayed out in several directions from Radecki's legs and he crumpled to the floor, screaming, his gun clattering off out of reach.

From the corner of her eye, Petra caught sight of Krasic charging down the Special Ops commander. She swung round and, without pause for thought, squeezed out a single shot. It hit the Serb in the gut, felling him instantly.

Petra stood frozen to the spot, her ears ringing from the gunfire, her nostrils filled with the smell of cordite. Radecki was still squealing like a pig, while Krasic gurgled like a half-blocked drain. She heard running feet, then The Shark's voice. 'Fuck, I always miss the action,' he complained.

'We need ambulances, Shark. I don't want these two bastards to bleed to death. Go and radio for the paramedics. And you better get KriPo along too,' Petra said dully. She dropped her gun to the floor and walked like a zombie to Tony. She crouched down beside him, slipping her jacket off and putting it over his shoulders. His face was a mess, though nothing like as bad as Carol's had been. 'Somebody get a knife over here,' she called.

One of the Special Ops guys trotted over, opening a Swiss Army knife and handing it to her. For the second time that night, she freed someone she liked and respected from their bonds. Tony gave a shuddering cry as his arms and legs cramped at their sudden release.

Morgan knelt down by Tony and started massaging his legs. 'It's a bastard, but it passes quickly,' he said.

Then Tony thought he was hallucinating. He heard Carol's voice, riven with concern. 'Tony? Tony, are you OK?' He struggled to roll on to his back, but his arms had no strength. Gently, Morgan grasped his shoulders and turned him towards the door.

Petra jumped to her feet, astonishment on her face as she registered the arrival of Carol and Marijke. 'What the fuck are you two doing here?' she said, half-laughing, half-crying.

Carol ignored her, making for Tony like a pigeon for home. Gandle stepped into her path. 'DCI Jordan?' he said uncertainly, putting a hand on her arm.

'Take your fucking hands off me,' she snarled, brushing past him and continuing on her way. Unconscious of her own injuries, she knelt on the floor beside Tony, cradling his head against her breast. 'I'm so sorry,' she choked. 'I'm so sorry.'

Words were beyond him. He simply clung to her. There they stayed, oblivious to the hubbub around them as paramedics and police swarmed into the building. They were impervious to everything until Radecki's voice cut through the clamour in a roar. 'You think you've won, bitch?' Suddenly there was silence. 'I might be going to jail, but compared to you, I'm free. You'll never be free of me.'

39

Petra let herself into her apartment and closed the door quietly behind her. It was early evening, but she didn't want to risk waking Tony if he'd managed to fall asleep. He'd been staying in her apartment at her insistence ever since his discharge from hospital. They'd kept him in for a single night, out of concern about possible hypothermia rather than his acute injuries. Three broken ribs, two broken fingers and a shattered cheekbone weren't enough to justify occupying a hospital bed, the doctor had firmly told Petra when she had protested against so swift a release. 'He'll probably need some reconstructive surgery on his cheek, but that'll have to wait for a while,' he'd said.

So Petra had brought him back to her place. She didn't think he was fit to be left alone, and he didn't want to return home until Wilhelm Mann had been arrested. Now his involvement in the case was out in the open, his profile had been shared with the German police teams investigating the murders. She knew, because he'd told her, that he'd been taking phone calls from the officers in Heidelberg, Bremen and

Köln, but he'd said little about their content, merely that they seemed to be taking his analysis seriously. In truth, he'd not said much about anything, spending long hours staring into space, apparently oblivious to Petra's presence.

Carol of course had been whisked away to Den Haag by Morgan and Gandle. They had informed Hanna Plesch that they would debrief Carol there and pass on all their information to the Berlin criminal intelligence unit, who were working flat out to roll up Radecki's networks across Germany and beyond. Petra had complained about this too, but she might as well have saved her breath. Plesch was perfectly happy to have one less thing to think about in the aftermath of the dramatic and unorthodox climax to the operation against Radecki.

Petra had endured an uncomfortable interview with her boss on the subject of Tony's presence in Berlin and her own involvement in the serial killer investigation. But once it looked as though nothing was going to emerge in the media about the more bizarre elements of the showdown, Plesch had relaxed. She'd been more concerned over the possibility of having to answer questions about the presence of a Dutch cop and two British intelligence officers in a Special Ops action than she was about what she called Petra's anarchic behaviour. She could afford to be indulgent after such a good result, Petra thought.

Marijke had left for Köln the next morning on an early flight. They'd managed to spend rather less than an hour alone together in the course of that chaotic night, and they'd both been too dazed by events to be capable of anything other than bemused, sporadic conversation. Petra had a horrible feeling that they'd never find a way back to their previous ease with each other, and she regretted the loss already.

She walked quietly through to the living room, where Tony was sitting upright on the sofa. 'Hi,' she said.

'Good day?'

She shrugged out of her leather jacket and tossed it over a chair. 'Hard work. We've been pulling in Radecki's underlings all day and trying to find enough bodies to interview them. Even with all leave cancelled, we're struggling.'

'But at least you feel like you're getting somewhere,' he said.

'Oh yeah, we're making real progress.'

'That's more than can be said for Marijke.'

Petra gave him a quizzical look. 'Have you been talking to her today?'

He nodded. 'She called this afternoon. She's got to go back to Köln tomorrow, and she wanted to know if she should come via Berlin. She couldn't get hold of you at the office or on your mobile, so she rang here.'

'What did you tell her?'

Tony smiled. 'I told her she'd better book a hotel room since I'd turfed you out of your bed and I didn't think the two of you would fancy sharing the sofa.'

Petra felt a blush spread up her neck and across her face. 'So when does she get here?'

Tony looked at his watch. 'She'll be walking through the door any time now.'

Her face crumpled into a mask of consternation. 'Oh shit! I need to shower, I'm disgusting.'

'I don't think she'll care about that.'

'I care!' Petra started for the bathroom, but before she could get there, the door buzzer sounded. 'Oh shit,' she repeated.

'Too late.' Tony edged forward on the seat, wincing as his ribs protested at the movement. 'I'll just go and have a lie-down.'

'No, stay,' Petra commanded, looking worried. She pressed the door release and wiped her mouth with the back of her hand. 'Jesus, I am so nervous about this.' She swallowed hard and went to open the apartment door. She leaned in the doorway and listened to the footsteps echoing in the stairwell.

Then suddenly Marijke was there, grinning from ear to ear. 'Hello,' she said. 'You don't mind?'

Petra opened her arms and enveloped her in a hug. 'I'm so glad to see you,' she mumbled into her hair.

'I booked a hotel, like Tony said. But I wanted to talk to you both first,' Marijke said, pulling away to plant a kiss on the corner of Petra's mouth.

'Both of us?'

Marijke nodded. Petra took her hand and led her inside. The three of them exchanged greetings and commiserations over Tony's injuries while Petra opened a bottle of wine. 'So,' she said. 'What is it you need to talk to us both about?'

'I have to go back to Köln to discuss what we do about Mann,' Marijke said. 'They have been looking at him for four days now and he has done nothing at all suspicious. And they tell me that tomorrow the Rhine will be reopened to commercial traffic, and it will be difficult to keep him under surveillance once the *Wilhelmina Rosen* is under way.'

Petra snorted. 'What they mean is that it'll cost too much. Jesus, I hate those tight, stupid provincials.'

'They might also be afraid that they'll lose him and he'll kill again and they'll get caught up in a firestorm of media blame,' Tony pointed out.

'I don't think they want to call it off. But we know now that the *Wilhelmina Rosen*'s next destination will be Rotterdam. Mann must be aware that he's the subject of a manhunt here in Germany, but so far we have managed to avoid anyone in the media making the connection with our case in Leiden, so I think he'll feel more safe to kill in Holland.'

'So you're going to continue the surveillance once he crosses the border?' Petra asked.

'This is what we will discuss tomorrow. If he comes to Holland, I want to end it. I don't want this to drag out. But unless he makes a definite move, we will have nothing against him except circumstantial evidence. So I need your help. I am thinking maybe you will have better ideas than me?'

Petra stood up and paced the floor. 'Let's look at what we've got. We have the car that Dr Schilling's boyfriend saw and a matching car with Hamburg plates near the scene of de Groot's murder, which gives us Wilhelm Mann. We have a smear of marine engine oil on the folder he left in Pieter de Groot's filing system . . .'

'And no forensics from any of the other three recovered files,' Marijke chipped in gloomily.

Petra continued undaunted. 'We also have a sailor's knot, which leads back to Wilhelm Mann.'

'And thousands of other people,' Tony pointed out.

'Thank you, Tony,' Petra countered with a sardonic

smile. 'Thanks to the work the river police have been doing over the last week, we can put the *Wilhelmina Rosen* at or near all four murders, which also gives us Wilhelm Mann. We have a killer who uses the alias Hochenstein. Tony's list from Schloss Hochenstein gives us an Albert Mann who was a child survivor of psychological experiments.'

Marijke butted in. 'Yesterday we heard from the cops in Hamburg. They did a records search on Wilhelm Mann which gives him a grandfather called Albert Mann with the same date of birth as the man on Tony's list from Schloss Hochenstein. He died two years ago. The inquest said it was an accident, but if you look at it with the idea that his grandson is a killer, it is not hard to see that it could have been murder.'

'Christ, with that much circumstantial evidence, why don't Köln just bring him in for questioning? I would,' Petra complained.

'It wouldn't do any good,' Tony said. 'I doubt he'd say anything.'

'So what do we do?' Marijke said plaintively.

There was a long silence. Petra threw herself down on the sofa, making Tony flinch. He gritted his teeth and said, 'I think I could break him.'

'They wouldn't let you interrogate him,' Petra pointed out.

'I'm not talking about a formal interrogation,' Tony said. 'I'm talking about me and him, one to one.'

Petra shook her head. 'No way. You're not fit enough for anything like that. He could kill you like snapping a stick.'

'I'm not that pathetic,' Tony said. 'I've been moving

around a lot more today. The painkillers are starting to kick in. I can do it.'

'I thought you said his English was poor,' Petra objected.

'*Ich kann Deutsch sprechen*,' Tony said.

Petra stared at him open-mouthed. 'You kept very quiet about that.'

'How do you think I managed to read the case files?' He dipped his head at Marijke in acknowledgement. 'I was very grateful that you had your material translated into German, because I really can't manage Dutch.'

'It's still far too risky,' Marijke said.

'What choice do we have? Do we just sit back and let him kill again?' Now Tony sounded angry. 'I came into this business because I wanted to save lives. I can't do nothing while a serial killer is left at liberty to take more victims,' he said vehemently.

'Marijke's right. It's insane,' Petra insisted.

Tony shook his head. 'One of two things is going to happen here. Either the police are going to help me, or I'm going to do it alone. So, which is it to be?'

Every day, he was growing stronger. Because at first he had thought what he did with Calvet was a weakness, he had nearly let it destroy him. There had been days and nights when he feared he'd never chase the darkness away again. But he'd gradually come to see that his first reaction had been the correct one. Making her his had been the ultimate demonstration of his power. It took a special sort of person to carry a plan like this to the limit, and he knew now that fucking her hadn't tainted his mission. The realization had brought peace, and with the peace came a lightening of his spirit that was all the confirmation he needed. The headaches disappeared, and he felt released.

As if mirroring his personal relief, he heard the news that the river would be open again the next day. He would be able to continue his work. He'd been scanning the papers and the internet, and nobody seemed to have realized that he had crossed borders and killed in Holland. He had to believe that, there, his victims would still be oblivious to risk. He couldn't afford to think otherwise, or the fear would eat into his soul and make it impossible to act.

With the news that life would soon return to normal, he had e-mailed his next target and rearranged their appointment. He'd have to be cautious, just in case the police were trying to trap him by deliberately keeping de Groot's death out of the picture. He would have to make sure he wasn't walking into an ambush. But in three days' time, he felt confident that he would be knocking on a door in Utrecht. Professor Paul Muller would have to pay the price for what he'd had no right to inflict on others.

He leaned on the stern rail, watching the mourning pennant flutter in the gentle breeze. It was the fifth one he'd hung there since the death of his grandfather, a constant reminder of what he had achieved. It was pleasant to contemplate what he was going to do to Muller. Just the thought of it made his blood pump faster in his veins. Tonight, he'd go ashore and find a woman to fuck, fuelled by the fantasy of what Utrecht promised. He really had made progress. Now he could use their bodies for rehearsal as well as release.

Carol stared out of the window at the fat russet buds on the tree outside. She had no idea what kind of tree it was, nor did she care. All she knew was that there was something profoundly restful about gazing at it. Every now and again, the counsellor would ask her something in an attempt to provoke some response, but she'd found that it wasn't hard to ignore the banal questions.

She wanted her life back. She wanted to be where she was before, in a place where betrayal was not a common currency used as cavalierly by those who claimed to have right on their side as it was by those who knew they were the bad guys. She wanted to be somewhere she could escape the conviction that her own side had treated her worse than the enemy.

Radecki had raped her. But that was something she could survive, because in a sense that had been a legitimate act of war. She had done everything in her power to destroy him; the risk she had taken was that he would fight back.

What Morgan had done was infinitely worse. He was supposed to be on her side. In her book, that meant he owed her a duty of care. Or, at the very least, honesty. But he had thrown her to the wolves in an act of cold-blooded calculation. He had set her up as surely as he had set up Radecki.

She knew now that Radecki had been telling nothing less than the truth when he had accused her of being part of a conspiracy whose first act had been to murder his lover. She knew because on that first morning in Den Haag, she had sat in the briefing room and refused to say one word about what had happened until Morgan had answered her questions.

She hadn't spent a single night in Berlin. Morgan had accompanied her to the hospital and stood over her while a harried doctor had reset her nose. He'd had the decency to leave her alone while they gave her an internal examination and confirmed that she had sustained no lasting physical damage in spite of the brutality of Radecki's attack. Then he'd insisted she be discharged into his care. She hadn't had the energy to argue. There had been a car waiting to take them to the airport and a private plane to carry them on to Den Haag.

Then they'd left her in peace in a silent room inside the Europol complex for twenty-four hours, the only interruptions being from a blessedly uncommunicative doctor who regularly checked she wasn't suffering from concussion. The following morning, Gandle had appeared, telling her Morgan was waiting. She'd demanded time to shower and dress, then she'd walked into the briefing room.

Morgan had stood up, wreathed in smiles. 'Carol, how are you feeling? I can't tell you how sorry I am about the way this turned out.'

She'd ignored his proffered hand and sat down opposite him, saying nothing.

'I realize you must be feeling terrible. But I want you to know that whatever support you need, it's there for you. We've set up counselling sessions for you, and you must tell us whenever you get tired during these debriefs so we can take a break.' Morgan sat down, not in the least disconcerted by her apparent rudeness.

Carol maintained her silence, her grey eyes cool and level amid the puffy purple bruising that surrounded them. Let her face be his reproach, she thought.

'We need to go through your reports in detail. But first, I'm afraid we're going to have to ask you about what happened between you and Radecki at the end. Is that OK?'

Carol shook her head. 'I have some questions first.'

Morgan looked surprised. 'Well, fire away, Carol.'

'Were you responsible for murdering Katerina Basler?'

Morgan's eyes widened, though the rest of his face remained immobile. 'I don't know where you got that idea from,' he said.

'The bike that caused the accident that killed Katerina was registered to the National Crime Squad,' Carol said flatly. 'Radecki knows that. It's not much of a step from there to the assumption that you were behind her death.'

Morgan tried an indulgent smile. 'None of this has anything to do with what happened the other night. So why don't we just concentrate on that?'

'You don't get it, do you? I'm not saying a word until you answer my questions. And if you won't answer them, I'll keep on asking them until I find someone who will.'

Morgan recognized steel when he saw it. 'Radecki was a cancer that was spreading through Europe. When you find cancer, you cut it out. And sometimes that means you cut away healthy tissue too.'

'So you did kill Katerina?'

'Katerina was collateral damage. For the sake of the greater good,' Morgan said cautiously.

'And what about Colin Osborne? Was he collateral damage too?'

Morgan shook his head. 'Osborne was no innocent abroad. You lie down with dogs, you get up with fleas. He hitched his wagon to Radecki, he paid the price.'

'But you had him killed too?'

Morgan raised his eyebrows. 'Carol, this isn't playschool. These people are responsible for untold amounts of human misery. You can't tell me you're losing sleep over a piece of scum like Colin Osborne.'

'You're right. I don't particularly care about some Essex gangster who traded in people's lives. But I care about *my* life. I care that you set this whole black operation up because somebody somewhere told you there was an ambitious detective in the Met who was the spitting image of Katerina Basler. And you thought that was too good a chance to let it go by. You set me up for this. You wound me up and let me go, and all the time you knew there was a bomb underneath me waiting to go off.' Carol's voice was infused with cold rage.

Morgan stared down at the table. 'I'm ashamed that you had to go through that, Carol. But if you're asking me whether that's an unacceptable trade-off for putting Radecki away and winding up his rackets, I'd have to say no.'

'You bastard,' she said quietly.

He looked up and met her eyes. 'You're a cop, Carol. It's bred in the bone with you, just as it is with me. If our roles had been reversed, you'd have done exactly the same. And that's what's killing you right now. It's not that I betrayed you. It's that you know you'd wouldn't have done anything different if you'd been calling the shots.'

40

Every day, he was growing stronger. Tony could feel the vigour returning to his body as bone and muscle gradually healed. He was a long way from full fitness, but he no longer felt the debilitation of the first couple of days following his beating at the hands of Radecki and Krasic. He still moved stiffly and awkwardly, but at least he could walk around without feeling his body was about to fall to pieces.

And he had to admit that there was something very healing about being on the water, especially after the bruising encounters he'd endured. He had insisted on accompanying Marijke to the summit meeting in Köln to put his case for confronting Mann. But while the German police had been grateful for his profiling advice, they remained adamant that they wouldn't support such an unorthodox operation. Senior officers had argued that it would be seen by their courts as entrapment, and refused to risk any potential trial by going along with Tony's proposal. He'd argued as persuasively as he knew how, but they'd remained obdurate. All they were prepared to do was to maintain surveillance on Mann and his boat.

After the meeting, Marijke had grabbed him and hustled him off to a quiet bar near the police headquarters. 'I didn't agree with you at first,' she'd admitted. 'But I listened to you today, and I think maybe yours is the only way to put a stop to this.'

Tony stared at the table, knowing that if Marijke understood why he was so keen to confront Mann she would withdraw her support. There was nothing more dangerous in a police operation than personal feelings that spilled over into professional actions. He felt as if all he'd achieved since he'd arrived in Germany was to make things infinitely worse for someone he loved, and he desperately needed to do something that would feel like an atonement. Keeping these thoughts to himself, he'd simply replied that what they needed now was a plan. 'The academic community is going to be buzzing with rumours,' he added. 'Like I said in the meeting, either he's going to go to ground until the fuss dies down, or the chances are anyone he targets now will refuse to have anything to do with him. There's no telling what he'll do if he's thwarted like that. I know they talked today about trying to set up a sting, but there are just too many potential targets for that to be practical, especially if he changes the way he makes his rendezvous with victims. I understand why the police are reluctant to endorse me going head to head with Mann, but there's no other way. So how do we persuade your people to back me?'

So they'd tossed suggestions back and forth until finally they came up with something that had the feel of possibility to it. Marijke, who was flavour of the month with Maartens, had managed to convince her boss that she should take part in the pursuit. She had hired a twenty-nine-foot leisure cruiser with a couple of berths, a tiny galley and a pungent chemical toilet. The idea was to maintain visual contact with the *Wilhelmina Rosen* as she made her way up the Rhine towards Holland. If Mann appeared to be targeting another victim en route, the German police would do what was necessary. But if they made it over the Dutch border without incident, Tony would attempt to confront Mann and extract evidence from him, with Marijke's team providing back-up. It had taken all Marijke's powers of persuasion, but she'd eventually convinced Maartens to go along with the stratagem. The temptation of being the man who would succeed where the Germans had failed had proved too much in the end. Petra had supplied them with a state-of-the-art surveillance kit: a tiny radio microphone embedded in a pen whose signal could be picked up on a remote unit by Marijke. As soon as Tony had elicited enough evidence, Marijke and her colleagues would play the cavalry and come riding to the rescue.

It was a strategy fraught with risk, but Tony had been as resolute as Marijke that Mann's killing spree had to be brought to an end. 'With the last killing, the level of violence leapt dramatically. Now he's overtly sexualizing his murders, he's going to want to enjoy them more often. There's no reason why he should confine himself to Germany and Holland either. When it gets too hot for him in one place, he can simply cross a border and begin again. We can't hang back and wait till he finally makes a mistake that provides something harder than circumstantial evidence. I won't sit on my hands while a whole community is staked out like a sacrificial lamb,' he'd said to her as they'd boarded their boat.

And so they had spent the past two days meandering up the Rhine, sometimes ahead of the *Wilhelmina Rosen*, sometimes far in her wake, one or other of them in the cockpit with a pair of powerful binoculars, watching the movements of the three men on board. Every couple of hours or so, Karpf and Marijke would exchange phone calls, keeping each other up to date with the movements of the barge. The first night, it had motored until midnight, then anchored offshore, out of the shipping channel. Marijke and Tony had had to carry on downriver for another mile or so before they found a wharf where they could tie up. Marijke had insisted on sleeping for no more than four hours, lest they miss their target. 'I'm beginning to think the German police had a point about the difficulties of maintaining surveillance on a boat,' she'd said wryly as she zipped herself into her sleeping bag.

'At least we know he's not murdering anyone tonight,' Tony said. 'He can't get the car ashore from there.'

Marijke had been huddled in the cockpit over a steaming cup of tea when the *Wilhelmina Rosen* had passed them just after six. She called to Tony to take the helm while she cast off, and they were soon back on the trail. The day's journey brought them to the Dutch border, and the barge made its way into the first commercial harbour on Dutch territory, Vluchthaven Lobith-Tolkamer. 'What do we do now?' Tony asked.

'It's an hour since I put my team on stand-by. They should be able to get here very quickly. Now, according to the chart, we can use this harbour too,' Marijke said, turning the helm. 'We watch where the *Wilhelmina Rosen* moors up, I put you ashore, then I go and find a yacht mooring, no?'

It was easier said than done. They managed to keep their objective in sight, but there was no easy way for Tony to go ashore nearby. The only possibility would have involved climbing a dozen feet up an iron ladder set into the harbour wall, and Tony had to acknowledge that was far beyond his present capabilities. Eventually, Marijke found a pontoon where he could scramble on to dry land, but by then they were both in a ferment of frustration and anxiety.

Tony hurried back to where they'd last seen the *Wilhelmina Rosen*, a task that was easier in theory than in practice because of the pontoons and moles that stuck out at apparently random angles to the main wharves. Eventually, he found himself at one end of a long jetty. Towards the end of it, he could see the *Wilhelmina Rosen*. With a sense of relief, he saw that the Golf still sat on the stern roof.

There was, however, no easy vantage point from which to keep an eye on the barge. This wasn't the sort of place where people went for an evening out to sit around watching the water traffic. It was a working harbour where men went about their business. The only advantage he had was that it was already almost dark. In half an hour or so, nobody would notice him standing in the shadows of the low brick building at the landward end of the wharf. He tried to look like a man who is waiting to meet someone, pacing to and fro and looking at his watch.

Twenty minutes passed and the night gathered around him, broken by pools of harsh light from the lamps that illuminated the wharves and the softer hazes of brightness from the boats themselves. He was so intent on his surveillance that he didn't notice Marijke's arrival until she was right next to him. 'I spoke to the team. They'll be here in about twenty minutes. Anything happen?' she asked.

'No sign of life.'

'So, now we wait till my people get here.'

'We have to wait anyway. I need to get him alone.'

'OK, but we should be ready for when the others arrive.' Marijke fiddled with the radio equipment, clipping the pen to Tony's jacket pocket and inserting her earphone. 'Walk down the jetty and talk to me,' she said, readying the minidisk recorder that completed the system.

He set off, nerves jangling, forcing himself to walk at the right speed. Too slow and he'd look incongruously like a tourist; too fast and he'd draw attention to himself. Already his mind was racing ahead to the encounter with Mann, and he tried to calm himself by focusing on his surroundings. The evening air had a cool bite to it, counteracting the heavy stink of diesel fumes and the odd whiff of cooking food that came from the barges moored alongside. But Tony felt hot and clammy, perspiration making his shirt cling with all the discomfort of a wetsuit on dry land.

He was halfway along the wharf when two figures appeared at the wheelhouse of the *Wilhelmina Rosen*. 'Oh shit,' he said softly. 'Marijke, we have activity.

Two men, can't see if either of them is Mann.' Heart racing, he carried on walking as the pair came down the gangplank and headed towards him. They drew closer and he could see that neither was his target. They passed him without so much as a curious glance and Tony muttered, 'Negative. I think he's on board alone now. I'm going to turn round. If you can hear me, step forward into the light and wave to me.' He turned to face the direction he'd come from and saw Marijke emerge into a cone of light. She raised one hand and let it fall.

The sensible thing would have been to walk back to her and wait till the back-up team was in place. But by then Mann could have left the barge. Or his crewmen could have returned. And Tony was in no mood to be drawn by the sensible option.

He couldn't resist the sense that he was fated to be in the right place when opportunity opened up before him. He understood the risks, but he no longer felt sufficiently attached to the idea of living to care either way. His guilt over Carol was a maggot in his heart that would only grow fatter with time. He wasn't sure that was something he could live with. If it was all going to end here, then so be it.

'I'm sorry, Marijke, I can't wait. I'm going in. Fingers crossed.' Tony closed his eyes for a moment, breathing deeply. His body felt as taut as the bonds Krasic had fastened around him. There was no point in being afraid now. He needed all his concentration for Mann.

He stepped on to the gangplank of the *Wilhelmina Rosen* then called out. 'Hello? May I come on board?' He knew there were rules of courtesy about approaching a boat that was also a home and he didn't want to set Mann's alarm bells ringing too early.

There was no reply, although lights showed in the wheelhouse and in the cabin below. He moved closer to the deck and called out again. This time, a head appeared at the door of the wheelhouse. It was the young man with the ponytail that he'd seen previously at Koblenz, his face screwed up as he tried to identify the figure silhouetted against the quayside lights. Tony switched to German. 'Can I come aboard?' he asked.

'Who are you?' the man he assumed to be Wilhelm Mann said.

'I'm looking for Wilhelm Mann.'

'I'm Willi Mann. What do you want with me?'

'Can we talk inside? It's a private matter,' Tony said, trying to look innocuous, arms loose by his sides in an unthreatening posture. This was the key moment; it could all be lost now with a tiny nuance that made Mann suspicious.

Mann frowned. 'What sort of private matter?'

'About your grandfather.' Tony took another step forward, a relaxed move calculated to make him appear like a man with only the most casual of intentions.

Mann looked startled. 'I saw you at Koblenz. Are you following me? What do you want with me?'

'Just to talk. May I?' Tony carried on to the end of the gangplank, acting as if it was the most natural thing in the world.

'I suppose so. Come into the wheelhouse,' Mann said grudgingly.

It was a remarkable sight, Tony thought as he

walked inside. Everything gleamed. The woodwork was polished to mirror smoothness and the brass gleamed as softly as if it were lit from within. A rack held neatly folded charts, and there wasn't so much as a coffee stain on the chart table. The room smelled of polish and the sharp chemical fragrance of air freshener. Mann leaned against the wall, his arms folded across his chest. He looked young and defensive. Tony had a momentary flash of the troubled boy inside the man and felt the familiar wash of empathy. Who knew what he'd been through to bring him to this point? Tony could guess, and it didn't make for comfort. One thing was for sure. Even if aping the verbal savagery of the grandfather was the most likely way to break Mann, he wasn't going to go down that route. There had to be another way to end these killings, and it was up to him to find it.

'What do you know about my grandfather?' Mann demanded.

'I know what they did to him at Schloss Hochenstein.'

Mann's eyes widened and his arms tightened around him. 'What do you mean?'

'He was snatched away from his family and treated like an animal. I know about the experiments. I even know about the water torture. These were appalling, terrible things to do to a child in the name of science. It must have had a terrible effect on him.' Tony could see his words hit home. With every sentence, Mann seemed to shrink into himself. But what he needed to do was to make him open up. 'You must have paid a heavy price for what was done to him.'

'What does that have to do with you?' Mann's

voice was hostile and defiant, the attitude of someone who is determined to tough out the situation.

Tony made an instant assessment. However much he sympathized with Mann's pain, this wasn't a situation where the gentle therapeutic approach was going to work. It would take far too long to bring him to the point where he would be relieved to share his nightmares. It was time to storm the citadel. 'I think it's the reason why you have been killing my friends.'

Mann's eyes narrowed and his head seemed to shrink into his shoulders like a watchful bird. Tony could smell perspiration cutting through the artificial scents of the confined space. 'Your German is not as good as you think it is. What you are saying doesn't make sense,' he said in a pitiful parody of arrogance. 'Who are you, anyway?'

'My name is Tony Hill. Dr Tony Hill. I'm a psychologist.' He smiled. Walking out on the high wire without a net. And not caring. 'That's right, Willi. I'm the enemy.'

'I think you're crazy. And I want you to leave my boat now.'

Tony shook his head. The cracks were starting to show. But he still had nothing that would pass for confession. Time to find some more buttons to push. 'I don't believe that's what you want. I think what you want is for someone to recognize the significance of what you're doing. You didn't start killing because the idea of it excited you. You started killing to make them stop what they were doing. But if nobody understands that, then it's all been a waste of time. Nothing will change. They'll still keep messing with people's heads. And you'll be in jail. Or worse. Because they know it's you, Willi. And sooner rather than later, they'll prove it.'

Mann made a harsh sound that might have been intended as a laugh. 'I don't know what you're talking about.'

Tony sat down on the high chair by the chart table. The secret of making someone like Mann open up was to read his responses and shift the approach accordingly. There was no point in having a script meticulously worked out in advance. He'd already changed tack and it was time to alter course again. Now, the pretence of sweet reason was his best weapon. He needed to act as if what he was saying was casually self-evident. 'You can deny it all you like. But they're watching you. When you go out tomorrow night or the next night, or the night after that, they're going to be on your tail. They're not going to let you kill another one, Willi. Unless you listen to me, there are only two alternatives. Either you stop or you get caught. And either way, nobody will hear the message.'

Mann didn't move a muscle. He stood staring at Tony, breathing heavily through his nose.

Tony leaned forward earnestly. 'That's why you need me. Because I'm the only one so far who has understood what you're trying to say. Come with me. Give yourself up. I'll make sure they hear the message. Ordinary people will sympathize with you. They'll understand you. They'll be horrified at what happened to you and your grandfather. Any civilized person would be. They'll force the psychologists to answer for what they've done. They'll insist that they stop causing the kind of damage that made your childhood a misery. You'll have won.'

Mann shook his head. 'I don't know why you're saying these things to me,' he said doggedly. There was a light sheen of sweat on his upper lip.

'Because it's very nearly over. And you made a mistake, didn't you?'

Now the eyes were troubled. Mann looked away, chewing his lower lip. Tony could see he was finally making headway.

'Marie-Thérèse Calvet, that was a mistake. You gave them an excuse to treat you like any other sexually motivated psychopath. They're not going to be able to see past that to the reality, because they're small-minded and stupid. You might think you'll get a chance to explain yourself in court, but, trust me, you're probably not going to make it to court. After what you did to Dr Calvet, they're not going to need much of an excuse to shoot you down like a dog.'

Mann wiped a hand over his mouth, showing his distress at last. 'Why are you talking to me like this?' His voice was a plea that Tony needed to answer.

'Because it's my job to help people who get themselves into a tight corner. Most people will look at someone like you and they'll think you're evil. Or sick. Me, I just see somebody who's been hurt. I can't undo the hurt, but I can sometimes make it possible to live with it.'

It was the wrong thing to say. Mann pushed himself away from the wall and began to pace agitatedly in the tiny area between the bulkhead and the chart table. His air of vulnerability had vanished, replaced by an angry menace. His words tumbled over each other, his hands clenched and unclenched in spasms. 'You're a fucking psychologist. You twist words. You come here, to my boat, my place, and you tell lies about me. You have no right. You all tell lies. You say you want to help. And you never help. You make things worse.' Suddenly he stopped and took a step towards Tony, blocking his path to the door, looming over him. He spoke slowly and clearly. 'I could kill you now. Because I don't believe you. Nobody knows who I am. Nobody knows me.'

Tony tried not to show the fear that had surged in his chest. He suddenly understood that no matter what he had thought standing on the wharf, he very much wanted to stay alive. 'I know you, Willi. I know your motives were pure,' he said, feeling his throat constrict, knowing his only chance was to keep talking. 'You saw what had to be done, and you did it. But you've done enough to make your point. Let me speak for you. Let me explain.'

Mann shook his head vigorously. 'They'll take my boat away. I would rather be shot down like a dog than let them take my boat away.' He made a sudden lunge towards Tony. In his urgency to escape, Tony tipped off the chair and crashed to the floor, screaming in pain as his bruised shoulder and broken ribs hit the deck. He cringed against the wooden boards, waiting for the blow that never came.

For Mann had no interest in Tony. His goal had been the drawer of the chart table. He wrenched it open and thrust his hand inside. It emerged holding a large, clumsy revolver. He looked at it wonderingly for a moment then put the barrel in his mouth. Tony looked on, powerless and aghast, as Mann's finger tightened on the trigger. But instead of a violent explosion, there was merely a dry metallic click.

Mann pulled the gun from his mouth and stared at it with a puzzled expression. At that moment, Marijke burst through the wheelhouse door, her Walther P5 braced in her hands. Instantly she took in the scene: Tony helpless on the floor, Mann brandishing a gun. In a split second, she made her decision.

For the second time inside a minute, a finger tightened on a trigger.

This time, bone, brains and blood spattered the immaculate wheelhouse of the *Wilhelmina Rosen*.

It was over.

Epilogue

It wasn't that there was nothing to say; more that there was too much, and neither knew where to start. Or even whether starting at all was a good idea.

The ground they finally met on was as neutral as it could get. They sat opposite each other in a café in the international departures lounge of Schipol Airport. Not only was this a physical no-man's-land, it was also a meeting that had finite limits, since both had planes to catch.

For a while, they sat in a silence that felt easier than speech. Carol's nose would never be quite the same, but the Berlin hospital had done a good job of resetting it. The bruising had mostly subsided, though her eyes still looked puffy, as if she'd cried herself to sleep. Tony's injuries would take longer to heal. His broken fingers were still troublesome and his ribs a perpetual torment. But that would pass.

Both had done everything in their power to start mending themselves. But each feared that what had been broken inside the other might never be fixed.

It was Carol who eventually broke the silence. 'You remember what Radecki said at the end?'

Tony nodded. 'That he'd won because you'd never be free of him?'

'Yes.' She stirred her coffee. 'He was wrong, you know. You see, he never got inside me. Only my body. And that doesn't count. Not really. He's the one who's never going to be free. Because I did get inside him. So he didn't win, Tony.'

Tony's smile was barely perceptible, but it reached his eyes. 'I'm glad. You're going to stay in the police?'

'It's the only thing I'm good at. I won't work with Morgan and his people, though. I don't care what he thinks. I'm not like him and I won't let him convince me otherwise. They're giving me some time to decide where I want to go, what I want to do. What about you? Are you going to keep hiding?'

'No. I can't. If the last few weeks have proved anything, it's that profiling is what I do best. I'm going to put out some feelers when I get back, maybe see if there's something for me with Europol. I can do good work alongside cops like Marijke and Petra.'

'That's a relief. I was scared you'd been put off again.'

Again, they grew quiet. This time, it was Tony who spoke first. 'So, where do we go from here?'

Carol shrugged. 'I have no idea. Onwards and upwards somehow.'

'I'd like to be there for that,' he said.

She smiled. 'I don't think you've got any choice.'

The Grave Tattoo

Val McDermid

Summer in the Lake District and torrential rain uncovers a bizarrely tattooed body on a hillside. But that is not the only thing to come to the surface: centuries-old tales involving the legendary Pitcairn Massacre are being told again. Did Fletcher Christian, mutinous First Mate on the ill-fated Bounty, stage the death of his men in order to return home in secret?

Wordsworth scholar Jane Gresham wants to know the truth. There are persistent rumours that the Lakeland poet, a childhood friend of Christian's, harboured the fugitive and turned his tale into an epic poem – a narrative that has since remained hidden. But as she follows each new lead, death follows hard on her heels. Suddenly, a 200-year-old mystery is putting lives on the line. And against the dramatic backdrop of England's Lake District, a drama of life and death plays out, its ultimate prize a bounty worth millions.

The superb new thriller from Val McDermid. Available now in hardback.

'Our leading pathologist of everyday evil' *Guardian*

'McDermid's capacity to enter the warped mind of a deviant criminal is shiveringly convincing' *The Times*

'Val McDermid is a roaring Ferrari amid the crowded traffic on the crime-writing road' *Independent*

ISBN-13: 978-0-00-714285-9
ISBN-10: 0-00-714285-4

Wire in the Blood Series 1 & 2
Available Now on DVD